HIGH WIRE

Books by Candice Fox

Standalone thrillers

High Wire

Devil's Kitchen

Fire With Fire

The Chase

Gathering Dark

The Ted Conkaffey series

Crimson Lake

Redemption Point

Gone by Midnight

The Bennett/Archer series

Hades

Eden

Fall

With James Patterson

Never Never

Fifty Fifty

Liar Liar

Hush Hush

The Inn

The Murder Inn

2 Sisters Detective Agency

Black & Blue (BookShot novella)

CANDICE FOX

HIGH WIRE

PENGUIN BOOKS

UK | USA | Canada | Ireland | Australia
India | New Zealand | South Africa | China

Penguin Books is part of the Penguin Random House group of companies whose addresses can be found at global.penguinrandomhouse.com

First published by Penguin Books in 2024

Cover design by Adam Laszczuk © Penguin Random House Australia Pty Ltd
Cover photography via Adobe Stock
Author photograph by Steve Baccon
Typeset in 12.5/17 pt Adobe Garamond LT by Midland Typesetters, Australia

Printed and bound in Australia by Griffin Press, an accredited
ISO AS/NZS 14001 Environmental Management Systems printer

A catalogue record for this book is available from the National Library of Australia

ISBN 978 1 76104 904 0

penguin.com.au

We at Penguin Random House Australia acknowledge that Aboriginal and Torres Strait Islander peoples are the Traditional Custodians and the first storytellers of the lands on which we live and work. We honour Aboriginal and Torres Strait Islander peoples' continuous connection to Country, waters, skies and communities. We celebrate Aboriginal and Torres Strait Islander stories, traditions and living cultures, and we pay our respects to Elders past and present.

For Lee

CHAPTER 1

There was a car on fire up ahead.

Harvey stopped his vehicle, got out, looked all around. Saw the same thing he'd been seeing for the past three and a half hours. Emptiness. One flat black mass, slightly darker than the black mass blanketed over it, peppered with stars and milky galaxies he'd known the name of once. The burning car was just a hazy dome of light rising beyond the curvature of the earth, maybe a minute and a half on. Harvey had seen plenty of cars on fire, from all possible distances. Knew that's what it was. Petrol stink and menace whispered past him on the wind.

He got back behind the wheel, gripped it and watched the dark, shut his headlights off. A set-up with a burning car was just the right kind of bullshit for the High Wire. The secret track that cut through the Australian Outback from Broome to Sydney had started out as a trucker-only thing; a flat, even, mostly hazard-free route that skirted Indigenous conservation areas, cattle farms and small towns. It was far enough into the dusty forgotten corners of the states that joined hands across it that each jurisdiction liked to think any problems on the Wire weren't theirs. Satellite coverage was patchy and routine patrols weren't feasible, so after the truckers let slip about it, the track became party central for drug traffickers trying to move cargo from the south-east corner of Australia to the north-west. And for the bandits who wanted to take advantage of that. Bandits who liked to set cars on fire, draw people in, rob and murder them.

Harvey had two choices now.

Drive on.

Or turn away.

He liked to weigh things. On one hand, he had the knowledge and experience to know that a burning-car ruse was the most basic of all honeytraps, that the kind of idiots who spent their life out here on the Wire trying to ensnare Good Samaritan truckers and hopelessly lost tourists probably weren't more inventive than that. There was a good chance Harvey would pull up to investigate the fire, only to turn around and find a gun in his face. The bandits would have it in their minds to beat the snot out of him, take what little he had and bury him alive out here. That wouldn't happen, of course. But Harvey was already in a hurry. He didn't need to add putting space between him and a pile of dead bodies to his schedule.

He tapped the steering wheel and thought about the other hand; a natural curiosity he'd never grown out of, and the idea that the burning car did indeed belong to one of the Good Samaritans or hopelessly lost tourists he'd just been thinking about, and if he wandered up he might see them in the process of having the snot beaten out of *them* or the whole alive-burial thing. So, on the scales was him having to live with seeing two grinning backpackers in the newspaper the next day, public puzzlement about where they disappeared to.

Harvey huffed a sigh.

Then he drove on.

The haze became a glow and the glow became a wobbly ball of light. Harvey kept his head on swivel, looking for figures out there in the blackness, his night vision compromised by the fireball. He got within about twenty metres and the figure, standing a good distance back from the car, heard his tyre pop a little stone on the hard earth and turned. She was tall. Ponytail, jacket, jeans. Instead of coming over to the car she backed away beyond the glow of the fire in a way that made Harvey's stomach turn. Because that told him something. An ordinary citizen with their car on fire in the middle of nowhere would welcome the help, at least come around the driver's side to get a look at who was offering it. He cut the engine and pressed the cigarette lighter in the console so that a hidden panel in the door popped open. He took his pistol out, opened the door and put one foot on the ground. He kept a hand on the wheel and his gun by his side.

'You okay?' he shouted. He had to raise his voice over the roar of the flames, but he raised it more than he needed to. It was an intentionally dumb question. If this was a trap, he'd want to be underestimated by whoever was waiting to pounce. 'What happened?'

The woman came into the light again. Tears glistened in her eyes, but her face was hard, determined. 'It overheated!'

Harvey beckoned her. 'Come here so we don't have to shout!'

She hesitated, then came. Harvey hadn't completely let go of the idea that this was a play, but he was loosening his grip. The woman walked with the mechanical numbness of someone grateful to be told what to do for a minute, but she stayed out of swinging distance.

'Are you hurt?'

'No, no, I'm okay. I just . . .' She gave a helpless, embarrassed laugh, swiped at the tears. 'I didn't know what to do.'

'Why the hell are you out here?' He watched her eyes. 'This is not a good area.'

'I'm uh, I'm from uh . . .' She flung a hand south. 'My friend has a farm. Down there. Near Co– Co– Cowarie? I was bringing her . . . supplies.'

Harvey stiffened. He looked out into the dark again, but it was a pointless exercise. The cabin lights in the car had ruined his night vision further. 'Lady, don't feed me any bullshit. Okay? I'm trying to help you out here.'

'I'm not—'

'Cowarie's that way.' Harvey jerked a thumb behind him. 'If you were from around here you'd know that, and you'd know how to pronounce it.'

She opened her mouth, shut it without speaking.

'You haven't come from anywhere around here in that car.'

'Yes I have.'

'There's enough fresh dirt and dust on that car to tell me you've been on the road at least half a day,' he said.

'I'm not lying to you, mate,' she scoffed. 'I don't even know you.'

'Have you rung the police? Called anyone at all for assistance? There's no coverage out here, but you should be able to get an SOS call through. Although if you really did live out here you'd have a satellite phone.'

'My phone's in the car.' She gestured at the flames. 'I forgot to grab it.'

Harvey dropped his eyes to the front pocket of her jeans, where the outline of her phone was clearly visible. She tugged her jacket down.

'Get in,' he sighed.

'No way.' She rubbed her turned-up nose, stepped back fast like a spooked deer. 'I'm fine where I am, thanks.'

'Just get in, would you?'

'No.'

'Why the hell not?'

'Because I don't know you,' she said, jutting her chin. 'And I don't – I don't . . . I don't like your attitude, if I'm honest.'

He had to laugh at that.

'I'm fine where I am,' she insisted.

'No, you're not,' Harvey said.

'I—'

'Look, I don't know why you're out here, but it's starting to become a moot point for me. Either you know you're on the High Wire because you're doing something sketchy, or you don't know you're on it and you're just an idiot with a secret. In both cases, you're alone and you're in one of the baddest places in the country and I can't leave you here.'

'Why not?'

'Because I don't do that,' he said. 'I don't leave people in bad places. Especially women.'

'Oh. Well.' She rolled her eyes. 'Lucky me. I got a hero on my hands.'

'You getting in?'

She did a little uncertain shuffle in the dark beyond his reach, looked like she was about to bolt, but didn't. When she slid into the seat beside him, she filled the space with woman-on-the-road smell. Sweat, sugar, coconut deodorant slapped on over the sweat, a nice laundry detergent trying to make itself known. It stirred up all kinds of things inside him that had been settled at the bottom of his mental swamp for decades. He slid his gun into the makeshift holster in the car door and nudged it shut with his thigh.

'What's the High Wire?' the woman asked.

'It's the road we're on.'

'There is no road.'

'That's the point.'

'So how do I know *you're* not out here doing something sketchy?'

'Maybe I am.' Harvey leant back in his seat, drove on, still watchful for figures in the dark. 'There's water here.' He pointed to the bottle in the cup holder between them, half full.

'Thanks,' she said, but didn't touch it, because apparently she was dumb enough to let her car overheat in the middle of the outback moonscape but smart enough to know not to drink from an open bottle offered by a guy she didn't know. 'You can just drop me at the next town.'

'Oh, believe me, I'm getting you out of my car as fast as possible.' He was following shallow grooves in the desert floor, the only physical evidence of the track's existence. 'I'm in a hurry and this'll set me back, whatever the hell this even is.'

'What's the hurry?' she asked. She was settling in now. Tired. When she reached over to turn the warmer up, he noticed bruises on her wrist as the jacket slid up. The distinct pattern of a finger grip. He was starting to paint a picture.

'A friend of mine called this afternoon from Sydney,' he said. 'She's dying.'

'Oh.'

'Yeah. Cancer.'

'So you – you're going there?'

'The doctors are telling her it's days, not weeks,' he said. Harvey had no idea why he was saying all this. He sure hadn't said it to anybody else, but something about the situation felt so temporary it didn't seem to matter. 'I didn't know she'd been sick or I would have gone earlier. I'm trying to get there in time. Alice airport is shut.'

'What? The whole thing?'

'Some arsehole called in a bomb threat, about a minute after I got to my gate. All planes grounded. Word was getting around that it was gonna be at least six hours before they opened up flights again, and even then, we'd be in the queue.'

'Jesus.'

'Yeah.'

'So you're gonna drive all the way to Sydney, then?' She glanced in the back, saw the bag.

'I was gonna try my luck with Durham Downs airstrip. Can't get Birdsville on the phone.'

She nodded, her mind already trailing off, eyes on the blackness. He guessed the story was good enough to let her get back to her other worries. Whoever was after her. Whoever had grabbed her wrist so hard they'd marked her for the next fortnight. Harvey let his mind wander, because he had other worries, too – whether he was going to make it to Sydney before Shayna slipped away. Her voice on the phone had been thin. Scared. And he'd never heard it like that before; not when they were sitting knee-to-knee in a rattly old MRH-90 helicopter over flat blue ocean off Sumatra and the thing got engine failure.

Not when they got word their wing of the multi-national army base at Tarin Kot was about to be rammed by a suicide bomber in a stolen troop carrier. Harvey hadn't been able to get Shayna on the phone since she dropped the news on him. Six hours, and all he could do was hammer it for the horizon and try not to think about what his world would be like without her in it.

'What's that red light?' The woman was leaning forward in her seat, staring at the sky.

'What light? Where?' Harvey looked.

'It's gone now. Blinking red light.'

'Probably a satellite.' He shifted upwards in his seat, tried to shake off the fatigue. 'I'm Harvey, anyway.'

'I'd rather not, uh . . .' She cleared her throat.

'So make something up,' he said. 'It's two hours until we hit civilisation. Don't make me sit beside a ghost the whole time.'

'I'm Clare,' she relented, and he got the weird feeling that she was not, in fact, making it up. They started picking up speed. 'Should you put your headlights back on?'

'Not yet. I want to get clear of the fire,' Harvey said. 'There's a chance it got someone's attention. And I don't need any more tr—'

The tyres blew out. Both sets, one after the other, two great explosions that made the car buck and then fishtail in the sand and gravel. Harvey's mind split in two; one half trying to wrangle control of the car before it flipped, the other half trying to wrestle his nerves back from panic mode. Because he knew what had happened in an instant, and it was all confirmed for him when he ground to a stop and above Clare's screams he heard the barking of a man in a balaclava, who approached the car at a run.

'Hands in the air! Hands in the air!'

The guy didn't wait for compliance, just punched two bullets through the driver's-side window to show he was serious; one whumping into the back seat, one hitting the headrest an inch or two behind Harvey's skull. Cubes of glass showered all over his lap. A second guy emerged out of the moonlit night and stood by Clare's window, his gun trained on her face. Harvey did what any smart person would do. He put his hands up and looked out at the man on his side of the car holding the pistol, and tried not to think about how bad this all was. The road spikes. The shooter's excellent aim. The speed and accuracy of the takedown. This wasn't the work of road bandits.

This was something else.

CHAPTER 2

Edna heard the shotgun blast take out something big and glassy, like a cabinet full of china, she guessed. Things inside the nearby house clunked and shattered on the floor, made that wobbling sound plates do as they're settling. The boy in the house gave an animalistic roar that morphed into a string of language so colourful it gave Edna cause to raise an eyebrow. The homeowner, one Alan Jacob Horn, had been standing at the roadside mirroring her with his arms folded, but now he raised them in dismay, and Edna prayed quietly that his burgundy bathrobe would stay fastened.

'So are you going to go in, or what?' Horn asked. 'We've been out here talking for ten minutes!'

'I'll go when I'm ready,' Edna said. 'First I want to know how the shotgun came to be in the young man's possession.'

'It was in the kitchen, beside the fridge.' Horn shook his head, blew out a chestful of hot frustration. 'He spotted it. While we were . . . arguing.'

'While you were discussing your little case of mistaken identity,' Edna said.

'I told you; it's not like that.'

'I'm really trying to understand what it *is* like, Mr Horn.' Edna nudged her glasses back up onto her nose and eyed the man through them. 'Because the story you've been telling me reminds me of a movie I saw once. It was called *Catfish*. You seen it?'

Horn folded his arms again.

'It's a good movie. Vulnerable young man falls in love with a beautiful, caring, kind, incredibly good-looking woman he finds on the internet. Drives a long way to meet her and discovers – holy shit! – she's not that person at all.' Edna looked Horn up and down, from his hard, bare, yellowed toes to his sweat-beaded and balding scalp.

'You can be whoever the hell you want on the internet.' Horn's voice was low and full of dangerous shame. 'That's not a crime.'

'It is if you're luring a minor for sexual purposes.'

'He's *eighteen*! He's not a minor!'

'You sure about that?' Edna asked.

Another shotgun blast. The sound rippled out across the open plains, nothing standing in its way for a hundred kilometres in every direction. The windows of the small house flashed white like the kid was throwing lightning bolts in there.

'*You piece of shit! Motherfuckerrrr!*'

'You've been lying to him. What if he's been lying to you?' Edna asked.

'Look, his age doesn't matter. I wasn't talking to him for . . . for sexual purposes,' Horn said, jaw tight with defiance. 'I'm not a fucking faggot.'

'So what *are* you, then, Mr Horn?' Edna squinted. 'Because that kid and me . . . All we really know is that you sure as hell aren't a seventeen-year-old girl.'

'I'm-I'm-I'm . . .' Horn threw his hands up again. 'I'm someone who made a mistake, okay? I was playing a game. I was bored. It was wrong and that's very, very clear to me now.'

'Uh-huh.'

'He was never supposed to find out where I lived. Coming here? He did that. That's on him, not me.'

'Oh, so this is *his* fault?'

'Would you just get up there and deal with him?' Horn's eyes grew wide. 'I'm standing here having my integrity questioned and he's *destroying* my house! What are you going to do if he shoots himself dead in there?'

'*Fuck you! Fuck you! Fuck yoooou!*'

'How many shells did you have in the cupboard, Mr Horn?'

'Oh my god, you're not listening to me!' Horn turned in a circle. 'I'm asking questions and you're answering them with questions!'

'How many shells?'

'Two packs of a hundred?'

'So we've got some time.' Edna leant against her cruiser. 'People tend to wait until the last bullet to do themselves in.'

A shotgun blast took out the side window of the house, glass spraying against the wood paling fence.

'Please do something!' Horn cried. 'Please! Please! I'm begging you, okay? Please!' His pitch was high, desperate, pathetic, the type Edna had been waiting for. She gave it another thirty seconds, just to let him taste his own cruelty, then eased herself off the bonnet, passing Horn a look that she hoped told him exactly what she thought of him. She walked slowly towards the house, not bothering to unclip the pistol on her belt. There was dead silence from inside the dwelling now. The sound of curiosity. Edna walked up the three creaky wooden stairs to the front door, knocked on it, and took a step to the side.

The shotgun roared, a hole the size of a bike tyre punching through the timber front door at head height and spewing woodchips all over everything; the little cane settee, the straggly pot plants, the woven grass rug. Edna kicked a big chunk of wood off her boot, but didn't cower, because she'd expected the shot. It hadn't been designed to kill her. The outback night was so silent and still, probably every soul in this part of the state had been able to hear the music of the floorboards beneath her feet; the plain-as-day fact that she had stepped to the right after she knocked on the door. The shot was designed, instead, to intimidate. Edna didn't feel intimidated. That took a lot, these days. Instead she felt tired. The drive out to the isolated property had tacked on an extra two hours to the bottom of her shift that she just didn't appreciate.

'Well, what kind of a hello is that?' she asked.

'Fuck you, you old bitch!' a voice boomed through the hole. The shotgun crunched twice as he pumped it. 'Get away from the door before I blow your fucking head off!'

'"Old"?' Edna felt her mouth fall open. She looked at Horn to see if he'd heard, but the robed man was cowering behind her cruiser. 'I'm fifty-eight!'

Another blast. Edna heard ceiling plaster and wood splinters rain over the floor inside the house.

'Listen, mate. Enough with the gun, okay? You're probably giving yourself permanent hearing loss.'

'Fuck you!'

'I'm serious. Your hearing is important. Especially when you get old. Which I, apparently, would know something about.'

'Fuck you!'

'Listennnn,' Edna said again, lowering her voice so he'd be forced to do just that. 'I've come up here tonight with a deal in my hand. Okay? Because nothing would please me more than to let you keep punching holes in this arsehole's house. I think you deserve to do that. But when my backup arrives, the deal I have is going to be off, the moment his tyres come to a stop on that road.'

Silence. Edna powered on. 'Mr Horn is in a lot more trouble than you right now. On his own admission, he has fraudulently presented himself to you online. That opens him up to a world of hurt once we start digging around in your chat logs. If this whole thing started before you became a legal adult, that's using a carrier service to procure sexual activity with a minor. If you've ever sent him a racy picture, or a single dollar of your money, there'll be child porn and cyber fraud charges in the mix. And I'm willing to guess you're not his only victim, mate.'

'Stop talking! Get off the fucking verandah, bitch!'

'How long has he been selling you his cute little story that he's a girl?' Edna asked. 'I bet it's at least six months. I know it would take me more than a couple of months of falling in love with someone to go so far as to track them down and drive nine hundred kilometres to surprise them with a visit.'

The boy walked off. Edna heard his footsteps retreating. Deep inside the house, she thought she heard a tightly stifled sob.

But he was back before long, his rage reignited. 'I'm gonna kill you. I'm gonna kill you both!'

'You?' Edna carried on calmly. 'You've done a lot of property damage here tonight. And I assume the car in the driveway there is stolen. The plate check is taking longer than it should.'

A roar of fury.

'But that's not jail-time-worthy.' She shrugged. 'That's not make-the-news-and-ruin-your-life-worthy.'

A threatening grumbling from inside.

'You've got the upper hand here,' Edna said. 'So use it.'

Silence.

'Put the gun down and come out of there. It's your only way out of this. You take the deal. Horn forgets about the property damage and you forget the online dalliance. I forget the stolen car and we all get to go to bed at a reasonable hour.'

'That's bullshit! You're lying!'

'Yeah, well, whether you think the deal is a lie or not,' Edna went on, 'you've got about twenty minutes to decide if you'll take it. Because, like I said, my supervisor is on the way. I'll deny ever offering it. My boss is not as creative as I am about how to resolve a thing like this. But I'm tired and I want to go home and have a shower.'

She waited.

Out on the road, Horn stood looking at the stars, shaking his head, huffing midnight mist. The boy inside wandered around a while, coming to the conclusion, Edna guessed, that there were in fact two ways out of this mess and one was more permanent than the other. When she heard the sound of the gun being placed on a table, Edna stepped forward and looked in through the hole in the door. The boy was mountainous, broad-shouldered, roped with muscles and veins he could only have got from working bricklaying or construction jobs between school terms, if he still attended school at all. His black hair was shaved close to the skull, dusted with ceiling plaster, and there was fluff at the corners of his upper lip that would probably be a full and striking beard in a year. With his wild, agitated eyes and hard, downturned mouth, Edna was taken to thinking about all the cell windows she'd peered through in her career at young men like this; men choosing between death and consequences.

The shotgun was on the table, within the kid's reach. Edna took the cuffs off her belt and held them up to the hole in the door. 'You'll have to wear these,' she said.

Horn went in to inspect the damage. Edna and the kid sat in the cruiser, watched him go.

'Didn't even say thanks,' Edna sighed.

The kid said nothing. She could smell him through the plexiglass. Nitro. Sulphur. Teenage funk.

'The papers are gonna love that prick.' Edna started the engine. 'Weirdo loner out on the plains pretending to be a teenage girl? Jesus. We might even get a visit from *A Current Affair*.'

'You said you weren't gonna report him.'

'I say a lot of things.' She rolled out, grinding gravel. 'Saying things to get people to put their guns down is easier than shooting them, usually. I don't have a supervisor. That was bullshit, too. I'm the senior officer out here. So, I can still cut you a deal, but it won't be a straight walk. You did steal a car. You can't go around stealing cars, hun.'

'I didn't steal that fucking car,' the kid grunted. 'I've never seen it before in my life.'

'Sure.'

'And everything he's saying about . . . about . . .' the kid glanced back at the house in the distance, 'some online relationship? That's not me, okay? That didn't happen. I came out here in my *own* car, which, like, got a flat tyre. And so I just started walking and stumbled on his, uh . . . his house. It was totally random. I don't know the guy. He doesn't know me.' The boy stared at the roof of the cruiser, searching for inspiration. 'I was just going to use the phone, and—'

'And what? You thought you'd help the guy out by adding some ventilation holes to his ceiling?'

'The dude wanted to fuck me. I was defending myself.'

'Okay.'

'It's true!'

'He told me your name is Talon Crest.' Edna was driving with one hand and tapping on her mounted laptop with the other. 'Is that right?'

'Nope.'

'Never heard of Talon Crest?'

'I said no.'

'This isn't your picture?' Edna turned her screen so it pointed towards the plexiglass. 'You're not Talon David Crest of 5/139 Beaker Street, Smithfield, Adelaide?'

Edna and Talon both looked at the screen, at what was probably the best picture of the kid that was ever taken. Better than school-photo quality, high res and glowing in the dark of the car.

'Nope.'

Edna laughed. 'You're right. Couldn't be you. Says here Talon Crest has no car, and isn't registered to drive, whether it's his own car or a stolen one.'

Talon cursed, kicked the partition between them.

'I like the name, though,' Edna said. 'Shame about "David" for a middle name. Missed opportunity. Could have been "Beak".'

'Do you ever stop talking?'

'Or maybe "Wing".'

The kid slumped back in his seat, making the cruiser sway. 'This is bullshit, man.'

'You really need to clean up your language. My ears are bleeding.'

'*Fuck* you.'

She pulled over. Got out. There was a wind up here on the higher plain and it ruffled her short silver hair. She opened the back door of the vehicle and waited, but Talon didn't get out. 'Did I mention I'm tired and I want to go home?' Edna asked.

He frowned.

'Get out,' she said.

He looked all around. 'You can't leave me here.'

'I'm not leaving you here, idiot. I'm moving you to the front seat.' She beckoned him. 'The cuffs and the perp seat were all for show for that dickhead Horn. Up here is less awkward. And guess what? There are snacks.'

Talon thought about it. Got out and stood there while she uncuffed him. Edna opened the front passenger-side door and the kid looked down at the seat, and at her, his frying-pan-sized hands just hanging by his sides. 'Aren't you, like . . . scared of me?'

Edna snorted. 'I wasn't scared of you ten minutes ago and you had a twelve-gauge in your hands. Why would I start now?'

'Because you're half my size.'

'Mate, if I was scared of everyone who's twice my size, I'd never leave the house.' Edna gestured to the seat. 'The glove box. Take what you want, but don't touch the Twix. They're mine.'

The young man thought for a few seconds more and then went with it. Edna walked around and slid into the driver's seat again, put the cuffs back on her belt. The smell was stronger now. It made her think of past cases. Bad cases. The way the gunshot residue hangs in the air after firing, the way it lies like dust on blood-spattered bed sheets. Cattle farmers who watched too many animals starve to death and didn't want to watch their kids do the same. The radio crackled as Talon was crunching loudly on a KitKat.

'*Ed?*'

Edna picked up. 'Yeah.'

'*How'd the call end up? Was it a prank?*'

Edna reached over and poked the kid with a finger. 'Seems real enough, Dispatch.'

'*Well, I got another job for you. We got a burnout up on the Wire.*'

Edna closed her eyes, let her shoulders sag. 'I'll be two hours into overtime by the time I—' She stopped. There was no point complaining. While it was an hour north to the High Wire and an hour east to her station, only she was available to drive that far from home base to investigate something as innocuous as a burning car. Rebecca Stevenson, the only other officer in their two-hundred-thousand-square-kilometre jurisdiction, would be tied up for the entire next day with a theft case that was threatening to turn into a neighbour war. Neighbour wars out here meant murders. If Stevenson didn't throw some water on it now, she'd be a whole lot busier in the coming months. Edna had a choice. Go north now, or do it the following afternoon. And by then, it might not be such an innocuous case.

Edna started the car and put it into gear. 'Buckle up, kid,' she said. 'We're taking a little detour.'

CHAPTER 3

Clare was trembling all over, looking from the men outside the car to Harvey in the driver's seat beside her. 'What the hell is this?'

'You tell me,' he said.

'This has nothing to do with me!' Even her voice was shaking. 'Wh-wh-what do we do?'

'You're gonna run,' Harvey said. 'As soon as you get the opportunity. Run for your fucking life. Don't look back. Just go.'

Clare said nothing, not 'But what about you?' or 'What are you gonna do?' Harvey liked that, because a woman with any kind of sense would know that as terrible as this could end up for him, it would be worse for her. There was no kind of loyalty that could possibly be established in the fifteen minutes they'd known each other that was worth that.

'With your left hand!' the guy on Harvey's right barked. 'Turn the car off! Take the keys from the ignition! Throw them out onto the ground! Keep your right hand up!'

This was bad. Very, very bad. Because whoever these guys were, they had either law enforcement or military training. The style of takedown was telling Harvey that. Everything about it, from the road spikes to the warning shots to the 'big-dog' voice the guy was using, the one they taught in the academy, the one from the gut. He reached across himself with his left hand and switched the car off, then silently unclipped his house keys from the car key and tossed the bundle out the window, leaving the single car key sitting in the ignition. Harvey had been keeping his car key on a separate clip to the rest of his keys for decades in case this very situation arose, and it seemed comically sad now that it finally had. With all four tyres flat, there was no chance of making a getaway in the car. But Harvey was hoping the man on the left might cross the bumper, in which case he'd start the car up and floor it, ram the guy, use the distraction to get the upper hand.

No luck. The man on the left walked forward and yanked open Clare's door. He grabbed her by the arm and pulled her out, shoved her so that she arrived at the front left-hand side of the car. Harvey kept watch on the other guy, waiting for the split second he took his eyes off Harvey to check his partner's activity, get confirmation to go to the next step. The moment came. The guy looked at his partner. Harvey dropped his left hand, punched the cigarette lighter in the console and then shot his hand back up to the ceiling. The panel in the door by his thigh popped open, the butt of his pistol pointed downward in the makeshift holster.

The second moment Harvey was waiting for arrived. Once his partner and Clare were in position, the man came forward to grab Harvey's door handle, taking one hand off his gun, halving the steadiness of his aim and his willingness to use the weapon. Harvey grabbed his own pistol, shoved the door open so that he smacked the guy in the thighs, and in the same motion, shoved his gun up through the broken window and into the man's ribs. Harvey fired twice. He felt the man's breath on his face. Coffee. Cigarettes. Blood mist from the bullet that just smashed its way through his ribcage and into his lungs. Harvey stepped sideways, shoved the man aside and double-gripped his own gun, swinging it towards Clare and her captor. But by this time, the guy's wide eyes were howling out of his balaclava and he was holding a fistful of Clare's hair in one hand and the gun to her temple in the other.

'Don't!' the guy hissed. 'Don't! Don't! Don't! Don't!'

Harvey didn't. He was a good shot, but taking out the black-clothed man as he cowered behind Clare in the moonlit night was a shot he wasn't confident in, not then, not when it had been some years since he'd had to fire a gun at all and he was tired from the road and shaken from Shayna's news and a million other things. So he just stood and aimed and breathed and watched the little prick in the glow of the cabin lights and waited, waited for moments, opportunities, mistakes, drawing on a sense of patience he'd spent a lifetime cultivating.

The man on the ground at Harvey's feet gurgled and rolled over and vomited blood. They all listened to it, to him choking and aspirating and dying near Harvey's right boot.

And Clare's captor did something that made the hair on the back of Harvey's neck stand on end. He let go of Clare's ponytail and pressed a finger to a little piece in his ear.

'How far out are you?' he asked.

Harvey glanced out into the dark for the third guy. He saw nothing. Heard a buzzing sound. The sound was fluttering, nothing to bounce off to give it a source, just a soft humming out there in the blackness that was growing louder. The spiralling dark formed a thousand figures. Harvey made a decision. He advanced on the man who had Clare, because walking backwards over uneven ground is hard enough at the best of times, and doing it while dragging a hostage is almost impossible. He strode fast and long and kept his gun up, waiting for the man to roll a foot on a rock and fall and give him a shot. But Harvey was only three strides in when the buzzing rose suddenly to a roar and something smashed into the side of his head.

Silence. The sickly, rusty glow of headlights. Harvey gripped the dust and dirt and tried to decide how much time had passed, whether he was clinging onto a rocky cliff face or the flat, barren earth. Something was tapping his heel. He looked around and saw the woman whose name he had forgotten now sitting with her back against the closed driver's-side door of a car he didn't recognise. Her hands were bound behind her back. She was knocking his boot with her own.

'Hey!' she hissed at him. 'Hey! Hey! Wake up. Wake up. Please wake up.'

There were other voices. Harvey rolled onto his side. Pain soared through his ribcage. He didn't remember being hit or kicked. Must have happened while he was out. The pain thrummed down into his hips and up into his shoulders, stole his breath, made him cough and choke on dust.

There were voices nearby. Two men.

'. . . waited for me! Five fucking minutes! That's all it would have taken!'

'We couldn't wait for you! He'd picked up a passenger, Darryl. We had no idea who she was! We had to shut it down before . . .'

Something fizzed in Harvey's brain. The name. Darryl. The thought fluttered away, uncatchable. He clawed his way towards Clare, shifted himself up against the car she was leaning against. 'What happened?'

'They flew a drone into the side of your head,' she whispered. Her eyes were on a hunk of robotic debris lying two metres or so from where they sat. In the darkness and swirling dizziness Harvey could see shattered pieces of black and white plastic in the sand. 'The third guy. He must have been controlling it. He drove it into your head, and you went down, and then he got here, in a truck. They kicked the shit out of you while you were out.'

Harvey put his hands out, caught a stream of blood dripping from his jaw.

'What the hell *is this*?' Clare snarled at him, panic giving way to fury. 'Who are these guys? They know you, Harvey. They were saying your name.'

'Lean forward,' Harvey said. She did. He'd just snagged a finger under the cable tie binding her wrists when two hands seized his shoulders. He was dragged away, dumped on the gravel, kicked in the stomach. He tried to get up but his head still wasn't right, his limbs seeming to be moving through water.

'Nice try, shithead,' one of the men said. Harvey was wrenched into a sitting position. The world buzzed and spun. His T-shirt was dragged over his head. Cold night air on his chest and stomach and back. Something heavy was dragged down over him. A coat or vest. Both men were on him, holding his wrists, guiding his arms, dressing him like a sleepy child. There was dirt in his mouth. His vision was blinking in and out. Harvey spat blood and dirt and looked up at the masked faces.

'Oh Jesus,' one said, crouched before Harvey, trying to wrestle the vest down his aching ribcage. 'It's too small. Tell me this isn't—'

'That's the medium.'

'Fuck. Good. Okay. Get the large. Get it. Get it.'

Harvey lined up his shot, swung out, got the man keeping guard over him in the kneecap. The punch wasn't effective. His brain was slush. He was smacked in the jaw for his trouble, an open palm that coloured his world red.

'Careful. Not the face. You did enough damage with the drone.'

The heavy vest was tugged off. Another was shoved on. Harvey's arms were wrenched through the armholes. He tried to shake the concussion off, got his eyes clearer, the fibres in the men's masks coming into hyperfocus while his hearing sunk out completely. It took a second or two to get feeling back into his fingertips. When all his systems were online he was sitting at their feet with a heavy black vest strapped to his bare chest and they were both looking down at him, their smiles clear even through the balaclavas, two proud dog owners who have just taught the thing to sit.

Harvey ran his bloody hands over the hard fabric of the vest, fingers wandering over sharp grooves and angles beneath the Kevlar. The vest was skin-tight, cut perfectly around his arms, cinched at his waist, dipped at his neck without exposing his collarbones. It was so tight around his aching ribs it caused a pounding through his middle every time he exhaled. Made to measure.

'What . . . the fuck . . . is this?'

The men laughed at his words. One crouched before Harvey, eye level, and even before he pulled the balaclava away Harvey saw something in those bright beady blue eyes that made his stomach plunge. A memory. Something buried deep in the blackness of his past.

'Harvey Buck,' the guy said, pulling up the wool. 'Welcome to your nightmare.'

CHAPTER 4

Edna passed the kid her glasses. 'Wipe these, would you?' she said. 'I can't see shit out here.'

Talon put down the packet of Tiny Teddies and took her spectacles, polished them on the edge of his T-shirt.

'I bet this is the first arrest you've had where you get to go on a ride-along afterwards.' She gestured to the horizon before them, featureless and unmoving beyond the headlit blacktop. 'Take a good look. Most people don't get to see this kind of thing until they're retirees going across country in a caravan.'

The boy handed her back the glasses, didn't answer.

'I mean, okay, so there's not much to see right now.' Edna looked out at the blackness. 'But tomorrow, when I drive you to the airport, you'll get to see all this. It's beautiful out there.'

'Uh-huh.'

'You should cheer up,' Edna said. 'Clifton Hills Police Station has one holding cell and a drunk woman pissed in it about a month ago. I've done everything I can to get the smell out but it's still there. You could be sitting in that cell right now becoming a connoisseur of *Odeur de Incarceration*.'

The boy shook his head. They rolled on, only the roar of the tyres beneath them dispelling the silence.

'You're not very chatty, huh?' Edna asked.

'I don't need to be,' he grunted. 'You're doing enough chatting for us both.'

'Look, Talon, you got duped by that idiot back there. You didn't deserve it. It was cruel and embarrassing. But you can't let something like that get inside you, hun. For every minute you spend hating yourself for what went down tonight; that's another minute you're *giving* to that guy.'

'Man, you sound like you're trying to comfort some little bitch about a break-up.' Talon looked her over across the space between them, head to foot. 'I told you, all that stuff about an online relationship with that dude is bullshit. And how the hell are you gonna sit there and tell me what I deserve? You don't know me for shit.'

'I kinda do.' Edna smiled sadly.

'No you don't,' the boy scoffed. 'You don't know a thing about me. I could – I could grab the wheel right now and pull us over and kill you and dump you out here. You're playing a dangerous game, woman, uncuffing me and bringing me into the front seat like this. How do you know I'm not, like, some crazy killer type?'

'Because I know them, too,' Edna said.

'No you don't.' He gave her another full-body once-over, then settled back into his seat with his biscuits. 'If you were any good at your job you wouldn't be stuck out here alone in the . . . the nothingness like this. You're just a cop reject on outback duty babysitting cows and weirdo farmers. Save the life advice for the shrinks.'

They watched the horizon, the GPS in the dashboard showing a blank green square cut through with a grey line. Their blue bubble worked its way along the line, the numbers ticking slowly down. Green was the wrong colour for the world out here. It was black now, but by daylight, Edna knew, the earth here was dried-blood red and tossed with boulders, car-sized, wind-rounded rocks left over from some devil's game of marbles. Edna thought about how rehearsed the lines from the boy had been. *You're playing a dangerous game, woman.* Almost as though the kid had heard those exact words said a thousand times before. She tried to recall a statement she'd made in the past ten minutes that the boy hadn't contradicted. She picked up the mic in the dashboard.

'Dispatch, I'm about to roll up on the site.'

There was a double click in response. Edna picked out the shape against the distant mountain range. The shell of a car, still lazily leaking smoke as the fire chewed through a back seat. The sight had Talon's interest. Edna parked and flicked her head towards the shell in the low scrub.

'Might as well take a peek,' she said. 'You can give me your assessment.'

Talon was out of the cruiser like it was the one that had caught alight. Edna watched him walk a slow circle of the burnt vehicle. Kids and fire.

'Where's the driver?' the boy said when he'd completed his circle.

'Probably at home by now, eating Twisties and playing video games.' Edna kicked the bent and buckled number-plate off the front of the car and examined it in the light from her cruiser. 'This area is called the High Wire. It's a track that runs from Sydney to Broome in a beeline across the middle of the country. Kind of like a shortcut for losers and drug runners. Kids come out here sometimes from the conservation areas, joyriding stolen cars.'

The plate was unreadable. So was the one on the back. Edna popped the still-warm bonnet and licked her thumb, used the spit to clean the soot off the chassis number. She read it into her mic.

'Who called this in?' Talon was staring out at the dark.

'No idea. Might have been a pilot. There's an airstrip north of here. Birdsville. More likely a plane than a passer-by, around here.'

Her radio coughed.

'*Clare Holland,*' the dispatch officer said. '*Thirty-eight. Alice Springs.*'

'Is the car stolen?' Edna asked.

'*Not reported as such.*'

Something stirred in Edna's chest, a growing sense of unease. She told Dispatch to send her all of Holland's contact details. Talon was watching her, feet braced, ready for action. It tickled her heart a little, seeing him like that, so eager to leap into a distraction from his current predicament. She decided to let him tug on that line, pull himself hand over hand into a zone of mental comfort.

'So where's Clare Holland?' Edna asked the kid.

'I don't know.'

'Take a guess.'

'Maybe she, like, started walking.' Talon strode out of the reach of the cruiser's headlights, squinted off into the dark. 'Like, the car overheated and caught fire and she thought, *Fuck it, I'll walk.*'

'Well, the evidence doesn't say that.'

'What evidence?'

'I've got two sets of tyre tracks coming through here recently.' She crouched. The boy just about ran over to see. Edna pointed. 'This is her vehicle. See the chevron pattern?'

'Yeah.'

'Then we have someone pulling over to pick her up. See how their tyre track crosses hers? That's how we know they came after. Different pattern on this one. And we can see she got in. See her shoeprint?'

Talon nodded gravely.

'Then a third vehicle comes along. Heavier. Thicker tyres. Deeper tracks. See?'

'Yeah, I see. So, like, a truck or something?'

'Maybe. All we know right now is the order. Clare's car, then someone else, then someone else.'

They walked over to the car, peered in. The rear bench seat was a glowing, smouldering sponge, the upholstery coiled back, tiny embers being lifted and tossed like fire fairies as the breeze came through the busted windows. Edna went to the rear of the vehicle and kicked the boot open, looked inside. It was mostly intact. She reached in and flipped over the rough grey carpet liner, stared into the empty wheel bay.

'Weird.'

'What?' Talon appeared by her side.

'No spare tyre,' Edna said. 'Who sets out to drive across the country without a spare tyre?'

'There's also no bag.' Talon's tone was mildly hopeful. He shrugged to take the edge off, in case his suggestion was stupid. 'Like, if she's driven from Alice Springs all the way here, why didn't she pack her stuff? You know?'

'She might have grabbed the bag before the car caught alight,' Edna said. 'Taken it with her when she got picked up. But it was a good observation.'

'Do you think she's dead?'

Edna looked at the boy, laughed.

'Nah, serious.' Talon pointed at the tyre tracks. 'Like, she might have been picked up by a serial killer. You know? He followed her out here. *Hunted* her. Maybe he did something to her car when she stopped at a petrol station, so the car would overheat. Maybe the second vehicle, the truck, is part of it, too. Like, maybe that's a . . . a kill van. Maybe it's a *pair* of serial killers.'

Edna appraised the enormous teen, supposing the same overactive imagination that was carrying him away now with thoughts of outback murderers and kill vans was the same kind that convinced him that his soul mate was a stunningly beautiful seventeen-year-old girl who lived alone in the middle of the desert.

'Let's just calm down a bit.' Edna put a hand up. 'We might be getting ahead of ourselves here.'

Talon frowned.

'It's possible the car *is* stolen out of Alice Springs,' Edna went on. 'And this Clare Holland person just hasn't got around to reporting it yet. The first set of tyre tracks could be the joyrider in Clare's car. The second set are the joyrider's friends, who were following, maybe in another stolen vehicle, picking up their mate after they torched Clare's car. The third set is just some other unrelated driver in a truck or a van using the Wire to get from here to there.'

Talon looked at the burnt car.

'I know you'd like this to be something really exciting,' Edna said. 'But most of the time – in fact, almost always – it's not.'

A coldness had come over Talon's features. A blankness Edna had glimpsed so many times in her career, she knew what was coming even before the kid opened his mouth. She knew in her heart that the total lack of emotion she was seeing now had been seen only hours earlier by Alan Jacob Horn, right before Talon picked up the shotgun from beside the fridge. It was an absence, that look. It was the space that hope left behind when it fled.

'I'm not a fucking idiot, you know,' Talon said.

'Oh, I know.' Edna nodded. The kid again looked her over, as if she'd just disgusted and disappointed him at a level no other person ever had. Or maybe in exactly the same way many, *many* people had before. He shook his head, walked back to the car and slid in. He rolled down his window and leant an elbow on the sill.

'Hurry up with this, woman, so you can take me to jail,' he barked.

CHAPTER 5

Harvey was sinking. The weight of his horror was so large, so fast-moving, it came down like a hydraulic press and squeezed all the air out of him, made him bend double in a way the kick to the stomach hadn't. Darryl and Tizza. Harvey looked over at the man he'd killed, still sprawled on the dirt, one arm twisted behind his back, his corpse already stiffening in the frigid night air. His balaclava was still on, but it was painfully obvious to Harvey now who he was. He didn't know how he couldn't have seen it, heard it in his voice. That was Parker.

Darryl, Tizza and Parker.

His victims.

Tizza had dragged his balaclava off and was smiling in Harvey's face. The small, rat-faced man was as lean and angular as Harvey remembered; taut, freckled skin stretched over sinewed muscle.

'Are you happy to see us, Bucko?'

Harvey couldn't speak. There were no words for this. 'Nightmare' didn't come close. Tizza came behind him and cable-tied his wrists. He looked over at Clare, who had her head bent low, her chin tucked into her chest and her eyes squeezed shut.

'Listen, guys, I'm not looking,' Clare said. 'I'm not looking at your faces. Okay? I haven't seen you. You need to listen to me. I'm . . . I'm not a part of all this. Okay? There's no need to do an-an-an-anything to me. Okay? Okay? People are going to come looking for me, so—'

'I'm Nathan Tizza and this is Henry Darryl.' Tizza gestured at Darryl with his gun. 'So you're a part of it now, honey buns. Sucks to be you.'

'Please let me go.' Clare's cheeks were wet with tears, her eyes still squeezed shut. 'Please. I can't do this. I-I-I'm not – *involved in this!*'

Darryl went over and Clare cowered, tried to tuck herself into a ball. Harvey watched as the older man felt her pockets, back and then front, and pulled out her phone.

'Who are you?' Darryl asked. He pointed at Harvey. 'How do you know him? *Do* you know him?'

'No. He picked me up after my car overheated.'

'What are you doing out here?'

Clare's head was low, between her shoulders, shaking slowly. Darryl pressed the gun to the top of her skull. 'I asked you a question!'

'I'm Clare,' the woman said miserably. 'I'm thirty-eight. I-I-I . . . I fix dolls for a living, for god's sake. I have a dog. Her name is Shelley. She's a golden retriever. I have *nothing to do with this and you have to let me go. Please!*'

'Let her go.' Harvey locked onto Darryl. The older man had put on pounds since Harvey had last seen him, but the blond, tanned man was still straight-backed and rigid. A commanding presence. 'Whatever you've got planned for me; she's only going to complicate it.'

'Shut up, Buck, you piece of shit.'

'Be smart about this,' Harvey warned, still appealing to the older man, who he knew would be the brains of the operation. 'You're one man down, Darryl. Don't double your prisoners when you're already short-handed in containing them. It's a dumb move.'

Harvey was working backwards as he spoke, reverse-engineering and retracing the plan from where they were now. The vehicle Darryl had apparently arrived in was a medium-sized box truck, parked at an angle to the car Clare was leaning against, the one Tizza and Parker must have been following him in. The height of the tyres of the truck told Harvey it was almost certainly empty. There was only one reason they'd brought an empty truck out here. Only one reason Harvey wasn't dead already.

He was going in the back of that truck.

Then there was the drone. It must have been Darryl who was driving the truck, screaming towards the takedown, 'only five minutes out' when Tizza and Parker pulled ahead of Harvey, stopped, and threw the road spikes out for Harvey's car. It must have been Darryl who, seeing things were getting out of control up ahead, stopped the truck and flew the drone desperately into the side of Harvey's head, a last-ditch move to stop him from murdering Tizza. The smashed drone had to be the one Clare spotted from the car; the red flashing light Harvey had dismissed as a satellite. Darryl, Tizza and Parker had probably been tracking him through the desert with the drone auto-synced to follow his vehicle, maybe all the way from Alice, so Harvey wouldn't spot them tailing him on the long, barren plains. This was a creative venture, whatever it was.

A carefully planned abduction. Months, maybe a year, to set up. Harvey could only guess what kinds of pain and torment lay ahead of him, because to catch him and contain him alive like this meant his execution would be prolonged. If they didn't intend for him to suffer, they'd have come up behind him back in Alice on some ordinary morning while he was getting petrol and blown his brains out. No, Harvey knew it in his gut: there were bad things ahead for him.

But Clare, whoever she was, was tangled up in it now, and that was his fault. He'd brought her into this. Harvey had to do something before Darryl and Tizza turned their creativity on her.

'You already have Parker's body to deal with,' Harvey went on. 'Don't add another one to your workload. Load me up and leave the woman here.'

'"Load me up,"' Tizza snorted. 'Listen to him. You're already resigned to what you think is gonna happen here, Buck, aren't you?'

'I know what this is.' Harvey tapped the front of the vest. 'Doesn't take a genius.'

'What is it?' Clare had her eyes open now, her mouth downturned, miserable.

'These guys are weapons experts,' Harvey said. 'We were all in the army together. This is a bomb vest.'

Clare curled her feet up, looked at the men for confirmation. Tizza gave a round of applause. Darryl cocked his head. He was examining Clare as she cowered against the vehicle.

'It's not just a slap-together bomb vest, Buck.' Tizza nudged Harvey's knee with his boot, playful. 'Give us some credit. You've got 2.36 kilos of C-4 plastic explosive strapped to your torso right now. That's enough juice to vaporise anything within twelve metres of you. Whatever's within fifty metres after that will be air-fried at two thousand degrees Celsius. Anybody standing in the next fifty metres outside *that* is going to need some serious skin-graft action.'

'Don't start tooting your own horn,' Darryl moaned. 'I can't take it right now.'

'What's the detonator?' Harvey asked. 'Is it a phone? A remote?'

'You think I'm gonna tell you that?' Tizza shook his head. 'Give you something to shoot for? Fuck you. Could be anything. Could be my watch.' He showed Harvey his wrist. 'Could be my dick.'

'What's the detonation range?'

'That, I *can* tell you,' Tizza said. 'This is not some haji-made IED you're wearing. We don't need to have line of sight to turn you into the pink mist.'

'So don't try to run,' Darryl said.

'But the real art of this thing is in the construction.' Tizza shoved Harvey from the side, made him sway. 'Look at that. It fits you like a glove. I took three measurements to make that vest for you, Buck. Your army dress shirt from back in the day. A T-shirt I stole from your clothesline in Alice and a photograph I took in the street that I basically *forensically examined*, mate.'

'You stole a shirt from my clothesline?' Harvey squinted.

'I deep-dived into your personnel files.' Tizza grinned. 'I accessed your purchase records for your dress measurements. I was like a fucking detective. An old-school private eye.'

'Nathan,' Darryl growled.

'And I made three different-sized vests, just so we were prepared.'

Harvey looked wearily at Darryl. 'Wow. You've enjoyed every step of this. You really haven't got over what I did to you, have you? How long has it taken to cook all this up? The whole twelve years?'

Tizza punched him in the side of the head. Harvey swayed but didn't go down.

'I told you to lay off the fucking face,' Darryl snapped.

'I can't believe this is happening,' Clare was muttering to herself. 'I can't believe . . .'

'Now the only question becomes,' Tizza said, 'do we just shoot the woman, or do we put one of the spare vests on her and use her for a demonstration?'

'I don't need a demonstration.' Harvey dragged himself to his feet. 'Let her go.'

'Look at him standing there making demands,' Tizza giggled at Darryl. 'Bound and trussed up like a fucking turkey.'

'It's not a demand, it's a bargain,' Harvey said. 'An exchange. You let her go, and when the time finally comes, I'll make sure it's fast for you, Tiz. I won't make you suffer again.'

Something washed over Tizza's face.

'Because that's what's going to happen here,' Harvey said. 'I'm going to get free and you're going to die. This is all falling apart. It's already started. Parker is dead. Listen to me carefully. Your plan . . . is falling . . . *apart.* We're gonna be right back where we started, you and me.'

The smaller man stiffened, and through all the pain and exhaustion and terror Harvey saw something that gave him a little spark of joy in his heart. It was Nathan Tizza remembering, with cold and agonising clarity, those last days they'd spent together. Tizza the one bound like a turkey. Harvey with his bargains and demands, his promises to make the suffering stop. Darryl must have sensed a change in his partner, because he stepped forward and grabbed the gun before Tizza could raise it. Tizza's whole body jolted. His grip on the pistol was that tight.

'Keep it together. Go get a vest from the car,' Darryl murmured. 'The small one.'

Tizza walked stiffly around the car Clare was leaning against. Harvey had just begun to form the thought that now was Clare's chance, that with a car between her and Tizza, and Harvey between her and Darryl, this was the perfect moment for her to seize and use whatever she had left inside her. Then a snap noise sounded and the woman's hands came apart suddenly. Harvey's whole body lurched with exhilaration as Clare leapt to her feet holding the rock she'd been using to grind her cable tie off. He side-stepped out of the way just in time for her to hurl the rock directly at Darryl's head. The shot was beautifully on point. The tennis-ball-sized piece of sandstone slammed into Darryl's face directly beneath his left eye, snapping his head backwards. Harvey gave a roar of triumph as he watched the big man fall, and when he turned back, he saw what he'd longed with all his heart to see.

Nathan Tizza struck dumb with surprise.

And the woman named Clare sprinting away into the vast and empty darkness.

CHAPTER 6

Edna pulled up outside the tiny property and sat before the closed iron gate, staring at the shadows it made on the long gravel drive. The house was a one-bedroom truck-in job, a bungalow-style thing that had arrived on a semi-trailer some five years earlier. It had probably perched in a spritely fashion for its original owners in Cairns, but out here, it sagged on the exposed brick pillars under the verandah like a sad parrot in a cage, dreaming of the rainforest. Three decades of baking heat had weathered its boards, split its gutters, wreaked havoc on the eaves. The original colour, a cheerful apricot, was now the same colour as the soles of Edna's feet and was, like them, peeling. Talon woke in the seat beside her and stared in bewilderment at the unlit house, perhaps taking in the starkness of the dwelling on the barren landscape and wondering if Edna had tired of his attitude and driven him right back to where she found him. A house without a garden, a lawn, a garage or a driveway was an odd sight. Incomplete. A crude base on an unpopulated planet. Edna herself took a while to get accustomed to it when she arrived out here.

Talon turned his head and spotted the only other building visible for hundreds of kilometres around – the moonlit police station, which was a stone's throw from Edna's house. Its blue-and-white checked side was also blistered. 'You live right next to the cop shop?' Talon asked.

'I used to live *in* there.' Edna pulled up the handbrake. 'Until I got the house trucked in.'

'Why?'

'Because there was no Clifton Hills Police Force before me.' Edna got out. 'I started it. How good am I? Its members have doubled in number since then, too.'

She pushed open her gate and came back, drove in and parked the cruiser on the bare earth. Talon got out and stood guiltily by the corner of the verandah, hands in his pockets, staring at the hard, cracked ground.

'I'm not gonna make you go sleep in the station cell.' Edna rolled her eyes. Talon's face lifted slightly. 'I've got phone calls to make. As long as you're useful, you can keep hanging around with me.'

'Okay.' The boy followed like an eager hound.

'If you don't know how to make a good coffee, you better learn quick.'

They went inside. He was like an adult in a child's play kitchen, picking open the cupboard doors with tweezered fingers because his huge digits wouldn't hook around the handles. He grabbed the kettle and started filling it. Edna opened her laptop on the dining room table and tried not to gawk.

'So where's the man?' the boy asked, fishing around in the pantry.

'What man?'

'*Your* man.'

'I didn't know I needed one.'

Talon baulked, looked around the cupboard door at her. 'You tryin' to tell me you just live out here with no guy protecting you? No dog? No cameras? What's to stop a bunch of dudes just walking right in here and taking your stuff?'

'Me.' Edna smiled. 'And my .45.'

'That's crazy.' The boy made a loud click noise, sucking air down the side of his teeth. 'This whole area, no cops around, people just living out in the open all alone. It's not safe.'

'Talon,' Edna said. 'I *am* the cops.'

The boy muttered to himself.

'I don't know how you missed that fact.' Edna whipped quickly through her empty email folder. 'I'm literally working on dissecting a possible crime right in front of you. Open your eyes, kid.'

'But seriously, though,' he said, 'you'll have a crack at it and then they'll like, bring in a team, right?'

Edna sighed.

'They can't just leave it up to you. You could search this place with six hundred people and never find a bone or anything. If Clare Holland's body is out there, there are probably dingoes and—'

'You're getting ahead of yourself again,' Edna cautioned. 'We don't even know if Clare *was* out there. We don't even know if she's missing.'

'So how you gonna—'

'We start slowly.' Edna patted the chair beside her. 'And we inch our way forward. You sit here and dig up everything you can on Miss Holland. Join me in the year 2024 where women are allowed to live on their own and you can research people using the wonders of the internet.'

The boy brought the coffees over, sat at the laptop and started tapping. Edna texted Rebecca Stevenson an update, went to the wall by the front door and looked at the huge, laminated map she kept there. The map took in the upper right-hand corner of South Australia, a plain of almost entirely empty red desert walled in on the eastern side by both New South Wales and Queensland and in the north by Queensland and the Northern Territory. Edna's house and the Clifton Hills Police Station, a kilometre from the tiny town of Clifton Hills, crowned the top of her jurisdiction. In its entirety her area of responsibility stretched seventy-five kilometres to the upper border, one hundred and fifty kilometres to the border on the east and three hundred kilometres into the land mass on the west, extending five hundred kilometres south. Overall, Edna and Stevenson, along with Indigenous leaders in the communities that dotted their jurisdiction, enforced law in a land area almost as large as New Zealand.

Edna found the High Wire, a solid red line she had charted on the map herself with a marker. It crossed her territory like a jagged scar, lifting and falling as it avoided small towns and Indigenous communities. She traced a finger up from Alan Horn's property at the edge of the Simpson Desert Regional Reserve, across what she knew were blank, featureless fields of cracked red earth, and touched the approximate area where she and Talon had stood two hours earlier with Clare Holland's burnt-out car. She took a purple pin from a cannister on a table beneath the framed map and stuck it into the Wire.

'Middle of nowhere,' Talon said. He was standing just behind her now. Edna turned and looked at him, shrugged.

'Yes and no.' She put a finger on a spot on the map sixty kilometres south of where the pin stood. 'We have eyes out there. We're not blind.'

'What, satellites?'

'If some are going over and recording, sure,' she said. 'But there are other options. Here, for example. There's a sort of cult community settled here. Doomsday weirdos. With a little cajoling, and offers of money, maybe, we could try to get access to their security cameras. They're paranoid. They have their whole property marked out with heavy surveillance and if you go anywhere near them they know about it. Send guys out on horseback to stop you wandering in.'

Talon lifted an eyebrow. 'So they have cameras up here near the High Wire?'

'No, no. But maybe whoever picked up Clare, or whoever was in Clare's car, was from the settlement. Or came by there on the way to the Wire. Maybe it's nothing, but we need to work with what we've got here.'

'What else *have* we got?'

Edna noted the boy's use of the word 'we'. Her own use of it. Guilt was twinging in her chest. 'Ah, well, there's also a line of electric grid towers that crosses from here to here.' Edna tapped the map. 'It carries power from Birdsville all the way down to these townships. I've actually dealt with the guy who services them. Some have cameras. We had a bit of trouble last year with kids going out there trying to climb the towers.' She traced the powerline, a thin blue cord that was marked on the official map. 'When this line was put in, it crossed over the High Wire. That was a problem. Because the whole point of the Wire is that it skirts all civilisation. People can travel on it without being picked up by cameras, running into tourists or cops. So when the powerline was built over the top of the Wire, they had to change it. The Wire now runs down past here.'

'I don't get it.' Talon squinted. 'If the High Wire is a secret road, and it's unsealed, how do you know you're even on it?'

'It's marked in certain places,' Edna said.

'What, with signs?'

'Not with sign-signs,' Edna said. 'With "signs".'

'What the hell are you talking about?'

'You have to know what you're looking for.'

'Well, it doesn't seem to me like Clare's on that side of stuff, anyway. Like, the badass side.'

'What do you mean?'

'She's not in the life,' Talon said. He went to the laptop and turned it towards Edna. 'She's not cutting through the outback on a secret road to do shady shit.'

'Why not?'

'Because she's the top cop's wife.'

Edna went to the laptop and looked at a newspaper article that dominated the screen. She could see that Talon had Facebook, Twitter and Instagram open on other tabs, but it was Nine News that had a picture of tall and tanned Clare Holland wearing a white skirt-suit and watching demurely as her husband spoke at a podium. Garreth Holland was blinking in the photo, his square jaw tight, a hand on the mic. The article was about a renewed search for the remains of missing backpacker Peter Falconio, presumed murdered in the desert between Alice and Darwin. Edna took in Garreth's steel-rimmed glasses and the dark five o'clock shadow trying to hint through the taut muscles of his throat, and something uncharacteristically shallow fluttered in her mind, a knee-jerk revulsion. She saw images of steel and razors and aftershave and sticky lotions. Edna told herself it was a symptom of dealing with police bureaucracy for too long.

'What does she do?' Edna asked.

'She's got a weird-ass job,' Talon snorted, flicking over to a Facebook page. 'People send her their old dolls and she, like, cleans them and fixes them up.'

Edna scrolled through the images of wet-the-bed-style vinyl dolls, naked and dishevelled, being measured by careful hands, she assumed, for custom clothing. A heavily filtered artistic shot of Clare in a messy ponytail bent over a porcelain doll dominated the cover page. She was peering through a specialised set of spectacles, painting eyelashes on a bald doll's face. The image was strangely maternal, Edna thought. Clare gripped the doll's whole head in her palm like an apple.

'I guess she doesn't need to make any actual money,' Talon said. 'Commissioner of Police. You'd be rolling in it, right?'

'There could be big money in dolls, you never know.' Edna shrugged. 'Collectors and stuff.'

'Should we ring the number?'

Edna checked her phone. The mobile number given on Clare's Facebook page was the same as the one listed on her business website and her car's registration. She dialled it. An automated voice message told Edna her call could not be connected.

'She's out there.' Talon nodded gravely. 'See? That proves it. She's got no reception. It's because she's out there rotting in the desert and her phone is with her.'

'Or she's in the bath and her phone is switched off,' Edna sighed. 'Talon, you've got to reel in that imagination.'

'One thing I did see. There's an event. For tomorrow afternoon, I think.' Talon clicked and the page disappeared, making way for a different one. 'Ah, where is it . . .? Yeah, okay, look.

Right here. An auction. Clare's selling dolls at a show in Alice Springs. Or she's supposed to be.'

'So if Clare was planning to still be in Alice twelve hours from now,' Edna looked at her watch, 'what's she doing out here in the middle of the outback?'

They sat in silence, side by side, their coffees on the table and the laptop between them.

'It can't be her.' Talon's shoulders sagged. 'It's like you said. Someone's stolen her car. Driven it out here. She's, like, gotten too busy to report the car stolen. Or she hasn't bothered because her husband is the police. You don't need to report something to the police if you're married to the police. She's in the bath, I guess, with her phone switched off.'

Edna looked up at the huge teenager, who had deflated a few inches in his disappointment. Because while she hoped deep down in her soul that Clare Holland was indeed alive and well, Edna knew that the unlikelihood of the case being anything titillating would quickly start dragging her young charge back to reality. And Talon's reality wasn't good. There were the charges for the car he'd stolen and driven to Horn's house. The plane trip back to Adelaide. The currently sidelined grief over the girl Talon had fallen in love with, the girl Horn had been pretending to be. Minute by minute, the boy was nearing the inevitable return to whatever awaited him in his life back home. Edna didn't know for sure, but she was starting to feel as if the kid's propensity to leap at anything that might take him away from thinking about that life was a hint that it was less than wholesome. The boy was like a bird smashing itself against anything that looked like a window as it tried to escape a house. She took a chance and patted his warm, wide back.

As soon as her fingers met the cotton of his T-shirt, he stiffened and shifted away.

'Don't lose heart, big fella,' Edna said anyway. 'Clare Holland could well be out there, having her femurs munched on by dingoes.'

Talon smirked.

'Let's take it slowly for now, discover what we can discover.' Edna took up her coffee. 'There's no need to go to panic stations just yet.'

CHAPTER 7

Darryl threw him into the back of the truck, just to be a prick. Harvey fell on his knees, rolled, tucked himself into a ball. No further violence came. There wasn't time. Clare was out there somewhere and the big man needed to join the search. The doors slammed shut. Harvey scooted over in the pure blackness until he found a corner in the truck bed and felt for the sharp metal edge of a seam in the wall to rub his cable tie against. But the truck started and swerved hard before he got the chance, sending him toppling sideways. The truck turned around and accelerated into the uneven desert, and all Harvey could hope to do was hang on. He lay on his good side and pulled his knees against his chest and squeezed his eyes shut.

Don't panic, he said to himself. *Don't panic. Don't panic. Don't panic.* He drew a deep breath, held it, counted off seconds, let it out. Because the panic was *right there*; closer than arm's reach, as alluring as sleep to the exhausted. And while most people thought they knew what it was to panic, Harvey knew what it *really* was, because he'd done it. He'd panicked so hard he'd lost all control of his body, tucked himself into a ball on the desert floor, the huge sky above him raining down its hellish heat from every possible angle, the horizon a blinding, endless nothingness, a scream of helplessness exiting his lips and going nowhere, because there was no one out there to hear it. Being burnt alive, slowly cooked, a bug on a grill.

No, no, no, no, no. Harvey opened his eyes, sucked air in through his nostrils, blew it out through his lips hard. *I'm not there. I'm not there. I'm here.*

There was a tiny pinprick of green light high above him. It shuddered and shook as the truck crashed over clumps of spinifex and rocks and whatever else, racing across the outback. A camera. Harvey latched onto the sight of it. Pushed away the memories. He listened and picked up the sound of Tizza's car out there in the desert hunting Clare alongside the truck. It seemed an hour he lay there listening, breathing, the truck stopping, idling, the two men shouting to each other through open windows, the truck going again. In time he heard a scream and a scuffle and he knew with a sickening despair that Clare had been caught.

The truck doors opened. Moonlight poured in. Harvey pushed himself into a sitting position and immediately found a seam in the wall, started aligning the tie between his wrists with it.

The run had taken all the fight out of Clare. She lay on the wood and sobbed while they dragged the vest onto her and zipped it up along the spine. Harvey watched carefully, squinting, eyes fixed on what he could see of how Tizza's hands worked.

'Look at that.' Tizza stood back. 'No room for tits. But it's nice and snug.'

'It's like you made it just for her,' Darryl smirked.

They dragged her wrists behind her back and cable-tied them.

'Break your ties again and I'll knock your teeth out.' Tizza was standing over her, the little man pointing down at the helpless woman curled on the floor at his feet, an image that made Harvey's blood boil. 'You understand?'

'Don't get any smart ideas about the vests, either of you.' Darryl was leaning against the truck wall. His face was lit for a half a second, gold and hollow, as he sparked a Zippo against the end of his cigarette. He exhaled towards Harvey. 'The zipper is wired from inside the vest. Pull it down, you'll complete the circuit and it's *kablowie* for the two of you.'

'Same if you try to slip them off.' Tizza was a streak of darkness against the flat blue moonscape outside. 'There's a tension wire running the full circumference. Break that and you're gone. I wouldn't even breathe too hard, if I were you.'

'What are you gonna do with us?' Clare was huddled against the wall, close enough that Harvey could feel her body heat from the sprint into the dark. 'You can't – you can't be serious with this. You're not going to-to-to *blow us up*!'

The men looked at each other. Harvey could see Tizza was grinning in the dark.

'What do you want from us?' Clare screamed. 'Just tell us what you want!'

They didn't answer. Darryl jutted his chin and the two men hopped down from the back of the truck. The doors slammed, sealing Harvey and Clare in darkness.

'I can't breathe.' Clare was panting hard. 'I can't – I can't – I can't—'

'You have to breathe.' Harvey rubbed his bound hands hard against the seam. 'Deep breaths, in and out.'

'He said there's—'

'That was bullshit,' Harvey said. 'The zipper, sure. I can see that. The zipper comes down far enough and it flips a switch on its way. Same switch it flipped on its way up. Boom. But they dragged that vest over your head without any concern at all for expanding a tension wire. You can breathe all you want.'

Clare sucked in a shuddering breath, blew it out hard. Harvey's tie broke. He flexed his wrists, then shifted over and reached out, tried to put an arm around her.

'Don't *fucking* touch me!' Clare nudged him away. 'This is all your fault!'

'All right. Understood.'

'What the hell are we gonna do?' It was her shifting over to him now, second thoughts about the physical contact probably spurred by pure terror. 'We've got to work together. Tell me what you know. I mean, you know these guys, right? From the army? You must know how we can get away from them.'

'We'll talk about all that later.' Harvey dragged himself to his feet and stood back, tried to get a full picture of the truck wall, looking for cracks where light was showing. He backed into a large trunk he half-remembered spotting when the truck doors were open, almost sat on it. Then he noticed a tiny sliver of light where the seams of the steel panels on the side of the truck met. He went there, pressed an eye to the gap. 'Right now, we need to listen.'

He'd heard Tizza and Darryl out in the dark. Their conversation had lowered and slowed from the jubilant and quickened chatter he'd heard in the background of Clare's panic when the men first exited the truck. Now he could see them, standing maybe twenty metres away, two cigarettes glowing in the night.

Harvey felt Clare shifting around at his feet as she tried to find an edge to cut her ties. He pressed his ear against the gap in the truck wall, closed his eyes and listened hard.

'. . . her as leverage, just in case.'

'No. That's not smart. Someone will know she's out here. The husband. The boyfriend. Whoever the fuck. We don't need to complicate things. We'll take her a few kilometres down the road and use her to show Buck how the vest works. I'm dumping the phone here.'

'Shouldn't we look through it? See who she is? What if she's someone?'

'I don't want to know who she is, Nathan. I'm about to make fertiliser out of her.'

'Okay, but, we should think about this. I mean, sure, it could end up that Buck doesn't feel anything for her at all. Maybe he won't factor her into his next few moves. But if we keep her alive, Dar, she could be a useful backup option.'

'You're talking about doubling the prisoners, with one third of our party gone.' Darryl gave a sharp, disappointed sigh, the voice of reason arguing with a moron. 'It's exactly what Buck called it: a dumb-as-shit move.'

'But she's a woman, Dar.'

'So? You've killed plenty of fucking women. Don't give me that. You weren't sitting in that control room pushing buttons and blowing up cows.'

'I mean she's hysterical. It's not two against two here.'

'Yes, it is.'

'If we do her now, it'll be fun, but we might regret it down the track. Imagine if Buck pulls something. And you *know* he's going to pull *something*. He gets one foot on the road to freedom, say. Without her, we'll have no way of drawing him back in.'

'He won't get a *half* a foot out of line,' Darryl growled. 'He makes a break for it; we toast him. That's what we agreed.'

'Yes, but—'

'We said it from the start: we keep our eye on the prize. We don't get fancy.'

'They are literally out there discussing whether or not they're going to kill me,' Clare said. Harvey looked down but could see nothing but a black mass by his feet. He slid to crouch next to her. 'How did this happen?'

'Doesn't matter how it happened,' Harvey said. 'We've got to plan how we're going to deal with it. First things first: we need to make a pact. Either of us gets an opportunity to run, we run. You demonstrated a willingness to do that already. And that's great. But you gotta understand; the best thing for me to do if I get a shot at freedom is to beat it and get help. Understand?'

He heard her sniff. 'Sure. I get it.'

'It's not very chivalrous, but—'

'No, no, I get it. It's smart.'

'Second thing we have to get our heads around is the fact that this is a long game,' he said. 'They've put a camera in the ceiling. See the green light up there? And that box—'

'What box?'

'There's a box in the corner. Probably full of supplies. Food. Blankets. Water. We might be out on the road for a couple of days with these pricks.'

'For what? *For what?* I don't understand!' Clare's voice was thin and rattling with frustration. 'Why are they *doing* this to you?'

'It's a long story,' Harvey sighed. He sat with his back against the truck wall. 'Point is this: they're going to exhaust us. We have to exhaust them right back. If they're exhausted and frustrated they'll make mistakes that one or the both of us can exploit to get free.'

'Okay. So how do we do that?'

'Every time they come for us, we fight,' Harvey said. 'We try to run. I mean every single time, whether it's viable or not. We need to be really annoying. We keep cutting our binds. We fuck with the vests.'

'If we fuck with the vests they'll blow us up!' Clare said.

'Unlikely. These guys are weapons specialists. Tizza, in particular, is very talented. At least, that's how I remember him. He'd have sewn these vests by hand. They'll be beautifully designed and constructed. You heard what lengths he went to to get my measurements. We'll get a proper look at them when we have light, but they won't want us detonating our vests unintentionally when we're standing right next to them. The vest won't blow until they're finished with . . .' He searched for words, couldn't find any. '. . . With whatever they're going to do to us.'

Clare's breaths had slowed.

'We have to undermine their confidence in their plan, relentlessly,' Harvey said. '*This is all falling apart.* We have to repeat it. Get that into their heads: This is all falling apart.'

'This is all falling apart.' Clare's voice was tinged, slightly, with certainty. There was a mere whisper of it. They sat in silence. Harvey's vision was adjusting to the interior of the truck. He was picking out the makeshift blast screen welded to the front of the truck bed that would protect the driver and cabin passenger from an explosion if their vests went off unexpectedly.

Although he'd just done a lot to sell the idea to Clare that her vest, or his, would not explode if she breathed too hard or moved wrong, the blast screen undermined that completely. Harvey tried not to think about that. Or about the capture in general, and how Darryl and Tizza and Parker had known exactly where to catch him, and when. Had known so precisely that they'd set all this up; packed the box of supplies, been following him with a fucking drone, for god's sake. Harvey willed himself not to think about what that meant for Shayna. For the phone call. The cancer. Her impending death. The frightened tone to her voice. For him being out on the Wire that night in the first place.

Instead, he went on. 'While we're in here, we need to spend every second we have trying to come up with something we can either use to escape or use to fuck with their minds. I know them. I know their relationship dynamic. We need to start digging away at that relationship at every available opportunity. You're a woman. That's been an issue for them already. We need to use that. Darryl in particular, it'll be a big thing for him. He won't mind if you die but how you're treated will be important.'

'Won't they be listening to us through the camera? If that even is a camera. Although I suppose they didn't bank on me being here when they put it in.' Clare sighed. Harvey knew she was swallowing some pretty hard resentment. 'You were supposed to be back here alone.'

'Right. And it's a loud truck,' Harvey said. 'Not worth the effort to rig audio decent enough to pick up anything above the background noise.'

'How do you know them?' she asked. He knew she wasn't going to give it up. And pure instincts were telling Harvey he wouldn't be able to resist forever. 'I need to understand why they're doing this. I think . . . I think I'd be able to cope better if I just knew what the hell happened between you all.'

Harvey chewed his lip in the dark, listened to the men grinding out their cigarettes and climbing back into their vehicles. He'd overheard a little of their plan. All he could do now was sit and wait for the next phase of it to play out.

Harvey sighed. 'I kind of deserve all this,' he said.

2011

Harvey should have listened to the dog. Even before they'd set out for Tarin Kot, he'd been overseeing his guys packing the Bushmaster to roll out and Jafna had been walking around panting and wild-eyed, occasionally coming up to paw at his shins, which wasn't like her at all. A skinny desert mongrel Harvey's section had brought back to base as a puppy, Jaf had almost certainly been born out here in the scrubby, rocky wilds of northern Afghanistan and could tolerate the blinding heat of the day as much as a mild night. Harvey had seen the dog walk on still-smouldering ashes, bury herself under a blanket to sleep when the surface temperature of the trucks lying out in the sun was enough to scald a guy who brushed past. She wasn't hot, he would think later. She knew what was coming.

Their vehicle was in the middle of the convoy, right behind the Bushmaster carrying the booty. As Harvey rode shotgun beside his sergeant, Sav, he could see the back of the head of the guy they were escorting. The stocky, balding American weapons expert was an asset being moved from a stronghold in Durji to the multi-national base at the bottom of the mountains, and it had been communicated to Harvey and all the mission leaders in no uncertain terms that loss of the booty, either through his death or capture, would be like losing a nuclear missile. For a man who was apparently so important he required two whole sections and four heavily armoured vehicles to make sure he made it to his rack safely, the man's gratitude was non-existent or masterfully disguised. Harvey had introduced himself to the guy, Sheerwater, before they loaded up, and it was like he hadn't been standing there at all, watching the man trying to fit a combat helmet on his fleshy skull, his brow wanting to fold down over his eyes. Harvey had struggled with the impulse to hammer his fist on top of the lid and jam the helmet on the man, the way he'd done to recruits a couple of times at the academy, because a too-tight helmet was better than a loose one. But in the end he'd just offered the guy his own lid, because if he'd learnt anything since his enlistment it was that you didn't piss off important people.

Harvey rode now with Jafna still whining in his lap, held onto the window frame beside him and watched the back of that head in the next vehicle bobbing around, wondering how much genius it took to invent bombs that could seek out people the way bees sought out flowers from miles away, with no visual clue. Flying killer robots that ran on instinct and rechargeable batteries. And okay, so maybe there was a little resentment bubbling in Harvey's chest that night. Since the war started, he had four confirmed kills to his name, all close up, and although they weren't fucking him up yet, he knew they almost certainly would. Maybe when he returned home to Sydney and bought a property out west, maybe at the foot of the Blue Mountains, no town water, no fences. Ghosts would wander the tree line, creeping over his verandah, whispering in the crackling of his firepit, dancing in Jafna's eyes. Did Ole Mate look forward to the same kind of haunting? Did Sheerwater – hell, it was probably *Doctor* Sheerwater – get printouts of how many empty-eyed, half-starved, war-exhausted Afghans his weapons had blown apart at the end of the month and go twisting and turning in his sleep? Would Sheerwater be that twitchy, disgruntled crone in the corner of the nursing home too ravaged by his active service to hold a conversation without dissolving into shaking, spittle-flying rage? No. Harvey knew that grunts like himself ended up in nursing homes, and weapons experts died in their beds in their harbourside mansions. He patted the dog on his lap and listened to Sav take the order from the guys in the back seat.

'Carro, what you havin'?'

'Big Mac meal. Six-pack of nuggets. Coke for the drink. No ice.'

'What sauce?'

'Huh?'

'What sauce for the nuggets?'

'They never give you the sauce.' Carro chuckled.

'Yes they do. The sauce *comes* with the nuggets, dipshit.'

'Not in the drive-thru. It's a deliberate corporate strategy. You've got to go inside to get sauce.'

Harvey turned around in his seat, told himself not to encourage Carro but did anyway. 'What?'

'Think about it.' Carro yawned, shifted his rifle against his chest. The only ADFA graduate in the vehicle. 'One McDonald's restaurant directs its staff working the drive-thru window to "forget" the sauce tub on every second order that comes in. Driver doesn't discover there's no sauce in the bag until they pull over somewhere to eat, and they don't go back for the sauce because hey, it's just sauce. Doesn't make a complaint or leave a bad Google review because—'

'It's just *sauce*,' someone moaned. 'Jesus, can we not?'

'In a year,' Carro continued, 'the restaurant that keeps forgetting the sauce racks up a couple of hundred bucks in savings. Expand that policy and those savings out across hundreds upon hundreds of McDonald's restaurants all across Australia, year after year. That's a sizeable dent in expenditure.'

'It's true, you know.' Sav nodded sagely beside Harvey. 'I've had it happen to me. You look in the bag. No sauce. You do nothing about it.'

'Your life is really hard, isn't it, Sav?' someone said.

'It is.'

'The rich are getting richer and the poor are getting poorer,' Carro sighed. 'One packet of sauce at a time.'

'I'm going to need you guys to stop pretending you're hitting the McDonald's drive-thru every time we go out.' Harvey rubbed his temple. The small helmet was like a vice on his skull. 'Find another game.'

The games. The rivalries. The weird 'Pussy Pool' the section had created, where each man contributed a picture of his girlfriend or his cousin or his sister into a communal pot for wank material. The reality of day bleeding into day and night bleeding into night with no action and nothing to do dissolving the boundaries between kinky and mundane, laughable and dangerously weird. Harvey's job was closer to high school teacher a lot of the time, only his class was carrying weapons that could end lives, and some of them were too eager to do that, and some of them weren't eager enough. He and the other teachers were coming together whenever they could to exchange ideas about how to keep their students from shooting each other or themselves or an ally while Command seemed determined to make them do just that.

Jafna sat up in Harvey's lap suddenly, started barking at the two vehicles ahead of them rolling through the desert. The bark was so loud it seemed to pulse against the windows. Harvey flipped his night-vision down and for a moment it seemed it was faulty – the glass showing dim outlines of the cars ahead in a wash of white light. Then he felt Savage whip his head around beside him.

'What the fuck is that?' Savage was looking at Harvey's helmet, at the top. Harvey reached up, saw the shadow of his arm on the dashboard.

'What?'

'There's a light.'

'Where?'

'On the top of your helme—'

The crack came before the gunshot sound, a sonic snap as the tracer round passed the front of the car. They were bathed in light, a roaring rush of noise mistimed to the explosion of the rocket-propelled grenade coming out of nowhere and colliding with the side of the vehicle ahead. Savage slammed on the brakes and Harvey felt Jafna tumble into the footwell, a collection of pointy, hairy limbs. The Bushmaster was a tough vehicle, but not tough enough to withstand the force of the grenade, which made a direct hit with the side and torched every man in the vehicle, crushing them against the doors and ceiling, a charred box of bones and flesh. Harvey moved on autopilot. He opened his door and slid out at the same time as Carro and English and Bak-Li, just as a tracer round took out Savage in the front seat, light like an enormous halo expanding out from the back of his head as his face was blown off from behind.

Nobody shouted in combat. It wasn't like the ambushes and coordinated attacks the guys so loved to crowd around and hoot and holler at on someone's laptop at the base. *Get down! Get down! Run! Run!* Everybody knew what to do, and shouting over the gunfire was pointless. Harvey's mind was quiet; gathering information, planning, reacting. There were two layers of enemy combatants; a group on the shallow hillside and a second group, close in, popping up from the scrubland like so many apparitions materialising out of the dark. Harvey looked behind the burning truck that Sheerwater was cooking in and saw the lead vehicle from the convoy was gone. He hadn't fired a single shot yet, though his guys were exchanging pot shots with the approaching footmen. This wasn't right. Any of it. The front vehicle should have backed up, joined the formation as a blockade behind which the soldiers could shelter. There were too many hajis out there for this to have been an accident. Harvey leant on the bumper of the Bushmaster and lined up a shot and blew off the head of a guy who was trying to approach from the north.

Five, he thought. He clicked the radio on his headset.

'Mayday, mayday, mayday, sec—'

Harvey paused, clicked the receiver a bunch of times, got no feedback rattling in his earpiece. No static. Nothing. He crouched behind the bumper of the Bushmaster and felt his sweat turn cold the instant it rose on his skin.

'What the *fuck?*'

Harvey tore his helmet off, tossed it to the ground beside him. For the first time, he saw what Savage had seen in the truck. A tiny green light on the crown of the helmet, no bigger than a grain of rice, a micro-bulb he hadn't noticed in the light of day that was nevertheless giving off a powerful light now. Carro was lying slumped against the back tyre of the Bushmaster, death-dancing, a hole in his neck. Harvey crawled there and dragged off his helmet, pulled it on, clicked the receiver.

'Mayd—'

No sound. No life on the radio. It didn't make any sense. Harvey bashed the receiver on the side of the helmet with his palm.

A shape materialised out of the dark in front of him. Harvey fired, teeth gritted, bullet holes from the guy's AK punching into the door of the vehicle beside his head while the man took a double-tap from Harvey's rifle in the chest. *Six.* There was another combatant behind the man Harvey killed. They just kept coming, one being replaced by another. How many were there? Harvey's rifle clicked. He popped and loaded another magazine, a half-second max, but by that time the guy was right up on him, toe to toe, the barrel of an old AK in his face. Harvey squeezed his eyes shut and prepared to die.

'Hu huna! 'Linah huna!'

He's here! He's over here!

The guy wasn't pointing at Harvey. He was pointing to the helmet beside him, the tiny green light. He took his eyes off Harvey, and a hand off the rifle, and though Harvey was too stunned and confused to take advantage of the moment, Jafna apparently wasn't, because the dog slithered out of the gap in the open front door like a collection of black smoke and flew at the man with the rifle and took him down, the dog somehow twice as big as Harvey remembered her being, her shoulders hunched and head tossing back and forth as she tore out the man's throat.

Harvey got up and sprinted off into the dark, trying to get away from the lights, the vehicles, the flames roiling and licking up over the roof of the Bushmaster in front of his. He huffed and ran and huffed and ran, cold night air in his lungs, eyes dancing across the rocky hills in front, trying to find a good place to set up with the rifle to give cover fire to the guys down at the convoy, if any of them were still alive. He tripped and fell over a body twenty metres out. The body sat up. Harvey swung his rifle up, almost lined up and shot the guy until he recognised the shape of his helmet against the burning truck and the tracer rounds, the stupid little devil horns Bak-Li had glued there.

'Boss! Boss! It's me!'

'Come on.' Harvey hooked the rifle across his body. He dragged Bak-Li up onto his shoulders. One of the soldier's legs stayed on the rocky, dry ground, the boot slick with blood. 'We gotta go.'

'My radio—'

'They're all out. We can't call for help.'

'What the fuuuu—'

'Shut up.' Harvey started running towards the mountains, Bak-Li's head on his shoulder. 'Just shut up and hold on.'

CHAPTER 8

Harvey was just thinking about those guys, his dead section: Bak-Li with his devil-horned helmet, and Carro with his damn business degree, and Savage with the five or six photographs of busty women he'd contributed to the Pussy Pool – the one picture Harvey knew he'd kept back for himself and only looked at when he thought everyone was asleep; a smiling shot of a guy in a suit and tie at a function, maybe a wedding. Harvey couldn't think of any nice things about the six men he'd led in Afghanistan, about where they were today. They were all in the ground. But now and then, he liked to imagine Jafna had managed to escape the fray and was still out there in the mountains north-east of Tarin Kot, most of her mind given over to the wilds, her first couple of years as his section's mascot faded to flashes in her brain. Somehow, he ached for her the most just then in the back of the box truck. He put his hands on his thighs and remembered the weight of her lying there.

He had let his words about what happened way back when die down to nothing as the truck stopped, and they listened to Tizza dumping his car and sliding in with Darryl. As the truck roared on, he hadn't picked up the thread again. It seemed to weigh more than he had the strength to lift.

'So,' he said to Clare, running from it as he always did. 'A golden retriever?'

She looked at him.

'Shelley? You said she was back home, waiting for you.'

'Oh.' She rubbed her face hard. He could see her more clearly now as the truck rattled along. Morning was coming. 'No. That was bullshit. I just . . . I was trying to give them something to humanise me. They say to do that. On the true crime shows.'

'So I guess you don't have any kids.'

'No.'

'The doll-making stuff?'

'I mean . . . I repair them.'

'You got to study for that?'

'No.' She huffed a tiny laugh. 'It's just . . . a profession that finds you. Latches onto you. Gets into your blood.'

'Like a parasite.'

She actually laughed. 'Jesus, mate.'

'It was your metaphor, not mine.'

'I found a doll,' she said. 'In the gutter. I was walking home from school. It was lying face down. I took it home and cleaned it up and . . . I mean, I was too old for dolls, you know? I was a teenager. But she just seemed so sad. And I felt good afterwards. Like I'd done a nice thing for her.'

Harvey smiled now, understanding.

'Then I sold her for four thousand dollars.'

'*How much?*'

'It was my neighbour, actually, who noticed she was worth something.' Clare nodded. 'She said she used to have a doll just like that one when she was a kid. Well, this lady was in her eighties, right? So I got to thinking: if the doll's that old, it must be an antique. And it was. I had a buyer inside of a week. A guy in Russia. This was back in the early days of eBay.'

Harvey felt his mouth twist, found himself not knowing what to feel. The story about the sad, face-down doll had sucked him in. The eBay deal spat him back out.

'I bought my first car with that money,' Clare said.

'That's a hell of a trick, for a teenager.'

'Yeah, I got a real hunger for it.' Clare shook her head. 'Everywhere I looked, there was money to be made. But I'm rambling now.'

'It's interesting. Keep going.'

'I've found three-hundred-dollar dolls at garage sales with fifty-cent stickers on them. Whole doll collections going free from deceased estates, worth tens of thousands of dollars. People don't know what they're worth. And they don't care! They think dolls are creepy. And yeah, a lot of them are. Artists were terrible at getting the faces right, up until the 1980s. And the plastics were all yellow and the eyes were all glass. Before nylon came in, these dolls had animal or human hair, which stinks after a while. But, if you look past all that, doll trading and repair is big business.' She glanced over at him. 'Oh, god. Listen to me.'

'You're very defensive of your job.'

'I am.'

'Because people look down on it,' Harvey surmised. 'They think it's a weird hobby. A grown woman playing with dolls.'

'I'm just an antiques dealer,' she said. 'But the antiques have faces.'

'What does your partner think about it?'

A muscle in Clare's jaw twitched. Harvey watched as she twiddled the wedding ring on her finger, probably deducing quietly that he'd noticed it, that it had inspired his whole line of inquiry, which it had.

'He thinks . . . what most people think.' She shrugged.

'You didn't mention him.'

'Well, this isn't a date,' she snapped, her eyes suddenly fierce, turned on him.

'I didn't mean to me. I meant to Darryl and Tiz,' Harvey said. 'You mentioned your job. You mentioned a fictional dog. You were trying to get into their minds that you're a person and not a game piece to be used or thrown away. You were trying to create empathy. And that's smart. So why not mention the husband? Why not say, "I have a husband who I need to get back to. A husband who loves me."'

She pressed her lips tightly, didn't answer. Harvey looked at the bruises on her wrist. She saw him looking and let her hand flop down beside her so that her legs blocked his view.

The truck slowed and then stopped and Clare's whole body seemed shot with electricity. She scooted over next to him. Harvey could feel her shivering. The voices of Darryl and Tizza in the cabin beyond the reinforced wall were too dim to decipher.

'Where are we?' Clare whipped around, pressed an eye to the seam between the steel panels. Pale light illuminated a slice of her face. 'I don't see anything.'

'We're about to find out. Remember. Mind games, Clare. If we see an opportunity, we use it.'

She made an uncertain sound deep in her throat. The truck doors opened. Harvey hung cut and bleeding wrists over his knees.

Darryl pointed his gun at Clare. 'You get out first.'

While Clare climbed awkwardly out of the truck, Harvey used the precious seconds of filtered light falling into the truck's interior to take in what he could of his prison. The camera in the ceiling was a cheap model, as he'd expected, nothing that came with audio as standard. The box he'd almost fallen on was maybe a metre long, half a metre wide and insulated, two latches in the front. He scanned the floor quickly for signs of a nail or screw he might be able to use as a weapon or to pick at his vest's stitches, but there wasn't time. Tizza had his gun trained on him now.

'Get out,' Tizza said.

Harvey went to the end of the truck bed, sat down on its edge and slid out. He landed hard on one foot and pretended to stumble, and Darryl was close enough in that he bent at the waist, automatically, hands out, as though to catch him. It was the same instinctive bodily response that made people stick out their palm when offered one from a stranger, the training to shake hands instilled in most people since childhood. Darryl checked himself in time, but it was too late. They were close. Face to face. Harvey pretended to right himself with a hand on the ground, scooped up a fistful of sand instead and pitched it as hard as he could into Darryl's eyes.

'Argh! *Je*-sus!'

Harvey didn't wait. He punched the dark shape of Darryl's head, a devastating downward blow he hoped caught him right where the lump of sandstone Clare had hurled at him earlier. Darryl went down backwards, rolled, gripping his face. Harvey had hoped to draw Tizza in, to give Clare a chance to run again, even if she wouldn't get far, even if the vest she was wearing really could be detonated from long distance. It was worth testing the theory by seeing if either man tried. But Tizza had backed up, his pistol wavering between the two hostages.

'Hands up! Hands up! *Hands up!*'

Harvey put his hands up. Darryl was groaning, pulling himself by the edge of the truck bed. Clare was three large steps back from where she'd started, seemed set to sprint again, but Tizza wheeled the gun around.

'Don't even fucking think about it.'

'I'm going to enjoy killing you so much, Buck, I swear to god,' Darryl was muttering, clawing at his eyes. 'You piece of shit. You piece of *shit*.'

A blinded Darryl climbed onto the truck bed and fumbled his way to the box. Harvey stood and watched Tizza and let a defiant smile play about his lips. The smiling was definitely unhinging something in the little man's confidence. He kept cocking his head like a dog, glancing towards Clare, trying to weigh Harvey's apparent assuredness against hers. Harvey let his hands come down eventually and folded them over his chest, a power pose.

'I fucking told you we should have brought cuffs,' Tizza called to Darryl.

'He knows how to slip them, you idiot.' Harvey could hear the water Darryl was pouring into his eyes spattering on the truck-bed floor. 'Then he's got a fucking pair of handcuffs to use as a weapon. He can double them up and use them as brass knuckles. He can cuff the doors of the truck shut.'

'Oof, good idea. Why didn't I think of that?' Harvey mused. 'Does anyone have a pen? I'm getting hot tips here.'

'How do you know he knows how to slip them?' Tizza asked Darryl.

'Because any capable soldier does.'

'Do you know how to slip handcuffs, Tiz?' Harvey asked. 'Are you a capable soldier?'

'Shut up.'

'Are you happy with how he keeps referring to you, Tiz?' Harvey asked. 'Calling you an idiot in front of the hostages. Shouldn't you two be presenting a united front?'

Tizza licked his lips, didn't answer. Clare was trembling from head to foot, staring off at a collection of black lumps on a nearby hillside, kangaroos. Tizza turned to her, keeping the pistol trained on Harvey, a bully searching for a weaker target in the playground. 'You cut your ties again.' Tizza pointed to Clare's hands. 'What did I tell you I was gonna do if you did that?'

'You said you were gonna kick my teeth in.' Clare looked back. 'Well? What are you waiting for?'

Tizza thought. Darryl was sliding back out of the truck. His right eye was already swelling shut, the brow black and blood-flooded in the dim light.

'What are *you* waiting for?' Harvey asked Darryl. 'You going to let me just manhandle you like that? Is that how this partnership works? He's the idiot. You're the pussy?'

Darryl smiled. 'I'm a patient guy, Buck. You know that. I won't forget about this little love tap. I can bide my time. I've got something special for you, later. When we have a moment. We're on a deadline here.'

They faced each other, two captors, two captives.

'Here's the deal.' Darryl pointed to a ridgeline maybe a hundred metres beyond the truck, a jagged line of blackness against the stars. He was still blinking, rubbing sand and grit from his eyes. 'Over that crest, about two clicks, is Cooper Creek township.'

Harvey glanced at the ridgeline, calculating. They must have continued south-east from where he and Clare had been abducted, still following the High Wire, dropping down from where the secret road threaded the needle between tiny Indigenous townships.

'Buck, you're going to go into town and rob the bank,' Darryl said.

'*What?*' Harvey let the word come out as a laugh, though his stomach was plunging. 'You can't be serious.'

'I'm not serious?' Darryl adjusted his grip on the gun hanging at his side. 'You got enough explosives strapped to your chest right now to paint your guts over a five-kilometre radius.'

'What would be the point of robbing a bank in a place like Cooper Creek?' Harvey glanced at the ridgeline. 'They service a land mass with a population of ten thousand people at best. Their vault will be stacked with twenties. That's if they even have a vault.'

'You're not getting it, Buck,' Tizza smirked. 'This is not about money. It's about playing with you. The way you played with us.'

Harvey felt Clare looking at him. The memories, tickling at the corners of his vision, of Darryl on his knees in the dark, begging Harvey for mercy. Tizza curled in a ball in a corner of the cell, flinching as Harvey yanked open the door.

'Have you told her what you did, yet?' Darryl asked. 'Why we're all here?'

'I started,' Harvey said.

'You started?'

'I'm not trying to explain to her how to peel a banana,' Harvey said. 'I'm trying to explain why someone would do something as fucked up as all this.'

'Won't that be an interesting conversation, when you get to the juicy parts.'

'You want to play with me. Fine. I get it.' Harvey kept his voice steady. 'Let's get in the truck. You, me, Tiz. We find a quiet spot somewhere and you can do as you please. But let's get this straight. I'm not going anywhere near civilians in this thing.' Harvey hooked a finger into the armhole of the vest, flicked it out. 'You can forget that.'

'You're going to do as you're told,' Darryl said clearly. 'Or we'll make you watch as we blow her to pieces.' He stabbed a finger in Clare's direction. 'If you're still noncompliant after that, we'll hit the button on you.'

Harvey shrugged, looked at Clare. 'Sorry, Clare. It's been nice knowing you.'

There was an icy pause. Their captors stared at each other. Harvey noticed that it was Tizza who waited for Darryl's direction. Darryl shrugged, just the way Harvey had, jerked his head. The men closed the truck up, hopped in and started the engine. Harvey and Clare watched as the two men drove away, the red taillights like angry demon eyes shrinking and bumping in the purple light of early morning. Harvey and Clare were silent. They both knew this wasn't, couldn't possibly be, what they both desperately wanted it to be.

The truck turned, made a wide circle, then stopped with the headlights cutting yellow towers of light across the uneven sand and rock, making enormous spidery figures of the spiny desert plants. The two hostages were, for a moment, surrounded by silence and spectres and kicked-up desert dust that glowed gold.

Then Harvey felt Clare twitch beside him, and the exhausted, battered woman gripped the front of the vest, where a tiny red light was now visible, dim and struggling to make itself known through the heavy black Kevlar. Then a pealing sound started up at the centre of the vest, a sharp and consistent alarm. Clare turned her wild and terrified eyes on Harvey through the pre-dawn gloom.

And she let out a scream.

CHAPTER 9

'I've got you on the two o'clock flight out of Moomba,' Edna said. When she got no response, she pushed the screen door open and looked out. Talon was slumped in the corner of the mustard-yellow corduroy lounge she kept on the verandah, his eyes on the pink-hazed horizon, watching the oily sunrise drip upwards into the heavy liquid night. Only hours before, Edna had let those old behaviours slip into her speech and her body, the way they had once before when a vulnerable young person had come into her life. Started saying things like, we could do this. We could do that. For a while, as she strolled around and made phone calls and sent inquiries, Talon had occupied what she'd already begun to think of as 'his' chair at the dining room table, and she'd taken 'his' mug back to the sink. But those precise behaviours, those words, those thoughts felt so familiar and so warm they'd become like a heater left on at the feet of a deep sleeper. Delicious at first. Potentially deadly. She forced herself to stop. The boy at the table had looked up when she started making calls that related not to Clare Holland, but to flights and pick-up arrangements for a trip to Adelaide. He'd slunk to the verandah then, letting the door slap closed behind him. Edna steeled herself now.

'Couldn't get Birdsville,' she said. 'Somebody called in a bomb scare to them as well. Same jerks who cleared Alice Springs, probably.'

Talon spoke without even looking at her. 'So the cops will be waiting for me at the other end?'

'No.' Edna came out onto the verandah. 'I plead your case to the Salvation Army. They've got a volunteer who's going to pick you up and take you home, maybe have a chat to you on the way about whatever it is that's going on there.'

'Nothing is going on there.' Talon's voice was flat.

Edna didn't answer.

'I came out here because of Rosie,' the boy said. 'What I thought was Rosie. My home life is fine. I don't need fucking charity losers crawling all over my mum and dad trying to figure out if I'm being abused. Those people feed all their information to CFSS. And CFSS make your life a nightmare.'

Edna tapped her utility belt, wanted so badly to point out that Talon's intimate knowledge of the Child and Family Support System and how they operated was almost certainly an indication that he had needed their help before, and only strengthened her belief that he needed their help now. Instead she felt the warm fingers of her old habits creeping around her shoulders, and the sight of the boy slumped in the chair like a kicked cat made her bend to them again, if only a little.

'We got two choices about how we get to the airport,' she said. 'We can go directly south from here, follow the highway down until we have to cut bush. There's a nice roadhouse on the way. Makes good muffins.'

Talon gave no clue he was listening.

'Or we eat toast here and go southeast through the desert instead, find the High Wire again and take *that* until we have to bush-bash south to the airport.' The boy froze. 'If a serial killer really has killed Clare and dumped her body and it's being torn apart by dingoes, we might be able to spot it, by the time the sun is up.'

The boy's head turned slowly towards her. Edna could see the whites of his eyes.

'So what'll it be?' she asked. 'Highway or High Wire? Muffins or toast?'

Talon got up and ran down the verandah steps towards the car. Edna went back inside to put on the toast.

They drove for an hour in silence, Talon's head on a swivel, watching the featureless desert with narrowed eyes like he really was going to see a body out there being ravaged by native dogs. It wasn't impossible. Once or twice, Edna had been called to bodies in the desert. Not freshies still being picked over, but dry, shrivelled husks that might have been mistaken for kangaroo carcasses were they not encased in sun-faded jeans and boots. Edna knew that it was more likely, in the heat of the day, to find a fresh body being tugged at by a wedge-tailed eagle than a dingo. But she didn't mention all that to the boy. He had a fierce certainty to his gaze that made Edna smile.

Talon had toast crumbs all over his lap and he'd sucked down the coffee she'd made for him in a plastic go cup like he was a seasoned detective gearing up for an all-nighter watching a perp through binoculars from a darkened car. They passed an

Indigenous couple walking slowly through the eternity of flat earth and hard plants. Edna recognised the pair as coming from Gidgealpa, guessed they were probably heading to see friends in Cowarie. She slowed, but when they didn't flag her down, she pressed on. She wasn't surprised. The chances these two people had actually seen anything overtly nefarious the night before, something that might help her discover the situation surrounding Clare Holland and her burnt-out car, were slim. And living so close to the Wire, it was debateable whether they'd tell her anything, even if they had. The best hopes Edna had for criminal tips from locals generally came anonymously through the Aunties and Uncles; the Indigenous Elders who organised the communities in her jurisdiction. The Elders routinely fed information to her when it became unavoidable that she or Stevenson, and through them, the state, got involved in happenings in the area. Or when they failed to stifle discord in the townships under their watch themselves. Edna made a mental note to text a few of them, put the feelers out for tips.

After forty-five minutes, she slowed and Talon looked over at her.

'This is it?' he asked. 'The Wire?'

'Yep.'

'How the hell do you know?' He looked out at the flat slabs of red desert and blue sky. Edna pointed to the cow skull the boy hadn't noticed, perched atop a chunk of reddish-brown rock, too high off the ground to be anything but intentionally placed. There was no sign of the rest of the animal's skeleton. The skull was bleached white from the sun, one hollow eye staring unblinking at their car as the nose pointed east and the base of the skull pointed west.

'Like I said,' Edna swung the wheel east, 'you've got to know what you're looking for.'

They turned. It was only ten minutes down this new trajectory before they spotted the car; a wet, inky dot shimmering through the heat haze a kilometre away, widening and solidifying as they neared. This vehicle wasn't burnt. But the way it sat, pointed south-east with the driver's-side door hanging open, brought an unseasonal chill into the car. Edna slowed to a stop a hundred metres away. Talon was leaning forward in his seat, gripping the dashboard with both hands, the seatbelt straining to contain him.

'Come on. Let's get closer.'

'I don't think so.' Edna pulled up the handbrake, left the engine running for the aircon. 'I'm going to go check it out alone.'

The boy wheeled on her. '*What?* Why? You let me go look at the last one.'

'Yeah, but I've had abandoned cars in the desert. Plenty of them. When they're burnouts, they're usually empty. But most of the time when the door is hanging open like that, it's because there's a body nearby.'

'Why?'

'Dunno. That's just how it works. Law of the desert.'

'I want to see it.'

'I want to see it, "please".'

'I want to see it, please!'

'No.'

'Aw, what?'

Edna patted him on the shoulder. 'You're a kid, Talon.'

'I'm a legal adult!'

'Come on, mate. It's a dead person. It's not a museum exhibit.' Edna opened the glove box and took out a pair of gloves, slipped them on, plucked her hat off the dashboard. 'I'm sure someone with your technological prowess can find all the corpse pictures you want online.'

She shut the door on the protesting teenager, walked through the desert with the morning sun cooking the crown of her skull even through the Akubra. She kept to the left of the fresh tyre tracks leading to the vehicle. From twenty metres away, Edna could see that all the tyres were blown, the belly of the car hovering over a nest of spinifex like a weary bird about to sit on eggs. To the right of the car, in a depression in the desert floor, she spotted the body. The figure lay curled on its side with its face twisted towards the low mountain range to the south. A man. Black flies were buzzing at the eyes and mouth of his balaclava. The night wind had kicked sand up against him, so that the arm that flopped awkwardly behind his back seemed fingerless.

'Well, this isn't good,' Edna muttered, taking out her phone and snapping a dozen pictures in quick succession. The car. The body. The footprints. The scene as a whole. There were four bullet casings on the ground on the driver's side of the vehicle. Two different brands. Edna snapped them, then leant into the car and saw a bullet hole in the driver's headrest. Glass in the footwell and on the seat. There was a weird panel cut into the moulded plastic on the driver's door, leaning open. She reached in, gave it an experimental push, heard it click closed against a makeshift latch. She looked around the car for an obvious switch to open it again, but found none. She saw the panel was connected at the base with a store-bought hinge that was painted to match the colour of the inside of the door.

As she went to take more photos of the body, she noticed Talon standing, hands on hips, halfway between her car and the open one. 'Get back!' Edna barked at him. Talon didn't move. She took the satellite phone from her belt and called Dispatch, still clicking off pictures on her personal phone. There were deep puncture marks in the tyres of the vehicle and a single key in the ignition. The key was turned to the off position. When Dispatch picked up, Edna looked back at Talon and saw he was closer again.

'Dispatch, we – *I've* got a body on the Wire, maybe twenty k's further south-east than the burnout from last night,' Edna said. Talon was walking uncertainly towards her now, even as she gave harsh, angry waves to direct him back. 'I'll let Stevenson know. Can you get me a unit from Cooper Creek, if they've got someone free? I'll send you a pin. And can you get me a plate read?'

Edna ended the call. The big lad was on the scene now. His lips were pressed into a thin, twitchy line, a mixture of guilt and defiance, even as his eyes danced over everything, trying to take in as much as he could in case Edna said or did something that would force him back to the cruiser. She let him do it, giving him a disappointed glare that went ignored.

'Satisfied?' Edna asked. 'There's the dead guy. There's the car.'

'Whoa,' the teenager breathed. 'Bullet casings.'

'You want to take a selfie with the body, Talon?' Edna asked. 'You bring your selfie stick?'

Talon crouched as near as he dared to the body, lips still tight, craning his neck to see into the eyeholes of the balaclava.

What he saw there made him shoot to his feet again, a shudder through his shoulders. 'So many flies. Where do they all come from?'

'Talon.'

'What the fuck happened here?'

Edna waved the kid off the scene, into the dry, rocky surrounds and away from the footprints in the sand. It was clear he wasn't going back to the cruiser unless she carried him there. 'Someone got ambushed,' she sighed. 'The car was taken out by road spikes. Two people, maybe three, came and tried to hustle the driver. He didn't like that. The dead guy is collateral damage. His friends left him here and took the driver, I suppose. That's as much as I've got.'

'How do you know all that?'

'Well, I've got at least two shooters, one probably the driver, seeing as he's got a homemade gun holster in the car. From the look of that body there, the bloating of his belly, and the bloody vomit on the ground, I'd say the dead guy came up and fired through the driver's-side window. The driver gave him two in the guts from close range in response. Firing upwards as he got out.'

Talon nodded, appreciating everything. 'Couldn't he be the driver, though?' The boy pointed at the corpse. 'I think he's the driver. He's right next to the driver's-side door. Like, maybe he fell out when the door opened, tried to crawl away.'

'He's wearing a balaclava,' Edna pointed out. 'He's not the driver. No reason a guy would be driving along wearing a balaclava.'

'Unleeesss . . .' The great waterwheel in Talon's mind was beginning to turn. Edna could see it in his eyes, digging a river heavy and slow-flowing with ideas, one paddle at a time. 'Unless *he* was the guy who abducted Clare Holland!'

The cop squinted at the kid.

'Okay. Here it is. He's – He's abducted her, right?' Talon's voice quickened as the wheel started making waves. 'He was wearing the balaclava so she wouldn't be able to identify him. He was going to take her off somewhere and-and-and . . . you know . . . *you know* . . . But then, these guys have jumped in. The guys with the road spikes. They've put out the spikes to stop the car and try to save her.'

'So who are the guys with the spikes?'

'I don't know. Friends of hers.'

'How did they know she'd been abducted?'

'She might have called them. You know? Secretly. With her phone down by her side, where the driver couldn't see.' Talon pulled out his phone, feigned dialling down by his thigh, chin to his chest and eyes low.

'So they were just out here,' Edna said carefully. 'Those friends of hers. Hanging around. With road spikes in the back of their car. Waiting to rescue a friend in need?'

Talon stroked the fluffy beginnings of his moustache, frowning at the corpse. Edna licked her teeth and tried not to laugh, made sure she nodded like she was giving it consideration.

'Man, this is crazy, trying to piece it all together.' Talon put his hands on his hips, surveying everything. 'Fun though.'

'This is fun?'

'I think so, yeah.'

'Well.' She wiped away the smile threatening the corners of her mouth. 'Good thing I got you here, mate, to help me work it all out.'

'And to spot things. I'm very observant.' The big kid walked a few metres out into the desert and pointed to the ground. 'Look. Check it out. Bet you hadn't noticed this, yet.'

Edna went to him. There was a set of keys lying at the base of a clump of spinifex, protected from the night wind by the dense, bulky plant. Something slithered in the clump as Edna came over and photographed the keys.

'Nice,' Edna said, truthfully for once. 'Nice.'

'Or *that*.' The boy pointed to a spot at the front of the car. Edna followed his pointed finger. There was the husk of a black-and-white device lying almost buried in the sand. Shattered, a spidery carcass with tiny screws and panels and exposed wires. She kicked over a shard of plastic shaped like a small propeller. It was dotted with a dried black substance.

'Huh,' Edna said. 'Very observant indeed.'

'There's also *that*.' Talon pointed. 'Man, I'm on a roll here.'

Edna looked up in the direction Talon was indicating. There was a shape materialising on the horizon, swimming through the haze. The sound came afterwards. A car. But it wasn't coming from the direction of Cooper Creek. It was travelling south-east along the Wire. Edna felt the first tingles of apprehension at the back of her neck. She opened the text app on her sat phone, pulled up the same message she'd just sent Dispatch with the dropped pin and squinted to get the approaching car's numberplate. She punched it into a message, sent the message off and put her hand on her gun.

'Get behind me, would you, kid?'

Talon did what he was told. The car slowed as it passed Edna's cruiser, but kept coming, pulling to an abrupt stop some twenty metres from where she and the boy stood.

Garreth Holland stepped out, gripping the car's window frame, his eyes huge as he took in the car, the open door, the body lying slumped on its side.

'Is she there?' the Northern Territory Police Commissioner asked. 'Oh Jesus. Jesus. Is it her?'

CHAPTER 10

'No, please.' Clare wrapped her arms around him, the two vests pressed together between them, her fingers for a second gripping the hair at the back of his head and her face buried in his shoulder. 'Please, please, please! No, god, no!'

He held her tightly. 'It's okay,' he lied, even as the alarm whined. 'I'm here with you. I'm here.'

'You gotta go.' She suddenly shoved him off. 'Run!'

'No way. I'm staying with you.'

'But we made a pact!' She was pushing at him again. 'D-d-don't let them blow us both up, Harvey, Jesus!'

'I'm staying. I'm staying.'

'But—'

'I said that to make you feel better about running.'

'You arsehole! You arsehole!'

'I'm sorry. This is all my fault.'

Clare fell back into the embrace, sobbing, shaking hard. 'I don't want to die. I don't want to die. I don't want to die!'

Harvey looked at the distant truck. His own vest began to squeal, the sound of it making both of them jump. He put a hand up, over her shoulder, searching the blank windscreen for

Darryl or Tizza's eyes. The sunlight was glancing off the glass. He couldn't see them, but he knew they were smiling behind there. 'Okay, you fucking pricks. Okay. Okay.'

The truck didn't move. For a shrill moment, Harvey saw his end coming. Wondered what it would be like. He'd seen some things in Afghanistan. The rocket-launched grenade making mincemeat of Sheerwater and everyone in his vehicle. No time to scream. He'd seen the handiwork of IEDs. People moving even after their spinal cords were severed. Eyes in detached heads swimming, rolling. Harvey knew they were probably just muscle twitches, the finger taps and leg kicks he saw after death. But the idea that he might feel the explosion rip his body to shreds, even for a second, made him shamefully afraid, and not just for himself. He waved harder. 'I'll do it!' he called.

The truck started rolling forward. He held Clare's head and rocked her a little. 'I'm so fucking sorry about all this.'

'It's not your fault.'

'Oh, yes it is.'

'Are they coming?'

'Yeah, they're coming.'

The vests stopped squealing. The silence pulsed, but no relief came with it. Harvey didn't know if he could unlock his arms from around this woman he barely knew, but told himself he had to do it, couldn't let her feel his fear and uncertainty, or it would worsen her own. She staggered when he let her go, wiping her eyes, shuddering. Harvey waited for the truck bumbling slowly towards them, their mobile prison, a grim kind of guilt lodged in his chest like a knife.

Then Clare said, 'We have to kill them both.'

He looked at her. She was watching the truck come, and the flat, quiet tone she'd used seemed to hang in the air between them. A tone that demanded, almost assumed, an agreement. It was the familiarity with the concept he could hear slithering through her words that made Harvey freeze. She'd spoken about killing the way he'd heard army captains speak about it. Men who only got to where they were in their careers because they'd cultivated the ability to talk like that, about lives like they were minor inconveniences. Like they were dreaded housework. *We have to put a load of washing on. We have to kill them both.* He felt an unsettling kind of flip inside his own mind, the same he'd felt when Clare revealed she'd sold the doll she'd rescued from the gutter, only on a much, much larger scale. He thought he'd begun to know her. But he didn't know her at all. Harvey stared at the woman in front of him and told himself that she was just a shocked and numb person speaking unemotional sense.

Still, he felt unsettled.

Tizza and Darryl parked the truck and hopped down from the cabin. Tizza tossed a small Kevlar pouch at Harvey's feet.

'What is that?' Harvey asked.

'A pair of glasses,' Tizza said. 'There's a camera in the frame and speakers inside the ear hooks. Your eyes are gonna be our eyes. The glasses have a mic, so you won't be able to play any games when you're in town.'

Darryl tossed a wad of clothes at Harvey's chest. He caught a black cotton T-shirt and a jacket and pulled them reluctantly on. He felt something heavy in the pocket of the jacket bump against his hip. A 9 millimetre. As he pulled it out, he could already feel from the weight of it that it was unloaded.

He checked the chamber anyway. Eternal optimist. It was empty.

'What do I need the gun for?' Harvey lined Tizza up with it. Looked down the barrel of it at him, imagined himself shooting the man in the head with it, hoped the little prick was doing just the same. 'Why don't I just walk in and say, "I'm wearing a bomb vest"?'

'You're not to refer to the bomb vest,' Darryl said.

'Why not?'

'Because I just told you not to.' The older man smiled.

Harvey nodded. He understood. He met eyes with Clare, and he could see her curiosity there, and he wondered how the hell he was ever going to explain all this to her. That Darryl and Tizza's mission, which was now clear to him, made all the sense in the world. It made so much sense, in fact, that he was surprised he hadn't seen it coming.

'Where's she gonna be?' Harvey gestured at Clare.

'I don't know. We might put her in the truck and park it right next to a playground,' Darryl mused. 'Or a daycare centre. You try to whisper to someone at the bank, or write a note about what's going on, and we'll blow you and then her.'

'Or her and then you.' Tizza shrugged happily. 'Let's see what mood we're in.'

'I want her with me,' Harvey said.

'What?' Tizza frowned. 'Why?'

'I can't be sure you'll park the truck somewhere and leave her alone in the back of it, unharmed. I don't know that she's safe with you. And I won't do it unless I know that she's safe.'

Darryl scoffed. 'Are you kidding me?'

'I know *you* won't touch her.' Harvey looked at Darryl. 'You don't really believe in that kind of thing.'

Darryl's lip twitched.

'Do you trust *him*, though?' Harvey nodded at Tizza. 'Do you know his history?'

'What history?' Darryl asked.

'Wait, wait, wait.' Tizza put his small hands up. 'You're not doing this, Buck. You're not playing these games with us. He's trying to make you think I've got a sick little box of secrets that you don't know about hidden away somewhere. Stuff he might have found out about me in the container. But I don't, okay?' He looked at his partner. 'You can trust me on that.'

'Can you, though?' Harvey squinted at Darryl.

'He's been looking at me,' Clare said. Harvey felt a tingle of excitement in his chest as Clare finally joined the game. She pointed a trembling finger at Tizza. 'Since the beginning. He's been looking at me. At my legs. At my breasts. Smiling at me in that dirty fucking way while your back is turned. I don't want to be alone with him.'

'What are you *talking* about?' Tizza's eyes were wide.

'I want her with me,' Harvey pressed. 'You don't know him, Darryl. Not like I do.'

'Enough.' Darryl marched over and grabbed Clare's arm. 'You can all calm down. She won't be left alone with him. We'll be together the whole time.'

Darryl dragged Clare to the back of the truck and shoved her in. Tizza and Harvey stood in the desert, watching each other, the small, freckled man appreciating Harvey as he unpacked the little pouch and put the glasses on, calmly and slowly, like he was dressing for a meeting and not the possible violent deaths of several people, including himself.

'This isn't gonna work, you know,' Tizza said.

'What? This whole plan?' Harvey raised his eyebrows. 'You're right. It's not. You should quit now, before it all falls apart.'

'I mean the mind games.'

'We're playing mind games?'

'When you had us in that box back in Tarin Kot, you had all the control,' Tizza said. 'You had all the power. But you have to understand, Buck, *you're our victim now.*'

'Am I?'

'This is happening to you,' Tizza said. 'That's what you kept saying to me. In the box. *This is happening to you, Nathan.* I've spent years and *years* trying to scrub those words from my brain. Every time I think they're gone, I'll be somewhere and I'll hear your voice whispering in my ear. Well, guess what, Buck? Those words are going to haunt *you* over the next few hours. Like they haunted me.'

This is happening to you.

Harvey eased a long, painful breath, focused on one thing only: not losing it completely. Because he'd spent even longer running from those words and had thought he was free of them until that very second. Free of what he did.

Darryl came back from the truck and handed Harvey a black baseball cap. 'Get going.'

Harvey went. The sun hammered down on him, and he walked towards town and kept his pace steady, but his thoughts were hurtling, smashing into each other, none of them even related yet to the insane act he was about to commit. Because he was lagging desperately behind Darryl and Tizza and their plan, and now had the time, and the silence, in which to try to catch up.

He'd planted a seed in Darryl's mind, planted it in a carefully selected place, used those secrets he'd learnt about the older man long ago to make sure that seed had enough water and sunlight and nutrients to grow. But how else could he mess with the two of them? What else did he know? He remembered Tizza with his head hanging in the chair, broken, crying, the words dripping miserably out of him like the spittle hanging from his lip.

I'm a bad, bad man. I know it. I'm sorry.

Harvey hadn't heard anything from the tiny speakers embedded in the ear hooks of the glasses. Crazy thoughts pulsed within him. About tossing the camera glasses away. Crushing them under his foot. Running for his goddamn life. But he knew how would end; with him blown to pieces on the outskirts of Cooper Creek, a dark red stain and a depression in the soil the only evidence to mark his existence. He stopped and crouched and put a hand on the already warm earth and steadied himself, tried to weigh things, make a decision. Keep walking, or give in and start running. Let them end it for him now. Could he really go into a town full of innocent people, walk among them with a fucking bomb vest strapped to his chest, to save his own life? To save Clare's life? No. He couldn't. The maths didn't work. He needed to give up, to accept death.

'*Get up.*'

Darryl's voice in his ear. Harvey didn't move.

'*Get up, Buck!*'

'I'm dizzy,' Harvey said. He adjusted the sweat-damp cap where it was rubbing against the gash in the side of his head, a gaping wound it barely covered. 'I've got a fucking head injury.'

'*Don't give me that,*' Tizza cut in. '*You move your arse or we hit the button. We've just come up on a netball field. Bunch of little girls on it. You've got ten minutes to get into town, before I rid the world of eight future teen mums from Bumfuck Nowhere.'*

Ten minutes. Harvey counted them off in his head, making his way step by step across the plains. He tried not to think about another desert death-march he'd taken, how the sun had seemed to choke him from behind, a steel claw locked on the back of his neck. Sun-baked asphalt appeared under his feet. He joined the road and let the hill give him momentum. A house materialised from nowhere, three mongrel dogs on the verandah, standing up and barking half-heartedly as Harvey walked by. The main street sprawled before him. Little buildings clustered in the distance. A sign by the roadside read *Only beer for 16,000 km!*

A potbellied man in an Akubra was standing outside the first shop Harvey passed, nibbling on a fingernail and looking at his phone. He clocked Harvey at ten metres, stood back and frowned deeply at the unfamiliar face. Harvey nodded and received no response. Felt the man staring at his back as he passed.

'*What the fuck was that?*' Tizza said. '*Did you signal that guy?*'

'He's probably wondering what the jacket is about,' Harvey murmured. 'It must be thirty degrees already. You didn't plan this very well, did you? I'm drawing attention to myself just walking around in this.'

'*Keep your head down. Watch your hands. You signal someone, and we'll—*'

'What am I gonna do?' Harvey went past a shop selling farming supplies. 'Sign *Help me, I'm a hostage wearing a bomb vest* in Auslan? What's sign language for *My captors have a woman in their custody, also strapped up with explosives*?'

'*Shut up, Buck,*' Tizza snarled.

'Seriously, I can't be watching my hands the whole time. It's weird.'

'*You'll do what you're told, or you're red mist, and so is anyone who's near you,*' Darryl said.

A little woman with a stroller emerged from a barren front yard, the blonde-haired toddler wobbling in the pram as the woman turned and shut the warped wrought-iron gate behind her. She smiled at Harvey as he passed quickly by.

Harvey tried not to slow his pace when the words in the ear-hook speakers started up again, lower and less filled with vitriol, as whoever was controlling the feed apparently switched the mic back on accidentally.

'*. . . nothing to know, Dar. I don't have a "history". It's mind games. It's plain as day that it's mind games. Why can't you see that?*'

'*When I was in that room with him, he came out with things I didn't even know about* myself. *Nothing was off limits. He had access to personal documents. Bank accounts. Fucking sealed childhood records.*'

'*I know.*'

'*That bitch Shayna must have been feeding them to him.*'

'*What's your point?*'

'*Buck knew me better than anyone who I've ever—*'

'*I know, man. It happened to me too, don't forget.*'

'*If there's something that he learnt about you back then, something that he's hinting at now, that you haven't told me . . .*'

'*What? You'll what? We're in this together now. All the way to the end. You said it. We have a pact.*'

'*I just don't want to discover I've made that pact with a person, only to find out they're someone else enti—*'

The line cut out. Harvey smiled. He turned right at the town's only intersection and looked at the front of the bank; a tiny sandstone building that must have been two rooms deep at best. There was a roll-away iron grill behind the shopfront window, and strands of tinsel still stuck to the corners of the plate glass, leftover Christmas decorations being bleached white by the sun. Harvey could see a woman inside, Blu-Tacking a sign about high-yield savings accounts to the wall.

He went in.

The bell above the door tinkled. Harvey was struck by that. It was a small thing, but within it, the sheer absurdity of the whole situation rang impossibly loud in his brain. That anyone would rob a place like this. A place that required a brass bell to be hung above the door, because it was frequently so quiet and calm at the front of the bank that the single teller standing there might need to be roused from the back room, having snuck there to put her feet up and have a cup of tea. The teller was an Indigenous woman with a pink scarf in her hair. She was clicking through something on a computer, probably still booting it up this early, the shop draped with the dusty smell of carpets ground in with desert earth.

'He-ey,' she said in greeting, without looking up.

Harvey stood at the beginning of a long aisle of shelves. There were toys here. Gift cards. Notepads. The bank obviously doubled as a post office for the tiny town. Made sense. The security of the only stone building would protect both its mail and its cash. Harvey glanced at a display rack to the left of him, which was full of different-sized envelopes, and the one to the right, which was stacked with stationery.

'*What the fuck are you waiting for?*' Tizza said in his ear. '*Go.*'

Harvey didn't move.

'*Go, Buck,*' Darryl's voice. '*My finger is on the button.*'

Harvey saw his vest exploding. The woman at the counter being hurled against the cool stone wall behind her, obliterated against the rock by a pressure wave that would simultaneously cook and pulverise her. The blast would take out the bank's front windows, lift the roof off its rafters, torch the shelves, their contents, the carpet, the walls. Paint would blister and peel in the ensuing fire. The lights and electric fixtures would melt. If there was anything left of the teller after the fire, she would be handed to her family in a ziplock sandwich bag.

'Hey,' he said to the teller, trying to will his legs to move, to carry him up there. Harvey had done a lot of things in his life. Robbing a bank wasn't one of them. He gripped the useless pistol in his jacket pocket and figured drawing the weapon might inspire his feet to become unplanted. He had the butt out of the pocket when the bell above the door rang again, making his heart thud against his ribs. The door bumped into his shoulder. A woman pushed her way inside.

'Ah, sorry, mate.'

The cop strode past him without waiting for a response. Harvey stared at the tan uniform, the dusty boots, the glossy brown braid at the back of the woman's head. He put the gun back in his pocket.

Silence on the airwaves. Harvey went to the stand with the stationery, put his hands on the uppermost shelf.

'Hi, Carol.'

'Oh, hey. You're in early.'

'I'm still working on this bloody thing between Vinnie Stone and his neighbour,' the cop said. 'About the tractor.'

'What? It's *still* going?'

'It is,' the cop sighed. 'Look, the neighbour's now saying he gave Vinnie the money in December last year, not September. Can we get a look at his deposits from that period . . .'

The cop trailed off, looked back at Harvey, took her elbow off the counter. Harvey knew he was staring but couldn't bring himself to stop.

'Shit! Sorry, mate.' The woman, whose nameplate said 'Stevenson', made an exploding motion against the side of her head with her hand. 'I wasn't even thinking. You were here first.'

Harvey stiffened. Then he turned, went to the shelves nearest to him, and grabbed two handfuls of pens from the canisters. Black Artline pens with numbers indicating their nib sizes. He shuffled them in his fingers. 'Oh, no, don't worry about me.' Harvey waved a pen at the women at the counter. He spread a collection of pens on the edge of the shelf and dumped the rest back in their cannisters. 'I'm just browsing. Urgh. The stationery. The choices, you know? Of these pens. Heh! Too many choices.'

The women looked at each other.

'*You'd better get your act together, and fast, Buck,*' the voice came in his ear. Darryl, low and deadly. '*Think carefully. There's a lot on the line here. You blow this, and we'll blow you.*'

'You go ahead,' Harvey urged.

'No, no. You do your thing. I'll wait.' The cop stood back. 'I shouldn't really be discussing matters of law in front of civilians, anyway. Caro, I'll hang out over here and we can get back into it after you've seen to our friend.'

She moved to the end of the counter, took up one of the brochures stacked there in neat little piles. Harvey stifled a curse word. He heard the mic in the ear hooks stutter on.

'. . . a good time to do it anyway. A cop and a bank teller? That's not a bad take.'

'It's a thought. What's he doing?'

'Hey Buck, move your arse. You're being awkward.'

'Listen, I need to . . .' Harvey started. His words ran out. He thought of movies he'd seen. Cartoons. Men with laundry bags with dollar signs on them. Westerns, where men rode in on horses. He started again. 'This is actually a . . .'

A what? A robbery?

He couldn't continue. Didn't have words for what this was, or how ridiculous it was. How dangerously, wildly evil. More crazy thoughts pushed their way into his brain. He imagined himself telling the cop, Stevenson, that he was a hostage. Screaming for them both to run. Or turning and running and pushing his way back out the door, waiting for the light at his chest and the beeping and the inevitable bang. Would he even hear it? But then he remembered the little girls at the netball court. Clare. With terror pulsing in his brain, he went to the counter, where Carol was beckoning him, if reluctantly.

Harvey had one pen still in his fist, the plastic tube swimming in sweat, the hook on the cap cutting into his thumb as he squeezed the item for dear life. He drew a long breath and let it out slow. He walked to the counter, passing loaded shelves on either side, a stiff-legged groom walking to a horror-show marriage before a hellish altar. He reached the counter. By the register was a rack of hand-beaded friendship bracelets made by local kids and discount slips for entry to the Umoona Opal Mine and Museum.

Harvey put the pen down on the glass. Both women stared at it. By now, they knew something wasn't right. It was in the air. It was in his eyes. Harvey knew it would come out in his voice; the urgency, the wrongness, which they would interpret as malicious intent. But he had no choice. He sucked in another long breath, and the teller locked her curious eyes on him.

'Anything else?' she asked.

'Yeah,' Harvey relented. 'This is a stick-up.'

CHAPTER 11

Edna got the same inexplicable icky feeling meeting Garreth Holland in person as she had when she saw him on her computer screen. Everything about him seemed pleasant enough, on the surface. The light desert wind tugged his clean, pressed collared shirt gently against his frame as he approached. Big, soulful eyes took in the scene before him with a desperation Edna knew should have been plucking at her heartstrings. Edna knew people. Had a sense for them. Sometimes it was a certain gait, or a tone of voice, or a gesture. The flick of a hand. But there was nothing here to point to. Nothing yet, but a measured man on the verge, just holding it together, locked in a tightly bound crisis. Despite all this, she found herself walking forward without completely being able to take her hand off her gun. Though she had no plans yet to pull it, she knew the power of the gesture, the fingers resting there over the holster guard. She held up her hand as Holland approached what she had decided was the edge of the crime scene. He seemed to have a slightly stiff walk, like he'd been driving for a long time and everything had seized up.

'Whoa, whoa, whoa. I've got to stop you there.'

'I'm Garreth Holland.' The big guy swallowed. 'My wife's—'

'Missing. I know. I found her car last night, burnt out, a couple of kilometres back that way.' Edna nodded. 'She's not here, Commissioner Holland. The deceased hasn't been identified yet, but I can tell you one thing: it's not Clare.'

'Jesus. Okay.' Holland turned away, let his shoulders rise and fall with a long breath. He looked over at Talon but seemed not to take the kid in. 'So what . . . I mean . . . What do we know? *Was* she here? Are any of her things in that car? Whose car *is* that?'

'I haven't searched the scene properly yet,' Edna said. 'I just got here myself.'

'Who's the dead guy? Is it his car?'

'Commissioner Holland—'

'Let's just take a look.' The man tried to side-step Edna. 'We're wasting time, standing here chatting about it.'

'I knew you'd say that.' Edna put a hand up again, higher this time, right under the guy's nose. She matched his step with her own. 'Commissioner, with all due respect, I can't have you anywhere near this scene. And I sure as hell hope you haven't just come from messing around at the site of your wife's car. Considering what's happened here, I'm going to have to lock *that* space down as a major crime scene, also. At least until I can figure out if they're connected.'

'You're not serious,' Holland scoffed. 'Step aside.'

'I'm deadly serious,' Edna said. 'And no.'

'Officer,' the commissioner said carefully, 'as I'm sure you're aware, the Cross-Border Justice Scheme gives me jurisdiction here, and seniority over you.' He took her in, seemed to think he had the measure of her in seconds. Like most people did.

His interest was again drawn to the teenager, the unknown quantity, who was by now standing off to the side, staring at his shoes, the vicarious discomfort reddening his face. 'Whoever the hell you even are, you need to—'

'My name is Norris.' Edna tapped her nameplate. 'Senior Sergeant Edna Norris. Says so right here.'

'Great,' Holland said. 'So, move the fuck out of the way, Senior Sergeant Edna Norris.'

'Ay!' Talon barked. Edna looked over. All the inhibition had suddenly fled from the boy. He was wild-eyed, puffed up. 'Who *da fuck* you think you're talking to?'

'Settle down, kid. Settle down,' Edna said.

'She said to get off her crime scene, bro.' Talon took two steps forward, boxer's steps, his feet never leaving the ground. With those couple of strides he was now in swinging distance of the Police Commissioner. The fist by his side was clenched, a mallet waiting to be swung. 'Or do you have a hearing problem?'

'Talon!'

'Because I can help you out with that, if you want,' Talon said. 'I can be the interpreter.'

'Talon, for fuck's sake!' Edna tried to push the big kid back. He didn't budge. It was Holland who stepped casually out of strike range. 'I've got this handled, mate. I didn't ask you to play a bodyguard.'

'Jesus.' Holland laughed. 'Who is this thug, anyway? Don't tell me it's Bring the Local Delinquent to Work Day here in the southern state. Or were you already at the scene? Are you the assailant? Let me guess.' Holland pointed to the body nearby. 'He tripped on a bullet and you found him like that.'

'He's a charge I'm escorting to the airport,' Edna snapped. She got in front of Holland. 'Back away from the crime scene, now, *sir*. Regardless of Cross-Borders, and regardless of rank; a conflict of interest excludes you from having access to this scene. Return to your vehicle immediately and wait for further instruction.'

Holland thought about it for a while, then limped back to his car, slid into the driver's seat and immediately took out his phone. Edna let hot air out of her lungs. The sun was blinding off the abandoned car's windscreen. There were already twice as many flies crawling and buzzing around the body's balaclava as there had been when she and Talon arrived. She looked at the sweat running down Talon's neck and felt dread for this, all of this, the car and the body and Holland and his wife, wherever the hell she was. Right in the middle of the slowly expanding mess was Talon, whose face was rigid under the dangerous blankness that had overcome him once before in her presence, the same kind feral cats got before they pounced on baby possums.

'Talon, that guy is the commissioner of the fucking Northern Territory Police,' Edna said.

'I don't care if he's John Cena!' Talon shouted. 'Where I come from, you get your head smacked in for talking to women like that.'

'That may be true. But it doesn't change the fact that Commissioner Holland is sitting in that car, right now, trying to dig up everything he can on you and me.' Edna pointed to Holland's windscreen. 'This is what they do. Smart men with power, who don't get their way. They don't smack people's heads in. They take a minute and they arm themselves.'

Talon looked at Holland. The commissioner was leaning back in his seat, watching them, the phone pressed to his ear.

'All we can hope is that he gets so interested in what he finds on me that he doesn't bother about you,' Edna said. 'Or you can forget about the Salvos and Family Services being the ones waiting for you when you get home, Talon. He'll have the big guns locked and loaded.'

'Oh come on.' The kid rolled his eyes. 'I'm not scared of some old puss in a fancy shirt. And you shouldn't be, either.'

'Just get in the car.' Edna took out her satellite phone. She noticed her hand was shaking. 'I've got to get Stevenson here. I need someone to take you to the airport.'

Talon leered down at her, turned and marched off towards her cruiser. Edna called Stevenson, but got no answer. She called again and watched the flies crawling around, the dirty black creatures walking lazily down the slope of the dead man's forehead and into the murky black holes in the front of the mask.

CHAPTER 12

The cop's phone rang. It was exactly the moment Harvey needed to split the air, divide the women's attention so that he could act before they could *re*act. He pulled the gun from his pocket, stepped back and pointed it at Stevenson's face. Her hands were hanging by her sides. Her right one twitched, the hand by the gun, but Harvey's voice stopped it in place.

'Don't,' he said.

Carol exhaled. Harvey swung the gun around at her, just for a second, let her look down its empty barrel before swinging it back and lining the cop up again.

'You don't, either,' he said to Carol. 'Get your hands up on the counter and take a step back from it. Don't hit any alarms.'

Carol did as she was told, flattened her palms on the counter and took a step back so Harvey could see her to the waist, see she wasn't hitting a trigger or button with her knee.

'Don't touch anything,' he repeated.

'I'm not. I won't. The alarms . . . they . . . they only call *them*, anyway.' She glanced at Stevenson.

'*Keep going,*' Darryl said in his ear. '*Move fast. Don't stop. Watch the cop. If she shoots you, you'll all die.*'

'This isn't a joke,' Harvey told Stevenson, who was frozen on the spot. 'I'm seriously robbing the place. So we can get through this, all of us. But it'll mean doing exactly as I say and not trying anything funny. Okay?'

Stevenson nodded.

'Put your hands on the counter by hers,' Harvey said. 'I'm going to take your gun and your taser.'

'This is just . . .' Stevenson ran out of words. Couldn't believe it was happening, Harvey supposed, just like he couldn't. That a man who was smart enough to speak and breathe and function on his own was also dumb enough to rob an outback bank with an armed cop standing smack bang in the middle of it. Stevenson put her hands on the counter, slow and numb, the shock probably trying to take hold. All her mental power fighting to prevent that from happening, to stay calm and remember her training. 'This is some incredibly stupid shit right here, man.'

'I don't need the commentary, thanks.'

'What's your name?'

'Mr Bankrobber,' Harvey said. 'No more questions.'

'Jesus.' Stevenson shook her head, dismayed, bewildered. 'Jesus.'

Harvey grabbed her gun and taser and slipped them into the waistband of his jeans. 'The two of you, hold hands. Interlace your fingers. I'm going to back up and lock the front door.'

He watched them, made sure they did as he said, gripping each other's hands across the counter, fingers intertwined, like lovers on a date. Harvey was working on pure adrenaline and instinct, but he figured that if either woman made a snap decision and a sudden grab for something – a weapon, a phone, anything – the manoeuvre might be made marginally harder by having to unlock her hand from the grip of the other.

He backed to the door, flipped the deadlock and turned the sign to *Closed.* Anyone looking in would see what was happening. There were no blinds or curtains. But he was hoping to be out the back door with the money before the next customer arrived at the building for their business.

'Sir,' Carol said as he marched back to the counter, 'I-I-I gotta tell you. There's like, twenty grand in the safe at best. We don't keep a lot of money here. We – I – It's a pretty small town, you know?'

'It doesn't matter.' Harvey walked around the counter.

'The most we ever pay out is, like, if someone wants to buy a car or something. A couple of thousand.'

'It doesn't matter,' Harvey repeated.

'So we don't have—'

'Carol.' Harvey was behind her by now. On his way to the safe. He put a hand on her shoulder. It was slick with sweat. She flinched under his touch, and Harvey's heart burned. 'Just tell me the combination to the safe, and then keep quiet.'

She told him the numbers. Somebody's birthday, for god's sake. The safe was a two-hundred-dollar job, the size of a slab of beer, bolted to a hand-welded stand that was itself bolted to the floor. It was hidden from view of the public at the counter by a corkboard partition, so that, standing by it, he could easily see the women clutching hands over the counter, their wild eyes trained on him. The kick to the heart as Carol shrank from his touch was nothing compared to when Harvey went around the partition and spied the staff area behind it, two rows of shelves packed with the personal items bank workers left for their shifts. Carol's shelf had one of those glittery water bottles with the times marked on the side so she could stay consistently hydrated all day, purple and pink, filled with water and lemon slices. There was a paperback of some well-thumbed crime thriller poking out of her handbag. Some guy named Bob had a shelf with a Sudoku pad in it and a neatly folded grey cardigan. Harvey wondered if Carol would ever be able to read crime thrillers again after she'd stared down the barrel of a weapon she surely thought was loaded. Whether Bob would wish he'd been here at that moment to take the attack in Carol's place, whether he'd open the bank the next day while she had time off to recover and would stare impotently at the front doors, willing Harvey to appear and try it on again so he could kick his arse.

'Why are you doing this?' Stevenson asked as Harvey punched the code into the safe. It gave a tinny, cheap squeal as the door popped open. 'This doesn't make any sense.'

'Shut up,' Harvey said. There were several dozen notebooks in the safe, and two unsealed cloth bags of cash. He upturned one cloth bag on top of the safe, keeping his eye and gun on the women.

'I don't know if you realise this,' Stevenson pressed, 'but you're basically in space right now, man.'

Harvey could feel his heartbeat pulsing in his ears. Beyond it, Tizza and Darryl's mic seemed to accidentally crackle on again.

'*. . . so fucking good. I could watch this all day. I could jerk off to this.*'

'*Do me a favour, Tiz: don't.*'

'I don't know what you're talking about,' Harvey said.

'You're not from around here,' Stevenson said. 'You don't have the tan. So maybe you don't realise it, yet. But out here? You're basically in outer space.'

Harvey looked at her, stuffing stacks of hundreds into his pockets.

'This town is its own little planet,' Stevenson said. 'The closest planet to this one is Clifton Hills. It's even smaller, and it's sixty k's from here.'

'So?' Harvey's pockets were stacked with notes. Twenty grand. Not even enough to buy a decent car.

'So between here and there, there's no cover,' Stevenson said. 'You're out in the open. Outer space.'

Harvey noticed that Carol was crying. At her feet lay a puddle of liquid. She hung her head. Stevenson's eyes were blazing at him; big whites, dark pupils.

'We're gonna find you out there, motherfucker,' Stevenson promised him. Between the two women, their clasped hands were shaking. Harvey didn't know if it was Stevenson's rage or Carol's terror or a bit of both. He went to the back door of the bank, pushed it open, and bolted out into the blinding light of outer space.

CHAPTER 13

Edna slipped into the car beside Holland. He was leaning back in the leather seat, his arms folded, and the immaculate space that enveloped Edna in icy air conditioning and new car smell gave her the odd sense that she'd just sat down in the middle of a luxury car advertisement. There was a small bottle of rubbing alcohol in the cupholder between them. She had to force herself not to start speculating about whether the guy actually sterilised the entire car every time he used it, and get to her queries about his wife.

'Why was your wife out here, Commissioner?' she asked. 'Should we start there?'

'I don't know how useful that would be for you, me answering that question.' Holland stared into the rear-view mirror, through which Edna was sure he was keeping an eye on Talon, the boy sitting sulking in her cruiser. 'I'm going to have a specialist team from Adelaide meet a team from Alice Springs, here, in about three hours. I've just organised it. They'll be taking over this case, and I'll have to repeat my entire story to them anyway.'

'It's still my duty to take a full and proper report with any and all witnesses involved in this case, as soon as I'm able,'

Edna said. 'Regardless of who'll be taking over. I need to hand over the freshest information to the lead investigator when they're assigned.'

Holland sighed long and hard through his nose. Edna took out her phone and hit record and read him his rights. She dated the recording and identified herself and Holland.

'Why was your wife out here?'

'She decided she needed some time to herself. She said she was driving to Sydney, where her mother keeps an apartment.'

'She just randomly decided she needed some time to herself?' Edna asked. 'What, following an argument, you mean?'

'I did not say that.'

'So it did not precede an argument.'

'I didn't say that, either. Jesus. Is this your first day?'

'What spurred the decision, then?'

'My wife's motives for wishing to spend time by herself were not clear to me at the time she left.'

'So the trip was spontaneous. It was not planned. She made the decision that she needed some space shortly before she set out to achieve that goal?'

'Yes.'

'She left from the family home?'

'Yes.'

'What time would you say your wife left, approximately?'

'I don't know. Quarter to six?'

'Were you present when she left?'

'No. I arrived home at six.'

'Did she call or email you to let you know she had made the decision to leave?'

'She called.'

'When, exactly?'

Holland took out his phone. Fished through it.

'Five thirty-one.'

'And she was not home at six p.m.? Is that how you approximated what time she left? Because you arrived at that time and she wasn't present in the house?'

'Yes.'

'Your wife seems to have made some strange decisions yesterday evening, Commissioner Holland,' Edna said.

Holland paused for a long time. Then he raised his hands, opened them, palms out. 'Was that a question?'

'She seems to have just rushed out suddenly. A half an hour or less after she let you know she had decided to leave, to take some time to be alone in Sydney.'

'Your listening and interpretation skills really need some work, Norris,' Holland sighed. 'I told you that the phone call to let me know of her decision was at five-thirty. Perhaps she had *made* that decision much earlier, and only let me know about it at that time. She was home all day. Perhaps she'd given it several hours' thought.'

'Did you regularly arrive home from work at six p.m.?'

'Yes.'

'If she knew you were due home only minutes after she had decided she was going to leave, why not wait to say goodbye to you?'

'Are you really going to spend the next three hours, before this case is handed over, dissecting the idiosyncrasies of my marriage?' Holland folded his arms, cocked his head at her. 'Because whether or not a wife is in the practice of modifying or delaying her activities so that she can kiss her husband goodbye in person is surely an individual thing, isn't it? Something that varies marriage to marriage?'

'Why did she decide to take the High Wire to travel to Sydney, rather than a safer, more traditional route?'

'I don't know the road you're referring to.'

'Oh, come on.' Edna smiled. Holland smiled back.

'Clare couldn't fly,' the commissioner said. 'There were bomb threats called into both Alice Springs and Birdsville airports at about four p.m.'

'So why didn't she delay her alone time until flights opened back up?'

'Are you asking me to retrospectively read my wife's mind, Senior Sergeant Norris? Because I can't even do that in real time. No one can.'

'How does she know about the High Wire?'

'I have no idea.'

'Did she learn about it from you? Had you had occasion to mention it in casual conversation, in your work pursuing criminals who might be using it?'

'I was not in the practice of talking about my work with my wife.'

'Did she tell you that she planned to use the High Wire to get to Sydney?'

'No.'

'Then how did you think she would get there? You just said you knew about the airport shutdowns.'

'I'm the Northern Territory's Police Commissioner. Of course I knew about them.'

'So how did you think she'd get to Sydney?'

'I thought she'd take the trad—'

Edna waited, her breath seized in her throat. She could see Garreth's mind ticking away, trying to avoid the next question. 'If you didn't know that your wife knew about the High Wire, and planned to use it, why were you looking for her here?' she asked. 'Why didn't you assume she'd driven south from Alice on the Stuart Highway?'

'A gut feeling told me she went this way,' Garreth said.

'A *gut feeling*?' Edna's voice was high. Outraged. She tried to swallow her excitement, the wild thing pulsing in her brain, telling her to grab the animal she had just cornered, to slit its throat. 'That's what you're going to go with?'

'Do people not have gut feelings, Senior Sergeant Norris?' Holland watched her carefully. 'Are they a myth?'

'Well, no, but—'

'I'm sorry? What was that?'

'No. I said no. People do indeed have gut feelings.'

'Oh, they do, do they?'

'Had you placed a tracking app on your wife's phone, Commissioner Holland? Is that how you knew where to find it?'

'How absurd.'

'It's a yes or no question, Commissioner.'

'My answer is no, Sergeant Norris.'

'Clare set out without a spare tyre in the vehicle. The vehicle itself was not roadworthy. It appears to have overheated,' Edna pressed.

'Were those questions?'

'Look, I have to put it to you, Commissioner Holland, that I believe that you are being evasive with your answers to my queries here today.'

'Excuse me?' Holland's brows popped up on his forehead. 'What did you just say?'

'I believe you're being evasive, Commissioner.'

'And I believe you're being an idiot, Senior Sergeant.' Holland's smile was hard and ugly. 'How dare you launch an accusation like that at a distressed and emotionally vulnerable witness. And on completely baseless grounds.'

'It is not baseless, sir. Clare didn't—'

'Isn't it possible that Clare *did* in fact set out for Sydney with a spare tyre in her vehicle, and found herself with occasion to use it? Tyres do blow, Norris. That's what we have spare tyres for.'

'Perhaps. But she would have put the blown tyre back in the wheel well after she swapped it out so that she could have it replaced or repaired without having to buy a new rim.'

'Or, equally, she might have dumped it by the side of the road, rim and all,' Holland snapped. 'It would have been illegal. That doesn't make it implausible. You're making an enormous number of assumptions about my wife and her propensity to follow the law without, to my knowledge, ever having met the woman.'

Edna felt her neck burning.

'Further, isn't it possible, Senior Sergeant, that Clare's car was *indeed* roadworthy when she left Perth,' Holland continued, spittle gathering at the corners of his mouth, 'and that some misfortune along her route caused it to become not so? Have you conducted a forensic examination of the vehicle already? Have you confirmed that a rock did not flick up and puncture her car's radiator, causing the coolant to leak and, in time, the car to overheat?'

Edna licked her molars, looked at the car's ceiling, told herself not to reach over and punch the Northern Territory Police Commissioner square in the teeth.

Holland sucked in a huge breath, and let out an enormous sigh. 'Jesus.' He shook his head. 'You know what, Senior Sergeant? I've breathed two enormous sighs of relief today. The first was at arriving at this scene and finding that the deceased is not my wife. The second came just now, when I remembered that you won't be lead on this case for much longer. Because, damn'—he laughed—'I think the desert heat has cooked your brain.'

Edna terminated the interview, got out of the car and stood there in the heat and light and willed herself, with everything that she had left in that moment, not to kick the side of the car. Holland was back on his phone before she had even caught her breath. She took out her own phone when it started buzzing and prepared herself to feel the sweet relief flood her when a friendly voice came on the line.

Instead, Stevenson's voice crackled with horror-tinged energy. 'You're never going to believe this,' she said.

2011

Americans were on the gate. Harvey started hearing them from eight hundred metres out, laughing and shooting the breeze. He dumped Bak-Li on the roadside and carried on alone, knowing Americans would shoot at anything with a pulse that approached the base unannounced and not showing hands, even if it was a half-dead man with another half-dead man on his back. Harvey had walked through the desert carrying his section private Geon Bak-Li for three days, out of the mountains where the ambush had happened and straight into the blazing white, sandy eternity, no choice but to make a beeline for Tarin Kot across the surface of the hottest place on earth. He'd figured the Taliban fighters who had attacked them would look for him in the foothills below Durji, rather than guessing he'd be insane enough to go out into the desert. He'd been right. Step by step, kilometre by kilometre, he'd carried his wounded cargo and used the stars and the trajectory of the sun to find his way home, and he had not encountered a single other human being along the way.

Now, as he set that burden down, he expected his whole body to hum with relief. But it didn't. While Bak-Li had spent the first day crying and pleading, and the second day sweating and shivering, he was unconscious and cold and silent now, and the clock was ticking. Harvey needed to get medics to the man as soon as possible. But third-degree sunburn, extreme dehydration and impossible amounts of muscle fatigue meant he wasn't walking fast or straight.

At four hundred metres, the yanks on the gate clued to his approach and hit the floodlights, lighting up the desert for miles around. Harvey put his hands up as high as he could, which was about eye level, and kept shuffling. He'd torn down his uniform shirt to use as a tourniquet for Bak-Li's leg and a head shade for himself, jettisoned all his gear and weapons, and his undershirt, pants and boots were so filthy from the dust storms and blood they appeared black as he looked down at them. He was certain he wouldn't be recognised. So when the voice came through the megaphone he dropped to his knees.

'Stop where you are. Do not take another step. You have entered a restricted military zone. Leave, or you will be shot.'

Harvey didn't leave. He knelt and waited. Dogs started barking. A gate lifted. Figures in the murky brightness, big and small.

'Get on the ground! Get on the fucking ground!'

Harvey sank slowly to his hands and knees, everything popping and trembling and shaking with effort, the palms of his hands so scorched he couldn't feel the gravel at all. He lay down on his chest, hearing more encouraging sounds that he wasn't about to be shot – boots and buckles, radios growling. Paws sounded on the gravel and then a huge black German Shepherd came out of the brightness. Harvey let himself be sniffed for bombs, the insistent nose pushing at his belly, his armpits, his head. The dog whined and disappeared. Harvey tried to speak when he heard the boots getting louder, but all that emitted from his lips was a rasp. 'Australian.'

He reached for the dog tags hanging around his neck. It was a stupid move. At least four rifles cocked.

'Move a muscle and I'll blow your fucking brains out!' someone shouted. Harvey froze. The pain was everywhere. His hips and lower back were throbbing weirdly from being locked in position so long, bearing the weight of Bak-Li across his shoulders. His knees were spasming. It felt like his crotch was on fire.

'I'm army.'

'Do not! Fucking! Move!'

All the barking died away and Harvey listened to the squall of radios and tried to wet his lips, but his tongue was like sandpaper. 'Australian Army.'

'Tower one, we got some fucker out here who's been – I don't know – hit by a car or something,' a guy with a heavy Texan accent was saying. 'Give October a sitrep, will you, and tell us what he wants.'

Harvey turned his head on the gravel, looked up at the black shapes of the soldiers moving towards him. A couple were right up on him, rifles raised, pointed at his head. Others were further back on their radios. There was enough ambient light from the moon for Harvey to get a look at the man closest to him, who was behind a rifle. He sucked in a lungful of air and tried again. 'Harvey Buck,' he wheezed. 'Australian Army.'

'*Buck?*' The guy's head popped up. He remembered himself, put his head back behind the scope. 'Sergeant? Sergeant, get up here.'

A pause. Harvey closed his eyes and prayed. He wasn't even a praying man. They came in a rush, boots and dust and hard breaths, someone grabbing his wrists and twisting them behind his back, someone else patting his pockets. Tendons popping and crunching. Pain shooting down his arms. His head was shoved back, the dog tags fished from around his neck and yanked off. The lights swirled red and green against the backs of his eyelids.

'Jesus fucking *Christ* ! It's Harvey Buck!'

He was dropped like a sack of shit on the gravel. Shock, rather than anything else, he told himself. A flurry of radio activity. He was dragged up and his arm slung over someone's shoulder. A bunch of questions were fired at him, all at once, a spray of verbal nonsense he couldn't follow. Where had he come from? How the fuck was he alive? All the rifles were pointed at the ground now. Harvey raised a finger towards the dark, hoped he'd lined up the road out into the wildlands. 'Back there,' he said.

'What? Is there someone else?'

'Yeah.'

'Get a medic. Jesus. Shit. *Shiiiit!* Get a team! Go! Go! Go!'

Harvey had his feet on the ground now. Here was that relief he'd so longed for. It was energising him, getting into his veins, swimming around, loosening hard muscles. He could walk, at least stumble-step, between the Americans. He could see. The gates of Tarin Kot were rolling over him. The air was thick and moist and carried with it so much blessed humanity. Gun oil, motor oil, whatever tasteless, mass-produced slop they were serving over in the chow house. He could hear music. Hendrix, of course, because it was a regular Tuesday night and everyone was swimming around in their stupid little fantasies of Vietnam like they weren't literally inside their own war at that very moment that deserved its own music, its own culture. By the time they were taking him through the second perimeter Harvey could almost walk on his own. Bent and shuffling and zombie-like, but unaided.

'Sit here, Corporal. We'll put you on a stretcher.'

'Forget that.' Harvey gripped onto the guy who was trying to sit him down. 'I want to go straight to Command.'

'Sir, you're in bad shape right now.'

'Fuck you,' Harvey snapped, held on harder. 'I need to speak to Camp Russell Command. Now. Take me there.'

'Yes, sir.'

He didn't need to argue his case further. By now, word was spreading all over the base that someone had returned from the carnage of three days earlier. Harvey stood there and watched the crowd gathering, guys running out of the open doors of the mess rooms, standing, pointing, staring. Someone handed him a water bottle and he sipped from it, expecting the world's greatest relief, but the liquid was like fire roaring down his throat. Already there was misinformation. He heard someone tell someone else he'd been captured and tortured and dropped back at the gates. Bak-Li was whizzed past him on a stretcher. The guy looked gunmetal grey in the face. There was more fussing about Harvey getting medical treatment, but he ignored it all, stood there waiting until a carrier pulled up. He searched every face, looking for *them*. Parker, Darryl, Tizza and Lipton. He didn't see them.

Major General Evan Leasing came around the corner of the briefing room where they put Harvey so fast he almost bounced off the door on the way in. The guy was wearing sweats and a T-shirt, was all puffed up like he'd been working out when he got the call. Beads of moisture on his bald scalp, big veins in his temples. Harvey had never seen him like that. Probably no one in the room had, and there were plenty of people in the room; basically anybody who had managed to tag along with the procession without being scolded and sent away for gawking. This was going to be a story to dine out on for the rest of a guy's life. People wanted to be there.

Leasing pulled a chair out from the table without even slowing his stride and slid it in front of Harvey and sat down. 'What the *actual living fuck*, Corporal Buck.'

'My thoughts exactly, sir,' Harvey said.

'We chalked you up as a dead man, the past three days.' Leasing sat rigid as a stone, his big hands on his thighs, eyes bright and locked on Harvey's. 'We hit that area outside Durji with everything we had. Took us a day and a half. We recovered the remains of some, but not many. Everything was torched. It was assumed you were among those lost. We held a fucking memorial for you. For all of those guys.'

'"It was assumed"?' Harvey said.

'Excuse me?'

'*It was assumed* I was among the dead . . . or *you were told* I was among the dead?'

Silence enveloped the room. Whispers drained away. A medic came in and dumped his bags and knelt beside Harvey and started hooking him up to an IV bag, huffy and pouty, presumably about Harvey refusing to be seen at the medical centre.

'There were four survivors of the massacre,' Leasing said carefully. 'Tech guys who were—'

'Who were in the first vehicle in the convoy,' Harvey said. 'They told you there were no survivors.'

'That's right.'

'It's because they set the whole thing up.'

There was no collective gasp. No cries of protest or outrage. The room was so quiet, the humming of the fluorescent lights in the ceiling sounded like a jackhammer. Harvey's skin was so ravaged, the medic was struggling to find a vein. Harvey just sat there while he fished around and around with the needle, finding nothing, turning Harvey's wrist to try to go in behind his thumb joint. Harvey told Leasing and the audience about the green light on his helmet. About the lead vehicle in the convoy taking off right after the RPG hit. About trudging through the desert, mentally raking over who had been in the convoy, every soldier, what their role was in the transport mission from Durji to Tarin Kot. Coming to the inevitable conclusion about who had access to the helmets. Who was leading the convoy. Who had survived the entire thing unharmed.

'It makes perfect sense,' Harvey said. 'Those weapons tech nerds. Parker, Darryl, Tizza and Lipton. They would have been working closely with the American guy, the expert, Sheerwater, before he arrived in Durji. They would have known his routine. What he was carrying. What might be valuable to enemy fighters. Parker and Darryl and Tizza and Lipton, they would have been briefed on the transfer to Tarin Kot. The timeline. The route. I'm telling you right now, Major General. Those guys hooked up with some Taliban arseholes and decided to sell Sheerwater to them as a hostage and everything Sheerwater had on him as intel.'

Leasing's mouth was small and hard, his eyes fixed.

'The green light on my helmet,' Harvey went on. 'It was supposed to turn on when we were in position and show the fighters lying in wait for us in the hills which guy Sheerwater was. They wanted to make sure they captured him. That he didn't get hurt. But the plan went south when Sheerwater and I swapped helmets.'

'Buck,' Leasing said. 'Listen—'

'The light was tiny. So small, I didn't notice it on the helmet when I put it on. But it was bright enough that it lit up the whole vehicle,' he said. 'We were riding dark. You would have been able to see it from the roadside.'

Leasing nodded.

'They hit Sheerwater's vehicle with the RPG instead of mine because they thought I was Sheerwater. When they came for me on foot, a guy pointed a rifle at my face. He didn't shoot me. He called to the others. He said, "He's here."' Harvey was getting a sinking feeling. He didn't know if it was the fluids laced with drugs that the medic was now pumping into him, because he'd finally found a vein. Or if – horror of all unspeakable horrors – what he was saying was not being believed. He searched Leasing's eyes and saw nothing. Not denial. Not affirmation. Just placid alertness. Harvey told himself not to think that way. He just *couldn't* think that way. 'Those guys. The tech guys. Parker and the others. They're traitors. They set up the ambush and fled the site when the attack started.'

Leasing said nothing.

'The comms were dead,' Harvey pleaded. 'I mean completely dead. No signal. No power. Nothing. I checked multiple radios. Who would have the ability to do that? To wipe out comms for an entire convoy?'

'It would take an electromagnetic pulse,' someone said.

Leasing held up a hand. Silence followed.

'You believe me about all this, right?' Harvey asked.

'Corporal.' Leasing exhaled.

'Tell me you believe me.'

'Corporal, we're going to deal with this.'

'I need to hear that you believe me.' Harvey could feel the painkillers creeping up his arm. Warm, tickling, humming in his throat, making the lights above him shimmer. 'It's all there. It makes sense. It's the only thing that makes sense.'

'I believe you,' Leasing said. He looked over Harvey's shoulder. 'Sergeant? Bring me those guys. The weapons techs he's talking about.'

'You got it, sir.'

'Buck, you're a fucking hero.' Leasing stood. 'Get to your rack. Your watch is over.'

They lifted Harvey and walked him out into the hall, the huffy medic squeezing the IV bag, Harvey's little unofficial entourage following. Harvey saw Shayna arrive at an intersection of hallways ahead of him, looking around, a couple of women from her section right behind her. He couldn't feel the floor under his feet, was walking on balloons, pushing through curtains of light, the pain that had been a fire roiling and turning in the hollows of his bones now a memory. Shayna flew at him, and his entourage of handlers all protested, worried he'd drop dead right there in her arms. Harvey held his girlfriend and smelt her and felt her fingers in his hair and her sobs against his chest, and he pushed down the slowly intensifying sense that everything he'd just said had been wasted breath.

CHAPTER 14

He walked out of town the same way he'd come in, arrived in the little valley two kilometres or so from Cooper Creek township. The cop, Stevenson, hadn't followed, as Harvey predicted. She would be as powerless outside the bank as she'd been in it, with both her weapons in his possession. He guessed she'd stayed to comfort the teller he'd terrorised, Carol.

The kangaroos who had lounged on the hillside at the break of dawn had moved on. Harvey stood in the sunlight and put his hands on his knees and stared at his shadow on the ground, tried not to think about those days in the desert, the times he'd had to put Bak-Li down and walk away, sit on his arse on the desert floor and try not to weep at the hopelessness of it all. He remembered that time now, gripping his sandy knees, the trauma aftershocks coming out of nowhere from the battle, as they always did, flashing and stuttering over his view of the desert. Carro's brains on the inside wall of the Bushmaster. The burst of light that had ended the lives of the men in the vehicle in front of them. Between the paralysing episodes of memories of the ambush, he'd also been besieged by guilty urges to leave Bak-Li in the middle of nowhere and walk on alone. He must have thought about that ten thousand times while he counted his steps over unending sand dunes, rocky valleys, featureless plains, the sun searing him from the side, then above, then the other side of him. A live rotisserie chicken dripping his sweat, and Bak-Li's, reeking, huffing breaths through a seared windpipe. The same guilty feelings were pressing at him now, about leaving Clare in their hellish predicament and taking an out. Because he could do that. It would mean his death, but he was sure he'd be able to get a couple of rounds out of the cop's gun and into Tizza or Darryl before that happened. But who would he aim for? Who was more dangerous? He certainly wouldn't be able to get both of them before he was blown to pieces. And that would leave Clare at the mercy of the survivor. But would his death cancel out that murderous fury the two men held for him? Would it mean Clare's freedom?

The truck ambled down the slope from the roadside and stopped a hundred metres away from where Harvey stood. The tiny speakers in the glasses crackled.

'*Place both guns and the taser on the ground and take twenty steps back.*'

Harvey took the gun out of his waistband. He actioned it and pointed it at the truck. It was Tizza behind the wheel. Harvey saw the man shrink slightly.

'*What the fuck, Buck? What are you doing? Drop the gun!*'

'This is going to be what it's like, Tiz,' Harvey said.

Harvey felt, rather than saw, the red light blink on at the centre of his chest. The mechanical squealing followed. He stood there for a moment in the sickening discomfort it gave him, the vest armed and ready to blow. Wondered if he could ever become accustomed to the feeling. Then he lowered his aim, hoped the mind games were working. He wanted Tizza to be able to envision the situation falling apart. See it acted out in real time, Harvey with a weapon. Him, helpless. The bullet coming. Harvey had spent a lot of his time in Afghanistan preparing young men to kill for the first time. Most had never so much as hit a bird with their car. Visualisation was important. The academies drilled into the men that they should never point a gun at another man. Terror of headlines about accidental shootings on bases. Harvey was more worried about his men seizing up when the moment came. He'd encouraged them to face each other, to look down the barrel of each other's loaded weapons, to feel the power in their hands.

'*This is what it's going to be like.*'

He was hoping the same principle that had helped him calm his soldiers about taking lives would be the one to unnerve Tizza now.

'Our time is coming, Tiz,' Harvey said. 'A bang. And then darkness.'

'*Jesus, he's lost it, Dar.*'

'*Push the button, then. End the motherfucker.*'

Harvey put his hands up. The men in the truck were still.

The vest stopped squealing, and the light went out.

Harvey walked forward, put the guns and the taser down, then stepped back. Tizza drove the truck up and parked a few metres behind the weapons. The pair got out and Tizza snatched at the taser a little too fast. Harvey smiled.

'Did you enjoy the show?' Harvey asked. He took the glasses off, folded them, placed them inside the cap. 'What'll I do to entertain you next? You know, I've never skydived.'

'Where's the money?' Tizza asked. Harvey took the sad little cloth bag from his back pocket and tossed the measly stack of cash into the breeze. It didn't even make a good plume. They all stood and watched the notes fluttering away.

'Turn your pockets out,' Tizza demanded. 'Lift the waistband of your jeans and turn 'em out.'

Harvey did as he was told. 'I didn't pocket anything. You had eyes on me the whole—'

'Shut up, arsehole.'

Darryl slid a packet of cable ties out of his back pocket. He walked towards Harvey and tossed them on the ground at his feet. Harvey dropped the cap with the glasses in it just near the cable ties. When Darryl bent to pick them up, Harvey faked forward, and the man snapped up at the waist, his back foot grinding in the gravel.

'Ooh-hoo-hoo.' Harvey grinned. 'I've got you on edge, haven't I, Dar?'

'You sure do, Buck.' Darryl smiled and handed the cap and glasses to Tizza. His bruised cheekbone was navy blue, bulging and shining in the sun. 'Fool me twice, right?'

Harvey took a cable tie from the packet, made a loop of it, and slid it over his hands, tugging it tight. Darryl came around behind him and yanked it tighter.

'Get down on your knees.'

'I'm not in the mood to suck your dick, Darryl. I've got a headache coming on.'

Darryl nudged the back of his right knee. Harvey dropped to the ground. As the older man came around in front of him, Harvey watched the gun hanging at eye level, the gnarled finger on the trigger guard, following the curve. The T-shirt and jacket he'd worn over the vest all the way into town, throughout the bank robbery and back again were suddenly stifling him. He knelt and wondered about the sweat rolling from his throat into the neckline, the effect of its dampness on the electrics of the bomb strapped to his body.

'What are we doing?' Harvey asked. 'Put me back in the truck.'

'I said I had a surprise for you,' Darryl sneered.

'I don't like surprises.'

'Tiz, give me a minute alone here, will you?'

Harvey's stomach dropped. Tizza gave an uncertain smirk.

'You're not really gonna—'

'Go,' Darryl snapped.

Tizza's tongue unadhered from the roof of his mouth, thickly, making an audible cluck. The smaller man glanced back towards the truck. 'But, dude, you—'

Darryl turned around. Tizza put his hands up, walked off. Harvey felt like the ground beneath him had been hollowed out. Like there was only a thin layer of red dirt between him and oblivion. He opened his mouth, sucked in air hot and thick.

'You know, I've had a lot of therapy about what happened in the container,' Darryl said. Harvey stared at the ground, concentrated on his heartbeat thumping in his hands and fingers. 'They make you do that. At Holsworthy.'

'Uh-huh,' Harvey said.

'Military prison isn't the same as regular prison. You get your own cell. There's a Bible in every room. They load you up with a lot of airy-fairy shit about honour and brotherhood. And then there's the therapy. Lots of therapy.'

Harvey exhaled.

'We tried to work out, my therapist and I, how you learnt how to do all the stuff you did to us,' Darryl continued. He reached over and put a hand on Harvey's head. Fingers spanned across the crown of his skull. Harvey stiffened, forced himself not to resist, as the muscular man dragged his head towards his thigh. 'How you got so deep inside our heads.'

Harvey couldn't bear it. He tried to pull back. Darryl dug his fingernails in, scraped up a handful of hair, locked Harvey's head to his crotch. Harvey could smell him. Feel the zipper against his brow through the denim. He told himself if Darryl's other hand came for the zipper, he'd kill the man right there. With his hands bound behind him, and a bomb vest on his chest, he'd kill Darryl. Whatever it took. His teeth were clenched so hard they were squeaking and grinding in his jaw.

'When you had me tied to that chair, and you brought up my daughter and what happened to her,' Darryl was saying. His voice was soft. Distant. High above where Harvey knelt. 'How I didn't protect her . . . I felt what she had felt. In that moment. With the guy. At the party.'

Harvey concentrated on the hammering in his ears.

'The *powerlessness*,' Darryl was saying. 'I felt it. I became it. And that's what you wanted, huh.'

Harvey tried to speak. All that came out was a low, furious growl.

'I'm not gonna make you suck my dick, Buck.' Darryl ground Harvey's head against his thigh. 'But I could. And I want you to take that in for a second. Think about all the different things I could do to you. Right now, you're exactly who I was, in that chair, in that shipping container. You're powerless. You're my victim. *This is happening to you.*'

'*Fuck* you,' Harvey snarled. It wasn't articulate, or well thought out, but it was all he had. Darryl let his head go and came down into a crouch before him. Harvey watched him pull a Polaroid picture from the breast pocket of his shirt, but before the older man could flip it and show him the image, he squeezed his eyes shut.

'Oh, Jesus, no.'

'You must have been wondering, this whole time, about how we got you to come out here, Buck,' Darryl murmured. Harvey tucked his head down, tried to hide in the darkness, but he could feel the corner of the Polaroid picture stroking his cheek. 'How we got set up so fast, with Tiz and Parker behind you, and me coming from Sydney with the truck all ready to go. The drone already in the air. The vests designed, built, tested. Shayna calls you, and suddenly the airports are out. You hit the road, and wouldn't you know it? We're ready to go.'

'Don't do this,' Harvey broke. He shook his head, looked at the ground, at Darryl's shoes. 'Come on. Come *on*. Please, man, just . . .'

'Maybe you've been avoiding it,' Darryl said from somewhere above him. 'Focusing on the minute to minute. Trying to survive. But it's okay. We've got plenty of time, Buck. Let's stop and smell the flowers for a second.'

The Polaroid fell on the ground between Harvey's knees. He glimpsed her. Shayna. Harvey didn't recognise the place, not from what he remembered of her apartment, but he'd been there once, years ago. He and Shayna had run into each other randomly in a bar in Parramatta, her blowing off steam with the other military recruiters after work, him being blown in by some unpredictable wind, the same kind that had been carrying him from job to job and place to place since he came back. They'd come together. They'd talked, about whose fault it was, about whether he'd forced her to do what she'd done in giving over those men to him, in helping him with the information he needed to break them. He'd taken all the blame. He'd assured her she hadn't known how far he'd go. They'd managed to put aside all the horror of what had happened in Afghanistan for a single night, before he woke in the early hours and looked at her sleeping face and remembered it all. Remembered what he'd done to her. To *them all*; Shayna, and the traitors.

He'd moved to Alice Springs the next day.

Knew she hated the desert and wanted to avoid ever running into her again.

In the photograph, she was slumped over the edge of a bathtub. Her bloodshot eyes told him she'd been strangled.

'Where is she now?' Harvey whispered. 'Will someone find her?'

'No,' Darryl said. 'She's somewhere west of Wanaaring. I had to make sure I could get up the Wire after the phone call, get to the meet point before Tizza and Parker jumped the gun and grabbed you on their own. I was only seconds away. But Tiz, he's been hungry to grab you for months. I should have known—'

'You buried her in the desert?' Harvey's voice was low, weak. 'She would have hated that.'

'She doesn't hate anything anymore,' Darryl chuckled. 'And to think your last words to her were about how you were coming, and you'd be there as fast as you could. I feel sorry for you, Buck. Just a little bit. I know what it feels like, to fail to be there for the one you love.'

Harvey let air out through his teeth. He couldn't speak.

'Cut your ties again,' Darryl said. 'Play your mind games. Go on. Try it. I'll reach my breaking point eventually, Buck. And when I do, I'll bind up that woman in that truck over there, and I'll put a cable tie around her neck, and I'll yank it shut. And you'll have to watch her fight off the darkness closing in all around her with everything that she has.'

Harvey tried to breathe.

'I wonder if she'll fight as hard as Shayna,' Darryl pondered aloud. He rose to his feet. 'Or take as long to die.'

CHAPTER 15

Edna slid into the cruiser beside Talon, reached across him, flipped open the glove box and took out a Twix. In the vehicle ahead, Holland had an elbow on the sill and was watching them in the rear-view mirror as he talked on the phone. Edna scoffed the chocolate bar wordlessly and took a deep breath, hoping it would relieve the rolling feeling in her stomach. It did not. 'We gotta get you to the airport,' she said.

Talon's lip twitched. He sucked in a breath that was big and fast enough that Edna knew he was gearing up to state his case. She spoke before he could.

'No, I'm serious. This is turning into something.' Edna shook her head. 'Something . . . weird.'

'What do you mean?'

'I mean a bank just got robbed.' Edna glanced at the desert. 'Out *here*.'

Talon sat frowning at her.

'I've had all kinds of cases since I arrived in this job, you know,' Edna said. 'Killings. Bashings. Rapes. I had to arrest a guy last year because he wouldn't stop sending this woman in Darwin jars of his own kidney stones.'

'What!'

'Yeah. But this is weirder.' Edna tossed the Twix wrapper into the back of the cruiser, popped the boot, opened her door and got out. Talon followed her. 'Stevenson, my colleague. She was there for the robbery. Said the guy hardly seemed interested in the money, which there would have been shit all of, anyway. So why the hell have I got a burnt-out car, a missing woman, an ambush, a shooting and a . . . a *symbolic* fucking bank robbery all happening within twenty-four hours?'

'I don't know.' Talon watched her slide the crime scene pop-up tent from the back of the cruiser. 'But I can be here to help.'

'No you can't.'

'What? Are you kidding? You just finished saying you were glad I was here to help you work it all out.' Talon pointed to the spot where they'd been standing twenty minutes earlier, where she'd said precisely that, by the still-open door of the flat-tyred car. 'Those were your exact words.'

'I was joking.'

'You were *joking*?' Talon's eyes narrowed to slits. 'Fuck you, Edna.'

'Fuck you, *Senior Sergeant Norris*.' Edna turned on him. 'Not Edna. Listen, Boy-o. It's been fun. It really has. But we've got to stop playing around. We started out as police officer and legal charge and we've ended up as . . .' She gestured to him, herself, the invisible space between them, criss-crossed with god-knows-what energies and complications. 'Whatever the hell this is. It should never have got this far, Talon. It's my fault it did.'

The boy glared at her, his jaw muscles flexing.

'You're not my investigative partner, okay?' Edna went on regardless. She slammed the boot closed. 'So stay here.'

She went to the body by the roadside, walking past Holland's car. The man was writing on a notepad balanced on the dashboard. Talon was right behind her, of course, an unspeaking ball of hatred and fury coming to a stop and watching impotently as she unzipped the tent.

'The team from Adelaide will be here in a couple of hours,' Edna said. 'I'll get one of them to drive you south.'

'I'm not leaving.'

'Yes, you are.'

Edna's phone beeped in her pocket. She picked up the satellite call.

'Hi, Ed,' a smooth male voice. 'This is Richie on Dispatch.'

She held her head. She hated Richie. Never met the guy, but his unshakeably honeyed voice reminded her of late-night radio, not emergency services.

'I just took over from Jane Heywood, and I'll be your dispatcher for today.'

'Great,' Edna sighed.

'I got a numberplate read you were apparently waiting on?'

'Yep.' Edna watched Talon unloading the fold-out tent from its case with dismay. 'I'm with the car right now. Who's the owner?'

'Harvey Michael Buck, forty-eight,' Richie said. 'There's an address in Alice Springs. You want it?'

'Phone number, too.' Edna switched to speaker phone and opened her notes app. As she typed in the details, Talon unfolded the tent. It's concertina-style structure fanned out and snapped efficiently as the legs locked into place. The boy gave

Edna a defiant glance as he shook out the reflective tarpaulin cover and started applying it to the frame. Edna watched him lift the whole tent by one aluminium corner and walk over to the body, where he plonked it down and started unfurling the sides to shield the body from view.

'Richie, are there any missing persons reports or Keep A Look Out For orders with Harvey Michael Buck on them?' Edna asked. 'Who's his next of kin?'

'Woman named Shayna Kinthrop. Sydney. And I've got . . . ahhh, let's see here. Nope. No sign of a "Buck" on the open call sheets from missing persons.'

'Give me Kinthrop's number.'

'Consider it done.'

Edna ended the call feeling vaguely slimed. Talon was standing by the tent, chewing his nails, looking at his phone. The stomach-churning anger she'd felt as she watched him rig her crime scene drained away as she approached.

'Listen.' Edna put her hands up in surrender. The boy didn't look up. 'Just listen to me. There's something you need to understand.'

Talon spat a gnawed nail on the desert floor.

'I brought a young person into my life once,' Edna said. 'Someone like you. A person who was in the midst of very, very bad things. She was really drowning. I thought I could help her, so I . . . I pulled her into my boat, you know what I'm saying? And all the boundaries and rules and structures went to hell. It ended up going as wrong as it can possibly go. Not just for her. For both of us. We sank.'

'Harvey Buck.' Talon turned his phone screen towards her. Edna glimpsed a fit, middle-aged guy with salt-and-pepper hair and a beard posing with a bunch of men in army desert camos. 'He's some kind of war hero, I think.'

'Talon, did you hear anything that I just said?'

'Maybe that's him.' Talon pointed to the tent, the body encased within it, protected from the desert breeze, the sand. 'Should we pull the balaclava off and see?'

'Talon, you are not my partner!' Edna snapped. 'You're not a cop! You're barely an adult!'

'I can't go home!' the boy roared back. Suddenly tears were welling in his eyes. His phone was forgotten, his face twisted. 'Please, Edn— *Senior Sergeant Norris. Please.* I can be helpful here. I know I can.'

'You are being helpful, but that's not appropriate.'

'But I said please!'

'That's nice but it doesn't help in this situation.'

'But this is all I have right now.' The boy was huge, trembling, every muscle tensed, trying to contain the pain. 'Last night, Rosie was all I had. And today, *this* is all I have. If I lose this, I'll have nothing.'

'That's not my problem,' Edna said. The phrase wasn't her own. She'd opened a tightly locked door in her mind and those words had come through, straight from her past, spoken with someone else's voice. Now they were adapted and fitted to her lips, carrying no meaning whatsoever. *That was not your problem, Norris.* 'That's not . . . my . . . problem.'

Talon's mouth pressed shut and he turned, and Edna saw the telltale dust cloud on the horizon that meant a car was coming. It was moving fast, from the direction of Cooper Creek. Stevenson.

'Send me the link about Buck,' Edna told Talon. 'Then go wait in the car.'

Edna stood there, doing her own googling, listening to the kid's footfall fading and the gentle roar of Stevenson's car getting louder. She could feel Holland's eyes on her, so she retreated from that searing gaze into the images she flipped under her thumb. Buck's face provided a strange sanctuary in that moment. He wasn't smiling in any of the photos, but had the lines at the corners of his eyes that came only from doing it a lot. In one image he was helmeted, crouching by the wheel of some enormous military tactical vehicle, his arm slung around a young mongrel dog. The headlines spoke of a massacre of Australian soldiers in Afghanistan. Some superhuman attempt made by Buck to save himself and a fellow soldier. There were no mentions of the man before or since his active service, no social media profile, no LinkedIn. Edna was deep in her analysis of a full-body picture of Buck in his ceremonial dress uniform, attending a funeral, it seemed, when Stevenson parked beside her. Buck seemed taller and broader-shouldered than the dead man in the tent. But Edna couldn't be sure. She called Dispatch back.

'Send out a KALOF for Buck, will you?' she said. 'Just say "Police require his assistance".'

'Consider it—'

Edna hung up, looked back at the soldier on her phone.

'What the fuck?' Stevenson said in greeting. She'd come to Edna's side unnoticed and spotted something on her phone screen. 'That's . . .'

Edna looked up. Stevenson's mouth was agape and she was pointing at the phone.

'How the hell did you find him so fast?' Stevenson asked.

'Who?'

'The guy.' Stevenson pointed to the news article. 'That's the dude. The one who just robbed the Cooper Creek bank.'

'*This* guy?' Edna's mouth fell open. It stayed open as she heard her cruiser start up and the tyres grind in the dirt. She and Stevenson watched as Talon swung the vehicle in a tight circle and took off back down the Wire, the way they'd come.

Commissioner Holland opened his car door and slid stiffly out, leaning an elbow on the roof of his vehicle to watch the police cruiser disappear into the distance. Even from behind, Edna could see he was smiling.

CHAPTER 16

Harvey hit the floor of the truck bed and stayed there, the effort to scoot into a corner like trying to climb a mountain. Every limb was heavy, his spine was on fire, and his fingers throbbed from loss of circulation. The doors whumped closed behind him and he heard Darryl and Tizza walking off into the desert, the flick of Darryl's cigarette lighter telling Harvey he had a few minutes to languish in despair before he'd have to make the effort to get up against a wall or get tumbled around the truck bed when the thing took off. Clare was suddenly over him, trying to lift him, sliding down beside him when she couldn't. He opened his eyes to find her face centimetres from his. Her hairline was glossy with sweat, and the hand on his cheek felt damp.

'Are you okay? What did they do?'

'They . . . They killed someone. Shayna. It's how they got me out here.' Harvey shifted into a sitting position. It hurt to move, to speak. 'I just need a minute. Can you give me a minute?'

'No.' Clare hooked her hands beneath his arms and tried to drag him back towards the wall of the truck. 'You can grieve for your girlfriend later. Every second we're in here together, we've got to be working on our escape. That was the plan.'

'A fucking minute won't make a difference.'

'Yes it will. I'm going to help you grind your ties off.'

'I don't know if I want to do that.'

'Of course you do.'

'Get off me!' He twisted sharply, tried to push her away. He gave up. He scooted on his butt to the wall of the truck, gripped the sharp steel edge and tried not to think about this woman twisting and kicking and clawing at a cable tie cinching off her airway. Somewhere out there, he heard Darryl laugh at something Tizza said. Harvey shifted his legs in against his body and put his forehead against his knees.

'Until a couple of minutes ago, I had a hope that maybe we were going to get out of this alive,' he said.

Clare waited, daring to put one hand on his thigh.

'They're destroying my reputation,' Harvey said. 'That's what this is all about. I came out of the war with a lot of credit, for surviving the ambush. For making it back to base. For . . . doing what I did . . . to get the men who set up the ambush exposed. Lipton. Parker. Tizza. Darryl. The ones left behind, everybody but Lipton . . . those guys might have just sucked it up if they'd been caught in any other way. But the way I went about it . . . I went too far. I really messed them all up. And now they're going to make me undo all my good standing. They're going to make sure the world doesn't see me as a hero anymore. And then they're going to kill me.'

'That's what the bank robbery was about,' Clare said. 'Making it look like you've . . . you've lost your mind.'

'Turned over a new leaf. A criminal one.'

'And that won't be enough for them?'

Harvey shook his head. 'No. If they were willing to kill Shayna, they'll have some amazing plan to kill me. All I can hope is that it involves the vest. At least then it'll be fast.'

'So we escape.' Clare's voice was shaky. Uncertain. Shot through with a tenuous determination. 'We find a way.'

'We have to.' Harvey nodded. 'Because they've come this far. They'll kill you, just to make sure you don't tell the world the truth about me. They're not curious about who you are at all. You notice that? They don't want to know who might be looking for you. What kind of hole you'll leave in the world. What that might mean for them in the long run. That's a problem, Clare.'

She nodded. She was looking at the box in the corner, the insulated case strapped against the wall and clipped at the front. Out there in the desert, Tizza's voice drifted on the wind.

'. . . *best day of my life, man.*'

Harvey's first tie broke.

'Hurry up with that,' she said. 'I have an idea, but I need your help.'

2011

'We have a problem,' Shayna said.

Harvey slid his eyes over to her. It was a deliberate effort, just moving his eyes, like he was a heavy, lead puppet and every gesture required the working of levers and cables inside his skull. He got the sense, rather than knew, that Shayna had been sitting by his hospital bed in the Tarin Kot base medical centre for a while, but the painkillers were washing together pieces of time like slabs of ice floating on the Arctic Ocean. The word 'problem' pulled him far enough out of that dark, delicious sea that he managed to shift upwards on his pillow, a bunch of tubes and monitors coming with him, his puppet wires.

'Huh?'

'I said we have a problem.' Shayna was in her undershirt and combat pants. The hard, tight bun of blonde hair at the nape of her neck. 'Are you with me, Harvey?'

'Yeah, I'm here. I'm here.'

'Because we need to talk.'

'What happened?'

'A meeting happened, with Command.' Shayna was holding his burnt and bandaged hand. He hadn't even noticed until he looked. There was no feeling in his fingers. 'They got together to nut out the whole thing about the accusation. Nobody believes you, Harv.'

Now he was fully awake. Harvey pushed himself up higher in the bed. The rest of the ward was empty. He assumed that meant Bak-Li had been medevacked out. 'What are you saying?'

'I'm saying, it's not holding water,' Shayna said. 'The idea that the comms blinked out. That the first vehicle in the convoy fled. The whole thing about a green light on your helmet.'

Harvey stared at her.

'It all sounds insane,' Shayna said. She waited, but Harvey didn't speak. Couldn't. 'They're putting it down to combat trauma. Dehydration. Heat stroke. They went and looked at the carrier those tech guys were travelling in, and it was all shot up like it was there for the whole battle, just the way that Lipton, Parker, Darryl and Tizza said it was.'

'But it wasn't.' Harvey was shaking now. Wide-eyed. 'They were gone right after the RPG hit. They took off like a bat out of hell because they knew what was coming.'

'I know.' Shayna took his other hand now, held them both, squeezed them as hard as she dared. 'I know, Harvey. *I believe you.* But that doesn't mean shit, babe. Because they're shipping you out. Your entire section is dead, and you're medically unfit for duty. You're scheduled on a medevac out of base tomorrow morning.'

Harvey was getting feeling back in his fingers. He gripped Shayna's hands, and felt a god-awful love for her deep in the pit of his guts. Of course, that urgent love was there now, because it had only ever been present when it was wrong for them to be together. First as recruits sneaking off and fraternising in the armoury sheds at the academy. Then as frantic lovers catching each other when their deployments put them together. Three days here in Darwin. Two days there in East Timor. Stolen, forbidden moments, always in uniform, always in the dark. Being here with him now, alone in the hospital, when he'd sullied his survival act by making the worst accusation a person could make against a fellow soldier. The wrongness and rightness of it all was so familiar. The next question came out of pure terror, because of course, real love didn't exist without a deep layer of terror shimmering underneath it. The thought of the men who had almost killed him remaining on the base with Shayna made the hairs on the back of his neck stand on end.

'What's the plan for those guys?'

'They're scheduled on a flight out this afternoon.' Shayna shook her head. 'Command are swapping them for a team from Kuwait, just in case there's any hostility. The major feeling around base is that you were the one in the wrong, Harv. But Command doesn't want to risk there being a couple of dissenters.'

Harvey was silent. His mind was churning. 'Who's driving them to the airstrip?'

Shayna watched his eyes. Didn't speak.

'Who—'

'Harvey.' There was warning flash in her eyes. Dark clouds full of lightning. 'No.'

'You're head of transport. You can put yourself on that assignment.'

'Harvey.'

'Did Bak-Li make it?' Harvey asked. He knew the answer, even before she spoke. He could see it in the way her throat tightened.

'No,' Shayna said. 'He lasted about an hour after you both made it to base. The medics did their best. His family . . . they want to do something for you. For trying to save him. They sent an email for you through base command. There's a printout of it there.'

She gestured to the table. Harvey didn't look. He was thinking about a section of the base far to the south-west, just outside the guarded perimeter, where broken down and disused surplus items were dumped. There were shipping containers there. Some were loaded with military trash – the broken vehicles, packing material from the endless supply runs, bags and bags of domestic garbage from the troops. But some of the containers were empty. When he looked back at Shayna, he could see the acceptance in her eyes. The dread-heavy acceptance.

'You could let this go, you know,' she said anyway.

'Not on your life,' Harvey answered.

CHAPTER 17

Stevenson drove. There was no sign of the kid in the police cruiser, not even his dust cloud, which meant he was putting the pedal to the metal. Edna gripped her seatbelt in one hand and her phone in the other and dialled Talon every minute or so, but received no answer. For a long time, the desert rolled by them, the occasional ghostly or charred gumtree whipping by among the scrub, gnarled fingers pointing back down the Wire like desert demons urging them on.

Stevenson would have known Talon's story from the station run sheet from the night before, but Edna recounted it for her anyway, both their gazes on the horizon ahead.

'You're going to be in deep doo-doo over this, Ed.' Stevenson tutted. 'They'll start with you disarming the kid at the Horn residence without calling in a backup team. And they'll end with him being killed when he flips your stolen cruiser in about five minutes' time.'

'I know.'

'Then they'll have you for leaving Commissioner Holland, prime suspect in his wife's disappearance, alone with a crime scene that may be in some way *related* to that disappearance.'

'I know, Stevie. I know.'

'Jesus. No sign of him. He must really be fanging it. What is it with boys and stealing cars?'

'Someone's probably done a study.'

'Hey, this all works for me.' Stevenson shrugged. 'A mess this big will take the shine right off me letting some arsehole take my gun from me back in Cooper Creek.'

'You owe me a beer,' Edna said.

They rode on in silence for a while, the never-never sprawling on either side.

'So what's the theory?' Stevenson loosened her hair, shook it out, ran a hand through it. She was doing one-twenty on gravel and sand, one-handed and clear-eyed, because she'd been roaring through the desert on mopeds since she was a toddler. 'Clare Holland's on the run from her dickbag husband. Buck stumbles across her. Picks her up. Rapes and kills her. Then he . . . what? He keeps trundling along on his way to Cooper Creek . . . to rob a bank . . . when suddenly he's ambushed?'

'It doesn't make any sense.'

'I mean, it *does*,' Stevenson said. 'Because it has to. We just can't see it yet. We don't have all the pieces.'

'How lucid was he?' Edna glanced over at her partner. 'He's a veteran. He faced serious conflict. You know how those guys end up. They either get depressed and shoot themselves or put their tinfoil hats on and start wiring up their property.'

Stevenson laughed, because between them, Edna knew, the two outback cops could name ten combat veterans in their region who had moved there to try to carve out a safe place away from the nightmares, the visions, the sounds of cars backfiring and firecrackers going off and kids screaming in playgrounds. Some were successful. They bought large slices of land, rigged them up with cameras and tripwire alarm systems, and sat on their verandahs, growing withered and smoking weed and pointing rifles at anything that moved. Filling the comments section of conspiracy theory and doomsday prepper Facebook sites. Others were not so successful. The isolation and the quiet drove them to put their rifle in their mouths.

'He seemed sane enough,' Stevenson said after a while. 'Almost like he felt bad about what he was doing.'

'Okay.'

'I asked him, in fact, why the hell he was doing it,' Stevenson said. 'He said, "I have to".'

'"I have to" like "Voices in my head are telling me I have to", or "I have to" like "I need the money damn fast so I have to"?'

'No idea.'

'So he was already there when you arrived?' Edna asked. 'Take me through it again.'

Stevenson did. Edna listened.

'He wanted Carol alone,' Edna concluded. 'He stood there fiddling with the pens, trying to see if he could get you to move along with your business and go away. When you wouldn't, he pretended he'd come in the first place with the intention of robbing the joint.'

'So the real goal was Carol,' Stevenson mused. 'That might fit. He's picked up Clare Holland. Had some fun with her. Finished up. Headed out to find victim number two. Got side-tracked by some road bandits for a spell but inevitably ended up in Cooper Creek. He saw Carol opening up the bank alone and thought, *She'll do.*'

'I want to know if this guy has a history of violence, or has he just snapped recently.' Edna sat texting a request to Dispatch. 'This is the best theory I have yet for this whole thing, and it's thin, but it's all I've got. I also want to know what vehicle he's driving now. Whoever tried to nail him – the guy in the balaclava and his crew – they must have been out to get a tourist or a drug runner and they ended up with a rapist on a spree.'

'Maybe Buck's got their vehicle now.'

'Teams are coming in from Adelaide and Perth to deal with that crime scene.' Edna sat up as she spotted a dust cloud ahead. 'They should be able to get me an ID on the dead guy pretty fast if he has a record. Slower if he doesn't. Then I'll have a hint at what kind of car we're looking for, maybe.'

'You worried about the Commish back there at your scene?' Stevenson asked.

'Not terribly,' Edna said. 'I photographed it pretty well when I arrived.'

The dust plume ahead began to grow. Edna saw flashing blue and red lights in the heat haze. In time, the shapes materialised, her cruiser turned sideways by a huge collection of red boulders, the driver's-side door open. Stevenson was leaning forward, knuckles white on the steering wheel.

'How unstable is this kid?'

'He has my cruiser, Stevie,' Edna said.

'Were you riding hot?' Stevenson looked over. Edna's stomach plummeted. At the very same second that she recalled the rifle she kept in a zippered case in the boot of the cruiser, she saw Talon standing there with it, a pot-bellied, bearded man kneeling on the ground in front of him. There was a

Harley-Davidson motorcycle lying on its side in the gravel. Talon was yanking back the slide bolt on the rifle as the two officers pulled the cruiser to a stop.

CHAPTER 18

'Take your pants off,' Clare said.

Harvey did, because in his forty-eight years on the planet, no woman had ever said that to him and he'd thought it was a bad idea. He sat on his butt on the truck-bed floor and dragged his boots and his stinking socks off. Clare took the thick black jeans from him and went to the back door of the truck. She threaded a leg of the pants between the vertical swivel poles which, operated from the outside, locked the doors in place. Then she went to the big cooler, flipping the latches and shoving the lid open. Harvey found inside what he had expected to find: a couple of boxes of muesli bars, some bottled water, blankets. The box was way too big for what it contained, but Harvey saw the thinking behind it. If Darryl, Tizza and Parker's plans had gone awry, and they'd needed to transport Harvey's body for any length of time, the insulated box would prevent his remains from contaminating the truck bed. Clare took one of the eight water bottles and handed another to Harvey.

He didn't need to be told what to do. He took the cap off and drank. She did the same. They eyed each other, gulping, tossing the bottles aside when they were done. Clare got through a bottle and a half. Harvey, two. When they couldn't drink any more, they dumped the contents of the rest of the bottles on the floor. Clare flipped the lid of the insulated box closed and latched it. She gestured to the other side, and Harvey went there. They pushed the box across the floor.

There came a voice from outside. 'What the fuck are they doing in there?'

Harvey and Clare tipped the heavy insulated supply box onto its end. Harvey went to the truck-bed doors and grabbed hold of the legs of his jeans, doubled them over his hands, leant back and hung on. He heard one of the men outside flip up the levers on the doors, and the vertical bars twisted inside the makeshift rope brace made from the pair of jeans. Buck held steady. The truck doors jolted slightly, but no more.

Tizza's voice was already enraged. 'What the *fuck*?'

Harvey looked back. Clare was climbing up onto the box. One of her fists was wrapped in one of his socks. She steadied herself against the ceiling with her other hand, lined up her socked fist and punched the camera.

The punch had no effect.

'Pull up the camera feed.' Darryl's voice was low and dangerous with frustration. 'Buck, whatever you're doing, stop now. You get one warning.'

'Go!' Harvey yelled at Clare. 'Go, go, go, go!'

The truck doors jolted. Harvey set his feet. He knew there was pure science behind his advantage, that he didn't have to hold the doors with all his might based on the sheer fact that Darryl and Tizza would be pulling at them from ground level, a downward angle, his own angle of pull horizontal from the centre of the doors. He could almost hear them calculating this.

The metal steps that folded from the rear of the truck squeaked as one of the men outside flipped them down.

Clare was punching the camera hard. Harvey guessed the dome was made from plexiglass, and there was no reason it would be thick, but the dome shape itself would withstand a bashing. He heard a crack sound, and Clare give a laugh of triumph. It inspired his own grin as he heard the dome collapsing under her muffled blows. He glanced back and saw that she was un-socked now, ripping at the innards of the camera with her fingernails, pulling wires. The main lens clunked on the floor beneath them.

Harvey timed his move to the rhythmic yanks on the doors, then let go. The jeans whizzed through the gap between the bars, and the doors flew open. Harvey saw Tizza fall sideways, managing to keep his grip on the lever, his whole body smashing into the side of the door before he tumbled to the dirt. Darryl was standing nearby, staring up at the captives, a phone in his hand. Harvey guessed the now useless camera feed was playing there.

'You stupid, stupid bitch.' Darryl shook his head. Clare came to Harvey's side. He swung an arm around her waist, immediately regretted the decision, remembering how she'd blasted him when he tried to comfort her in the first few moments of their captivity. To his surprise, she put an arm around his shoulders. The ridiculousness of it all got Harvey again, right in his hollow, bleeding heart, and he stood there in his boxer shorts and bomb vest laughing down at the men who were almost certainly going to murder him and the woman at his side.

Tizza had recovered, spat blood in the dirt and wiped a smear of it off his busted lip. 'You morons. You dumped all your water.' He grinned. The blood between his teeth made the already small, square bones look like baked beans swimming in sauce. 'That wasn't the right move. Darryl and I have got all our own water up the front. You two just made the next few hours a nightmare for yourselves. You know how hot it's going to get in that truck when the sun's fully up?'

'You're right, Tiz. I already feel light-headed.' Harvey nodded solemnly. He stroked his throat. 'Parched. Did you two factor in the midday temperatures when you cooked up this little scheme? Couple of hours back here; no air flow. No water. I might slide right into unconsciousness.'

'Same.' Clare shrugged. 'We'll just have to run back into town. Stock up.'

'You walked through the fucking desert for three days without a drop of water, Buck, you stupid prick!' Tizza barked. Bloody spittle flew from his lip. 'You think dumping your water is going to shake our plans? You're out of your mind!'

Harvey kept smiling. It seemed to slice right through the little man below him.

'I hope you suffer in that box, the way you made us suffer.' Tizza thumped his chest. 'I hope you sweat and bleed and beg for mercy back there.'

'Are you okay, Tiz?' Harvey let his smile morph into a quizzical frown. 'You sound unhinged right now. Are you losing it? Is he losing it, Dar?'

'Fuck you!'

'You gotta be wondering, by now, about how things would be going if it was Parker who survived the ambush back there on the Wire, and not this idiot.' Harvey held Darryl's eyes. 'You've got a subhuman assisting you in this, Darryl. You'd be better off with a five-year-old. When Tizza came into the world, the doctor who delivered him went straight home to his wife and said, "Honey, I can't do this anymore." The guy retrained as a vet.'

Clare snickered.

'This is all falling apart, Darryl,' Harvey said.

'Enough of this shit.' Tizza grabbed the edge of the door. 'Let get moving.'

'Hold up,' Darryl said. He was the only person at the back of the truck who hadn't yet given a hard, evil smile. That made Harvey's skin prickle. The older man bent down and picked Harvey's jeans up from where they'd fallen in the dirt and threw them up at Harvey's chest.

'You wanted to go on a water run,' Darryl said. 'So we'll go on one.'

He gestured for Tizza to flip the truck doors closed. The little man did as he was told. Harvey and Clare stood arm in arm in the dimness and listened to the men climbing into their seats in the front.

'What did that mean?' Clare asked.

'I don't know,' Harvey said. 'But it didn't sound good.'

CHAPTER 19

Edna drew her gun, prepared to fire it. She'd done that twice in her career, and as the weapon slid out of its holster, she felt a different kind of energy in the metal to the thousands upon thousands of times she'd withdrawn it to clean it, check it, lock it away. The whole butt seemed to buzz in her fingers. Talon turned those fierce eyes on her as she and Stevenson exited the patrol car and stood behind their doors, their pistols trained on the boy. Even in a ready-to-fire stance, Edna found she couldn't line the child up directly in the gunsight. She was aiming well above his head.

'Put it down, Talon. Now!' she shouted.

'He ran,' the boy said. He edged closer to the old man, so that the rifle barrel was just centimetres from his cheek. 'As soon as he saw it was a cop car, he turned the bike and took off. He's out here doing something bad.'

'*You're* doing something bad, you idiot!' Stevenson barked. 'You are holding a man at gunpoint! You better snap back to reality in three seconds flat, kid, or I'm gonna blow your befuddled mind all over that rock behind you.'

Talon fingered the trigger guard. His eyes flicked between Edna and Stevenson. Some of the power seemed to drain from his shoulders. He was a slowly awakening sleepwalker trying to make sense of his surroundings. Edna was sure he was going to drop the gun, but the boy turned to the old man on his knees instead.

'What's in the bag, bro?'

'I'm just a guy delivering some food to a mate who's sick,' the bikie said. His forearm tattoos were so ravaged by the outback sun they appeared like dark blue bruises over his brown, sagging skin. When he waved his raised hands, the skin of his biceps flapped like crepe paper. 'I only turned because I forgot me phone back at the caravan.'

'Talon, put the gun down.'

'You turned because you saw it was a cop car!' Talon seethed. 'Don't lie to me!'

'Talon!' Edna snapped.

'Boy, I am going to pop the top of your head like it's the lid of a tube of Pringles.' Stevenson had one eye closed, the pistol trained on Talon's skull. 'It's going to make that air-sucking noise as it comes off. *Shlunk*.'

Talon looked over, his eyes bugging.

'Bet you didn't know bullets could do that.' Stevenson adjusted her stance. 'Peel back people's lids. They can do all kinds of things, if you know where to aim.'

'What the fuck are you saying?' Talon quivered.

'You heard me,' Stevenson said. 'I'm having a hell of a day. When I have a day like this, you know what I do? I go out looking for wild pigs. Scratch that itch to *pop* something.'

'Is she for real?' Talon turned to Edna.

'Unfortunately, yes.'

'What do you think, Ed?' Stevenson asked. 'Give him another three seconds to comply?'

'Just put the gun down, Talon,' Edna sighed.

'One.'

'You have to check his bag.' Talon jostled the rifle uncertainly. Seemed to want to put it down. Raised it again instead. The old bikie flinched. 'He bolted from me. I'm telling you.'

'Put. The gun. *Down.*'

'Two.'

Talon placed the rifle at his feet. Stevenson swapped her aim to the bikie, walked over and shoved the old man flat to the ground. Edna holstered her weapon and went right to Talon, grabbing a fistful of his T-shirt, the rage making her whole body feel like it was on fire. She walked him to the cruiser and threw him up against it. Being twice her size, that took some force. But she could get like that now and then. Driven by almost primal emotions that filled her limbs with liquid strength.

Edna cuffed the boy and shoved him into the cruiser, clambered in after him, slammed the door on them both. Outside, Stevenson was chit-chatting to the old bikie, hands on her hips, the cuffs she'd put on him as he lay on his belly shining in the hard midday light.

'How could you be so *fucking* stupid?'

A fire in the boy's eyes. Edna snapped again before he could fill the car with his own rageful ranting. 'No, don't even begin to tell me you're not stupid,' she snarled. 'That little moment of recklessness – that teenage brain snap you just had – is going to get you up to *ten years* in prison. Do you understand that? I'm not talking about juvenile detention, either, Talon. I'm talking about a men's prison.'

The boy blew out air, leant back in his seat. 'I can handle myself in prison. That's not what I'm worried about.'

'It should be!' Edna couldn't help herself. She reached over and scuffed the kid across the back of the head. 'Get a hold of yourself! You talk a big game, my child. A *huge* game. But I have seen the kind of things that go on inside correctional facilities. You think you got an impulse control problem? These guys don't know how to plan past the next fifteen minutes. They can't fathom consequences. They see what they want and they grab it. And when they see you? You're a handsome young man, Talon, and you're naive as a spring lamb. It's going to be a feeding frenzy.'

'I don't think so. I think it sounds like I'm gonna fit right in.' Talon shifted his cuffed wrists against the car seat behind him, trying to get comfortable. 'I might even end up in charge. I got no plan past the next *five* minutes.'

'Jesus.' Edna held her head. 'I haven't come across someone with so little regard for themselves in a long, long time, you know that?' She glanced outside. The bikie was sitting on his arse now, watching Stevenson, who was picking her way carefully into the saddle bag attached to the motorcycle, starting with the front pockets, tentative fingertips peeling back hems. Edna could vaguely hear the bikie protesting through the closed window.

'*. . . no legal right to search me stuff!*'

A tear was rolling down Talon's cheek. He swiped at it with his shoulder, gazing at the desert.

'You have so much to offer the world,' Edna said. 'I know you've heard that before. I can almost hear other people saying it to you. Because it's plain as day. You must have had teachers and social workers and whoever else tell you, Talon, that you're smart, and you're funny, and you're creative.'

The boy kept staring at the desert.

'Your creativity with this crime stuff is really . . . *something.*' Edna licked her lips, her mind racing. 'You're destined to do something like that, you know. If you stop doing everything in your power to fuck it up. You might be a cop. Or a writer. Or a lawyer. Shit, spinning together complex, convoluted possibilities to cast doubt on a perfectly obvious series of events is basically all that defence lawyers *do*.'

'My dad's gonna kill my mum,' Talon said.

Edna closed her mouth. She watched him.

'He raped her. Day before yesterday.' Talon rubbed his nose on the shoulder of his T-shirt. 'I tried to stop him but, you think I'm big . . . He's twice as big as I am. He goes to the pub and she texts him the whole time he's there trying to get him to come home before he gets too messy. Eventually she makes him angry enough that he does come home.'

Edna took her handcuff key off her belt. She reached over and pushed the boy forward. Once freed, his big, shaking hands came over his face, mashed his wet eyes.

'She just keeps going back, you know?' Talon's voice came from within the mask he made of his hands. 'Like, every man and his dog has been to the house to try to break them up. Family Services. The rape counsellor people. The police. She never does what they tell her to. Because at the end of the day, she's got no schooling, and no job history, and no skills. How's she going to survive? But it's not even that, in the end. It's because he says he's gonna kill her if she ever walks out. And she believes him. Man, I believe him, too.'

'We're going to fix this,' Edna said, without hesitation. 'I'll pull in every favour I have.'

'You can't fix it.' Talon waved her off. 'I figured that out for the last time, day before yesterday, standing outside their bedroom door listening to what he did to her. I thought, *I can't help here. I'm just making it worse.* Because half the time it's me that sets him off, you know? Not her.'

Edna listened.

'Rosie was a . . . a safe place to be during all that time.' Talon laughed sadly. 'The past year or so. Since it's been getting worse and worse. She was always there. Wasn't surprised by anything. I could tell her everything I felt. Like, I actually thought about killing him, so my mum could be free. I told Rosie that, and she didn't call the cops on me or anything. I also thought about . . . you know. Myself. Maybe if I was out of the picture, the grief or whatever would bring the two of them back together. Make him snap out of it.'

'Jesus.' Edna pinched the bridge of her nose.

'I guess Alan Horn liked all the drama,' Talon said.

'First thing I'm going to do is drive back there once all this is over and punch that man square in the mouth.' Edna shook her head. 'Right after I'm done making all the right calls and having your father locked up.'

Outside, Stevenson and the bikie were still arguing about the legality of her search. Stevenson made one last furious point and marched back over to the motorcycle.

'There's a way out of this, Talon,' Edna said. 'I'm gonna help you find it. I promise.'

'I thought it wasn't your problem.' Talon's voice was flat.

'It's not,' Edna said. 'It's ours.'

Talon didn't answer. Edna heard a yelp from outside, turned to look, and saw Stevenson approaching the cruiser at double pace. The younger cop wrenched open the door beside Edna. She slid out and stood, looked at Stevenson's face, which was bloodless and spotted with sweat.

'Go look in the bag,' Stevenson said.

CHAPTER 20

Harvey lay on the floor of the truck and looked at the broken camera in the ceiling, watched the loose wire waving back and forth. The truck had rolled onto the tarred road outside Cooper Creek for a while, but it was definitely off road again now, almost certainly back on the High Wire heading east. Clare lay next to him, sweat running from the middle of her forehead into her hairline. She was also watching the wire in the ceiling dangling and swaying.

'How do you know about it?' Harvey asked suddenly.

Clare turned her head and looked at him. 'Jesus, I was almost out.' She rubbed her eyes. 'It's so hot. It's putting me to sleep. Even with all this going on.'

'How does an antique-restoring, married city-woman in her late thirties know about the most dangerous cross-country driving route in the entire nation?'

'Mid-thirties,' she said. 'If you don't mind.'

Harvey looked at her.

'What says I'm a city dweller, anyway?'

'The full head of blonde highlights with the keratin blowout,' Harvey said. 'That's a three-hundred-dollar haircut right there.'

'How do you know so much about women's hair?' Her eyes were wide.

'The first section they ever gave me to command had four women in it. Answer the question. How do you know about the High Wire?'

'A friend told me about it.'

'"A friend" meaning the husband,' Harvey said.

'What says I meant the husband?'

'Your tone. What does he do?'

'This is not a . . . a relevant thread of conversation.' Clare looked back at the broken camera mount.

'It's not a thread at all. You're batting away every question I serve you. We're playing verbal ping-pong here.'

'We're trying to get out of this situation alive, Harvey.'

'Right,' Harvey said. 'So when you finally cut the bullshit, we can toss around the idea of who might come looking for you. Who knows you're out here. How we might communicate with them.'

Clare sighed.

'Listen,' Harvey shifted up onto his knees, 'they're about to make me do something really fucked up.'

She looked doubtful.

'That's the mission,' Harvey said. 'Destroy my reputation. Whatever's coming, it's going to be bad. We don't know what it is, but we need to have plans in place. Maybe I'm going to have an interaction with someone, like I did in the bank, and that person's going to survive. There might be a way I can say something or do something that they'll recount to the police, the kind of thing that'll give a signal to your husband that you're with me and you need help, without—'

'—without alerting Darryl and Tizza that you're even dropping that signal.'

'Right,' Harvey said. 'Your husband. He'll be looking for you.'

Clare's mouth clamped shut.

'I know what's happening.' Harvey held his hands up. 'You're on the run from him. The bruises on your wrist. The lies. The skittishness. It's obvious you're running from an abuser. Guess what? He's going to come looking for you. We both know that, because nobody runs from men like that. He might be your abuser, Clare, but he's the best chance we have right now of getting found. How do we say "mayday, mayday" to this guy so he doesn't just think you've gone to ground somewhere?'

He waited. Clare didn't answer, just lay there with her hands over her face. Harvey resisted the urge to bark at her. To reach over in the dim light penetrating the vehicle and shake her by the shoulders. Because he knew she'd probably had so much of that in her relationship with the dipshit husband that the neurological pathway that took her from perceived threat of male aggression to total mental shutdown would be deeply ingrained and lightning fast.

'Hostage movies,' she suddenly blurted out. Harvey cocked his head.

'What?'

'Whenever it happens.' Clare sat up beside him. 'The next time you get a moment to talk to a person out there, start talking about hostage movies. Mention two or three of them. They'll see the pattern, surely.'

'You think Darryl and Tiz aren't going to sense what's going on when I pull over a car full of young backpackers at gunpoint and start blathering to them about how much I enjoyed Denzel Washington's performance in *The Negotiator*?'

'Of course you wouldn't be that obvious.'

'I want something specific that your husband, and no one else, will recognise. That's our best bet. That's the way we're gonna get a signal out that Darryl and Tiz don't know is a signal.'

'We don't need to signal them that I'm in trouble,' Clare said. 'They'll know that. The cops are going to find my burnt-out car. Then they're going to find *your* car, and the dead guy. Parker. It must have been what, ten minutes down the road? They'll know the two are connected, right? I mean, surely they will. So they're going to get the sense that I'm in danger.'

'So long as they assume you're alive.'

'Why wouldn't they assume I'm alive?'

'Because I just turned up at the Cooper Creek bank alone.' Harvey shrugged. 'In their eyes, what the hell have I done with you? Dropped you at a pub so you can have a white wine while I rob a bank?'

Clare licked her teeth.

'They're probably assuming, right now, that I've killed you,' Harvey said. 'It's the only thing that makes sense. We need a message that says, "Hey, I'm still alive, and I'm in danger." It'll increase the urgency of the pursuit tenfold.'

'How are they gonna know I'm not saying, "I'm in danger from *this guy*"? From you? They might shoot you on sight. How are you going to say, "I'm also in danger"?'

'I left something at the bank.'

'What?'

'A little message. Maybe it'll work. Maybe it won't. It was pretty last minute. Very far-fetched. But it was all I could think of in the seconds I had to work with.' He heaved a heavy breath. 'My concern isn't me right now, Clare. It's you. Work with me. Think.'

She shook her head.

'You're so scared of this guy, you don't want him to find you,' Harvey said. 'Even if it means getting out of this situation. Jesus. What could he possibly do to you that is worse than this?'

He poked her in the chest, right at the centre of the vest, where the red light lived. When Harvey pulled his finger away, the red light was beaming, as though his touch had turned it on.

'What the . . .?'

Clare looked down at the light. It shuddered and shook as her body was jostled along gently with the truck's passage through the desert.

'Why is it on?'

'I don't know. It just—'

The squealing began. Harvey saw the woman's chest sink as all the breath left her.

'What's happening? What are they doing?'

'Maybe they're not doing it.' Harvey's mouth was bone dry. He spread a hand over the Kevlar of Clare's vest, pressed down, confirmed what he already knew. What he could see with his own eyes. That the tiny red light was on. That the vest was activated, ready to blow. 'Maybe I turned it on or . . . or maybe . . .'

'What? What? Maybe what?' Clare got to her feet, steadied herself against the wall.

'Their tech is sketchy.' Harvey could hardly get the words out. His throat was closing. 'The glasses certainly were. The glasses that they gave me, so they could communicate with me in the bank . . . They had little microphones in the ear hooks so they could tell me what to do. But I kept getting little snippets of their conversation in the truck. Bits I'm sure I wasn't meant to hear. It might be that Tizza kept his thumb on the mic at his end too long, or maybe the mic itself was faulty.'

'If their mic is faulty, then . . . maybe . . . maybe the *vests* are faulty.' Clare exhaled. She and Harvey locked eyes. The alarm squealed and squealed.

They moved. Harvey grabbed Clare's hand. They walked unsteadily together to the front wall of the truck bed, and began beating their fists on the reinforced panel between them and the cabin.

CHAPTER 21

'I have four separate crime scenes going on right now,' Edna said.

Stevenson didn't answer. Edna saw her glance behind her, to where Talon was slumped in the furthest end of the bench seat in the back, his long arm on the sill. Harry Starr, the bikie, sat at the other end, cuffed, watching the road ahead.

'The ratio of crime scenes in our region to policing staff is two to one,' Edna continued. When Stevenson wouldn't respond to her whining, she nudged her partner's elbow. 'Are you listening to me?'

'I'm listening to you.' Stevenson clamped the steering wheel with her knees and swept her hair up again, knotted it at the back of her neck. It was always hair-up, hair-down with Stevenson, the extreme heat giving her a headache that made her want to let the hair out, that same heat urging her to get it up off her neck. Edna had cut all her hair off within three days of arriving at Clifton Hills. 'You're exaggerating.'

'No I'm not.'

'Clare Holland's car. Okay. Yeah. That's a crime scene. The woman's missing. And I closed down the Cooper Creek bank so we could come back and take a look at it later. That's a legit crime scene. But we don't really need to examine it.' Stevenson patted Edna's knee. 'I saw the guy. I saw what he did. And we know who he is. It's not like we have to dust the place for prints or spray it with the blue light stuff.'

'Oh, good. We'll call that half a crime scene.' Edna rolled her eyes.

'Harvey Buck's car.' Stevenson nodded ahead, to the distant site at which they'd soon arrive. 'That's a crime scene. A full-blown one. You get one credit point for that. It's got a dead body and everything in it. Bullet holes. The works.'

'So what about the bag?'

'The bag is . . . that's a *contained* crime scene.' Stevenson took her hands off the steering wheel again, made a gesture like she was packing a tiny bag. 'It's transportable. We're currently bringing that contained crime scene *to* Buck's car crime scene. So when we get there, it'll kind of be like we're *combining two crime scenes* into one.'

'So two and a half crime scenes all up,' Edna said.

'Three at best.'

A mob of kangaroos raised their heads as the cruiser passed. Edna turned to observe them. The midday sun gave them no shadows at all. She wondered how they endured the gaze of the scorching eye hanging above them, its hellish light creeping into everything, drying, shrivelling and hardening all it touched. They lounged in the dust, fly-hassled and stoic.

Stevenson's phone started vibrating. She reached into her pocket and silenced it.

'Take your phone off silent,' Edna said.

'I like it on silent.'

'I tried to call you at the bank, you didn't answer. Shit's going down, Stevie. If I need you, I'm gonna really need you.'

'I wouldn't have answered even if it did ring, Ed. I was in the middle of a stick-up.'

'That's not the point.'

Stevenson drove, didn't touch her phone.

Edna sighed. 'So who was she?' The older cop lined up Harry Starr in the rear-view mirror. The ancient bikie slid a sidelong look to her, but didn't respond. 'The dead girl. Was she your girlfriend or what?'

'No comment.'

'Where's the rest of her?' Edna asked. 'You've got the head and hands. Has someone else got the body?'

'No comment.'

'You gotta say something, man.' Talon shifted in his seat. He was so big, his knees were wedged against the partition between the front and back. Edna felt it bow and push against her seat. 'They found the body parts in your possession. It's not like you're gonna get away with it.'

'There's nothing to say.' Harry Starr shrugged. 'Nothing that won't make things worse for me than they already are.'

The car fell quiet. Edna heard Talon's fingers drumming on the windowsill behind her.

'I mean, that's not *exactly* true,' the boy said after a while. His voice was low. Confidential.

'What?' Harry's leather seat creaked as he leant over.

'There's stuff you could say that's not, like, "I killed a woman and chopped off her head and her hands and you guys caught me dumping them in the desert."'

'Like what?' the old man snorted. 'That's exactly what – *what it looks like* – happened, mate.'

'Maybe not. What if you say, "Oh, I found them"?'

'What! Nobody's going to believe that.'

'I can see it. You were out riding your bike,' Talon said. Edna had to lean slightly sideways in her seat to pick up the low voices. 'You spotted something on the road. Stopped. Went over. Found the head and hands. You decided you shouldn't leave them to the, uh, the wilds. Right? Because there are animals out here, or someone could run them over, or—'

'Or it could rain,' the bikie said. 'It does rain out here. People think it doesn't, but it does.'

'So you picked them up. You were on your way to the police station to drop them off. Anonymously. Because you're, you know. You're someone who—'

'I've got a chequered past. That's what they say.'

'Right. And it's also what a good person would do, yeah? But when you noticed the cop car coming towards you, you panicked.'

'That's not bad, ay. You got anything else?'

'Well, maybe it's like, someone else put them in your bag, last time you stopped somewhere,' Talon went on. 'Maybe you stopped at a pub. At night. Went inside. Left your bike and your bag outside. Someone could have come along and put the head and the hands in there, then, without you noticing. Maybe to frame you. Because you'd be perfect for it, right? You have a chequered past.'

'But I didn't come from a pub. I came straight from home.'

'Oh, right.'

'But maybe someone put them in my bag at home.' The old man sighed heavily through his nose, thinking hard. 'I got no garage these days. I live in a caravan up Pandie Pandie way.

Leave the bike parked outside all night, I do, with the bag buckled on. Could be someone snuck up while I was sleeping.'

'Exactly.'

'Maybe I'll say that.'

'I would.'

'It won't fly though,' Harry said. 'Once they find out who she is.'

'Who is she?'

'She's a prozzie. Been working out in the mines, servicing the remote workers,' Harry said. 'But she's had long associations with my club. My old bikie club in Sydney. Makes sense that she's crossed the boys at the club somehow, maybe stolen some drugs from them or whatnot. Then she's done a runner, tried to escape into the outback, take up some work out at the mines. The club's found out she's there, remembered that I'm retired but that I live nearby, and asked me to go punch her ticket for them.'

'Right,' Talon said. 'That does make a lot of sense.'

'The pigs'll find out who she is, find out who I am, and put two and two together.'

'We're known to do that,' Stevenson leant over and murmured to Edna.

'Unless you can come up with somethin' else,' Harry urged Talon.

'I'll keep thinking.' Edna watched the boy in the rear-view mirror as he stroked the corners of his faint, starter-level moustache. 'People have told me that might be my thing, you know? Coming up with excuses like that. *Convoluted* stories to cover up crimes. It's what lawyers do.'

'Uh-huh. Met a few of them, I have. They make big money, the good ones.'

There were more people at the crime scene around Harvey Buck's car when they arrived. A couple of cops based in Oodnadatta, west of Edna's jurisdiction, a pair of Indigenous, younger people who she had called on frequently when the gap between her age or her culture and that of suspects in her custody became strained. Dot Storch was unloading the crime scene kit from the van the two had arrived in, while Rick Sutkin was talking to Holland by the bonnet of his car, his boot on the front tyre, a notepad on his knee.

Stevenson stopped the cruiser and Edna got out, opened the door beside Talon.

'Come with me,' she said.

'Why?'

'Because you're going to need to hear what the story is.'

Edna glanced across the bonnet as the big kid got out. Stevenson was giving her the kind of cautious, tight gaze of someone who knew they were about to be signed up to something they weren't necessarily going to enjoy. They approached Matt and Holland as a group, leaving Harry Starr to enjoy the cuffs and the silence and the air conditioning. Edna saw Stevenson and Holland lock eyes, an intense energy sizzling between them.

'Why isn't this man cuffed?' Holland pointed directly to Talon. Talon opened his mouth, and Edna slapped a hand against his chest.

'Mr Crest has not been involved in a crime this morning. I've established that. My partner, Stevenson, can back me up.'

'You've got to be kidding,' Holland smirked.

'I'm not kidding, Commissioner Holland.' Edna had to remind herself to take the malice out of her tone. Rick raised a quizzical brow under his Akubra. 'I'm not in the practice of providing light entertainment while surrounded by the remains of murder victims. Mr Crest has been instrumental, just now, in the recovery of further human remains and the possible intervention in a second major crime. His own actions were not criminal.'

'He just stole a police car.' Holland glanced at Edna's cruiser, at Starr sitting in the back, watching the distant clouds. 'I saw that myself. Whatever he's discovered while he was on the run—'

'Mr Crest was sitting in my cruiser.' Edna focused on Rick. 'I had been providing transport for him, following an incident yesterday, in which he also was found by me not to have been at criminal fault. He is a vulnerable and displaced youth who needs to get back to Adelaide.'

'Okaaay.' Rick was watching Stevenson for a reaction to Edna's words.

'He heard a call-out on my two-way radio for assistance. Someone had spotted a motorcyclist who had come off his bike. He gave an approximate location. Mr Crest, seeing that my partner and I were deeply engaged in an active crime scene, commandeered my police vehicle to render assistance to a possibly endangered citizen, which is not a crime.'

'Oh, for the love of god,' Holland scoffed. 'Are you hearing yourself?'

'Upon discovering Mr Starr at the accident scene, Mr Crest discerned his manner to be suspicious and threatening, and armed himself with the personal rifle I keep in the back of my vehicle for euthanising injured wildlife. My partner Stevenson and I subsequently attended the scene and discovered human remains in the possession of Mr Starr.'

'Who do the remains belong to?' Rick's upper lip was curled, a mixture of humour and confusion. 'Did you leave them at the scene?'

'No. We made the executive decision to bring them here. They're contained, as we do not have the capacity to cover multiple crime scenes right now. We believe they belong to a woman connected to Mr Starr through his alleged outlaw bikie club associations.'

'Is it clear that the remains are not, uh . . .?' Rick scratched his head with his pen, looked cautiously at Commissioner Holland, then Edna. 'Apologies. But, being blunt; it's not Commissioner Holland's wife in the bag, is it, Sergeant?'

'The deceased has six piercings on each ear, and appears to have a nose ring,' Edna said. 'Which is not the brief we have for Mrs Holland. Unless she did get some recent piercings that are not in her licence or online photos, Commissioner?'

'It's not her,' Holland said.

'Well. Isn't this a dog's breakfast.' Rick lifted his hat and wiped his brow on his wrist. 'Don't suppose whoever made the call on the two-way left a name, uh, big fella?'

Talon opened his mouth again to speak. This time it was Holland who cut him off. 'There *was* no two-way call. The kid *stole* the police car, and happened to bumble into a body-dumper going about his business.'

'What's your fucking problem, bro?' Talon barked.

Edna ground her heel into the toe of the boy's shoe. 'There *is* no problem here,' she growled. 'Mr Crest is going to remain in my custody until I have arranged his transport home to Adelaide.'

'I thought you had a flight booked,' Stevenson piped up.

'I did, but it's more complicated than that.' Edna felt Talon watching her. 'I have a duty of care to ensure he's returning home to a safe environment.'

'No you don't,' Holland said. 'The kid's eighteen. He's a legal adult. Your duty of care—'

'Extends to vulnerable people.'

'Jesus Christ.'

'All right, well.' Rick shook himself all over, gave a big, bright sigh. 'I best get to work, then. I got Dot processing Ol' Mate in the balaclava. I'll get her to take the remains out of your boot as well, Ed, and get 'em on ice. We'll have to drive both bodies to Alice so they can wait for a proper look-over. Happy with that?'

'Great. Thanks, Rick.'

'When do the city teams get here?'

'An hour or so.'

'We'll wait to do a proper handover.' Rick nodded, looked Holland up and down, pointed to him uncertainly again. 'Is the Commissioner, uh . . . Again, I'm being blunt, but, sir, are you—'

'I'm not in custody.' Holland gave a mean smile.

'But I would like you to return to Clifton Hills to await a formal interview, Commissioner Holland,' Edna said. 'From one of the specialist teams on their way from Adelaide.'

'Dream big, Senior Sergeant Norris,' Holland said. 'My wife is out here somewhere, and I'm determined to find her. I'll be heading to Cooper Creek with that pursuit in mind.'

'Well, I can't stop you,' Edna said. She watched Holland round the front of the car, heading for the driver's-side door. Talon muttered behind her as the commissioner started his car.

'"Dream big",' the kid said. 'What a dick.'

Edna was yanked aside. It was Stevenson, walking her into the desert beyond the crime scene. Buck's car was slowly collecting flies, the tiny, filth-covered creatures taking breaks from feasting on the body on the ground to wander the inner shadows, out of the heat. Edna watched them as she listened to Stevenson's harsh whisper.

'What the hell are you doing, Ed? This is exactly what got you all strung up down in Adelaide.'

'I know. I know. I'm sorry. I'll take the rap for all of this.'

'Damn straight, you will.' Stevenson shook her head. 'A two-way call?'

'It's all I could think of.'

'You know that old bikie isn't going to cop to any of that stuff about Talon rolling up to help him after a crash when they interview him.'

'I don't think the nuances of *how* he was discovered with that woman's remains are going to matter much in securing a conviction, Stevie.' Edna rubbed at a monster headache that was beginning in her left temple. 'If he's out here dumping body parts in the broad light of day, he's not a genius. We'll probably find the rest of her at his caravan, as well as text messages to the bikie leaders negotiating the hit fee.'

Holland's car was disappearing into the heat haze towards Cooper Creek. They both watched it fall below the horizon like a setting sun.

'I'm worried about you and this kid, Ed,' Stevenson said.

'So am I,' Edna agreed.

2011

Harvey opened the mini fridge in Major General Evan Leasing's room. That's what snapped the base commander awake; the sound of the rubber seals unsticking from the machine, the clink of bottles inside. Harvey took a James Squire ale from the top shelf, let the door rock closed, and walked to the bedside, where the startled major was gathering his starchy bedsheet around his balls and fishing for the bedside lamp. He shouldn't have turned it on. Seemed to realise his mistake when he did. Harvey knew he was a sight. The third-degree sunburn had leaked yellowish fluid into the bandages on his arms, and the blood spatter from the men he'd spent the past forty-eight hours working on in the heat of the shipping containers was splashed up to his elbows, dried and brown in parts, black under his fingernails. The skin was off all his knuckles. There was desert dirt and grime in the old sweat on his neck. Harvey was sure he held the expression of a man who had been out of control of himself for some time; probably since the ambush itself, the hard and hollow gaze of a cornered animal. He could do nothing to alter it.

Leasing watched him take the chair by the bed with his mouth gaping open and his eyes searching Harvey's face for some frankly magical evidence that this was a dream, that the real Harvey Buck was AWOL somewhere in Qatar, as he'd been told, having absconded from the base hospital in shame or fury or whatever the hell the consensus was. Harvey took a pair of pliers from his trouser pocket and used their teeth to take the cap off the bottle. Leasing twitched as the bloody pliers clunked onto the bedside table.

'I was right,' Harvey said.

Leasing reached for the phone beside him. Saw Harvey's eyes following his hand and thought better of it. 'What did you do?' Leasing asked.

'Everything I could think of.'

Leasing took a few deep breaths. Outside, the base was quiet. 'Are they still . . . alive?'

'Of course they're alive,' Harvey said. He drank the beer. It was painfully cold in his throat, and not in a good way, the liquid sloshing over open ulcers and burns. 'They're going to be held responsible for what they did. I need them to confess it all in your presence. In the presence of your superiors. Because I don't want it to look like what they're saying here, in these recordings, is only due to what I put them through.'

Harvey took a USB stick out of his other trouser pocket and put it on the table beside the pliers.

'Lipton was the leader,' he went on. 'He instigated the whole thing. Contacted the main guy on the Taliban side with the idea of selling him some weapons design plans. Parker, Darryl and Tizza got on board shortly after that point, because Lipton wasn't talking initially about killing anybody. They convinced themselves they were just selling information. From my understanding of what the four men told me over the past couple of days, it was Lipton who gradually led the other three into something more murderous. And even then, none of them had been aware of the scale of what was planned.'

Leasing put his head in his hands. He raked his fingers up over his skull, gripped the stubbled flesh, clawed his fingers back down his face, leaving pink marks. 'Fuuuuuu—'

He couldn't even finish the word. It wasn't anywhere near adequate. No word in the English language was. Leasing seemed to be torn. On the one hand, wanting to sit there stiffly and silently and think it all through, to plan and strategise and control the damage, and on the other, get away from the imminent physical threat that Harvey presented to him, sitting there in the chair by his bedside like the walking dead. Because any soldier who would abduct and torture his own men, and then stroll into the base command's personal quarters still covered in their blood and piss and sweat was clearly an unhinged person, however noble he thought his cause. Leasing kept letting his eyes wander to the bare corner of the room, before they snapped back to Harvey.

'You've got some cleaning up to do,' Harvey said.

'No shit.' Leasing's voice was high and tight. 'Where are they now? The men.'

'If they're smart they'll be heading back to their dorms to have a shower, dress and await their arrests.' Harvey shrugged.

'So you just . . . let them go?'

'I untied them and opened the container doors and left them to their own devices.'

'Containers?'

'The old ones out in the surplus area.'

'Jesus.' Leasing held his head. 'Jesus. I've . . . I've got to make some calls.'

'Before you start any of that'—Harvey held up a hand—'we need to agree to some things.'

'What?'

'You're going to keep this quiet,' Harvey said. 'I mean, of course you are. That won't be your decision. It'll come from higher up. Because the international scandal and outrage it would cause, let alone the tension between us and the Americans, would end up in the fucking history books. They'll be teaching it to teenagers in high schools all across the world for the next half a century. The great Australian traitors, and the men who failed to notice them hiding in their midst.'

Leasing held his face in his hands.

'You're going to lock Lipton, Parker, Darryl and Tizza up. That's for sure,' Harvey went on. 'But you won't hand them over for federal prosecution, because you can't rely on them to keep their mouths shut.'

Leasing breathed, open-mouthed, struggling to listen through the panic.

'Inside the cover-up, you're going to include my part in all this,' Harvey said. 'And Shayna Kinthrop's part, in dummying up the transfer records for the four men so I could get them to the surplus area. I'm not going to bother trying to make excuses for her right now. It would be easy enough for you to discover her involvement. But understand this. If there's any blowback for her – I'm talking so much as a dirty sideways look – I'll give my copy of the recordings I made out there directly to the *New York Times*.'

He pointed to the USB on the bedside table. Leasing looked at it.

'You're also going to make sure those men pay for this,' Harvey said. 'All of them. You'll come up with something to charge them with, something to keep them under lock and key until you can figure out what the hell to do with them. You're going to have a real problem on your hands, keeping them quiet. Because I broke them. I went too far. I guess I was angry.'

Harvey stared at the carpet, thought about what each of the men had told him as they begged and cried and twisted in the chairs he'd tied them to in their separate steel hellholes. Darryl weeping about his daughter's rape at a party when she was sixteen, about not being able to protect her, about feeling impotent and ashamed and hollowed out by what had been done to her. Tizza losing it completely as Harvey plucked and strummed the tight wires of pain criss-crossing his brain, plugged in one by one by his abusive father in a childhood that left Tizza with all the self-worth of pond slime. It had taken seven or eight hours of working on Parker to get him to give Harvey access to *his* inner ghosts; the high school best friend who had killed himself after a fight with Parker in the school yard. Of the four men, only Lipton hadn't given Harvey anything at all. The man was a cold, calculating psychopath, and he only relented and confessed to orchestrating the ambush after two hours straight of Harvey waterboarding him.

Footsteps in the hall. A sharp knock at the door. One of the stewards. He was in the room and blurting his words out to Leasing before he even noticed Harvey sitting there. 'Major General, there's been an incident over at T Dorm. Your presence is requested.'

'What is it?'

'Suicide in the women's shower block.' The young steward noticed Harvey, did a double take, seemed unable to compute what he was seeing. He turned back to Leasing. 'They're saying it's Greg Lipton. One of the techs. One of *those* techs. The guy just walked in and blew his brains out in front of three female soldiers.'

Harvey sucked down the last few drops of his beer, put the bottle on the bedside table beside the pliers and the USB. He didn't even look at Leasing before he got up and walked out the door.

CHAPTER 22

The truck stopped. Harvey and Clare stood in the dimness listening to the squeal of her vest. Harvey found that what might very well have been his final seconds on earth were besieged with memories of what he'd done to the four men in the shipping containers. His voice, lowered and thickened with a darkness that had frightened even him, as he wreaked slow agony on them individually, hour upon hour, unable to stop. *I guess I was angry*, he'd told Leasing. That wasn't exactly true. What he was, he couldn't really say, even now. 'Possessed' seemed closer. He knew a psychiatrist, presented with how he'd behaved in those containers, would have accounted for what he'd done with biological explanations. They'd say that when the ambush began, so too did a separation between Harvey Buck and reality at large, that catastrophic gap widened further by three days of trudging through the desert heat with a dying man slung across his shoulders, and a day in the base hospital being pumped with drugs. Harvey was sure, standing there beside Clare, waiting for her vest to blow the two of them to pieces, that he would never, ever be able to lie comfortably in the bed of unaccountability a psychiatrist might make for him.

Because no psychiatrist would ever learn about what he'd done to Lipton, Parker, Tizza and Darryl. What he'd done had been so bad, Lipton, the most callous of the four men, hadn't been able to endure more than a few minutes of life after the ordeal was complete.

The other three had managed to live on. But, perhaps they'd known, even in those first few moments, that they'd need Biblical levels of vengeance to get over what had happened.

The truck doors opened. Their captors were standing there.

'Did you fuck with the vests?' Tizza asked.

'No,' Clare panted. She went to the edge of the truck. Tizza and Darryl didn't back away. That told Harvey something. 'It just started up on its own. First the light. Then the sound. Turn it off. *Turn it off!*'

Darryl reached into his pocket. Harvey cocked his head. Thought he heard a double click. A button pushed down, and then released. But when he turned his eyes on Tizza, he saw the man's fingers were at the chest of his shirt, between the third and fourth buttons, fiddling with something. He wasn't certain where the clicks had come from, and Harvey needed to be certain. Clare's vest stopped squealing.

'What happened?' Harvey asked. 'Are the vests faulty?'

'Maybe they are.' Tizza shrugged, a smile spreading over his lips. 'Maybe we're just fucking with you. Who can really say, huh?'

'No. No. No. We need to know what the stakes are here. Okay? Did you mean to set it off or not?' Clare yelled. 'You have to be honest with us about that, at least. I mean, why would we do what you say when you . . . you might blow us up accidentally! If that's the case, we might as well both run, right now, take our chances out there.'

'Be my guest.' Darryl motioned to the desert. Harvey looked. Could see nothing but empty plains, lonely gums. Clare swiped her hands over her face and hair, tugged at the vest where it was rubbing at her collarbones.

'Jesus. I need to pee.'

'So do I,' Harvey said.

'Fuck you.' Darryl jutted his chin at Harvey. 'You can wait.'

He beckoned Clare. She refused the help, sat down on the edge of the truck bed and slid to the ground, stumbling a little when she hit the dirt. Harvey saw a slice of her face as she turned to walk out into the desert, her lips pinched tight and eyes wet. Harvey went to the edge of the truck and hopped down in front of his captors.

'You cut your ties,' Darryl said. 'I told you what would happen if you did that again.'

'Try it,' Harvey said.

Darryl chewed his tongue, considering, his empty eyes locked on Harvey's.

'You know, there's an aspect of this that you haven't considered,' Harvey said. 'You've told me how I can detonate my own vest. What's to say I grab my zipper, run at you and yank it? End this for us all?'

'Survival instinct,' Darryl said. 'You got it bleeding out your eyeballs. It's what got you through the desert, those three days you were out there. The pure will to survive.'

'Touch the woman. I dare you,' Harvey said. 'Fuck my survival instinct. I'm there when a woman needs me.'

His tone, the glint in his eye, hit Darryl just the way Harvey wanted it to. While the line about being there for a woman in need was chauvinistic bullshit, he saw a coldness come over Darryl's features that told Harvey he'd taken the man right back to the containers for an instant, to the howling despair of a father who hadn't been there for his baby girl in the worst hour of her life. Darryl's face changed again as he realised what Harvey was doing. He painted on another warmthless smile.

'You're too much of a narcissist shithead to kill yourself,' Darryl said. 'Especially like this. When, to all the world, you're looking like a psycho on a spree.'

'*War Hero Destroys Legend with Devastating Final Act.*' Tizza painted the headline in the sky with one hand. 'Can you imagine it? I can.'

Harvey felt a tingle in the tips of his fingers, a thought itching at the back of his mind, begging to be scratched. But he was so tired, and whenever he managed to wrench his thoughts away from his current circumstances, all that waited for him were bad memories or visions of Shayna hanging over the side of the bathtub. Her sightless eyes. All he could think was that Tizza's line seemed too rehearsed. Like he'd thought about the headline concept before.

Clare was out there in the scrub, standing, watching the horizon, her shoulders low and her hands by her sides. Harvey wondered how long shipwreck victims watched the curve of the empty earth before they gave up on spotting a ship bound for rescue.

'Go piss.' Darryl tried to wave Harvey away. 'We've got somewhere to be.'

'So. What was the alarm all about? Faulty vest?' Harvey asked, ignoring the instruction. It was important to defy directions whenever he could. 'Or was it butter fingers over here, with the detonator switch?'

'Jesus. You want me to hit you, don't you, Buck?' Tizza licked his split lip. 'Every chance you get, you badmouth me. It's like you *want* me to hurt you.'

'If anybody is going to screw up this whole operation with a slipped finger, it would be this guy.' Harvey kept his eyes on Darryl. 'I mean, you know that, Darryl, right? He's the weak point of the whole plan. He was the first to fold, out there, in the shipping containers. The fastest man to break and spill on the rest of you. You gotta be thinking—'

Harvey reached sideways, grabbed Tizza's fist out of the air as the little man came barrelling towards him, aiming for his temple. Harvey used Tizza's momentum to bounce him off the corner of the truck's door. Tizza collapsed onto his knees. Darryl took two steps back, drew his gun out of his pocket, but didn't raise it. Didn't need to. They all knew Harvey couldn't go any further. Darryl kept his eyes quiet and his face rigid but the ticking vein in his temple told Harvey the adrenaline was loose in his system now.

'Buck, you motherfucker—' Tizza rasped.

'Your daddy teach you how to fight, Tiz?' Harvey asked. 'Oh no, that's right. You told me. You spent half your childhood cowering in a corner while the old man wailed on you.'

'Fuck you!'

'You got two hits to the face,' Harvey said to Darryl. 'First Clare, and then me. Same spot. I've just smashed this little weasel for the second time into this same truck door. Do you feel like you're right back in those containers again, gentlemen? Imagine it. Imagine we're back there. I'm hitting you, and hitting you, over and over, in the same spot.'

Darryl didn't speak.

'I thought of that myself, you know,' Harvey said. 'I thought, *Why don't I try something different with these guys?* Maybe I don't break all your ribs. I just break one. Then I hit it, and hit it, and *hit it*, until it's pulverised. Until it's dust. Were they ever able to fix that rib of yours, Darryl? Does it still bother you, whenever you breathe?'

Tizza dragged himself up, held his head. Darryl went over and took his arm and pushed him towards the desert, where Clare was standing.

'Go watch the woman.'

Harvey and Darryl watched Tizza go, his step a little crooked and head bent low.

'Please tell me that you're the button man, Darryl,' Harvey said. 'And that you didn't give a detonator to that imbecile.'

'Buck—' Darryl started.

'I wonder how that played out, if indeed, you *didn't*,' Harvey mused. 'Because how do you justify that to the little man? How do you say, "Tiz, your father knew it, and I know it, too. You're barely competent enough to dress yourself. I'm not giving you the detonator to two enormous bombs, because it would be like giving a handgun to a toddler."'

'Buck.'

'Then again, it would be hilarious if you *did* give Tiz a detonator, in a way. Because that would put you in the same boat as me. Just wondering, from minute to minute, when I'm going to get my guts splattered all over the outback.'

Darryl beckoned Harvey to him. He went there, put his hands in his pockets, cocked an ear, two friends sharing a secret under the hellish sun.

'*Buck*,' Darryl whispered. 'You're misunderstanding something.'

'What's that?' Harvey asked.

'I don't care if I die.' Darryl grinned at him. 'Just as long as I take you with me.'

CHAPTER 23

Edna parked outside the Cooper Creek bank and post office, got out of the cruiser and eyed the crowd. The events of the morning were obviously a welcome quickening for the residents of a town accustomed to watching the days slide by like well-fed snakes. There were groups of men and women on the opposite corner of the wide street, a mixture of Indigenous and white, eyeing the police cruiser with the usual quiet scepticism remote town people applied to all police activity. An Indigenous Elder Edna recognised, Uncle Adam Bourne, started making his way over. He had to hustle children out of his way who were racing remote-controlled cars between opposing driveways. The biggest car, controlled by a boy in a big red baseball cap, was doing doughnuts and kicking up street dust. Stevenson had slid into the driver's seat by the time Bourne got there, and waved from the car as she drove off to track Garreth Holland in the town. Talon stood on the pavement outside the bank, flipping through his phone and chewing his nails.

'I need a description of this Harvey Buck fella you've got running around the countryside robbing banks,' Bourne said, pulling out his phone and spinning it between his thumb and forefinger so that the screen faced the right way. Edna thought of gunslingers in old Westerns. Bourne started trawling through text messages. 'We got the alert photo, and some pictures of Buck as a soldier, but all the shots look a few years old to me. Carol says he was all done up in a cap and glasses so she couldn't see his hair.'

'I really don't want too much public involvement on this, Adam.' Edna put a hand on the sleeve of his sun-warmed shirt. 'The last thing I need are residents pulling over tourists and farmers trying to hunt down an armed and dangerous man.'

'Well, hey, I guess you shouldn't have put an alert out on the guy.' Bourne showed Edna his phone. She glimpsed the text message that would have flashed up on hundreds of screens across the top half of South Australia. *POLICE ARE SEARCHING FOR HARVEY MICHAEL BUCK, 48, LAST SEEN IN THE COOPER CREEK TOWNSHIP AREA . . .* 'Assistance is coming, whether you like it or not. Everybody from here to Alice knows the prick stuck a gun in a girl's face. You had to know something like this would get everybody excited.'

'I have protocols,' Edna said. 'I couldn't avoid sending the alert. But I hoped people would use common sense for once.'

'High, high hopes, those were.'

'Yeah.'

'Look, I can't unlight a fire like this.' Bourne batted away a fly. 'But I can make sure they get the right guy and not some unlucky bloke who's got the same chin. Does Buck still look like that? Do we know?'

'I don't know. I haven't clapped eyes on him myself. I'm here to look at the footage of the robbery.'

'What's his story, then? Did he come down from the Wire?' Bourne asked. 'Some people are saying they've heard the name. Remember him from the news a while back. He's a war hero or something. Has he lost his marbles?'

'We're still working out what's happened,' Edna said. 'Please get the word out that Harvey Buck is not to be approached, followed or arrested if he's spotted by any residents of Cooper Creek or the surrounds.'

'Yeah, yeah.'

'If people really want to help, they can look for Clare Holland.' Edna waved at Bourne's phone. 'That alert should have gone out as well.'

Bourne frowned, looked back at his phone. His thumb yanked the thread of police-assistance-line messages down, then pushed it back up. Edna recognised all of the messages and their accompanying pictures. Runaway youths, dementia patients, a missing tourist from the year before. 'I'm not seeing a "Clare Holland" on here.'

'It should be there.'

'Well it's not.'

Edna left Bourne, hissing curses to herself, and went to the doors of the bank. Her stomach was unsettled. She had to get out of the heat. The lights were off inside, the door unlocked. Edna pushed her way in and listened to the bell jangle above her, waited for Talon to slide into the dimness beside her.

'I could go hang out somewhere, I guess,' the boy said. 'Maybe there's a cafe.'

'There's no cafe, but I appreciate you pretending you're not leaping out of your skin to get a look at your third crime scene in twenty-four hours.' Edna closed the door behind them, ending the display for the public, causing the groups across the street to turn inward to compare assessments. She flicked on the lights. 'We won't be here long. I just want to get a quick look at the CCTV. Get my head around this guy.'

They went to the computer behind the desk. Talon actually stepped on Edna's heel as he trailed behind her. He watched her, restless on the balls of his feet, as she followed the instructions Carol had texted to Stevenson, and Stevenson had texted to Edna, about how to open the device and pull up the security footage. Edna and Talon watched as crisp and colourless vision showed Buck entering the building. He hovered uncertainly just inside the front doors.

'What's with the jacket?' Edna asked.

'Got to hide the gun, maybe?' Talon squinted.

Mere seconds clicked by on the footage before Stevenson marched in and went directly to the counter to speak to Carol. Stevenson left the footage belonging to a camera mounted to a pillar at the side of the room, then reappeared on the feed from the counter's overhead camera. Her face was animated, a finger stabbing and drawing on the counter as she described what she needed. Edna was seeing the footage, but at the same time, not really taking it in. She was so distracted by the fact that Clare Holland's missing persons alert had not reached the public yet that she could barely focus. She decided to call Dispatch, swiping the mousepad to roll the footage back and watch the entry sightlessly again as she dialled with her other hand.

'What's he doing?' Talon asked, dividing her attention from halves into thirds.

'Hmm?'

'Buck. With the pens.'

Edna looked. 'I don't know. He's fuddling around waiting for Stevenson to get lost so he can come attack Carol.'

Talon smacked his lips, took the footage back and rolled it again. Then he turned and walked around the counter, went to the first row of shelves by the door where Harvey had hovered. Edna watched the footage roll on. Buck approaching the counter. Speaking to Carol briefly. Stevenson standing nearby, at the end of the counter closest to the wall. Buck pulling his gun from the pocket of his jacket, stepping back in the same fluid motion. He was definitely a man accustomed to using firearms. His aim was firm, confident, arm at a perfect right angle, supported with an elbow into the ribs, his position a tight triangulation that gave him a good shot at both women should either decide to make a move. Buck's shoulders were back and his head was up. Edna squinted, waiting for him to tilt his face to the camera. It was almost certainly Harvey Michael Buck behind the thick, black-rimmed glasses. The jawline and nose seemed right. The call to Dispatch connected and Edna cringed at the Love Song Dedications voice that came over the line.

'Edna. Good to hear from you again. How are you holding up?'

'I want to know why the alert I put out for Clare Holland wasn't approved.'

'Oh. Uh. I can chase that up,' Richie said. She heard keys tapping. 'The request definitely went in. No sign here in the system about why it was knocked back.'

'Find out. Let me know.'

'I'm on it, boss.'

Edna eased a sigh and screenshotted Buck standing by the counter with the gun pointed at Carol, the best shot of his face where his unsmiling mouth was open in speech. She emailed the picture to herself and tried to call Stevenson. The phone rang out.

'Hey.'

'What?'

'Come here.' Talon waved. 'Look at this.'

Edna went around the counter, walked down the aisle to the shelves where Buck had stood, messing around, waiting for Stevenson to do her business and get out of the bank. Talon's face was taut with anticipation. Edna looked at where he was pointing, at a handful of pens plucked from a display canister on the shelf and dumped on the long white pad where customers could test the colour and thickness of the pen's stroke.

'Look at *this*,' Talon repeated. 'Huh? Huh? What do you think?'

Edna looked. Shrugged.

'These pens,' Talon said. There was indeed a series of pens dumped haphazardly in a row on top of the pad, messy black piano keys. They were all the same brand, Artline, felt tip. Nine of them.

'You're going to have to be more specific, Talon. What am I supposed to be seeing here?'

'The nibs. Their sizes. They're written on the pens.'

'Okay . . .?'

'We got 0.2, 0.2, 0.2.' Talon pointed to each pen in succession, left to right. 'Then we got 0.4, 0.4, 0.4. Then 0.2, 0.2, 0.2 again.'

Edna felt the muscles of her shoulders drawing tighter and tighter. 'Talon, please tell me what you're getting at here. I'm not a mind reader, and I'm too stressed out to play games.'

'I think it's a code. Like, he's telling us where he'll hit next.'

'Oh my god.' Edna rubbed her aching eyes. 'Talon—'

'Look at the footage.' The boy marched back to the computer. He pointed, arm out straight, at the screen. Edna followed, her whole body heavy. 'See here? He's playing with the pens. Seems like he's just messing around with them. But look closer. See how he puts them down.'

'Talon.'

'He sets them down very carefully. They end up all in a row. See?'

'He's not even looking at the pens as he sets them down,' Edna sighed. 'He's looking at the counter. At Carol.'

'But—'

'Why would he leave us a message telling us where he was going to hit next?'

'Because he's playing a game with us.' Talon's eyes were full of sugary light. 'Like Kevin Spacey in *Seven*.'

'Is that the one with Brad Pitt?'

'Yeah.'

'Oh my god.'

'Maybe it's—'

'Talon, if Buck was going to leave us a special message, why wouldn't he just have *written it on the notepad*?'

'Maybe there wasn't time.' Talon licked his lips. 'Maybe . . . I don't know. He didn't want to make it that easy. Listen, Edna. There's something here. I can feel it. It's like when I felt it out there in the desert. With the guy on the bike. Starr. When he turned and ran, it was like I got these chills up my body, a big rush of them. *Boom*.'

Edna pushed away a mean impulse thought about Talon's ability to intuit the secret intentions of others, and how that had panned out for him in the case of his online girlfriend. 'Listen, kid—'

'We can figure this out, if we try hard enough. Like, Buck was in the army, right? Could the numbers be a location code? Longitude and lang . . . *langitude*. Or whatever?'

'No.'

'Maybe they're a phone number. I'm gonna dial it now.'

'Okay,' Edna surrendered. 'You dial 02-02-02, 04-04-04, 02-02-02 and see if a voice on the other end of the line tells you where Harvey Buck is going to show up next.'

The kid was actually dialling. Edna shut down the computer and called Stevenson as she headed to the front doors.

'You still on Holland?'

'Yeah, but he's a wily motherfucker,' Stevenson said. 'He drove right through town and out the other side, off road into the wilds to make sure he wasn't being followed. I had to track him with binoculars just to stay hidden. He came back, parked, and went on foot to the chemist.'

'The chemist?'

'Yeah.'

'That'll be Billy today,' Edna said. 'Do me a favour. Go ask him what Holland purchased.' Edna heard a car door open in the background of the call.

'Listen, Ed,' Stevenson said. 'Something you should know. Holland was on the phone the whole time I trailed him. Never let up once. I'd like to think he was trying to chase down any leads on Clare, or let her family know she's missing, or whatever. But I'd also like to believe in Santa Claus.'

Edna felt dread *whump* into her belly.

'He's got to be coming for you,' Stevenson went on. 'It might be time to leave this whole thing alone. Go home.'

'Forget it.' Edna waved Talon away from the pens. She went out into the wall of heat and shut the bank behind herself and the kid. 'Meet us at the bank after you're done at the chemist. I've got another call coming through.'

Edna looked at the number. Resisted the urge to go back inside and lie down in the cool of the shady interior. The crowd in the street had cleared. She picked up the call and inhaled two lungfuls of hairdryer-hot desert air before she spoke.

'Chief Inspector McEvoy,' she winced.

'I've had five years of peace and contentment in my professional life since you moved up there to Clifton Hills, Senior Sergeant Norris,' McEvoy started. Just the sound of his thin, faint voice gave Edna the chills. She had always been sure it was a strategy by her superior officer to make people fight to hear him, to never let them get comfortable in conversation. 'Now I'm hearing worrying things about your ability to perform in your police work. Again.'

'I'd just love to know what was said, chief,' Edna sighed. 'Because unlike last time—'

'Alongside a general comment about your nature and bearing, which the Northern Territory's Police Commissioner described to me as "frantic",' McEvoy sniffed, 'Holland says he personally witnessed you allowing a civilian male youth to drive your police cruiser, which, if true, is a scenario that beggars belief.'

'I'm not "frantic", chief.' Edna gritted her teeth. She walked away from Talon, towards the sunbaked street corner, giving up the thin strip of shade cast by the bank to get out of earshot of the boy. 'And that's not even close to what happened. I have, at present, a young man in my custody who requires my assistance in—'

'In what, Senior Sergeant Norris?' McEvoy sounded tired. 'I'm hearing this boy is from Adelaide. Is his presence up there due to his having been involved in a crime or the commission of a crime?'

'Yes, sir, it is.'

'Why, then, is he not under arrest?'

'In a certain fashion, he is.'

'"In a certain fashion", Senior Sergeant Norris?'

'He's under my care and direction.'

'How, then, was he able to forcefully commandeer your police vehicle, Senior Sergeant Norris? I'm being generous in assuming you didn't simply toss him the keys.'

'It's . . .' Edna gave a short, hard laugh. Couldn't help herself. 'It's not as simple as all that, chief. To put it in such simplistic and literal terms is frankly ridiculous.'

There was an icy silence. Edna leapt into it, terrified of the effect of it on her body, which was already gently trembling with fury and dread. 'It is essential for the wellbeing of this young man, for the *immediate short term*, in a psychological sense, that he remain with me.'

Another silence. Now it was McEvoy's turn to laugh humourlessly. 'It sounds like you're right back where you started, Edna.'

'Perhaps, sir.' Edna forced herself to unlock her teeth.

'Then I have no choice but to suspend you immediately, with pay, and restrict your access to police resources and equipment.' She heard McEvoy's desk chair creak as he sat upright.

'You're communicating to me that you feel it is your moral, spiritual or otherwise fantastical imperative to abandon your work on what I'm hearing is quite a handful of a case, to provide care for a wayward youth. Not even a youth, but a fully grown and legal adult, it should be noted. So I have to do what's necessary to ensure your mission doesn't interfere with police operations.'

'As you wish, sir,' Edna said.

'You can hand your gun and badge to Stevenson.' McEvoy heaved a sigh. 'And I'll let the specialist team I've sent up there know that they can go to her for assistance on the unfolding situation, as you have decided your calling in ad hoc social work is more important.'

The line went dead. Edna watched as Stevenson pulled into the kerb. Talon approached as she made a gesture at Stevenson to unlock the boot.

'It's not a phone number,' Talon said, oblivious to the icy awfulness coursing through Edna's body. 'It's not a landmark, either. I was thinking, *Maybe they're times*. Right? Maybe, like, he killed Clare Holland at 2.02 in the morning. And for Carol, he was going to do it this afternoon at 4.04.'

'Uh-huh,' Edna said. She opened the boot and took out her rifle, thumbed a pack of bullets into her pocket as Stevenson got out of the cruiser. 'You keep working on it, kid. You'll figure it out.'

'Gauze, tweezers, painkillers and a sewing kit,' Stevenson said in greeting.

Edna thought for a moment. Then she nodded. 'The bastard's been shot.'

CHAPTER 24

The truck parked. It had been another hour, maybe longer, of rumbling through the desert, the interior like a furnace, sweat prickling and running down Harvey's ribs and up his back as he lay on the floor beside Clare. He'd dozed a little, his body relenting to the constant adrenaline dumps over the past twenty-six hours, since the moment he received the call from Shayna that snapped the cable on an elevator that refused to stop plummeting and hit the bottom of the shaft. Clare popped up beside him and went to the wall, peering through the tiny crack between the steel panels. Whatever she saw had her scooting back to him quickly.

'They're walking away. Up the hill,' she said. 'Sit up and take your shirt off.'

Harvey did as he was told, raked his hands through his hair and stubble and tried to claw his way back to his dreadful reality.

'I found this when I went to pee,' Clare said.

She showed him a tiny shard of glass, curved, half the length of a sewing needle. It was brown. A piece of a beer bottle probably flung from a car. Harvey leapt back to wakefulness, gripped her hand so the edge of the glass turned into the light.

'I'm going to use it to cut into the seam of your vest.' Clare's eyes were hard and focused. 'If we're careful, we can just open a slit and take a peek inside. Maybe we won't do enough damage for them to notice.'

'Wait.' Harvey held on to her hand. 'We should cut into yours.'

'Why? If we cut a wire and your vest blows, I'm still mincemeat.'

'Yeah, but if we find an obvious way to disarm one of these vests, it should be yours. It's my fault we're in this mess, Clare.'

'I'm not gonna argue with that.' She peeled her shirt up. Harvey scooted close to her, ran a finger along the vest's armhole seam. Inside was damp with sweat.

'I guess we should go in under here.' He tested the seam carefully with a finger in the tight, dark space between the vest and her armpit. 'If we make a big hole, you can hide it with your arm.'

She put an arm up over her head, grimaced. 'Urgh. I reek.'

'You're all right,' he said. From the corner of his eye he saw her smile. 'I'm sure I don't smell like daisies, either.'

He pressed his fingers against the seam, pushed down and pried carefully at the two pieces of fabric. Sweat dripped from his eyebrow to his cheek, and wiping his brow against his sweaty forearm did nothing to alleviate the problem.

'Good thing the stitches are black, like the vest, and fucking *microscopic*,' he huffed.

'Don't worry'—Clare's sarcasm matched his own—'you've got plenty of time to get it right.'

He applied the sharp tip of the piece of glass to a gap between two stitches, began sawing experimentally.

'What are you thinking you're gonna find in there?' she asked. 'Do you have any idea about bombs and how they work?'

'Look, you don't need a degree in science to make a bomb,' Harvey said. 'All you need is an accelerant – something that'll explode. Then you get a detonator – something that'll cause a spark and ignite that accelerant. Then you need a trigger. Something that'll create that spark, either at a specific time or by remote.'

'Okay.'

'So in Afghanistan, you had rebels making bombs out of all sorts of things. You take a tin can. Pack it with gunpowder and roofing nails, chuck a piece of flint at the bottom and run a piece of wire from that flint. You put the can inside an object somebody's likely to pick up. Like maybe you put it inside a toy or a bag. You attach the wire to an anchor point. The victim picks up the object. The wire pulls tight. The flint gets struck and causes a spark which ignites the gunpowder. Kaboom. Blows some soldier's arm off. Or, you know, a kid who thought they found a free toy.'

'Jesus Christ.' Clare rubbed sweat out of her eyes.

Harvey popped a stitch, used the point of the glass fragment to unthread it from the fabric. 'The detonator for these vests won't be something as rudimentary as flint,' he said. 'We're moving around too much for that. It'll be an electrical circuit hooked up to a battery. And Tiz said it was C-4. Plastic explosive. A lot bigger bang than gunpowder.'

'So what's the trigger?'

'I've been keeping an eye on Darryl and Tiz. I saw Darryl go for his pocket and Tiz go for something at his chest, but they both moved at the same time. I don't know who set the light off. But you've got to think, whatever they're using, it's got to have three buttons on it. Because there are three stages to ignition. Light, then siren, then blow. That's a big object. A mobile phone, maybe. I don't know.'

'A remote control? Like for a toy car?'

'Maybe.'

'I don't think I can talk about this anymore.' Clare wiped sweat into her hairline.

'Tell me something,' Harvey said. 'Is this what you had planned for this afternoon?'

She laughed. 'Right now I should be at an auction in Alice Springs.'

'Houses or dolls?'

'Dolls.' Clare sighed. 'I stood to make fifty grand.'

'Such a weird job.' He shook his head. 'I'm sorry. But it is.'

'The weirder the job, the fewer people are qualified. The fewer people are qualified, the more money you can make.'

'That's true.'

'But the teddy-bear people are the real weirdoes in my industry.' She turned and watched him sawing at the stitches with the glass fragment. 'There was a big scandal last year. A teddy dealer stalking another teddy dealer because he blocked the sale of a Lemur-fur bear. The guy got arrested.'

'*Lemur* fur?'

'The exotics can get into the hundreds of thousands of dollars,' Clare said. 'They're illegal, a lot of them.'

'I imagine it's a business that makes it easy to hide your income.' Harvey had popped eight stitches, opened a pea-sized hole in the vest. Sweat was running down his temple, threatening to turn into the corner of his eye. 'An online transfer here. A cash sale there. Unless your husband is your business partner—'

'Harvey, I don't want to talk about my husband.'

'You *have* to.' Harvey stopped cutting and glared at her. His exhaustion had stripped him of his patience. The frustration was thick in his voice. 'Whoever this guy is. Whatever you think he's going to do to you. You can't stay here, in this situation, to try to avoid it. Because you'll end up dead, Clare.'

She let her head fall into her hands, put her elbows on her knees. 'I feel like I'm trying to escape the boiling pot so I can jump into the frying pan.'

'It's the only escape route,' Harvey said. 'Hot or not, it's the only way out.'

Clare chewed her lip. Tears rolled down her cheeks. 'Remember when you said that, uh . . .' Her voice trembled. She shook her head hard.

'What?'

'Just forget it.'

'Not a chance.'

'Remember when you said that in the containers, with those guys, you sort of . . . became someone else? That all the exhaustion and the rage it . . . brought out something in you that wouldn't have been there if . . .'

Her words choked off. She glanced at him, her face darkened with shame.

'Harvey, my . . . my husband has been trying to kill me for the past two years,' Clare said. 'But I . . .'

Harvey waited. He sensed, in some closed-off part of his mind, that he was gripping the piece of glass so tightly it was now cutting into his thumb but was unable to loosen his grip.

'I've been trying to kill him, too,' Clare said.

It had started with an anniversary getaway. Garreth and Clare on the Margaret River, fifteen years into their marriage, a childless and warmthless and mechanical affair that had begun as an accident and progressed out of habit. The two of them had showed up at an internet-organised singles meeting, devoid of marital options at their workplaces, and discovered the gap between them and the youngest other prospective partner was thirty years. Garreth had rescued her from the clutches of a handsy lawn-bowls enthusiast whose wife had just died of cancer, and she'd stuck with him, the rigid certainty and authority he presented as a cop like a broad umbrella under which she could shelter from the rain.

Garreth came with problems, sure, but so did everyone. He wouldn't so much as hold hands. His kisses were thin-lipped and hard, and sex departed the marriage within the first year, a sort of relief for them both; the fast and silent activity that was only performed in solid darkness a thing they both seemed to know was only necessary until something came along to do away with it. Like buying an electric car and letting petrol station visits become a curious inconvenience of the past. There was a quietly regretful understanding on her part that she was only with him because he reminded her of her father; her icy sanctuary, a quiet shoemaker who'd taught her to sew and cut fabric in his bolthole shop in Kings Cross. Her father had been a quiet man, too, but regular. Predictable. He brought money into the house. He decided how it went out again. With an alcoholic mother prone to disappearing for weeks at a time, Clare had delighted in all the things she could count on about her father. And it was the same with Garreth. If she cared to investigate the messages on his phone while he showered, she invariably found texts from police colleagues, operational in nature, with the occasional invitation to the pub for drinks, politely declined. Every Saturday evening at dusk, Clare could find Garreth cleaning and vacuuming his car. Every Sunday afternoon, she could find him in the kitchen meal-prepping for the work week. Broccoli and tuna. Every day he ate a single clove of garlic, swallowed whole before he brushed his teeth, to ward off illness. True to form, he was never ill.

Clare hadn't ever been able to figure out exactly why Garreth chose her. She suspected, in some way, he'd been waiting for someone to come along who met a minimum standard of features, abilities and intelligence, and when he alighted on her, he didn't question or evaluate the decision that she should be his life partner, because he wasn't a person who questioned or evaluated systems that worked. On paper, she was the quirky one in the relationship, with her garage workshop cluttered with dislocated doll parts and jars of buttons, vacuum-sealed pouches of carefully sourced vintage fabrics for those custom restorations she took on. But in truth their shared appreciation for order and quiet and solitude made them a perfect match. On Friday nights he sat at one end of the sofa, writing a speech or answering emails on his laptop. She sat at the other, bidding on glass eyes on eBay or flipping through monograms of doll catalogues from the 1920s.

Then came the trip to Margaret River.

It was their usual anniversary destination. A sparse rental house with a small dock, accessible only by boat, a setting that inspired all kinds of silly romantic fantasies in her. Wealthy women who owned big glassy remote riverside mansions, who took on hunky, dark-eyed men to repair their boathouses for cash and ended up uncovering their dangerous pasts. Because she was a little bit like that. Taken to fantasies, corrupted by the story winds of different lands, a woman who searched the shady pockets of sandstone and gums beside the river for wild men or witches. Garreth had never tolerated her musings, and neither had her father, so she'd learnt early in the relationship to hide them, to keep her whimsical wonderings about dolls that came into her care, their pasts and futures, to herself.

Garreth was out at 4 a.m. and 4 p.m. kayaking every day of the trip, making a black silhouette against the pink sunrise on the water, while she sat on the balcony and sipped tea and compared bulk deals for horsehair on her phone. One afternoon, completely out of the blue, he'd paddled in and she'd seen flickers of that romantic fantasy she'd been having about the dangerous man on the dock as he climbed, shirtless and hairy, onto the pier. He beckoned her down with a big, friendly hand.

'Let's go out together,' he'd said. 'It'll be fun.'

She'd leapt at the chance, though her stomach immediately plunged, because it was 6 p.m. now and night was falling, and the wind was picking up, and she knew from a decade and a half of being his wife that Garreth's idea of 'fun' wasn't this. Not at all. Garreth's fun was listening to obscure legal podcasts and running on his treadmill until the track became so damp with sweat it was dangerous, not splashing and laughing along a moonlit river with his wife. But she went, wrestling the second kayak down from its rack in the boathouse, batting away mosquitoes in the purple twilight. His gentle encouragement set her heart on fire, a smile and a piece of advice offered now and then as she fumbled with the big slippery paddle and blathered nervously about bull shark feeding times and winced in the wind. In a high-walled cove, she'd caught up to him, and he'd reached over with his long arm seemingly to take her hand and pull her and her kayak closer to his. But when their outstretched fingers met, instead of a gentle pull there'd been a sharp tug, and her kayak had flipped, plunging her into the icy black water.

Harvey watched Clare's eyes. His hands were still on her vest, the shard of glass clutched in his fingers, the gaping hole beneath where the vest looped around under her arm pinned open by a fingertip. He could feel wires inside the hole, but Harvey couldn't draw his gaze away from Clare's downcast lashes, the muscle ticking in her jaw as she remembered.

'At first I thought he was trying to, you know, to get his feet steady,' she whispered. She drew a rattling breath. 'He was standing right beside me. I was gripping onto his legs under the water, trying to . . . to climb up him. To use his body to flip myself and the kayak back over. When that didn't work I thought maybe he was trying to flip it *this* way, and I was trying to flip it *that* way, and we were working against each other. I was under the water, twisting around, trying to get my legs free from inside. I remembered I had a lap belt, and

I reached for that, and that's when I realised that Garreth already had a hand on it.'

'On the lap belt?'

'Yeah.'

Harvey went quiet.

'I think he had one arm around the keel of the kayak.' Clare put an arm out, hugged the air. 'And one hand up underneath, keeping my belt in place.'

'Jesus,' Harvey said.

'He only let go because I scratched the fuck out of his hand.' Clare rubbed her nose on the back of her wrist. 'I flipped myself back over. Vomited water everywhere. He said all the right things, of course. That he was holding the strap because he was trying to undo it. That he hadn't been able to flip the kayak because the air trapped underneath had suctioned it to the surface of the river.'

'Bullshit,' Harvey said.

'I know.'

'That's not how it works.'

'I know that now.' Clare nodded. 'But I lay awake all that night, trying to work it out. If he'd been trying to kill me, or teach me a lesson. If he had been trying to kill me, why? Why not just divorce me instead?'

'Did you ask him?'

'Of course I did. He was appalled. But . . . I knew. Sometimes I'd catch him looking at me and it was just . . . there. In his eyes. An intent.'

'Why do you think he was trying to do it?' Harvey asked. The words felt heavy in his mouth, weighted with dread and disbelief.

'It's going to be hard to explain, but . . .' Clare shook her head. Her eyes were distant. 'Killing me just made more sense than divorcing me.'

Harvey batted the idea around in his brain a little, tried to make it stick. It didn't.

'Nope. I don't get it.'

'It's like . . . We had an oven once,' Clare said. 'An old cast-iron thing that had been in the house when we bought it. It broke down. We ordered a council pick-up.' Clare turned to him. 'Garreth took the whole oven apart. Every nut and bolt. Every rack and rail. He kept half the pieces back from the roadside pile, stored them in the garage, so that if someone came along and decided they wanted to take the oven they'd never be able to put it back together and make it work. We ordered a second council pick-up for the rest of the pieces. No one was going to have his oven.'

'You're not an oven, Clare,' Harvey said. 'You're a person.'

'That's right.' She turned to him. Her eyes were fierce now, glittering in the furnace of the darkened truck. 'I'm a *fucking* person! I'm not a doll!'

Harvey watched her.

'So I put fentanyl in his aspirin.'

'Jesus *Christ*!' Harvey felt his eyes bugging from his head.

'I know.' Clare held a hand up. 'I know.'

Harvey bent his head, trying to hide his bewildered expression as he pried the hole in Clare's vest apart. He needed something to do, something to focus on, so that he could keep his grip on reality. What he saw inside the hole in her vest gave him no mental relief. Thin black wires, ten or so, bound by a tiny cable tie. Harvey stuck his finger into the hole, felt the sharp edge of another band of wires below the one he could see. He pushed a finger sideways and felt a box shape covered with fabric.

'What . . .' he fumbled for words. 'What was your plan, exactly, Clare?'

'I don't know.' Clare sighed, making the whole vest expand and contract. 'I just thought . . . I thought, *Fuck you.* You know? From the moment I met Garreth I . . . I went into *training* to be his wife. On our first date it was like; when you walk beside me, you walk on this side. Not that side. When you kiss me, you don't use your tongue. When we have breakfast, you don't clink your spoon on the side of your bowl. And I know what it sounds like. It sounds like that movie. The Julia Roberts one.'

'With the towels.' Harvey nodded.

'But that's not what it was.' Clare shook her head. 'Because for years, *years*, all that stuff was actually comforting to me. I didn't have to think how to be. I didn't have to "try to find myself". It was like Garreth knew who I was. I was his wife. And so I talked like this and I dressed like that and I squeegeed the shower screen every time I used the shower and I weighed myself on the first of every month and made sure I never went over seventy kilos.'

Harvey tried not to speak. Felt his jaw tighten with resistance. He really hated that shit, with the weighing and the dieting. He'd seen enough of it in the army, with both male and female recruits.

'Why would you train me for fifteen years to be something'—Clare wiped her eyes—'and then try to destroy me?'

Harvey listened. Said nothing.

'I thought, *I'm going to survive you, Garreth,*' Clare went on, her eyes narrowed, ignoring Harvey completely. 'Because it was pretty clear then, that surviving him was the only way out. He'd told me about his early days on the force. About the High Wire and the stuff that went on out here. He'd told me how easy it was to use the outback as an escape route and a body-dumping site. Your body doesn't stay intact out here. It bakes and turns to dust and gets blown away by the winds.'

Harvey picked up his discarded shirt and wiped cold sweat from his face and neck.

'I knew Garreth was trying to kill me on that river,' Clare said. 'And I confirmed it for myself when I poisoned him. I got the drugs from a nurse I'd sold a doll to. Half a speck, the smallest amount you can imagine, soaked into an aspirin. I had to peel the backing off the blister pack, heat-glue it back together. It didn't kill Garreth. But the dose made him sick enough that he . . . he *knew*. His behaviour changed. He took an aspirin for a headache, and suddenly he was out cold for sixteen hours. I mean, he knew.'

'Were you trying to kill him?'

Clare was silent for a long time. 'No,' she said. 'Or . . . maybe. I think I was trying to see how brave I was. Whether I could . . . play . . . with his life. The way he'd played with mine. Treat him like a doll. I stood at the foot of the bed while he lay there breathing shallowly, completely unconscious, and I felt such power over him. It's hard to explain. It's bizarre.'

'It is bizarre,' Harvey relented.

'Six months later, he was repairing the garage wall and a brick fell off the scaffold he was sitting on. Hit me right on the collarbone while I was walking underneath. Shattered it. If his aim has been a centimetre better, I'd have copped it in the top of the skull.'

'At no point did you ever talk about it?' Harvey frowned.

'What was I going to say? "Hey, honey. I have this feeling you tried to kill me on that river. So in response I poisoned you. Now things are getting silly. Should we call a truce? "'

'You might have started with, "I think we need a break. I'm going to a hotel."'

'You don't understand.' Clare shook her head. 'We didn't talk in those terms. If we ever had a fight, it was a cold war. One would do something to the other and he'd just go silent, and his silence snuffed out everything. It would drown out the words. It was like a black cloud falling over the house, choking out the air. I'd just wait until the cloud lifted, until we started talking and acting normally again.'

Harvey sat silently, listening.

'There were signs that running away wasn't going to be possible,' Clare said.

'He said that? That he wouldn't let you get away?'

'No, not in those words. But after the thing with the fentanyl, suddenly he wanted us to combine our bank accounts. He didn't ask me. He told me. We're combining our bank accounts. I've made an appointment for us, with the bank. We're going there. I knew then that I was being watched. My purchases. My savings. Everything was being tracked. Then he installed GPS navigators in the cars. Both of them. For a decade and a half he'd been a man who prided himself on his ability to know where he was going at any given minute, or to plan his routes with street directories. He liked the tatty old books. They'd been his father's. They were full of Post-It notes and highlighted sections, handwritten notes in the margins. But the GPS systems, they collected your routes. Listed your destinations. I turned that function off on mine. He turned it back on. Neither of us said anything about that.'

Harvey nodded.

'I know it sounds crazy,' Clare said.

'Did he make other attempts on you?'

'I think so. I got really sick last November. My liver almost failed. It was a mystery to doctors, what was wrong. Then suddenly it cleared up.'

'Did you make attempts on him?'

'I planned some things.' She nodded. 'Didn't carry them out. It was hard. Because I couldn't search for anything on my phone or computer. I didn't trust the devices to delete my search history completely, and getting to an internet cafe or a library meant driving there and leaving a trail.'

'What happened last night?' Harvey asked. 'To get you out here?'

'He arrived home earlier than he should have.' Clare wiped her eyes. 'I don't know why. I thought I had another hour to myself. He came in and caught me in the kitchen with a beer bottle presser. You know, the kind with the lever, that presses the cap on properly, seals it shut. I was recapping a Corona bottle I'd just slipped ricin into.'

Harvey laughed, covered his face with both hands, surprised that the sound coming from his lips wasn't a mournful howl. He might have been too exhausted for despair then. The laugh was an easier, lighter reaction to access in his frayed and burnt mind.

'It was an attempt that was several months in the making,' Clare said. 'I bought the bottle-cap presser from a craft beer supply shop in Braitling. Paid cash that I'd been skimming off the top of cash sales with the dolls. To get to Braitling I had to dummy up a fake Facebook Marketplace ad about a vintage doll collection being sold out of a deceased estate. While I was there I joined the library under a fake name, used their computers to search for recipes for poisons that don't show up in an autopsy.'

'Clare,' Harvey said, 'didn't you ever think of telling anyone what was happening? There are helplines and . . . shelters. There are abuse support groups.'

'I would never have got away.' Clare shook her head. 'He's the commissioner of the bloody Northern Territory Police, Harvey. He can pick up a phone to the top police officer in any state in the country and tell them whatever he likes about me. That's his power. Always has been. The phone. He wields it like a . . . a titan with a lightning bolt.'

'What did he say? When he walked in and you had the bottle capper there . . .?'

'He didn't say anything, he just looked at me in that . . . that way. It was like we'd had a curtain between us for two years, and we'd both been working secretly and silently behind the curtain, and suddenly that curtain had dropped.' Clare eased a shuddering breath. 'He turned to run to his study, where he kept his personal weapon. I got there first.'

'Did you shoot him?'

'Yeah.'

'Badly?'

'Not badly enough.' She shook her head. 'I hit him in the hip. The fleshy part, above the bone.' She pinched her waist. 'I think it went right through and hit the fridge, so it couldn't have been that bad. I just fired in a panic and ran. Got in the car.

I started heading for the airport, to try to make him believe that's where I was going. Then I ripped the GPS system out of the car and dumped it in a bin at a park. I turned and headed for the desert south of Santa Teresa. I knew the first sign that tells you you're on the Wire. The big broken-down semi.'

Harvey knew it. A huge rusted semi-trailer lying on its side in the desert, a random curiosity for tourists who might have ventured off road out of Alice Springs to see the red desert earth. Only certain characters knew what the big black arrow spraypainted along its length meant.

'I followed the other signs, until I knew I was on the Wire. I figured he would never think to look for me out here. I'm not the kind of person who would ever travel a road like this. But now I'm caught between wanting to have been right and wanting Garreth to have guessed I'm that cunning. That I'd have gone this way.'

Harvey sighed.

'The car broke down just before I met you.'

'What happened there?' he asked. 'What do you mean it just broke down?'

'I have no idea. I heard a big bang. Stopped. Got out. There was smoke coming out of the engine. It was making a horrifying noise. Then it caught on fire. And then, there was you.'

Harvey took a deep breath. Let it out slow.

'I feel like he's after me,' Clare said. She rubbed her sternum. 'It's like a prickling feeling in my heart. That he's guessed I've come this way. That he's out there. Getting closer. It was always meant to be quiet, my . . . my ending. Neat. An accident. But this is way out of hand now. He'll want to clean up the mess.'

'So now, with everything that's already going on, we've got the Northern Territory's top police officer on our tail.' Harvey smiled. 'And he's probably going to shoot you as soon as he lays eyes on you, without knowing that if he does, he'll blow everyone within fifty metres to pieces.'

Clare nodded.

'I guess I feel a little less guilty about drawing you into this disaster, Clare,' Harvey said. Clare gave a lopsided smile.

'I've come on our road trip with some pretty good baggage of my own.'

They heard footsteps on the gravel outside. Darryl and Tizza approaching from the hill.

'What did you see inside the vest?' Clare lifted her arm, tried to tilt the hole he'd made towards her.

'Nothing that'll help us,' Harvey said. He flopped onto his back. 'I guess I'd hoped to see what you see in the movies. A couple of wires, one green, one red, a clear place to cut the connection to the explosives. But the vest is riddled with wires, all black bundled together and cable-tied. They won't all have a function. Most will be decoys. There are boxes inside which are probably the bricks of plastic explosives Tiz was talking about. But they're individually sewn in their own Kevlar pouches, probably to hide the connection points and disguise the decoy wires from the real ones.'

'There's no way to see what you're doing without taking the vest apart completely.'

'Yuh.'

'They're so well made.' Harvey heard her running her fingers along the Kevlar neck of the vest.

'He was a tailor,' Harvey said. 'Tiz. Learnt it in high school. He had someone send him a sewing machine from home to the base, and ran the unofficial uniform repair shop out of his dorm. Your uniform got torn or wasn't the right fit, you could take it to him and he'd fix it for cash. I had him let down the hem on a pair of trousers for me once, a few months before the ambush. It was a civil exchange. Not friendly, not unfriendly. Just a business dealing on base. I go on a bit about how much of an idiot Tizza is, but he's actually a gifted craftsman. The vest's design will be all him.'

Harvey stared at the hole in the ceiling, the broken and scarred mounting where the camera had been, wondering what filled him with more despair; Clare's story, or how familiar it was. Because he understood deeply what had drawn the woman beside him into her deadly alliance with the police commissioner. It was the same thing that had led him into the army. Harvey's own childhood, tumultuous and uncertain, had created a brain that thrived on predictability, rigid systems, unquestioning faith in processes. He'd loved the routine. In the service, every process – from what time he went to sleep to how he made his bed, from how he walked to what words he used to express himself – was tried, tested and optimised. Harvey's happiest years in the army had been his grunt years, when his brain was forcibly quietened into automation, working like a machine in its on-duty hours, relaxing into mindless activities like counting when it sought entertainment: kilometres marched, operations manual paragraphs memorised, one-arm push-ups performed in a single minute. Harvey had recovered from his childhood in his early years in the army like a drug addict in rehab, forming new neural pathways, taking out and folding traumatic memories like sheets and arranging them neatly in a linen cupboard.

Sadly, he'd needed to progress into leadership roles, which required him to constantly test and update those processes with more creative thinking and humanity, leaving him ultimately edgy and irritable. Harvey imagined Clare relishing in Garreth's dominance of her thoughts, feelings and impulses like a soldier bending to the will of the great military system. Faithfully following, knowing that all things were done for the good of one *and* the good of all.

The problem was that Harvey's relationship with the military had almost got him killed. It had taken him, and held him, and loved him, and then tried to destroy him. Because while in its better parts it was deliciously protective; at its worst it was infected with terror, secrets and suffering.

The dark hole above Harvey was cut through with light as the truck doors opened.

'Get out,' Darryl said from somewhere to Harvey's left. 'It's time for your next mission.'

CHAPTER 25

'You're coming with me,' Edna said, pointing at Talon. She kept her rifle by her side, swivelled, pointed the same finger at Stevenson. 'You're going to need to be our man on the inside, Stevie. I've just been suspended.'

'What?' Stevenson blurted. 'What for?'

'For this.' Edna gestured at Talon. 'Holland's phone calls. He got to my chief, down in Adelaide. He probably called around, learnt what he could about my history, and made a pitch to the chief that I was back to my old tricks. Anyway, I'm suspended. You'll need to confiscate my service weapon and the car.'

Stevenson glanced at the cruiser beside her. She took Edna's pistol and taser numbly as the older officer unclipped them from her belt. 'So what'll you do? Go back to Clifton Hills?'

'Forget that,' Edna said. 'Me and the kid are going off road.'

'Oh, *shit. Yes!*' Talon clapped hard, punched the air. 'Off road, baby! Are you fucking kidding me? This is *wild*!'

'Edna,' Stevenson's gaze was steady and brimming with caution, 'is this the best course of action right now?'

'The kid's big, strong and dangerous looking.' Edna took her badge off her belt. 'If I run into any trouble on the Wire his appearance alone might come in handy. Besides that, he's sharp as a tack, if a little prone to fantasy.'

'Shouldn't he go home?'

'He's at as much risk there as he is with me.'

Stevenson looked doubtful for a moment, seemed to shake the doubt off like an oversized coat. She flung back her shoulders. 'All right, Ed. If this is what you want.'

'It is.'

'I haven't been able to push you off course in something like this even once, in all the years we've worked together. No reason this time would be any different.'

'Exactly.' Edna nodded. 'So you're gonna get in the cruiser and go back to the site of Buck's car. The team from Adelaide should have arrived by now. They'll be setting up a ground zero.' Edna knew the scene around Buck's vehicle out on the Wire would be a slowly expanding hive of activity. The same chopper that dropped the team from Adelaide in would begin a land-search grid, looking for signs of Clare Holland, Harvey Buck, or anyone else who might have been involved in the incident. They would divide officers into groups, tasking some with an inspection of the scene and the surrounds, and others with driving between Cooper Creek and Clifton Hills to canvass for witnesses. There would be officers arriving in tactical vehicles from Alice Springs, who would hunker down in one of the towns and create a secondary command point, probably inside a pub, if Edna knew anything about cops. These officers would start digging into Buck and Holland's pasts.

'What are you two going to do?' Stevenson let her gaze drift to the big kid behind Edna. 'You don't have a car. You can't pursue Buck on foot with a bloody rifle, Ed.'

'We'll be fine. Tell me about Holland. What did the chemist say?'

Stevenson shrugged. 'Billy said the guy looked pasty and asked for the hardest thing he could get over the counter for pain. Showed his licence to get something with codeine. Left town heading north.'

'He's probably going back to the Wire. Going to keep pushing east. That's probably what Buck's doing.'

'Yeah.'

'Billy say he was shaking? Or just pasty?'

'Didn't mention it.'

'I wonder how badly he's hit. I think he was limping, out at Buck's car. He didn't seem too bad.' Edna sighed. 'But it's hot. If he's bleeding *and* he's dehydrated . . .'

'Clare must have tagged him,' Talon mused. The women looked up at him. 'They had a fight. She wounded him. Then she bolted. Went out to the Wire, got herself tangled up with Harvey Buck and the other guy, the balaclava guy, on the way.'

Edna and Stevenson stood silently thinking. Talon spoke again.

'Unlesssss . . .'

'Unless what?' Stevenson's face was twisted with scepticism.

'Unless he caught up to her. Holland. Just after she was picked up by Buck.' Talon's eyes searched the ground as he tried to follow his own thread. 'Maybe Holland *saw* her get abducted by Buck and the guy in the balaclava. Holland got out ahead of them, threw the road spikes out, stopped them and killed the guy we found. And Clare, he killed her, too. But Buck got away. So now Holland's out here pretending he's searching for his missing wife, while really he's . . . he's hunting Buck. Because – oh my god – Buck knows what he did!'

'You're gonna break my brain in a minute here, kid,' Stevenson sighed. 'I need a diagram or a flow chart or something.'

'Any and all theories I have for this woman end with her dead in the desert somewhere.' Edna massaged her brow. 'Whether it's Buck who's killed her or Holland or whoever the hell.'

'We'll get answers when we find Buck,' Talon said. 'We've just got to crack the code.'

Stevenson frowned. 'What code?'

'Don't.' Edna held a hand up. 'Just go back along the Wire and keep us updated. Take your bloody phone off silent, in case I need you. We're going to keep heading east, see if we can run across Buck before Holland does.'

2018

'Dispatch, we're on scene now. Got eyes on the suspect.'

Edna put the cruiser's radio down and watched the lone figure ahead of her in the street, an unsteady streak of blackness on the rain-hammered windscreen. Gordon took a large slurp of his coffee and fitted the thermal mug into the holder beside him, a wrist on the steering wheel, fingers hanging in the gloom. The dark figure in front of them beat on the big iron door to the front garden of 108A Caroline Street. Pushed the buzzer. Edna could hear the sound even over the storm. She bet the residents of the terraces all around them hated it.

'Fuck this shit,' Gordon sighed.

'Eloquently put, Gaz,' Edna said. She unbuckled her seatbelt, reached down and lifted an umbrella from the footwell. 'Come on. It's not going to let up.'

The two cops went out into the tempest. Edna had been trying to do the gratitude thing, a hangover from turning to yoga at fifty to try to fix her knees. So she thanked the universe that while it was freezing and the rain was falling in olive-sized droplets that made the whole umbrella tremble above her, at least it wasn't windy. Gordon had one hand on his umbrella and one on his taser. The guy had been itching to tase a junkie since Edna had met him six years earlier.

It became clear when the girl wheeled around that Gordon's dream wouldn't come true tonight. The alcohol reek coming off the young woman had somehow survived the rain drenching every inch of her body and clothing, and the hand that reached up and swiped at the water gushing off her chin was free of track marks. She was clearly on something beyond cheap bourbon – Edna could tell that from the slices of white visible above the woman's irises. But she was coming down, not going up, and the alcohol would soften everything. The girl reeled back, gave them the look that cornered dogs give; like she was actively fighting the instinct to bite.

'Oh good, you're here.' The girl stabbed the intercom button in the wall again, hard and rapid. *Buzz-buzz-buzz-buzz-buzz.* 'I've got an appointment. I'm – I'm not – This isn't – I really am supposed to be here. Okay? Okay? Can you help me get in, please? Some people came out, but they – they don't understand.'

'Ma'am,' Edna started.

'I've got a reference number for a bed.' The girl clawed at her saturated hair, tried to get it off her forehead. 'They won't let me in. I've got to get in.'

'This isn't a rehab anymore,' Gordon barked. 'It's a private residence. It hasn't been a rehab facility in half a decade.'

'It is, but.'

'No it isn't,' Edna confirmed. 'It closed down. Now it's just a regular house.'

'But I've got a placement.'

'It's not a rehab!' Gordon leant in, his umbrella bumping Edna's, which she'd tilted to protect both her and the girl. 'You get it?

You listening? It *used* to be a rehab. Now, it's *not*. Get that into your drug-baked skull. The owners are regular people. They're in there right now, trying to sleep. They called the cops on you because they *don't want you here*!'

'Gaz.' Edna held a hand up. 'Cool it for a second.'

'I'm getting drenched!' Edna's partner barked. 'I'm standing here getting drenched while we play reality games.'

'I know, I know. Just fucking cool it.' Edna turned to the soaked girl. 'Ma'am, you need to go home. This address is no longer a rehab facility.'

'Yes it is. I have a placement.'

'Oh Jesus.' Gordon turned and walked away. Edna tried to take the girl's arm, gripped the empty wet cloth of her long, heavy sleeve. When she finally got hold of the girl's upper arm, it was half the size she expected it to be.

'Come with me,' Edna said. She led the kid to the cruiser, guided her over the torrent coming down the gutter. Huge liquidambar leaves, brown, sliding over the sandstone like little boats. The cabin lights threw awful angles on the girl's face, her thinning, dripping hair. Gordon was watching Edna, twisted in his seat, his grip on the steering wheel white-knuckle hard.

'You serious right now, Ed? You're signing us up to be a taxi service for Adelaide's homeless?'

'Shut up, Gaz.'

'Listen, listen, listen,' the girl was saying. Her skeletal hands wrung Edna's as the cop slid onto the bench seat beside her. 'You don't understand. I was – I'm – I was supposed to clock into the rehab this afternoon.'

'No you weren't, hun,' Edna said.

'I was late. I missed my train.'

'No, you didn't!' Gordon growled.

'Honey—'

'I called. I told them my name. They said they'd hold my bed until seven o'clock.'

'It's midnight'—Edna squeezed the girl's fingers—'and the place you're trying to get to doesn't exist anymore.'

'Dispatch, we got the suspect. It's a catch-and-release.' Gordon sighed into the mic beyond the plexiglass barrier where Edna and the girl sat. He threw Edna a warning glance in the rear-view mirror. 'We'll be green in three minutes or less.'

'No we won't,' Edna said. 'The drive to Cremorne House is half an hour.'

'We're not dropping her at a shelter. It's like I said. This is a cop car, not a taxi service or an ambulance.'

'Gaz.'

'They'll all be overrun in this weather.' Gordon knocked a thick knuckle on the window glass beside him, gesturing to the black, wet night. 'You're really pissin' me off with this, Ed. Every time I go on shift with you, you get into another relationship with a fucking street cat. I still can't drive down Portrush Road without getting hassled by those window-washer freaks because you bought them doughnuts that one time.'

'What's your name?' Edna ignored Gaz, turned to the girl.

'Alicia Kleinmann.'

'Alicia, do you have somewhere you can stay tonight? A friend's place? Is there a family member who you can—'

'I need to get to my placement.' The girl's eyes were distant, sliding around. Edna tried to guess her age. She could be anything between thirteen and thirty. 'If I complete my rehab placement, they'll give me visits with my daughter.'

Gaz was typing on the mounted laptop in the front of the cruiser. Edna watched the water pooling on the creases in the leather seat beside her, a steady stream running from Alicia's sleeves. There were puddles on the floor. She glanced up and saw Gordon's screen reflected in the plexiglass. The words doubled and backwards. *Kleinmann, Alicia Bonnie, 21*.

'The daughter's a ward of the state.' Gordon slurped his coffee. 'Has been for the past two years.' The big cop twisted around in his seat again, pointed a finger at Alicia through the grimy plexiglass. 'You want some rehabilitation, Kleinmann? I'll give it to you, right now, for free. Stop drinking. Stop doing drugs. Stop stealing people's shit to fund your habit. It's as simple as that. Now get out of my car and get out of this suburb and get out of whatever alternate reality you're living in.'

'Gaz, shut the *fuck* up, will you?' Edna sighed.

'Join the rest of the fucking world, here, in reality,' he went on, gesturing to the car around them. 'It's nice. Trust me. You'll love it. You get a job. You get a house. You don't have to suck some random guy's dick under a bridge for half a bag of coke.'

'Stop!' Edna banged the plexiglass with her palm. 'She's a fucking kid, Gaz.'

'Once you have a kid, you stop being a kid.'

'I really need to get to my placement.' Alicia's eyes were glossy, trying to focus on Edna. 'Can you please help me?'

'Come with me.' Edna pulled Alicia sideways towards the door.

Gordon was still talking as Edna slammed the door on him and shepherded the girl back to the footpath. The rain had lightened and Edna leant her umbrella on her shoulder and turned her back to the cruiser.

'I'm going to give you a key,' she told the girl. Her hands were shaking, her mind twisting as desire and guilt wrestled for dominance. Cop brain fighting a bleeding heart. 'I'm going to order you an Uber. It'll take you to a house with a yellow door.'

The girl took the key Edna wrestled from her keyring. It dropped into her wet palm.

'Stand right here until the Uber comes,' Edna said. 'I'll give you my umbrella. When the Uber takes you to the house with the yellow door – Are you listening? Hey. Hey. Alicia? Use the key to go inside, hun. I'll be home in a couple of hours.'

'What is this place?' Alicia stared at the key, her lids heavy now, a drunk moth locked onto a flame.

'It's somewhere safe,' Edna lied.

CHAPTER 26

The heat was easing. Harvey got out of the truck, helped Clare down, and noticed the face-smack of warmth wasn't as startling as it had been the last time they stepped into the sunlight. Or perhaps it was that his body temperature was so high from being boxed into the mobile oven beside him, that he wasn't noticing the ambient heat. He didn't know. He tried to guess the time. Early afternoon.

They were in the embrace of a curve of low, rocky hills, not far from the Wire, Harvey guessed. There were large creatures on the horizon, but between the heat and the distance, they appeared only as brown blobs, anything from brumbies to feral camels.

Tizza tossed the pouch with the camera glasses in it onto the cracked clay in front of Harvey. The little man's lip was split and swollen, and he was running his tongue over it and smiling like a cartoon demon.

'There's a property,' Tizza pointed. 'Around that bend. You'll see it.'

'What kind of property?' Harvey asked.

'Somewhere with water.'

'What am I doing?'

'You'll get instructions along the way, Buck.' Tizza grinned. 'You've got to be patient.'

'He needs more information,' Clare said. 'At least tell him what you've got planned.'

'Don't worry, you won't have to wallow in the not-knowing for very long.' Darryl turned to her, his tone sweet. 'You're going with him. You're both going on a mystical journey of discovery together.'

'What? Me?'

'You broke the camera.' Darryl gazed at her, the faux sweetness gone. 'You tipped out the water. Seems to me like you were tired of sitting on the sidelines and you wanted to play. So welcome to the game, bitch.'

Harvey watched Clare. He saw no more than a tightening in the muscles around her collarbones, a remarkable refusal to let her terror and desperation show. 'You can stop this now, you know,' she said.

Tizza laughed.

'I'm not kidding.' Clare looked over at the younger captor. 'What he did to you in Afghanistan was fucked up. He told me all about it. How he needled stuff out of you. Your darkest traumas and your . . . your fears. But all this isn't going to cure you, you know. It isn't going to make you any less angry. You get that, right?'

'Is this where you tell me to *radically accept* what happened to me?' Darryl smirked, exposed a yellowed canine tooth. 'Offer Buck forgiveness? Because it's about me, right – the forgiveness? It's about deciding to heal myself?'

'She doesn't get it,' Tizza said. 'How healing all this is. How healing it's going to be, in the end.' Tizza put his lean, muscular arms out. His freckled forearms were lit up by the sun, the narrow curve of his chest bucked forward under his T-shirt. 'I feel like I'm being fused back together,' he said. 'Piece by piece. Like the old cracks and crevices are being filled in. I feel more whole every second you suffer in that vest, Buck.'

'Congratulations,' Harvey said.

'You couldn't possibly understand what healing from something like this *takes*,' Tizza said to Clare. 'What it feels like. Because nothing like this has ever happened to you.'

'What about you, Dar?' Harvey asked. 'Is your soul being healed?'

'I'm still waiting,' Darryl said. 'I haven't seen you cry yet. Do you remember the second day, when you played that little trick?'

'I do,' Harvey nodded. 'I do.'

'I want to make you cry like that.'

'What trick?' Clare asked. 'What's he talking about?'

Harvey cocked his head, gazed at the horizon, let a satisfied look play about his face as he remembered. 'I pretended they were being rescued.'

No one spoke.

'I'd been messing with Darryl pretty bad for a couple of hours and getting no traction,' Harvey said. 'Pushing on pressure points. Knocking him around. I thought he was on the verge of giving up, of telling me the names of their contacts in the Taliban group. He kept starting to. Then backing off. It takes it out of you, beating a man. And being beaten. We were both exhausted. I decided I needed to change things up.'

Darryl's eyes were full of thunder.

'So I gagged them all, went outside and waited a while,' Harvey said. 'Then I came back. Made some radio noises.

Put on a different voice. *I think they're in here! This way! This way!* I crunched around in the gravel. Shone a torch. They thought it was finally over. That they were being rescued.'

Harvey looked at Clare. Her mouth was hard, downturned.

'I played the trick on each of them in their separate containers, one after the other,' Harvey said. 'Darryl was the most broken by it. He'd been listening to the apparent rescue of the others. Waiting the longest. Hoping. Wondering. Crying out behind the gag. *I'm in here! Help! Help!* Oh, how you cried and cried, Darryl, when you saw it was only me.'

Harvey laughed. He hoped he was selling it; the sick, psychotic humour, but making the sound almost caused him to gag. Because Harvey had spent ten years trying to forget the noise of Darryl crying, bound in his chair, the wooden frame creaking as he twisted and howled with fury and sadness. Many a night after he'd returned to Australia, Darryl's crying had underscored the screaming of Harvey's section as the gunfire rained on them, the two traumas twisted together with others, a braided band of pain around his skull. Harvey had dreamt of lifting and hauling Darryl, running out of the combat zone with him, carrying him through the desert. For years he'd awakened drenched in sweat, the sheets and blankets and pillows all torn from the bed and scattered around the room. The nightmares had scared more than one woman out of his apartment, ruined one-night stands and casual flings, which was about all he'd been able to manage since his return.

He'd never asked Shayna if she had nightmares. Because she hadn't been at the containers, but what happened to the men Harvey tortured there wouldn't have been possible without her.

With a *whump* of pain to his chest, he remembered her eyes, black and hard, as she hung over the side of the bathtub.

Harvey looked at the brown blobs on the horizon, and for the first time noticed a thin string of wires and posts shimmering through the heat haze in the distance. Cows or horses. A farm.

'Leave Clare here,' Harvey said. 'You won't be able to keep an eye on us both. You've only got one set of glasses. She might drop a signal to someone.'

'You better hope she doesn't,' Darryl said. 'Because if we get an inkling that something's going on, we won't warn you. We'll just hit the button.'

'Get going,' Tizza said.

They walked. Harvey watched the red rocks and sand pass beneath his feet, unsure where to focus his mind; on the horrible possibilities that lay immediately in front of him, or the ones that lay behind. Clare was watching the world pass beneath her also, her mouth open, panting.

'Why Margaret River?' Harvey asked, deciding to go mentally backwards rather than forward.

'Huh?'

'Margaret River,' Harvey said. 'The anniversary trip. Why did Garreth choose that moment to . . .'

He remembered, looked up and met her eyes. 'We'll have to be careful'—he tapped the side of the sunglasses—'they're listening.'

'Okay.' She nodded.

'What did he choose that moment to do what he'd been planning to do?' Harvey asked.

Clare looked like she was struggling to pull her mind back from the brink of panic. She gripped the edge of the vest, her arms crossed over her chest. 'It, uh, it must have seemed like a good opportunity,' she huffed.

'But you'd been married for fifteen years without incident,' Harvey said. 'And you clearly didn't see it coming. One moment you're relaxing on holiday together. The next . . .'

'Right.'

'So there was no slow build? No arguments? Threats to leave, either on your behalf or his?'

'No.'

'So why then?' Harvey asked. 'What changed in the relationship?'

'I don't know.'

Tizza's voice in Harvey's earpiece. '*What the fuck are you two talking about?*' Harvey didn't answer. He heard the mic continue to pick up sound, as it had earlier, even after there was an audible click. Darryl, his voice softer. '*Let 'em talk. They're getting to know each other. It's to our advantage if a relationship forms.*'

'What changed between you and him?' Harvey asked Clare again.

'I said I don't—'

'Yes, you do,' Harvey said. 'Because, until that moment, you had been an appropriate fixture in this guy's life. If you've described him to me accurately, he was not a guy who fixed things unless they were broken. You served your purpose for him; emotionally, financially, logistically. What made him seek a different version of his life – one in which you weren't just divorced and living elsewhere, possibly with someone else, but . . . you know . . . you were where he planned for you to be.'

Clare didn't answer.

'There was another woman,' Harvey said.

'No way.' She shook her head. 'Not possible.'

'Why not?'

'Because he isn't that complex,' Clare said. 'Garreth wouldn't want the – the messiness – of an affair. The unpredictability of it. You have to worry you'll run into your partner out in the street. That someone will see you. Say something. You'll cook up a lie to explain where you were, and some unforeseen thing will unravel it. You'll have to have a contingency story. Garreth likes things straight down the line. Compartmentalised.'

'Wouldn't that explain his decision at Margaret River perfectly?'

'How?'

'Because divorcing you would be messy,' Harvey said. 'He'd have to worry about seeing you out and about, arm in arm, with whoever you chose to be with next. Then there would be all the heartache. The crying. What if you and your new partner had kids? What if you settled nearby? But if . . . what he had planned for you . . . actually succeeded . . . Things would be straight down the line. Compartmentalised. You'd be in his past, where you belonged, with no chance of messing up his future.'

Again, Clare was silent.

'You cheated,' Harvey said.

Clare gave a sudden, sad little laugh. 'This is what you did in the army, huh?' she said. 'You sat around and psychoanalysed people.'

'I had to,' he said. 'I was my job. I had to take eight guys in their twenties and make them killing machines. And *maintain* them as killing machines. That took psychoanalysis. Watching what they're doing, saying, reading, listening to, and what they're not doing, saying, reading and listening to. Because an Australian guy in his twenties isn't just going to wander up and tell you he's homesick, or suicidal, or scared out of his wits. It's sad but it's true.'

Clare licked her lips. Shrugged. 'He was a buyer.'

'What'd he buy?'

'A doll for his daughter,' Clare said. 'He was a widower. Handsome. Vulnerable and whimsical in a way that Garreth wasn't. He wanted the doll's dress custom made, and he provided me with a dress belonging to his late wife. It was so thoughtful.'

They walked in silence for a while.

'Garreth was a roses man,' Clare said. 'Long-stemmed. Red. That was it, always. I guess he decided at some point that when you buy a woman a gift, you buy her roses. It was a system that worked and so he didn't question it. Sometimes I would strip them, recut the stems and plant them in propagation soil. Regrow the rose plants and sell them. I'd use the money to buy what I really wanted.'

'You can do that?' Harvey frowned. 'Make rose plants from roses?'

'Yeah.'

'Huh.' Harvey put his hands in his pockets. 'Clare, I hate to break it to you. But Garreth found out about your boyfriend.'

'No, he didn't,' Clare said. 'He wasn't a boyfriend. It happened one time. In total, I laid eyes on the man twice. Once when I picked up the materials and then when I delivered the product and took payment. It happened then, the second time. In his car. We never saw each other again. Garreth would never have . . .'

Her words trailed off. Harvey waited. They walked.

'Okay.' Clare nodded, solemn. 'Okay. So he must have found out.'

Harvey's mind thrummed, a clanking engine interrupted by a noise ahead. He saw that the curved slab of rocky hills had lowered and flattened out, and before them lay a small farmhouse. Two children were standing on a wide gravel driveway, staring at them, their freckled and sun-bronzed faces curious. They were swimming in the lean, angular agelessness between small child and pre-teen, seven or ten or something like that. Harvey had never had much to do with children. Before he could react, the kids got up and ran inside.

He stopped dead. Clare did, too. The tiny speakers embedded in the ear loops of the glasses sprung to life.

'*Walk on,*' Darryl commanded.

'No,' Harvey said. 'There are kids in there. I'm not going anywhere near children in this vest.'

'*Walk on, now, or we blow you both,*' Darryl said.

Harvey reached over to grab Clare's hand, found hers was already on the way to his. He saw himself reflected in her eyes. It was like she could ear Darryl's voice in his ears. Knew the consequences. Harvey's heart lightened a little then at their solidarity.

'Fucking do it, then,' Harvey said.

The light on his chest came on. Harvey looked down at it. The sound of a screen door slapping up ahead sent a bolt of terror through his body that wasn't softened as he spied the two children sprinting back towards him.

'No.' Harvey took a step back, dragged Clare with him, but it was too late. The kids were within the blast zone and closing fast. He dragged his jacket shut over the light, the whole bomb vest. 'Shit shit *shit*!'

They were a boy and girl, the boy slightly taller and freckled, the girl missing her two front teeth and squinting under a battered Akubra. Harvey glanced down at the gap at the neck of his jacket. He couldn't tell if the light was still on down there under the thin cotton of his T-shirt.

'Heeeey.' The girl smiled in greeting. 'Are you here from Tommertons?'

Clare looked at Harvey, her eyes bulging. 'We – We – Uh . . .'

'*Tell them your car is broken down, and you need help.*'

'No,' Harvey said. The sound came out as a rasp. 'No. No.'

'*Tell them*'—Darryl's voice in his ear was seething, savage—'*your car is broken down. My finger is on the button, Buck. You want to see this little girl's flesh peeled clean off her bones? It'll be the last thing you ever see, war hero.*'

'What are you doing here, then?' the boy asked.

'We—' Harvey shuddered.

'*Three seconds until I end all four of you—*'

'We've had some, uh . . .'

Clare was staring at him. The kids were staring at him.

'*Three.*'

'Uh . . .'

'*Two.*'

'We've had some car trouble,' Harvey relented. Sweat burst at his brow, the baseball cap like a hot stone on top of his skull. 'Can you kids go inside and send your dad out?'

There was a woman on the distant verandah now. She hung a tea towel over her shoulder and waved at Harvey and Clare. 'G'day!' she shouted. 'Sorry, weren't expecting you lot until after lunch!'

'They're not from Tommy's!' the little boy turned and wailed. 'They've had some car trouble and they want Dad to come!'

Harvey was walking automatically, being dragged onward by the little girl's hand. His fingers were so numbed by the blood pounding in his ears and head and chest that he couldn't feel her skin, just knew he was being led and couldn't stop it.

'Car trouble? Oh. Shit. Well, the guys are just finishing up out back.' The woman looked Harvey and Clare over as they approached, her eyes lingering on the jackets. 'Can I do something to help? Where's the car?'

'It's just past the slope back there,' Clare said. 'We're fine. It's not a big deal.'

'Come inside. Lenny won't be long.'

'We . . . We don't need to come inside.' Clare turned desperate eyes on Harvey.

'She's right. We're fine out here.'

'Don't be silly. It's mental out there.' The woman held the door open. Harvey was getting feeling back in his hands. 'What's up with the car? I'm Daisy, anyway. Come in, would you? Come in! You're very welcome. We were just sitting down to lunch. Pull up a pew.'

Harvey's mind drifted away. He was somehow entering a small house, the number of lives in peril multiplying, until there was a dining room table spread out before him, cluttered with plates of food and the brilliant detritus of children's activities – paper, pencil cases, glue sticks, stickers, the lunch chaos and the kids' chaos like a meeting of two waves, a riptide of family life.

The little girl and boy who had been their escorts took up seats on either side of a toddler in a highchair who was mashing spaghetti into the plastic surface with her bare hands. Harvey was aware that Clare was carrying on talking with the woman, Daisy. Giving her fake names. Sally and John. Talking cheerfully, if a little too fast, about the heat. Harvey fell into a chair beside the young girl. Daisy was explaining that she'd thought Harvey and Clare were from a livestock supply company, due to arrive soon to deliver hay and medicines for the cattle. More lives. Harvey looked down and saw that his fists were clenched at his sides. He put them on the table, tried to unclench them and couldn't. He imagined a huge burst of fire exploding from his chest, torching everyone in the room around him to ash.

'*This is in* . . . sane . . .' Tizza's delighted voice on the radio.

'What do you want from me?' Harvey whispered. He was aware that the little boy with the freckles was frowning at him. He hid his face in his hand, pretended to swipe at the sweat pouring from his brow. 'What are we doing here?'

'*This is your mission, Buck,*' Darryl said in his ear. '*You have to choose someone from this family.*'

'Choose them?' Harvey whispered. 'What for? What do they have to do?'

Harvey heard both men laughing.

'*They have to die,*' Tizza said.

CHAPTER 27

'Maybe they're dates,' Talon said.

The kid looked more at home in Adam Bourne's Range Rover. He was able to straighten fully in his seat, the top of his close-cropped hair just brushing the roof lining. His long arm was resting on the sill, baking in the desert sun, fingers strumming. Edna, by contrast, felt completely out of place in her police uniform sans badge, the utility belt uncharacteristically light. She was still shaken from the phone call from McEvoy, embarrassed at having to borrow a vehicle from a resident of one of the towns under her jurisdiction, exhausted from the mental tug-of-war she was playing with herself. Being dragged constantly backwards to those days. The Alicia days. Yanked forwards then by the outback rumbling around her and the kid who was not Alicia but was as much a slow-motion car crash, a walking mistake. Edna's mistake.

She had headed north from Cooper Creek until she found a sign she recognised; a sun-bleached mannequin nailed to an old gumtree. Two enormous deer antlers were jammed into the sockets that had once connected the shop doll's arms, pointing east and west along the Wire. It was the most obvious of the

Wire signs she knew of, which could be as small as a black ribbon tied to a grass tree. The Wire, constantly being moved and adjusted to compensate for the presence of non-criminals, had been marked with this same abused and defaced doll in an area much further east, the last time Edna had encountered her. Talon wanted to stop to examine the snow-white antlers, the eyes and mouth of the mannequin spray-painted haphazardly red. Edna had taken one look at the fried and bedraggled wig bespeckled with brushfire ash and urged them onwards. She was so distracted now that the boy had to repeat himself.

'Dates?' Edna finally looked over.

'Buck would have been in the army in 2002.' Talon was scrolling on his phone. 'Just joined, from what I can see from articles about him online. Have you got anyone in the police who can look at his service record? Maybe something happened in February '02 and April '04 that—'

'Talon, Talon, Talon.' Edna reached over and patted his knee. 'This thing with the numbers on the pens . . .'

'What about it?'

Edna looked at the kid. His finger was hovering over his phone screen, eyes eager. She drew a deep breath, let it out slowly. 'When you're on a big case like this . . .' she said.

'Yeah?'

'You can get tunnel vision.' Edna looked back at the road, slowed to let a trio of kangaroos clear the path ahead. 'Sometimes you can focus so hard on a clue, you stop actually seeing it for what it is.'

'Right. Right.'

'Maybe draw back a little,' Edna said. 'Let the whole pen-code thing simmer away on the back burner.'

'Gotcha.'

She took her phone out and handed it to the kid. 'Dispatch should have texted me a phone number for Buck's next of kin, Shayna Kinthrop.'

'Who's she?'

'Dunno.' Edna waved at him. 'You're the one with the screen in front of you. Google her.'

The boy dialled, put the phone on speaker and set it in a cupholder between them. It rang and rang as he fished around on his own device. Eventually an automated voice asked them to leave a message for Shayna or try again later.

'She's not on the socials,' Talon said. 'Jesus. Not even Facebook.'

'LinkedIn?'

He tapped and scrolled. 'Yep. Yep. She's a consultant for a company that does, like, logistics . . .?' The boy shifted up in his seat. 'Okay so – wait – she was in the army, too. Left in 2011. Same year as Buck. Maybe she's Buck's girlfriend or something. No. Wait. Says here she lives in Sydney. Buck's last known address is in Alice. Maybe they're doing the long-distance thing.'

'More like he's a weird loner, and he knew her once upon a time.' Edna settled in her seat. 'We get that a lot with veterans out here. They elect someone as the next of kin so that someone knows when they die. I had to call a guy in Japan last year because some navy vet blew his brains out down south near Merty Merty. Took some effort for the guy to figure out who I was talking about. They'd been stationed on the ship together for only a week, more than a decade ago.'

'Sad.'

'Yeah.' Edna glanced over. 'Does she have a work number listed?'

'Yeah. I'll call it.'

Talon dialled. That number too rang and rang, unanswered. Another automated message. Edna felt a heaviness in her gut that wouldn't shift.

'This doesn't feel right,' Talon said, as though he could read Edna's thoughts.

Edna instructed the boy to dial Dispatch while she drove. The operator she'd previously dealt with, Richie, came on the line. His voice was slightly less smooth than the last time they'd spoken.

'Senior Sergeant Norris. Hi.'

'Dispatch, I'm hoping you can run another search for me on one Shayna Kinthrop. She's based out of Sydney. I'm wondering if she has any addresses in Alice or—'

'Ah, I'm so sorry, Senior Sergeant Norris.' Edna and Talon both looked at the phone as the operator cleared his throat. 'But, um. I've been acting as the liaison officer for the past hour or so with the team at the active crime scene west of Cooper Creek . . .'

'And?' Edna felt her jaw tighten.

'And I'm being told that you're – you're, uh . . . *not operational* at the moment.'

Edna sighed. 'You've got to be fucking kidding me. Who's the lead out there? Can you give me his number?'

'I've been instructed not to give you any information regarding current police operations in that area, Senior Sergeant Norris.' Richie grunted uncomfortably again. 'Your status is listed as inactive in the system, and I've got a note here to say you'll be contacted to give your debrief when—'

Edna picked the phone up and pitched it into Talon's footwell. The boy reached down numbly and ended the call. The car rumbled on, passing the huge, half-eaten carcass of a horse or cow. Yellowed ribs and limp, dusty hooves. A pair of startled ravens hopped out from behind the dead beast as the car passed.

'You know, when I've asked Adelaide for assistance on cases before, it's taken days, sometimes *weeks*, to get help.' Edna gave an angry laugh. 'I had a young guy here who wanted to go get a job in the mines. Had to have a warrant cleared, first. Took three days. I get sacked, however, and it's changed in the system within the hour.'

'You're not sacked-sacked, though, right?' Talon said. 'You told Stevenson that you were just, like, suspended.'

'I don't know, Talon,' Edna sighed. 'It's hard to care right now. Whether I'm operational or not, I'm going to keep looking for Clare Holland. You don't just down tools on a person who could be in grave danger because your boss is a dickhead.'

Another carcass, this one further from the road, being picked at by a pair of wedge-tailed eagles. This time the ravens were standing off to the side, not game to tango with the bigger birds of prey, waiting indignantly for their turn.

'The determination Garreth Holland displayed to get me off this case, after I asked him some uncomfortable questions about what happened between him and his wife, tells me something,' Edna went on. 'It tells me I need to be there when she's found. Because we might have to protect this woman as much from her husband as we do from Buck.'

'Do you think Clare was the one who shot him?'

'I can only guess,' Edna said. 'But why else would he be hiding his injury?'

'How do you know it's a gunshot wound, anyway?'

'The tweezers. Stevie said he got gauze, meds, a sewing kit and tweezers. I'm assuming he's not tidying up his monobrow right now. He'll be pulled off the side of the road somewhere removing a bullet and stitching himself up. But again, I'm only guessing.'

'A lot of guesswork in this job.'

'Sure is.'

A silence ballooned inside the car, heavy with potential. Edna waited, knowing what was coming.

'Why was it so easy for you to *get* sacked?'

'Talon, I let you steal my police car.'

'Yeah, but—'

'You mean, what did Garreth find out, when he called around about me?' Edna kept her eyes on the road.

'You don't have to tell me.' Talon gave a supposedly nonchalant shrug, but when Edna looked, the kid was watching her out of the corner of his eye.

'I took someone in,' Edna relented. 'Someone who needed help.'

'And it went bad.'

'Real bad.'

'How?'

Edna wiped sweat from her neck into the collar of her uniform shirt. She dialled the aircon up. 'It was a difficult time in my life. Things were very heavy at work. I'd been a witness to something while I was out on duty one night, responding to a fight at a nightclub. I saw a woman getting in the car with a known gangster scumbag. She was never seen again. I was supposed to go to court at the end of the year to say what I'd seen. Get up on the witness stand. And I was going to be a pretty credible witness. Because, you know, I was a cop.'

The boy watched her, listening.

'So it was stressful, is what I'm saying.' Edna took a deep breath, trying to alleviate some of the tightness in her chest. 'The gangster creep was having his cronies threaten me. Sending me awful messages at work, watching me walk to my car at night. And I was starting to doubt what I'd seen. I'd also just split with my second husband, so I'd moved house. I was living out of boxes because between the court case and my day job I could never find any time to unpack. I was working under a guy who hated my guts and always had. Not for any particular reason. Just didn't like the look of my face, I guess.'

'Okay.'

'So my . . . My decision-making powers weren't at their best.'

Talon nodded like he understood.

'One night, a girl turned up,' Edna said. 'A drug addict. She was homeless and out of touch with reality. There were a hundred things I could have done with her, including just shuffling her on from where I found her and letting her fend for herself. Because, as it was rightly pointed out to me later, she was not my responsibility.'

Talon chewed his lip.

'But I chose to *make* her my responsibility.' Edna struggled to get the words out. They were like rocks tumbling up her throat. She paused, and in the awful pause, the boy spoke.

'Why?'

'I don't know why, exactly.' Edna shook her head. 'Or maybe I do. I've just always been like that. When I was a kid I brought home wild animals. When I was in high school I made my house a sanctuary for outcasts. Goths. Losers. Bad kids. I had a string of boyfriends at uni who I thought I was saving. Fixer-uppers. Bad boys. It drove my mum nuts, all this mothering I was trying to do. Because it never ended well. The animals scratched and bit me. The loser kids stole my CDs. The bad boys took me for all I had, emotionally and financially. Mum used to say she couldn't wait until I was old enough to have a kid of my own so I could get over this *thing* that I had with needing to care for someone. But that wasn't meant to be, I would find out.'

Edna swiped at her eyes. Talon's discomfort was radiating off him like a heat. Despite it all, he reached over and patted her knee quickly and stiffly. Edna laughed.

'Thanks.'

'It's okay.'

'So anyway, yeah. My partner read out Alicia's date of birth in the cruiser. She was born the same year that I miscarried for the first time,' Edna said.

'You thought it was like, a sign?' Talon said.

'There are no signs.' Edna gripped the wheel. 'There are just good decisions, bad decisions, and consequences.'

Edna lost herself in memories of that night. Of arriving home at 1 a.m. fully expecting to find her front door swinging open, the rain coming in, her laptop, jewellery, pushbike and the girl, Alicia, missing in action. When she'd found the door closed, her next assumption had been that the girl was too whacked to make it inside and had given up and tottered off elsewhere. Edna had checked her phone as she fished for the spare key under the mat and saw that an Uber had indeed picked someone up at the spot in Norwood where she and Gaz had discovered Alicia, and that vehicle had driven to the very place where Edna now stood. She went inside and closed herself in pitch-blackness, noting every blind and curtain on the ground floor had been pulled closed.

She was snapped out of her reverie by the phone ringing in the cupholder where Talon had placed it. Edna picked it up and put it to her ear. 'Stevie.'

'Ed, I'm halfway back to Buck's car.' Stevenson gave a hard sigh. 'I'm gonna need you to turn around and come get me.'

'Why?'

'Because the cruiser just fucking blew something, that's why.'

Edna slowed the Range Rover. 'What do you mean? You blew a tyre?'

'No, it's engine related. I have no idea.' Edna heard Stevenson open her door. 'I heard a big bang, and now I got steam coming out from under the bonnet. It'll be too hot to do a diagnosis and I'm too annoyed, anyway. Will you just come and get me?'

'But—'

'I got other news for you, which you can chew on while you drive back.' Edna heard footsteps crunching in the dry desert gravel. 'Rick called me. Wanted to know why he's being told not to talk to you about the case.'

Edna pulled over completely, tried to settle the thumping of her heart in her throat.

'I didn't get into all that with him,' Stevenson went on. 'But he says the body from beside Buck's car has got a tattoo on it.

Noticed it while he was putting the mystery dude on ice. He thought it might help us identify him faster than a print search.'

'Stevie, forget that. Tell me about the car,' Edna said, her instincts twitching, skin prickling with dreadful foreboding. 'What's going on? That car was only serviced last month.'

'I have no idea, Ed. I'm not gonna lift the bonnet. I told you; it's too hot,' Stevenson snapped. 'I'm trying to tell you about this tattoo. It's a memorial tattoo. Says "Lippo". There are dates. Rick says he's gonna send a pic.'

Edna felt suddenly colder than the Range Rover's aircon could ever make her. Stevenson's words were sliding across the surface of her mind, finding no traction on the icy certainty. Talon's face was taut. Edna realised she was gripping his forearm with her free hand, her nails biting into his skin. 'Stevie, I really feel like you better—'

A sound like thunder splitting the air crackled over the line.

'Shit!' Stevie's voice was distant. 'What the fu—'

'Stevie!' Edna used all the air in her lungs to cry her partner's name. She had to gasp to speak again. 'Stevie, get back in the car!'

CHAPTER 28

'You can take your jackets off, you know,' Daisy said. She was standing in the entryway to the kitchen, keeping an eye on a pot of what smelt to Harvey like corn on the cob. 'Just take a load off.'

'You know what, I might just keep mine on.' Clare's smile was hard as she sat beside Harvey, smoothed down the front of the bulky garment. 'The aircon in the car doesn't work. We've been on the road since daybreak. I smell awful. I'm sure he's worse. Right, babe?' She slapped his chest. Harvey's mind was still entangled in visions of explosion. Fire. Mayhem. Pain. Children screaming. He flinched too hard, and the little boy frowned deeper.

'She's right.'

'What are you doing out here, anyway?' Daisy asked, disappearing into the kitchen. Harvey heard a wooden spoon on the edge of a pot. The woman's voice travelled from where she cooked. 'You're a hell of a long way from anywhere.'

'His mother's got a property east of here. A, uh . . . a cattle farm. Like this one.'

'East of here?' Daisy reappeared in the doorway. 'What, Durham?'

'A little beyond that.' Clare nudged Harvey's knee with hers.

'The Wakefield place?' Daisy looked at Harvey, eyes wandering over his face. 'Your mum's Georgette Wakefield, is she?'

'No,' Harvey managed. 'It's a little further out than that.'

Daisy cocked her head. '*East* of the Wakefield farm? There's nothing east of there but crown land. Not a blade of grass on it. Not until you get to – Jesus – Wyandra, I suppose.'

'Clare's being generous when she says it's a cattle farm.' Harvey tried to get his head in the game. 'It's a hobby farm. I'm pretty sure she's down to one cow.'

'I had no idea anyone lived out there.'

'You'd never know the property is there. It's tiny.'

'Well, you're a good son to drive all the way out to see her.' Daisy glanced at the food on the table, pointed the spoon at Harvey accusingly. 'Have something to eat, will you? I feel weird having guests sitting at my table staring at the food. There's plenty to go around.'

'Where's my corn?' the boy demanded, having given up on his analysis of Harvey.

'Hold on to your hat, will you?'

'You can have some of Belle's lunch,' the little girl beside Harvey piped up. He looked down and copped a face full of impish delight by his side. The child pointed at the mess the baby was making at the highchair. 'She spreads it everywhere but she never eats it.'

'I'm sure I've been offered worse.'

'Guess what, also?'

'What?'

'After this there's ice cream.'

'What flavour?'

'Banana.'

Harvey slapped his palms down on the table. 'Why the *hell* are we eating this healthy stuff when there's banana ice cream in the house?'

The child giggled.

'Don't encourage her,' Daisy called.

Harvey felt new sweat bead on his brow. The tiny foray into the humorous had been about all he could manage. There was numbness from his neck down, his body's revulsion against what he now was; a walking, talking death robot mounted with his own head. He reached out unsteadily and poured himself a glass of water from the jug sitting in the middle of the table. The girl watched him curiously.

'How old's your little sister?' Harvey asked.

'She's one. I'm six. Larson is seven.'

'And what's your name?'

'Frannie.'

'What's wrong with your car?' Larson, also, only had eyes for Harvey.

'I'm not exactly sure,' Harvey said.

'Is it just the air conditioning?' The boy picked his teeth with his fork, a tiny mechanic pondering an anecdotal diagnosis. 'Because you can still drive without air conditioning, you know. You just have to roll the windows down.'

'The brakes are faulty,' Clare blurted out. Seemed to regret it immediately.

'You drove out here with no brakes?' the boy said, incredulous.

'Not *no* brakes,' Harvey eased a quiet sigh. '*Faulty* brakes. We can stop but it just . . . takes an effort.'

'Well, that's weird.' Larson put the fork down. 'How are you gonna fix that? Do you have any tools?'

'I don't. And I don't know how I'm going to fix it, little man.' Harvey willed the child to be quiet with every fibre of his being. 'I'm at a loss as to what to do, at the moment.'

'My dad could probably fix it.'

'He'll be here in a sec,' Daisy called from the kitchen.

Clare leant into Harvey, rubbed his chest as though gently consoling him on his failure to know what to do with their troublesome vehicle. Her murmur in his ear was whisper-quiet as she straightened. 'Please tell me what the fuck we're doing here.'

'*You're getting water.*' Darryl's voice came down the line, crackling in Harvey's ears. '*Tell the bitch to drink up. It's her fault you're here.*'

'So, let me get this straight,' Harvey said to the little girl at his side. He pointed to the children in turn. 'You're six. He's seven. And li'l bubby here, she's one year old?'

'Seventeen months,' the girl said proudly.

'Ah, children,' Harvey said pointedly. 'So small. So innocent.'

'*If you're trying to guilt-trip us, Buck, forget it,*' Tizza said. '*Whichever one of these hillbilly fucks is about to die, it's on you and no one else.*'

Harvey wanted to scream about how little sense that made, but the men carried on. He couldn't tell whether they meant to broadcast their conversation to him, or if the mic was still malfunctioning.

'*The baby makes the most sense,*' Darryl said.

'*Shiiiiit, man.*' Tizza laughed. '*That's cold.*'

'*Take all the emotion out of it. If Buck chooses the father, he devastates the family financially. Daddy's the one who's out there working the farm. Keeping the money rolling in.'*

'*Why not the wife, then?*'

'*Same problem. In a purely economic sense, you take the mother out of the equation, and you've got to replace her, either with a nanny or another family member. And if Buck chooses the wife, he'll put a massive dent in Dad's productivity while the guy grieves. The smallest kid has been around the least amount of time. The grief period for both parents will be shorter than it would be for either of the others.*'

'*You think?*'

'*The kid's probably an accident, anyway. Look at the age gap between her and the other two.*'

'*Okay, but how's Buck gonna grab that baby and run out of there without the whole family trailing behind him?*'

'*That's his problem,*' Darryl said. '*Not mine.*'

'You guys ever just wonder, what the hell are we *doing* here?' Clare widened her eyes at Harvey, gave a dramatic shrug. Her voice was high, attempting to be light and playful, but her hostility weighed it down. 'What quirk of the universe brought us into the company of such *delightful little children*?'

'*Tell her, Buck,*' Darryl said. '*Tell her the mission.*'

The children started chattering among themselves. About the universe. About what the hell a 'quirk' was. Harvey heard a door open in the kitchen, a man's voice. A kiss and a greeting.

He leant into Clare, swung an arm around her, kissed her temple. 'We have to pick someone,' he murmured.

'For what?' she asked. Harvey didn't answer. Just waited. Clare seemed to shrink against him. 'Oh, Jesus, Harvey. *Jesus.* No. We can't. We can't. We *can't*!'

CHAPTER 29

They rode in thundering silence, Talon gripping Edna's phone, dialling Stevie's number unsuccessfully, over and over. Edna had her hands clamped on the wheel. The rush of the tyres on the crumbling desert floor and the roar of the engine was all she could focus on, noting to herself how much that vibrating hum sounded like the ocean, or the wind through a tunnel, or the whooshing of blood in her ears. Because beyond that level of thought lay a soul-destroying certainty about what she would encounter when she arrived at the cruiser. She could do nothing more than drive, and think surface thoughts, and wait, as the minutes turned to seconds, and seconds turned to moments, pages of unerasable horror she couldn't prevent from turning. This moment, now, as she spied the cruiser for the first time, sitting out in the middle of nowhere, tyres planted firmly on an invisible trail, slashing menace through the outback the way veins forged their vital paths under skin. This moment, now, as she parked and got out of the Range Rover fifty metres from the cruiser, hearing her own words to the boy that very morning about cars stopped in the desert with their doors hanging open.

Death was here. She could smell him. Talon went to Stevie where she lay on her stomach at the back of the vehicle, touched the nape of her neck, shaking fingers reeling back from the mess that lay higher than that still-preserved patch of tender skin as though the boy could feel the heat of the bullet that made it. Edna looked at the body, told herself to think about roadkill, and crime scenes, and marking distances and positions of objects in her mind, and not Stevie. Because she couldn't bear to think of Stevenson being dead. Culled like a kangaroo and left on the baking red sand to be discovered by lucky birds of prey.

Talon was swiping the flies away from the body. Edna saw them crawling on a shoeprint of blood near the rear tyre of the car. She glanced at the tooth-like hills, but whoever had shot Stevenson and then come to the scene and stepped in her blood was long gone now. The bullet hole in the front wing panel of the car was leaking smoke or steam. Edna walked there, reached out and put her finger on it, plugged it, felt the pressure. She wondered where the bullet hole in Clare Holland's car had been in relation to this one. Whoever shot Clare's moving vehicle had not only caused her to stop and get out, as intended, but had ignited something in the engine that set the whole vehicle alight. He hadn't been so lucky here. Neither had Stevie. Edna got her phone out and snapped a shot of the bullet hole and the shoeprint and didn't realise there were tears on her face until one dropped onto the back of her hand.

'Where's her phone?' Talon asked. His voice was heavy, shoulders high as he rose. 'All the car doors are open. He must have come here looking for something.'

Edna dialled Stevie's number. Half-expected her to pick up. Because that couldn't be her on the ground. She was too vital.

Too loud. Full of movement. Whoever lay headless in the dust in their blood-spattered police uniform had been killable. Stevie was not.

The phone was ringing down the line. Edna listened. There was no vibration sound near the body. Edna didn't want to go there, to fish around in Stevie's pockets like she was a victim.

'She put it on silent sometimes.' Edna wiped her face. 'Forgets to take it back off.'

Talon's eyes wandered the dirt as he listened. He went to the other side of the car, stuck his head in, froze. Then he picked up the phone and righted himself, showed it to Edna. The screen showed her call.

'It's right here. It was in the centre console.'

'What?'

'It was just lying here in full view.'

'So what was he looking for, then?' Edna asked. She stepped over to the vehicle. Thought about Clare Holland in the desert. The High Wire. Her car being tracked along it by a rifle scope in the darkness. No one out there hearing the shot, the sound echoing out across the empty plains.

'How did he know where she was?' Edna asked. Talon didn't answer. 'Holland. He went after Clare. I asked him how he knew she took the High Wire. If he downloaded a tracking app on her phone. But maybe I was almost right, just not right enough. Because if he did what he's done here, and shot her vehicle to stop her, make her get out so that he could . . . Then he'd have had to know *exactly* where she was, whether she had her phone switched on or not. Whether she had reception or not. Could a tracking app on her phone do all that? Or are we talking about something that's bigger. More reliable. Something that's—'

'That's an external piece of equipment,' Talon said. 'A unit on its own.'

Edna and Talon dropped to look under the vehicle at the same time. It was what saved their lives. The sonic crack as a bullet split the sound barrier right beside Edna's head made her eardrum pulse. Directly after it, she heard the boom on the horizon. Talon flattened against the earth, Edna with him, the two of them gripping the dirt, willing the shot to have been a figment of their shattered imaginations. Because this wasn't happening. This wasn't possible. Edna in the open like this, being hunted like an animal, a teenager she hardly knew cowering against her side, her partner dead in the dirt. Edna was suddenly breathing through a throat clamped in iron. To swallow felt like taking a punch. Another shot came, whining off the rear of the car. Talon jolted in the dirt.

'Oh god!' the boy howled, gripping his arm. 'I've been shot. I've been shot! I've been shot!'

'Get up!' Edna clawed at him. 'We gotta go!'

The shots were coming from the direction of the Range Rover, the low hills they'd passed through to reach Stevie's cruiser. Edna saw a sparkle of white light, heard the crack, then the boom. Talon leant against the car, took his hand away from the wound. Blood, thin, running freely in rivulets down his elbow, dripping into the red soil, painted solidly across his palm. They crab-walked to the front of the car, hugged the warm bonnet. Some detached part of Edna's mind marvelled at how she was already printed and smeared with the boy's blood. She didn't remember touching him after the shot. They huddled, shoulder to shoulder, waiting for the next shot. None came.

'I can't believe I've been shot. I can't believe it. I can't believe it.'

'You're gonna be okay. We both are.'

'*How?*'

'We know where he is. He's in those hills there. Look at the angle of the shot that took out the engine. Okay? Okay? Look at Stevie's body. He shot the car as it passed through those hills. It rolled to a stop where it is now. Then he sat and waited for us. Look, you can tell.'

'Okay,' the boy puffed. 'Okay.'

'If we run this way, and keep low, we can make it below that rise and we'll be out of range.'

'We gotta run?'

'We can't get back in our car right now. He'll light it up. We're a much harder target out in the open.'

The right-hand side mirror of the car exploded. Talon and Edna cowered, listened to the boom a second later.

'We need to get Stevie's gun,' Talon said.

'Not worth it.'

'What if he comes?'

'He's too far out. If he tries to come in to finish us off, he'll have to drive. He can't drive and fire at the same time.'

'What if there's two of them?' Talon tried to check the wound again. Gagged at the sight of the blood now soaking his lower arm. 'What if – What if he circles around? He could use those hills as cover to get a new angle on us.'

'Talon. Talon. Talon.'

'What if—'

'Talon!'

'Okay, I get it.' He let out a low, shuddering breath. 'We

can't think like that. How long until sunset? What if we die out there in the desert?'

'The search team from Buck's car will have choppers out doing a grid. They might even have drones. And someone else could come along from Cooper Creek any minute.'

The boy looked doubtful. The sun beat on the top of Edna's head, fingers gripping her skull.

'Get ready,' she told the boy. Talon came up into a crouch, braced his fingers against the gravel, an Olympic sprinter listening for the starting gun.

'Go!' Edna said.

CHAPTER 30

A man appeared in the kitchen doorway, burly and thick through the middle, short dark hair plastered to his head in the shape of a hat. Harvey could see the dirt under his nails and dusted through the hairs on his forearms from across the room. The bigger kids looked at him, while the baby sucked spaghetti sauce off her wrist.

'Where's! My! Corn!' the boy howled.

'Oi! Whatever happened to "hello"?' the man asked, gently scuffing the boy's head as he went by. He reached a hand across the table to grip and pump Harvey's. Hard, dry calluses. 'G'day, mate. Lenny. The missus says you're in from the wilds with a broke-down car.'

'John,' Harvey replied. He gestured to Clare, who was gripping the edge of the table, staring at a bowl of salad, shell-shocked. 'This is Sally.'

'*Pleased to meet you.*' Harvey could hear Tizza's smile. '*We'll be your murderers today.*'

'What's the problem with the car?'

'Brakes,' Harvey said.

'Well, I'm not the handiest bloke in the world with that

sort of thing,' Lenny said. 'It might be that me eyeballing the problem would be as good as you doing it yourself.'

'I could take a look,' the boy suggested.

'Could you, mate?' Lenny reached over and covered the entire crown of the child's head in his hand, gave it a playful shake. 'Thanks. That'll save me going back out into the heat.'

Daisy came in with the corn, scooped a cob out of the pot so that it fell steaming onto the boy's plate. 'Here you go, Mr Impatient.'

The boy rolled the corn into the centre of his plate.

'Tha . . .?' Daisy prompted. The boy didn't react. She nudged him with her hip. 'Tha . . .? *Tha . . .?*'

'Thank you!'

'That's right.'

'Now I need butter!'

'Oh, god. Yes, yes, hang on.' Daisy huffed a huge sigh and went back to the kitchen.

'You're not eating anything,' the girl said to Harvey. She took a bread roll and tore it in half. There was a transparent container full of beads at her elbow. Harvey moved the container as the kid's preparation of her roll scattered crumbs in with the beads. 'Aren't you hungry?'

'I'm okay,' Harvey said.

'Mum, I need the butter!'

'No, I need it!' the boy yelped. 'I said so first!'

'Kids, eh?' Lenny poured himself a large glass of water. He looked at Clare, who was staring at her plate. 'You got any?'

'No.' Clare's voice was flat.

'Well, they'll give you the runaround, that's for sure.' Lenny gulped the water. 'Can't live with 'em. Can't live without 'em.'

Clare gagged, threw a hand to her mouth. 'Oh, god. I need some air.'

'*Don't let her out of your sight, Buck.*' Darryl's voice was sharp. '*She tries to leave a cute little message somewhere, or get to a phone, and we'll take you all out.*'

'Just stand out on the verandah for a sec.' Harvey caught Clare at the front door, helped her through it. 'You're just feeling the heat.'

'*I think it's your turn to feel the heat, Bucko,*' Tizza said. '*This whole thing is really adorable, but we're not here to play happy families. You've got two minutes to pick someone and bring them out here to us.*'

'*Time starts now,*' Darryl added.

Harvey went out onto the verandah with Clare, wiped the sweat pouring down her temples into her hair, because he couldn't so much as lift her shirt or his to mop her brow. Her breath was coming in short huffs. He held her face and stepped close, his skin alive with terror, prickling as he pulled her into a hug. 'They're giving us two minutes.'

'We can't *do* this!'

'Well, we can't not do it, either.'

Clare turned, looked at the gravel drive leading away from the house. 'We can run. Right now. Let's go. Even if they blow us, we won't be hurting anybody else.'

'*Step off that verandah and I'll pull the trigger, Buck,*' Darryl said. '*I swear to god.*'

'That won't work.' Harvey put an arm around Clare's shoulder. 'Just leave this to me.'

He was suddenly back in Afghanistan, making decisions for his section that would leave his men the opportunity gifted to so many takers of lives in combat. *I was only following orders.* 'It's my choice. Okay? I have to take the father.'

Clare was staring at his eyes, pleading with him for there to be some other answer to all this. But there was not. Harvey had already done all those wretched calculations, even before Darryl and Tizza had weighed the infant's life like a pound of mincemeat. Yes, taking the baby made sense on paper, where reactions could be plotted and behaviour charted like sharemarket holdings. Projected output, minus grief period, minus funeral costs. Harvey was also cognisant of the fact that little Belle – sister of Frannie, sister of Larson, daughter of Lenny and Daisy, seventeen-month-old destroyer of spaghetti – wouldn't know what was coming. When Harvey got Lenny around the bend, and he laid eyes on Darryl and Tizza, he'd know. He'd feel it in the air. Belle would know something was wrong, sure. But she wouldn't know that death himself had finally come knocking.

'You okay?' Daisy's eyes were full of worry as Harvey and Clare returned to their seats. 'You should eat something. When it's dry like this, my stomach always plays up.'

'Mine too,' Frannie said gravely. She'd gone back to her beads, was threading them onto a piece of translucent nylon, making a rainbow. Harvey sat down beside her, looked at the craft supplies spread everywhere. Considered that, indeed, it would be smart for him to eat. Clare too. But neither had made a move to do so. To eat, in this moment, seemed absurd. Instead, he picked up the scissors that were lying beside the pack of beads.

'*Drop the scissors, Buck,*' Darryl said. '*And I see pens in the centre of the table. Forget about them, too.*'

'I *said*, my tummy plays up, as well!'

'You gotta stay hydrated,' Harvey said to the girl absentmindedly.

'My teacher says you have to drink eight glasses of water a day.'

Harvey took a piece of the nylon from a coil in one of the container's segments, started threading beads. He was willing himself to say the words, to remove this father from his family's lives, permanently.

'Listen,' Harvey said to Frannie, 'would you mind if I borrowed your dad for a minute or two to come look at my car? I know you're right in the middle of lunch—'

'*Forty seconds, Buck.*'

'—but we shouldn't be long.'

'I want to come, too,' the boy whined.

'It's too hot out, mate.' Lenny patted the boy's hand.

'I hope you don't mind.' Harvey tied the string of beads he'd been making around the little girl's wrist. Made a triple reef knot. 'We're just so keen to get to my mother's. She's been unwell, herself.'

'It's okay.' Frannie smiled.

Harvey looked her in the eyes. Her big, unknowing, chocolate brown eyes. 'I'm sorry that I have to do this.'

The girl shrugged.

'No worries, mate.' Lenny rose. 'We'll be back in a jiffy. Like I said – I reckon I won't be of any help. You'll probably still be here six hours from now waiting on the NRMA.'

'*Twenty seconds. Move it, Bucko.*'

'Come on, Sally.' Harvey looped an arm around Clare's waist. She got out of her chair weakly, walked hunched to the head of the table. 'We have to go.'

'See ya, kids.' Lenny waved.

'*Ten seconds,*' Tizza said.

Lenny was holding open the verandah door. Harvey felt Clare shrink as they approached. Then she twisted in his arm at the sound of a screen door flapping closed somewhere behind them. Harvey turned and saw an older man standing in the kitchen doorway before Daisy.

'Where the hell do you think you're going?'

Harvey and Clare froze. So did the children. From the corner of his eye, Harvey saw Frannie slide off her seat and retreat into the living room, taking her bread roll and beads with her. Larson was bent over his corn, eyes downcast. Even the baby started fussing. Daisy went over and lifted the sticky, squawking mess out of her highchair.

'Dad, this is John and Sally.' Lenny gestured to them. 'They broke down at the bottom of the hill. I was just gonna go take a look at their car.'

'In the middle of lunch?' The man took Harvey in. Gave him a real once-over, an assessment Harvey had endured plenty of times, in bar rooms and dark parking lots, the occasional late-night petrol station stop. Places where violent men sniffed around for trouble and seemed to catch its scent on Harvey's skin. 'You kidding me?'

Harvey did what he usually did. Held the guy's eyes. Said nothing.

'I've been out there on the land with this idiot for the better half of the day.' The older man dragged a sun-fried hat off his head. He was definitely Lenny's father. The same bulbous nose. Close-set eyes. The plastered, hat-shaped hair. 'I'm starving. Not only have you lot started without me, which was a cardinal sin in my household, but you're about to take off, Lenny, with a pair of blow-ins?'

Harvey slid his eyes to Clare. She was already watching him, her mouth hard and downturned.

'The guy's on his way out past Wyandra to see his sick mother. Been on the road all day. And this one's not feeling her best with the heat.' Lenny waved at Harvey, then at Clare. 'Least I can do is take a quick look at the car, Dad. Might be able to get them on their way. Lunch'll keep.'

'Will it?' Lenny's father put his knuckles on his hips. 'Shit. I wish you'd had this level of energy out there in the truck, Len. We might have been done with lunch an hour ago and been watching the cricket with our feet up.'

'Just take it down a notch, will you, Warren?' Daisy sighed as she went past. 'You're making the guests uncomfortable.'

'Isn't it "guests" when they're invited and "intruders" when you're not?'

'Maybe you should just go back to your lunch, Lenny.' Clare put a hand on the big man's arm. 'Your father's right. We've been really rude, barging in like this.'

'Too right.' Warren took hold of a chair at the head of the table.

'And you said you didn't know much about engines, anyway.' Clare's eyes sparkled with dark energy. Harvey felt a turning in the pit of his stomach.

'Him?' Warren snorted. 'Oh, Jesus. You wouldn't trust this bonehead to change the batteries in your TV remote. Cows is his talent, isn't it, Len?' Warren dragged the chair out and sat down. 'They're on the same level, Len and cows. Speak the same language.'

'Is it too early for a beer?' Lenny sighed and made for the kitchen.

'It's probably best if no one examines the car, babe.' Clare took Harvey's hand. 'You get that kind of thing wrong and you can end up with more damage than you started with.'

'What's the problem?' Warren asked.

'Brakes,' Clare answered.

'Thanks, genius.' Warren poured himself a water. 'What about them? Are they sticking? Are they twitchy? Are they dragging on the ground behind the car on a fucking cable?'

'They're weak,' Harvey answered. 'Lacking pressure. I put my foot down, don't get any traction until halfway down the shaft. It's getting worse the longer we drive.'

'Uh-huh.' Warren sipped his water. 'Smell of rubber burning, too? Puff of smoke when you really slam it on?'

'Yep.'

'The pads are getting jammed,' the old man said. 'They're not unclamping from the rotor when you take your foot off the pedal. What kind of car is it? Piece of Jap shit, I'm guessing.'

'Mazda 6,' Harvey lied, nodding.

'The air conditioning doesn't work, either,' Larson said, his voice full of scandal.

Warren gave a dramatic sigh and slid the chair out so that it groaned loudly against the floorboards. He waved impatiently at the door behind Harvey and Clare. 'Show me the fuckin' thing.'

'It's fine, really—' Clare started.

'No, no, no. Lunch'll keep, apparently.' Warren sneered. 'Not that anyone cares when I eat anyway.'

Harvey took a look around the room, at Lenny and Daisy standing in the kitchen doorway, the infant on her hip, a beer in his hand. He met eyes with Larson at the table full of picked-at food, and Frannie sprawled on her belly in the distant living room, sorting through her beads. The family looked expectant, and tired, and whole. Harvey held open the door for Warren, and the old man walked out. His muscles locked tight with a weird mixture of anticipated relief and soul-crushing dread. Harvey followed Clare out, and then began to close the door.

'I'm coming, too!' Larson called.

Harvey felt the cold hand of horror on the back of his neck. Sweat erupted there, icy, prickling. 'No, no, little mate, just sit and eat your lunch.'

'Let him come,' Warren barked, still walking. 'The boy could use a life lesson.'

2018

Edna opened the door to interview room eight and paused, her brain taking long, arduous seconds to compute what she was seeing. To overlay it against what she'd expected. She had been told that a repeat break-and-enter artist would be in the room, with his lawyer. Edna was so accustomed to seeing the career offender Jason Doltt around the station, she was carrying the bag of chicken-flavoured Twisties he routinely asked for upon arrest by her side. But Doltt was not in the room. Nor was his lawyer. Instead, Gene Gordon was there on one side of the table, with her boss, Chief Inspector Oscar McEvoy, on the other.

She sat beside Gordon, put the Twisties down, her stomach plunging and neck beginning to flame. McEvoy had a notepad in front of him. In it were words scrawled in his tiny, scratchy handwriting. Edna had noted McEvoy's chicken-scratch penmanship before, resented how it resembled the softness with which he spoke; neither being an accidental fluke of his personality, she was sure, but a deliberate strategy to make people uncomfortable. To make them work to understand him. There were many words in the notepad. Edna glanced over. Gordon's coffee mug was almost empty.

McEvoy looked at the notepad, said nothing, his hand resting lightly on the table beside it. Edna sat and sweated and willed herself not to give in and ask what this was all about.

'Alicia Kleinmann,' McEvoy finally said.

Edna looked at Gordon. He was stiff, silent, staring ahead.

'What about her?' Edna asked.

'Describe the nature of your relationship,' McEvoy said.

Edna took her time to answer. The room was so silent, her ears were ringing. There was a scuff mark on the wall just near McEvoy's elbow that was almost certainly a blood smear. A result of an injured suspect being brought in, or police roughhousing, she couldn't tell.

'Platonic,' she said.

'Cut the bullshit, Senior Sergeant Norris.' McEvoy's voice rose a quarter of an octave. Seemed somehow more dangerous. 'Everything is on the line here for you.'

'Why? What's happened?'

'Describe,' McEvoy eased the words out. The hiss of a snake. 'Your relationship.'

'I met Alicia Kleinmann for the first time on the beat.' Edna glanced at Gordon again. 'It was clear to me that she was vulnerable, at risk, and suffering from drug and alcohol dependency. Knowing a housing situation for her on that particular night would be almost impossible to secure, I offered her temporary accommodation at my house.'

'Your personal domicile?' McEvoy asked. 'Where you reside on a permanent basis?'

'Can we – *Jesus* – maybe we can talk about all this without the cop speak.' Edna laughed humourlessly, held her head. '"Domicile"? We talk like fucking robots around here, even when we don't have to.'

'Senior Sergeant Norris.'

'Yes, my house. My house where I live. I gave her a key.'

'You *gave* her a *key*?' McEvoy glanced at Gordon.

'Well, it was that or tell her which window she should climb through.' Edna looked at Gordon, too, who was gently shaking his head. 'It was inappropriate. I get it. What am I looking at, here? A suspension?'

'You met Alicia Kleinmann for the first time three months ago?'

'Yes, that's right.'

'So she's been going back to your apartment frequently, has she? To visit?'

'No, she's been living there,' Edna said.

'*Why?*' McEvoy slammed his hands on the table. His voice was finally at normal angry human being level. Thick, hard, ear-splitting. Edna flinched, opened her mouth to answer, found she couldn't. Because there was no explaining it, not in a way that McEvoy or Gordon would understand, men who came into policing for the age-old clichéd reason that the worst kind of cops did; because they'd been bullied savagely at some point in their lives, and they got addicted to the delicious vengeful power that a police badge gave them. There was no robot speak for what had happened between her and Alicia.

How could she explain that coming home that awful rainy night and finding Alicia Kleinmann asleep on the couch in Edna's study had filled her with a kind of worthiness and purposefulness that was as close as a non-spiritual person could get to the divine? That the days afterwards had passed with an inexplicable ease, in which the girl just . . . *hung around* and Edna just . . . *let her*. Alicia was like happy stray cat, sitting in the newly returned sunshine in Edna's tiny back courtyard, a broad straw Bunnings hat on her head, idly pulling weeds up between the recycled bricks or lying and watching the clouds go by. How could Edna explain that she had been able to *see the girl thinking*, see her unwinding problems in her head, soothing unspoken traumas, finally doing something in her mind, a thing Edna couldn't possibly guess, that she'd never been able to do. That she'd never been offered the time, and security, and silence to do. Edna couldn't even explain to herself why the girl had sweated and shaken and groaned her way past her withdrawals, had discovered strange solace in the contents of Edna's bookcase, could reliably be found lying on that same couch in the study, engrossed in a paperback, her bare legs hanging over the arm of the furniture, kicking and bouncing as she read.

No, it hadn't been sexual. It hadn't been romantic in any regard. Though they'd sat up into the night at the back table, talking and laughing and puzzling over all the ways they were alike – their narcissistic mothers, their terrible taste in men, their desire to be mothers themselves, and the tragedy of that not unfolding like a fairytale the way it seemed to for everyone else – the relationship hadn't turned bad in any of the multitude of ways Edna anticipated that it might. Alicia hadn't made a pass at her, or interpreted something she did as a pass, and there had come no awkward tiptoeing, no door clicking closed in the middle of the night as the girl fled. Alicia hadn't stolen Edna's car, or eaten her out of house and home, or started making gentle inquiries about how much money Edna had in her savings account. She hadn't come in late one night with a thug in silver chains and huge Nikes who decided he also wanted to take advantage of Edna's unspoken hospitality. The girl seemed determined to pay her way, and after weeding, sweeping and scrubbing down the courtyard could be found out there planting and nurturing cuttings she'd taken from a variety of flowers around the neighbourhood in the neglected flowerbeds. The formerly derelict garden seemed a healing place for Alicia. The very morning that Edna had left for the police station, and subsequently been called into this interview, she'd said goodbye to Alicia as the girl crouched by the front steps, planting an old sandstone pot with gardenias she'd nabbed from the next-door neighbours.

Edna explained to McEvoy and Gordon as best she could. The chief made notes, but the emptiness in his eyes told Edna he wasn't picking up the essence of it, just mining what she said for dates, times, physical arrangements.

'She needed help,' Edna said.

'That was not your problem,' McEvoy said. Edna saw real danger in his eyes.

'She's probably ready to go now, anyway,' she said. 'I mean, I haven't raised the idea. But Alicia is clean and sober. She's asked about a job at the cafe at the end of my street. They have a little garden there. If she can stay sober while living outside my home, she might have some chance of getting custody of her daughter, in the long run.'

Neither of the men at the table spoke.

'Her being there did something for me, sir,' Edna said in conclusion. 'And it did something for her, too. It did not start as a . . . a *malignant* arrangement, in any regard. And it did not progress into one, either. It's just something that happened that was good for two people.'

'Until it wasn't,' McEvoy said.

Edna held the edge of the table.

'Senior Sergeant Norris.' The chief put his pen down. 'Two hours ago, officers responded to an incident at your property, in which a woman was shot dead in the front garden. It is believed, from witness accounts, that Alicia Kleinmann was out there gardening, and that she was wearing a large sun hat that shielded her identity from onlookers. She was crouched, shot through the back of the head. Although we're still hunting for suspects, the execution style of the shooting is in keeping with the known techniques of a local organised crime association. At this time, investigators are trying to establish whether this incident may have occurred as a result of your forthcoming involvement as a witness in the case against the leader of that same organised crime association.'

Air wouldn't enter Edna's lungs. She held the table and felt the world tilt around her and tried to breathe.

'We think they were after you, Edna,' McEvoy said. His face was blank. Voice whisper quiet again. 'And they got Alicia instead.'

•

Edna didn't know how long they'd run for. Or how long they'd walked. It seemed within minutes, the backs of her hands were prickling with sunburn, the tips of her ears alight. Some of the blood from the boy's wound had dried, making black forked lightning strikes down his huge arm. Talon walked with his other hand gripping the wound. In a thin slice of shade made from a ragged sandstone boulder, they collapsed wordlessly, panting, wiping sweat. A huge desert honey ant the size of a grape had taken an interest in a spot of blood in the dirt near the boy's shoe. Edna kicked dust at it, before it could get a taste and go tell its brethren. She peeled the boy's fingers back from the wound, finding, as the blood began trickling again, that it was a through-and-through which looked just too small for her to put her index finger into.

'It's not a bullet wound—' Edna started. The boy's head, which had been hanging, snapped around.

'Yes it is. It *must* be.' He gripped the muscle hard. 'I heard the bang. We both did. I've definitely been shot. It was a bullet, no doubt about it. It's probably still in there.'

Edna looked at the boy. His eyes were huge and defiant. Her cop brain was telling her to lay the truth on the young man. That a bullet shot from a rifle across the kind of distance they were dealing with would have done to his arm exactly what it had done to Stevenson's head. There would be no through-and-through about it, no discernible entry or exit wound. They'd be picking up his severed arm and carrying it with them. Edna thought about telling the boy that his wound was almost certainly from a shot ricocheting off the back of the cruiser, kicking up a shard of shrapnel that punched through the front of his biceps and out the back, relatively cleanly. But she didn't. She instead helped the kid peel his shirt off and began folding it into a bandage.

'I was trying to say it's not a bullet wound like I've ever seen before,' she said.

'Why? How do you mean?'

'I mean most people who take a hit like this? This part of the bicep? They're dead inside of five minutes,' Edna said. 'Must have just missed the artery.'

'Jeez, man!'

'Yuh.' Edna wrapped the shirt around the wound. 'You're one lucky kid.'

CHAPTER 31

The old man stopped on the verandah, grabbed an ancient toolbox from where it sat on the edge of a low wooden bench. A screwdriver sat atop the box. Harvey turned away, watched from the corner of his eye as, rather than unclip the clasps on the front of the toolbox and place the screwdriver inside, Warren slipped the tool into his back pocket and snatched the toolbox up by its handle.

'Bloody kids.' Warren spat at the boy. 'Ya never put anything back where it belongs.'

Harvey said nothing.

They walked through the desert, Warren and Larson ahead, Clare and Harvey twenty metres behind. The gentle slope from the family home on the cattle farm felt like a walk down the inside of a volcano. Harvey could feel the heat rising, noxious fumes searing the inside of his nostrils. He was aware that Clare was staring at him, desperate. Ahead of them, the old man and the boy walked silently, two generations a million miles apart.

'Harvey,' Clare whispered. 'Harvey? We can't—'

'I'm thinking. I'm thinking,' Harvey said. There was no sign of the imaginary Mazda 6 at the base of the slope, of course.

The rocky hills that hugged the truck, a couple of hundred metres from the mailbox at the end of the drive, were growing larger. Harvey chewed his lip and turned, saw the little family home growing smaller. His heartbeat was thumping in his temple as the boy turned, apparently abandoning his grandfather's silent company, and approached Clare and Harvey at a jog.

'I'm gonna run this farm when I grow up,' Larson announced.

'Are you?' Clare said. 'That's nice.'

'We have fourteen hundred head of cattle,' the boy recited, beaming.

'More than a few,' Harvey said. They fell into silence, the boy twitchy, still longing for a string of comfortable conversation and banter no one seemed to have on offer today. Harvey knew they were making life difficult for the kid. A friendly, outgoing sprat who just wanted to take advantage of a novelty in his otherwise featureless existence. School. Farm work. Fights with his little sister, episodes of *Spider-Man* or whatever the kids were watching these days. Harvey tried not to think about what was coming for the child. How this apparently amusing interruption in his monotonous life was going to destroy his entire perception of the world. Instead, Harvey grasped desperately for an alternate path, and as his eyes wandered the blistering landscape before them, they actually fixed on something. A spiky desert plant lay off the tyre tracks in the dust ten metres ahead. Harvey glanced at Clare, locked eyes with her, glanced back at the plant, a vicious-looking thing covered in thorns. She nodded. They shifted position, sandwiching the boy between them. Larson was just beginning another bid for conversation with Clare when she jammed her foot in front of his.

'Do you think that maybe when—'

'Whoa!'

Harvey made a motion like he meant to catch the stumbling boy, guided him instead into the spiky plant, and dropped him hard. The boy fell in a heap into the arms of the thorny bush. A gasp. A yowl of pain. Harvey crouched over the child.

'Whoa, little mate! Watch your step!'

'Ow! Shit! *Ow! Ow! Ow!*' The boy let Harvey drag him to his feet, examining his prickled hands and scratched forearms numbly. The scratches, white and searing, began quickly to bleed. The kid's chin tightened and wobbled. 'Ow! Grandpa! I fell!'

'Well, what do you want me to do about it?' The old man stopped briefly, waved dismissively at the boy from his position up ahead. 'You fall on your arse, you don't get a letter from the Queen.'

'Go back up to the house.' Clare wiped at the tears springing in the boy's eyes with the hem of his T-shirt. 'You're okay, honey. You're okay. Go get cleaned up.'

The boy turned and ran. Harvey didn't watch him go. He quickened his pace towards the old man instead, who had just rounded the bend where the truck was hidden.

Darryl and Tizza were standing at the back of the truck, which was closed. At Tizza's feet lay a familiar object. The hard Kevlar and the layers of plastic explosive encased in fabric meaning the vest lay perfectly flat in the dust. Like a display model, laid out for inspection in a shopfront.

Harvey wondered what Warren noticed first about this hell-inspired scene. Would his mind pick at the details – Tizza's split lip, Darryl's black eye, the dark energy in their faces?

Or did those big, unexpected elements consume him first. The truck. The extra people. The gun hanging in Darryl's hand.

Harvey would never know, because Warren stopped dead in front of him and Clare, and simply said, 'What the *fuck*?'

'Put the vest on him, Buck,' Darryl said.

Harvey took off his cap and glasses, tossed them aside, unzipped the jacket and peeled it off. Immediately, he was five degrees cooler. Short-lived relief. Warren just stood there, the toolbox gripped in his fist, the terrified apprentice arriving for his first day. Staring at the gun in Darryl's hand. Harvey supposed it had been a while since the old man had seen a pistol, if ever. It would be all rifles and shotguns out here. Harvey picked up the vest, weighed it in his hands. Tizza, Darryl and Parker had been so consumed with their desire to do all this to him, they'd made three separate vests, just to ensure they would have one that fit his body perfectly.

Harvey stood there and thought about that. About the details. He wondered what ruse Darryl had given Shayna so that he could access her apartment building, get to her front door. Had he had three different ruses ready, in case one failed? The old man's voice, cutting through the heavy silence of a murderous afternoon in the middle of nowhere, pulled Harvey back to reality.

'What the hell is this? Somebody talk to me. Are you guys cops?'

Darryl and Tizza looked at each other, gave surprised laughs. It wasn't a bad guess, Harvey thought. The vest in his hands might have been mistaken for a police officer's bulletproof vest, at a stretch. But there was no police marking on it. And Clare's obvious horror as she stood pacing and shuddering now by the truck unravelled the theory quickly.

'No, mate.' Tizza chuckled at Warren. 'We're not cops.'

'Is this a robbery? Are – Are you out of your fucking minds?'

'The best thing you can do right now,' Harvey said to Warren, 'is try to stay calm.'

'Fuck you.' The old man dropped the toolbox. It banged on the unforgiving earth, things inside it clanking and rattling. He took a step back. 'We don't have anything. Okay? That farm up there is all my family's got. There's no point in all this.'

The old man's eyes were wandering over Harvey's chest. No doubt picking up the shape of the vest pressing against the inside of his T-shirt as he breathed. Harvey lifted the vest, showed it to Warren. 'Put this on, or I'll make you put it on.'

'What is it?'

'Just put it on.'

'No. No. I won't. I'm not doin' anything like tha—'

Harvey moved forward, closed the distance between him and Warren in one large step. In the same motion, he let the vest swing away to his left, while he drew his right arm back for a massive punch to the old man's face. His goal had been to knock the guy out cold, before he had a chance to think more about what was going to happen to him. The vests. The gun. The truck. Clare standing nearby, her hand over her mouth, tears of horror running down her cheeks. Harvey gave it all he had. Wanted to spare the man that fear. But Harvey was tired, and Warren had an outback farmer's brain; scorched by sun and dry air, mottled with decades of dread and foreboding about cattle disease, drought, flood, fire, locust, loneliness, the inevitable creeping in of dementia, the allure of the trusty shotgun in the shed. Warren's head snapped back, and his knees went, and Harvey got down over him in the dirt and flipped him onto his stomach and dragged the vest onto his thin, hard torso and zipped it up the spine.

Then he hooked his fingers into the nape of the vest's neck and yanked the old man to his feet, because he knew that if Warren had been given the chance to sit down and discuss his own murder, one of the main negotiation points would have been dying that way. Standing tall. Harvey shoved the old man back towards the farmhouse to get him going. 'Run,' Harvey said.

Warren looked back, his eyes wild, and then he started trotting unsteadily away. He thought about the farmhouse. Then banked left and made for the empty horizon.

Harvey went to Clare. Held her against his chest, with her head tucked into the hollow of his shoulder, seeking shelter in the very same style of explosive garment that could turn them both to pulp at any second, the way it was about to do to an innocent old man. A father. A grandfather. A curmudgeonly coot, bringer of awkwardness and shame and dismay to his family, frightener of children, bully of men. Harvey had held on so tight to those things about Warren that he hated on sight, but some corner of his mind slumped in sadness now at the possibility, the *probability*, that those things were all wrong. That Warren had simply been stressed, or tired, or hungry, or having a mad morning, and that Harvey was nowhere near knowing or understanding the man he was about to murder, probably never would be.

Tizza smiled. Harvey heard it through his words.

'Three . . .' the small man counted. 'Two . . . One.'

Harvey wished there was some way to cover Clare's ears, to swaddle her completely, take her into himself to shield her against the blast. But when it came, it seemed to shake the entire landscape around them, the thunderstrike echoing out across the plains and rocky hills, causing sand and rocks to tumble down the low hill into the shade beneath the truck, dust swirling around its tyres, around Clare and Harvey where they stood. Harvey felt the heat against his cheeks as he squinted into the light, determined to watch. He felt the electric pulse of nervous energy shoot through him, as he bore witness, not for the first time, to that unholy spectacle: a human life being taken by force. One second, the man named Warren was between Harvey and Tizza and Darryl and Clare where they stood in the curve of the rocky hill, and the edge of nowhere. Then he was in that nowhere. Gone. Replaced by a bloody smear and a hump of flaming meat and a plume of smoke and ash and corrupted air that hung in a dome over the space where he had been.

Harvey saw Darryl extract his hand from the pocket of his jeans.

And he saw Tizza take his hand down from where it had been slipped between the buttons of his shirt.

Harvey let Clare go. She went to a low boulder nearby, crouched by it, and vomited. Harvey gave Darryl and Tizza a look that he hoped made them believe he was unthinkingly consumed with hatred and viciousness, and not icily rehearsing movements in his mind. He walked over to the toolbox Warren had dropped, and just as Harvey knew he would, Tizza stepped forward and intercepted him, bent for the box at the same time, reaching it a good two seconds before Harvey would have. Only Harvey wasn't reaching for the box. He was play-acting, going through the motions, keeping Tizza's eye locked on his left hand, while with his right he slipped his fingers into the waistband of his jeans and brought out the screwdriver he had secreted from Warren's back pocket as he knelt over the man and pulled the vest onto him.

Harvey shot upwards, side-stepped and then entangled Tizza in a bearhug from behind. He reefed the smaller man's head sideways and jammed the screwdriver into his neck.

It was a jailhouse murder. Harvey knew, of course, how to put Tizza down instantly. How to wedge his jugular between the ball of his shoulder and the back of his wrist and turn his lights out before he thrust the screwdriver's blade and shank up and into the pressurised artery. But he didn't do it that way. Harvey jabbed the screwdriver in, hard, once into the internal jugular, yes, but once also into the trachea and once into the carotid triangle, because he wanted to see what he could do with the time it bought him. He wanted it to be a horror show. And it was.

Tizza fell to the ground and twisted and dug his heels into the dirt, a gurgling, howling mess, and Darryl just stood there and watched, stunned, for a good four or five seconds, long enough for Harvey to rip Tizza's shirt open and grab the object at the end of the chain hanging there, to yank it off the smaller man's chest. He didn't look, because he wanted to keep his eyes on Darryl. But he could feel, immediately, that the object was too small to be a detonator. Disappointment washed over him, taking the edge off the adrenaline that kept kicking and kicking from inside him, a beast trying to beat its way out of his insides. He rose slowly to his feet, and with the screwdriver in one fist and the chain in the other he levelled Darryl with his gaze.

'Two down,' Harvey said. 'One to go.'

CHAPTER 32

The scene leader was a woman named Zhang, who was wearing make-up. Edna stood there puzzling over it, the dark rims of the woman's eyes and her perfect mascara, because it was years since she had seen a cop wearing it. But Edna supposed that, before Detective Inspector Luqi Zhang received the news that morning that she'd be heading north in a helicopter to see about some hullabaloo in the middle of Woop Woop, the young woman had risen in her suburban flat outside Adelaide's central business district (or wherever the hell she lived) and put the make-up on, expecting that after work she might do the things that city cops did after a day shift. Meet friends at the pub. Go on a date. Catch a show. The make-up, requiring mild refreshment, would morph from day into nightwear.

Edna, by contrast, would have to drive an hour and a half to attend her local pub, and if that wasn't enough of a turn-off, the chances of running into someone she didn't know at that establishment were akin to zero. She hadn't had a date in the past ten years, and for a show she supposed Alice Springs was her best bet, approximately four hundred and fifty kilometres away.

As much as Edna puzzled over Zhang, Zhang puzzled over her and Talon as they leant against the cruiser that had rescued them out of the desert, a good hour and a half after they waved madly at a drone crossing the sky overhead. The pair were dusty, sunburnt and patched with blood. Talon had his arms folded across his bare barrel chest, the 'gunshot' wound still wrapped in the bandage made from his blood-soaked T-shirt. Cops were manning the command tent that had been set up some distance from Buck's car. They were crossing between the vehicle and the tent behind Zhang and eyeballing the half-naked teen and Edna, murmuring among themselves. Edna guessed there were thirty cops on site, half from Adelaide, half from Alice. Like an approaching storm, Edna could smell journalists on the wind.

'Two of my officers just arrived at the scene you described to me.' Zhang tapped a mobile phone against her thigh. 'They've confirmed what you told me. Your cruiser, the Range Rover and Sergeant Stevenson's body were right where you said they'd be.'

Edna said nothing.

Zhang's eyes were narrow, sceptical. 'Help me understand, again, why you followed Sergeant Stevenson to that site, when you had told her your intention was to continue east from Cooper Creek.'

'She called me,' Edna said. 'Said the cruiser had broken down suddenly. She wanted a ride.'

'And you closed that distance, from approximately ten kilometres outside Cooper Creek to the north-east, to where Stevenson's car was located, west of Cooper Creek, in just fifteen minutes?' Zhang cocked her head.

'That's right.'

'Why were you travelling with such urgency?'

'Because I was certain that the cruiser had not, in fact, broken down,' Edna said, for the third time that evening. 'I felt Stevenson was in grave danger.'

'Explain your reasoning.'

'Explain your reasoning, *please*,' Talon said. Zhang widened her eyes, but didn't look at the boy.

'The cruiser was in good working order,' Edna said. 'She and I had always ensured that. Breaking down can be a death sentence out here.'

'It seems that way.' Zhang gave a stiff nod.

'I held the same belief about Stevenson's car as I did about Clare Holland's car,' Edna said. 'That it had been deliberately compromised. I felt that, just like Clare, Stevie was about to come to harm.'

'She was right,' Talon piped up.

Again, Zhang didn't look at him.

'I am certain that if you examine Clare Holland's car, you'll find it was shot from some distance with a rifle, like Stevie's was,' Edna said. 'The intent, as demonstrated with Stevie, was to get Clare to exit the vehicle so that she could be executed. I believe that, unlike with Stevie, Clare managed to get away before she was killed.'

'Explain your reasoning,' Zhang said again. Edna felt Talon twitch beside her.

'The scene shows Clare was picked up,' Edna said. 'And from the lack of blood at that site, I'd say she wasn't shot.'

'Who was she picked up by?'

'Harvey Michael Buck,' Edna said.

'The bank robber from Cooper Creek?'

'Yes.'

Zhang looked around the camp. The great black dome of night was descending over them, the horizon a flaming golden ring that stretched uninterrupted in every direction. Officers were assembling a light system on a fold-out tripod to cast a white glow over Buck's car and a nearby table, where maps of the region were splayed for grid searches. Whatever answers she'd been searching for as she gazed across the developing crime scene-cum-search base, Zhang didn't seem to find them. She looked as tired as Edna felt.

'I knew it could get kooky out here,' Zhang sighed. 'But this is beyond reason.'

'Whoever shot Clare's car—' Edna began.

'That's not what happened.' Zhang put a hand up. 'Do you have any idea how difficult it would be to shoot a vehicle moving at one hundred kilometres per hour and hit it directly in the engine block from *any* distance? Let alone do it twice in a day? One of those occurrences in the black of night?'

'It would take a lifetime of firearms training,' Edna agreed. 'Perhaps a decades-long career in which weapons handling is commonplace. I would put money on it, that the shooter in both these instances had an interest in guns both on and off the job.'

'You sound like you know the guy,' Zhang said.

'Oh, I do. I believe the shooter was Garreth Holland. Clare's husband.'

Zhang's head dropped, her eyebrows straining into her forehead. 'Excuse me?'

'Garreth—'

'*Commissioner* Holland has been out all afternoon searching the countryside for his missing wife.' Zhang pointed across the campsite. 'He's right over there.'

Edna and Talon looked. In the distance, they could see Holland by the edge of the command tent, a paper cup in his hand. He was on his phone, then scanning the horizon. Edna stuck a hand out as Talon stiffened, made to stride across the camp towards the police commissioner. It was becoming a habit, yanking on his dog chain, an automatic reflex. 'Settle.'

'That arsehole shot me, too, you know,' Talon huffed. 'You get that, right? I've been *shot* with a *bullet*. Do you know how many people I know who have had that happen?'

'I have a feeling you're going to work through the pain of it all, Talon,' Edna said.

'Commissioner Holland,' Zhang interjected, 'has been updating teams on his progress all afternoon, clearing grids in the search pattern.'

'Has he been alone, or with someone else?' Talon asked. Zhang jutted her chin, still refusing to look at the boy.

'With Commissioner Holland's help, we have covered quite a lot of ground,' Zhang said.

'Are you going to double-check those areas?' Talon asked.

Zhang closed her eyes, pressed her mouth shut. Her farcical ignoring of the boy was becoming impossible.

'My colleague asked you a question, Detective Zhang,' Edna said.

'Your *colleague*?'

'*Has* Commissioner Holland been out all afternoon by himself, in his personal vehicle, or *has* he been in the company of other police officers?' Edna said.

'He's been calling in his progress.'

'That's not what you were asked.'

'Nevertheless, it's the answer that I'm offering you, Senior Sergeant Norris.' Zhang was starting to lose it, her whole body trembling gently with fury as she tried to maintain her composure.

'So he's been alone, is what you're saying.' Edna nodded. She looked at Talon. 'He's been keeping in contact with the other search teams by phone, so he can be sure of where everyone else is. Stevenson probably called base, here, to say she was coming in. Holland probably got word of that and he—'

'And he *what*, Senior Sergeant Norris?' Zhang's eyes were wide, challenging. Edna straightened. She never backed down from a challenge.

'And he tracked her, using a device he placed on the cruiser in Cooper Creek. He timed himself carefully, got into position ahead of her, lined her up, and shot her vehicle,' Edna said, loudly and clearly. 'When she got out of the car to check what had happened, he shot her, too.'

'Oh my god.' Zhang pinched the bridge of her nose. 'I didn't just hear that.'

'Then he went to the scene to retrieve his tracker,' Edna continued, 'and he left a shoeprint in her blood. I have that shoeprint photographed. I'd like it checked against the shoes Commissioner Holland is wearing right now.'

Zhang let her hand slap down against her thigh, looked defeated.

'I also want his car confiscated and searched,' Edna said. 'He'll have a rifle somewhere, in the car or secreted away close by. I suggest you have someone watch him for a little while before you arrest him. He won't go back out there unarmed. He'll lead you to the murder weapon first.'

'Senior Sergeant Norris.' Zhang filled her lungs with air, let the words out slowly. 'From what you've told me, your suspicions about Commissioner Holland's involvement in this are based on his being not forthcoming enough for your liking during an unofficial interview you subjected him to and a *chemist's* visit?'

'That's right.'

'In which you ordered your subordinate, the late Sergeant Stevenson, to invade Commissioner Holland's privacy by seeking to know what he purchased, and used that information to make a wild assumption about his current medical condition.'

'He's wounded,' Edna said. 'Probably happened while he was fighting with his wife back in Perth. Before she fled. He also did everything in his power to remove me from this case, starting the moment I began asking him hard questions about his wife, where she went, and how he knew she was out here.'

'Oh, sweet mother of Mary.' Zhang was shaking her head in bewilderment and disappointment, the stunned parent walking in on a child's disorganised bedroom.

'Have you asked him how he knew she was out here?' Edna asked.

'Edna,' Zhang said. 'I'm ordering you to return to your home in Clifton Hills and await a debrief from one of the detectives in my team. Go there now, *please*.'

'I'm a free citizen.' Edna shrugged. 'I can do whatever I want.'

'Your further involvement in this case, or matters relating to it, will be considered an obstruction of police processes,' Zhang said.

'I'll cross that bridge when I come to it, I guess.'

'Get off my crime scene.' Zhang pointed to the newly fallen dark. 'You and your son are not welcome here.'

'Her *son*?' Talon's eyes widened. He looked at Edna. The two of them stood there, silently, their mouths agape. All of the horror and heaviness of the past twenty-four hours seemed to fall on them at once, crushing out all remaining remnants of their sanity. Edna and Talon started laughing. Wearing their cloaks of dirt, and blood, and sweat and sunburn, they continued laughing as Detective Zhang turned and walked away.

CHAPTER 33

They rode for what he guessed later was about three hours. Harvey slept the whole way, Clare in his arms, her back against his chest and her head on his arm. He knew from the temperature drop that the day was wasting away outside. Harvey was still gripping the necklace he'd torn off Tizza as he slowly came to. He lay there, listening to the sound of the truck coming to a stop and Darryl getting out and walking into the wilds. Harvey felt the objects at the end of the chain; two Australian Army dog tags hanging from a little beaded cord. He recognised the octagonal shape of the first, and the sharp, circular shape of the second. He ran a fingertip over the letters stamped into the paper-thin metal, taking his time to pick out each number and letter individually, to be sure of it.

AS
8499099
NJ
TIZZA
RC
AB POS

He ran his finger back up the disc again, over Tizza's blood type to his religion. Roman Catholic. He was surprised, hadn't pegged Tiz as one. He wondered what the Catholics thought about revenge, about the killing of innocent civilians. Then he stopped treading down that extremely dark path and did a big mental about-face and wondered about Tizza in those last moments, gripping his throat, suffocating, staring wild-eyed as Darryl walked up and put the pistol to his forehead. Maybe Harvey had imagined it, but he thought his two captors might have shared a look then. A promise, silently made, silently understood.

Harvey thought about Tizza as he had known him before all of this, bent over his sewing machine on the base, headphones clamped to his ears. He wondered just how deeply the man had become involved in the plotting and planning of the massacre of Harvey's section, of the men in the other vehicles, or whether he'd been told some of the plan and not all of it. In the shipping containers, Darryl, Tizza and Parker had all insisted, once Harvey broke them, that they'd been led to believe the plan would involve only one casualty. Sheerwater. The potential Taliban hostage. Harvey rubbed his thumb over Tizza's dog tags and pondered them, tried to understand why Tiz had been wearing them at all. He'd betrayed the men of the Australian Army. He'd been incarcerated for ten years in various army barracks, the subject of a cover-up. Why had he let his fingers trail to these useless pieces of metal so many times over the past two days. What had they meant to him?

Harvey let the dog tags slip from his fingers. The sound of them clanking onto the truck-bed floor made Clare turn her head slightly. Harvey had an arm around her waist. She slipped her forearm over the top of his, interlaced her fingers with his, and he lay there staring at the blackness, having forgotten Tizza completely, wondering instead if she'd really meant to do that, or if she was caught in some kind of dream. Minutes passed. Long ones. Her stomach growled. Then his did, and the gurgling, grinding, empty sound went for so long she turned her head further and gave a soft little laugh and he joined in.

'Do you think they deliver pizza out here?' she asked.

Harvey laughed again, pulled her close. Her body was so tight against his, he could feel the heat of his own breath rebounding off the nape of her neck, hot on his upper lip. His mind wandered with exhaustion, a drunken night walker veering madly away from the edges of the path where traumatic visions lay, following the road, brick by brick, into weird places. He thought about Darryl standing out there in the desert darkness. Tried to make a bet with himself about whether the man was planning to come to the back of the truck and drag him out and shoot him, or if perhaps he'd given up on the whole mission and abandoned them there. Maybe it was all over. Maybe they were free. New thoughts crashed in, about Clare gripping and scratching at her husband's hands as he held her kayak upside down in Margaret River. Clare clambering, wet, up the rocky water's edge. Clare's hand squeezing his again now, guiding it further down her body, onto her hip.

Harvey jolted out of a thin half-sleep, realised the part about Clare's fingers and his hadn't been fantasy. His hand had definitely shifted. Onto her hip. She'd rolled over almost completely. Her temple was against his lips. Harvey followed the absurd mental path, took a chance, slipped his fingertips into the waistband of her jeans, just below the vest. She guided his hand down further still. She sighed, and he lifted his other hand and raked it into her thick hair. They stayed like that for a long time, her back arching, her gasps in the dark whisper-soft, his brain trying to drag him into all kinds of twisted territory; of Shayna, of their imminent deaths, of Clare's husband and his sadly cautioned and sterilised life, and whether Clare had been fucked hard and brought to orgasm even once over the past decade. And Harvey got to thinking that maybe she hadn't, because he had all kinds of plans for her, but she rolled over and dragged her jeans off and climbed into his lap and started undoing his jeans.

'Slow down, slow down,' he said, laughing.

'Speed up, speed up,' she ordered. He held her and scooted over to the wall until his back was against it, and they kissed and ground their hips together, and then he was inside her, and when they finished together she was holding him so tightly he could barely breathe.

Afterwards they lay on the floor of the truck bed, panting. Sleep pulled at him again.

'How did you do it, in the army?' Clare asked suddenly. Her hand was near his on the hard truck-bed floor, sweat-damp and warm.

'Do what?'

'Cope with the stress,' she said. 'Days and days of tension. Danger. Threat.'

'Shayna,' he said. Maybe he shouldn't have. He didn't know. There was no protocol for this. 'But we managed to find nicer places to do it. And we weren't usually wearing bomb vests. I mean, once or twice a year. Just to spice things up.'

She laughed. He wiped sweat off his brow.

'I didn't think about it all the time. The danger,' Harvey said, his fingers trailing over the shapes of the blocks of explosive on the vest. They rose and fell as he breathed, bricks of death right above his heart. 'I took little mental retreats. Went somewhere else.'

'Where?'

Harvey felt strangely embarrassed, took a few attempts to get the words out. 'A little property. Near the Blue Mountains, maybe,' he said. 'Somewhere a bit rundown that I could get cheap and patch up. I'd have a dog.' He cleared his throat. 'I had a dog for a while in Afghanistan. My first one. It was good.'

Clare was silent. He turned to her.

'What?'

'Nothing.' He felt relief as he recognised the smile in her voice. The light was fading fast. 'It's nice. You could grow your own vegies. Hardly ever drive into town.'

'Something like that.'

'Why didn't you do that, when you left the army?' she asked. 'Was it expensive?'

'Not the kind of place I was looking for,' he said. 'And the Bak-Lis left me money, after I tried to save their son. I said I didn't want it. But they've kept it aside for me, all this time.' He took a long breath, let it out slow. 'I don't know. I had some wandering around to do first. It didn't feel safe, settling down. I knew these guys would get out, eventually.' He gestured to the wall of the truck. To Darryl, and Tizza, and all of them. 'The cover-up meant they were being held on bullshit charges, but those charges couldn't be too heavy, or they'd make the news. I assumed I'd be told when they were released. I guess I was wrong.'

'How could they not have told you that?'

'My commander, Leasing, would be the only one who really knew the full story.' Harvey shrugged. 'There's a hundred reasons why he wouldn't have warned me that Darryl and everyone were getting out. Maybe he died. Maybe he's a drinker. Maybe he's pissed at me, about what happened.'

Silence fell between them.

'I also didn't want to be too close to Shayna,' Harvey said. 'In the mountains. Not far from Sydney.'

He had no idea why he was telling Clare all this. He'd never said it aloud to anyone. There were unspoken things he was afraid would come out now, if he kept talking. About how he felt about Shayna, how clear it was to him and always had been that she was the love of his life. About how afraid he was of the grief that was going to hit him if he ever got through this. About how devastating it would be to know he'd wasted all those years avoiding her, because he couldn't look at her and not think about Afghanistan. Like the trauma of war, he knew that pain would only come when he got far enough away from the site of what created it. When he thought he was safe.

Before any of that could come out, Harvey slammed the door on all the hurt and bolted for safer territory. 'Where would you go?' he asked. 'Where were you headed, when you ran from your husband?'

Clare was silent for a long time. Then she said, 'New Orleans.'

'New Orleans!'

'Don't say it like that.'

'I'm not saying it like anything.' Harvey laughed. 'It's just so far. That's all.'

'I'd have to leave Australia to get away from Garreth.' Clare shifted closer to him. 'I'd have to go to the other side of the planet to feel safe. He's like the sun. Everything he shines on, he can see. I'd need to stay on the dark side of the earth away from him.'

Harvey thought about that, frowning at the ceiling.

'Lots of oddities shops in New Orleans,' Clare went on. 'Antiques. Voodoo dolls. Porcelain dolls. Old surgical equipment and prosthetics. Books that are falling apart, and leadlight lamps. I'd have a little shop in the French Quarter, so tightly crammed with stuff you'd have to walk sideways, do a few loops around the store to see everything. I'd buy dolls at estate sales. Fix them. Trade them.'

'What is it with you and the dolls?' he asked, but he knew the answer. From the kind of husband she chose. By the way she talked about herself. She got a high from recognising the hidden qualities in discarded and unappreciated things, and enjoyed the sensation of having that discerning eye rewarded with money. It was the same reason she'd seen something in Garreth, something another person would have missed among the rigidity, coldness and aloofness of the man.

'It's a craft,' Clare said offhandedly. Because that's who she was. Who she'd been made to be. Someone who talked down or shielded their own hidden qualities. 'It's satisfying.'

Harvey smiled.

'You can jack up the price on a vintage doll by twenty-five per cent if you say it's haunted.' Clare yawned. 'And everything in New Orleans is haunted.'

'It sounds like a nice life.'

'It would be. I'd have beignets by the river every morning at the Cafe Du Monde until I was huge. Until I had tits the size of watermelons.'

Harvey laughed, hard and sudden, clapped his hand to his forehead.

'I would,' Clare chuckled.

'You'd have to change your name,' Harvey said. 'You couldn't be Clare Holland. You'd never fit in. It would have to be "Claudette Devereaux" or something.'

Clare laughed now. A tinkling sound in the dark. 'You could be Dave Smith from Oberon.'

'With my dog, Jafna.'

'Jafna?'

'Yeah,' Harvey said.

Harvey thought about it. The dog. The verandah. The shop in New Orleans selling glass eyes by the jarful, and Clare behind the counter with her hair dyed cherry red and a tattoo of a witch on her arm, so far from bathroom scales and daily clove of garlic that she was unrecognisable. Then the sound of footsteps in the dry desert earth came to him from outside. He pulled his underwear and jeans back on, and so did Clare. Darryl opened one of the levered doors of the truck, and placed a cable tie on the edge of the platform.

'You know the drill.'

Harvey patted the space where he'd left Tizza's dog tags, secreted them into his jeans pocket. He stood and walked barefoot to the edge of the truck bed, sat down in the moonlight and made a loop of the cable tie. He put his hands behind his back, looped the tie around his wrists, and zipped it shut. Darryl stood well back as Harvey slid off the truck bed and his bare feet hit the still sun-warmed soil.

He had no idea where they were or what time it was. A billion stars crowded overhead, so many they clustered into clouds and swirls, were dizzying to look at. In the moonlight, Darryl's features looked heavy, shadowed, the eyes hollow. Harvey watched him fix the door of the truck shut on Clare. Then he walked, guided by Darryl's gun, out into the nothingness, looking for a fence line or a powerline or the glow of a small town to tell him anything about his position. There was nothing. He might well have been on the moon. The horizon seemed impossibly flat and distant, and yet close enough to fall off.

Darryl walked him into the blankness until the truck was small. Harvey waited the whole time for the sickening click of the safety on Darryl's pistol being flicked off. An order to kneel. Neither sound came. He listened to the older man's footsteps, and when they stopped, he did, too.

'Is this it?' Harvey asked.

The older man just stood there, the gun by his side.

'Because that would be smart,' Harvey said. 'You're outnumbered now. Two to one. This plan was a failure in the making, and it's unfolded as a failure, one misstep after the other. If you continue with this, you'll get yourself killed. One way or another, I'm going to do to you what I did to Parker and Tizza.'

Darryl didn't speak. Harvey stared at the dark holes where his eyes should be, and forced himself to breathe.

'I'm going to leave you choking on your own blood in the dirt, Darryl,' Harvey said. 'And there won't be anyone there to put you out of your misery. That's a promise.'

The wind swept around them. Harvey felt it tussle his hair. Darryl was rigid as a stone, his silhouette sharply inked against the stars.

'That's not how it's going to play out,' Darryl said finally. Harvey realised, with terrifying clarity, that the man had been standing there making a decision. 'I want you to know how it's going to play out, though, Harvey. Because you'll be there for the big finish. But you won't get to enjoy what comes afterwards.'

Harvey sucked in the rapidly cooling desert air.

'Tomorrow evening,' Darryl said, 'the news programs are going to run a story on you. It'll take them that long to figure the whole thing out. But by then, they'll have the interviews. The sneaky little contacts in the army, who can read between the lines and piece together what happened back in Afghanistan. The first versions of the story will be a bit wobbly, but after a while, they'll get a full picture. That you, Harvey Buck, were a war hero. That you exposed four murderous traitors inside the Australian military presence in Tarin Kot, and intercepted a network of relationships between those four men and Taliban militants. There will be side stories about the cover-up. About Lippo's suicide, and the jail time the rest of us were landed with. But all that will be background stuff. The real focus will be on you and what you were. And what the hell happened to make you do what you're going to do tomorrow.'

Harvey waited, listening to the moaning of the wind and a ghost from his past foretelling his future.

'The news stories will begin to theorise,' Darryl said, 'that you stopped being able to live with what you'd done to us. That you reached out. That you met with us. Parker, Tizza and me.'

Harvey cocked his head.

'They'll learn that together we planned all this,' Darryl said. He swept his arm across the desert. To the truck. 'A spree. A last hoorah. A big-bang finish.'

'No,' Harvey said.

'I'll be there to tell them the story,' Darryl said. 'About how you turned on us. You murdered Parker. Then Tizza. You came at me, but I survived.'

'No one will believe you.' Harvey shook his head. 'No one who knows me will believe I would ever join you in something like this.'

'Who out there really knows you, Buck?' Darryl's teeth glinted in the moonlight as he smiled. 'Who's gonna speak up for you? Huh? Shayna's dead. You cut ties with everyone you knew in the force. You're a loner who reads and drinks coffee and takes the occasional lug-about job for cash. Don't look surprised. We've been watching you for a year now, Harvey. You're just the right kind of socially aloof weirdo who would flip out like this. Who would get sick in the head from all the trauma and institutional bullshit and plot something big. Because, let's face it, they fucked you, too. The army. They left you to die out there in the desert, after the ambush.'

'No they didn't. They tried to find us. The area was too hostile.'

'You had to believe that to survive. As you walked. Day after day. The sun beating down on you.'

Harvey shook his head, forced himself not to look at the desert around him. Not to remember those hellish steps, one after the other, the days growing hotter and hotter, reaching blinding, white-hot levels. Watching his skin blister and peel in real time, like he was actually boiling alive. Bak-Li moaning and crying, hanging on his back.

'Then you finally make it in, and no one believes your story,' Darryl continued. 'What you did to us in those containers, it must have fucked you up, too. Pulling Tizza's teeth out. Burning Parker's feet. Pulverising my bones. You dream about that, sometimes?'

'No, I don't,' Harvey lied.

'You were forced to do that, so that you could prove you were right.' Darryl shifted the gun in his hand, changed his grip. 'They ever tell you that they did, in fact, round up two of the Taliban guys Lippo had connected with? Yeah. He'd sold them designs for a drone-mounted missile. They were going to bomb a school. They tell you that?'

'No. I left that day. I gave them the USB of your confessions and I left.'

'Sad that you didn't find out,' Darryl said. 'I guess it's not too late. Congratulations, Buck. There's a whole primary school full of hajis who are still alive because of you. They'd be teen-agers now. Young men. Probably planning to hijack a plane somewhere. Kill a hundred white kids.'

Harvey didn't dignify the words with a response.

'Worst of the worst possible crimes,' Darryl said. Something sparkled in his eyes. 'Killing children.'

'No one will believe this,' Harvey insisted.

'They'll believe,' Darryl said. 'When they see what you do tomorrow.'

'What am I gonna do?' Harvey asked. Darryl just smiled.

'I told you,' the older man said. 'We're going to finish with a bang.'

CHAPTER 34

They were loaned a car belonging to a resident of Clifton Hills who had come out into the desert to join the search teams. Edna thought the move was smart, in a way; allowing her to drive the kid home on her own meant Zhang's operation in the desert would not be down one man for two hours while they were escorted. In another way, it was incredibly dumb. Because she had no intention of going home. She made her way with the shirtless teen towards a group of cars parked in the blankness far from the lights of the crime scene and search command tent.

Edna reached out and grabbed Talon's good arm as he veered towards the tent, where they'd last seen Holland with his phone and paper cup.

'Don't even think about it.'

'I'm going to knock him over and steal his shoes.' Talon yanked his arm away. 'There has to be blood still on them. Up in the grooves. We can at least get a picture for a match.'

'That won't help,' Edna said. 'We'll get him some other way.'

'The guy shot your partner dead.' Talon stopped walking. Shirtless, the police camp sprawling behind him, he was an absurd sight. 'You're just going to keep going and not do anything about it?'

'I'm on my way to do something about it, Talon.' Edna grabbed his arm again and pulled him onward. 'Kid, if you want to do this job, you have to understand something. It's like . . .' She took a breath, tried to find the words. 'Have you ever tried to catch a chicken?'

'Have I *what*?'

'You can't catch a chicken just by running at it,' Edna said. They walked on through the darkness, desert plants scratching at the bottoms of their trousers. 'I learnt that the hard way. I used to have chickens.'

'Where?'

'At the house. In Clifton Hills Station. It's a bloody long way for me to drive to get fresh eggs, where I am. And I like fresh eggs. So when I first moved here, I kept some chickens. Then I realised that if you keep chickens, you'll get rats. And if you get rats, you get snakes. And the snakes out here are the kind that can kill you just by looking at you.'

Talon's silhouette against the distant lights showed he was frowning deeply.

'My point is, you've got to come at a chicken like a snake. You act casual, sidle up slowly, and then you *snap*.'

'Okay? So what?'

'So we're going to get Garreth Holland,' Edna said. 'Just not by running at him.'

Edna recognised a few of the vehicles in the makeshift car park. Mothers, fathers, teenagers still on their P-plates. Teachers from the tiny school in Kaltjiti. Edna knew that some of the searchers had probably met here, and climbed into each other's cars to avoid driving alone into the badlands. Though local knowledge of the High Wire and its exact nature would be rare, the eeriness and vastness of the area at night touched the hearts of even those who had lived there the longest. The night desert was a place for predators. She unlocked the car she had been directed to take, a Kia four-wheel drive, and they got in. There was a big straw hat in the front passenger-side footwell. Edna shut her mind quickly on awful thoughts, picked up the hat, tossed it into the rear. Talon ratcheted his seat all the way back. A helicopter flew overhead, low enough for Edna to feel the *whump* of its rotors in her chest. Talon leant forward and watched it cross the desert before them.

'Whoa.'

'Yeah. Can you believe this morning it was just us?' Edna asked.

The boy shook his head, settled into his seat as Edna turned the car onto what were by now well-worn tracks into the desert. She figured driving east, when she had been told to drive west towards home and Clifton Hills, would be a bad move. She drove west, intending to cut through the desert plains back towards the Wire once they were a good distance from Zhang and the police presence behind her.

'Okay,' Talon said from the passenger seat. He slid a phone from his pocket and rubbed it against the thigh of his jeans, trying to clean the smeared screen. 'Lippo.'

'What the hell is that?' Edna looked over.

'What? It's Stevenson's phone.' Talon shrugged. In the glow of the centre console lights his cheekbones were green and his eyes wide. 'I found it under the cruiser. Before I was shot. You were there.'

'I just assumed you'd dropped it.' Edna shook her head. 'Jesus. Why didn't you tell me you had it?'

'I've been a little distracted,' Talon huffed. 'Did I mention that someone *shot* me? Like with a *gun*?'

'Only eighty-six times.' Edna eased an uncertain sigh. 'Crime scene techs will be looking for that.'

'We can start helping them when they start helping us,' Talon said. 'Okay. The picture is here.' He was silent for a moment. Staring. 'Man. That's a dead guy's arm right there.'

'What does the tattoo say?'

'Lippo, 9-9-78 to 7-3-11.'

'Any picture? In the design, I mean.'

'No. Just the name and the dates.'

'Well, she was right. It is a memorial tattoo,' Edna said. 'Guy was . . . thirty-three? No, thirty-two.'

'So who's Lippo and how can this tell us who the dead guy is?'

'It would be a stretch, trying to connect that to anything,' Edna said. 'We're armed with Google and our own imaginations and that's it. We've got a name and a couple of dates. And it's not like we even have a full name. Lippo sounds like a nickname. Which means it could be Lipman, Lipford, Lipper, Lipton, Lipley . . .'

'Lipcock.'

The boy fell to cackling. Edna groaned. 'Well, I've got nothing to do but sit here,' Talon said. 'I'm gonna start messing around. We know what day the guy died. Maybe, like . . . Okay, so . . . Look, there's a Georgina May Lipford who died on the third of March 2011. Is it her?'

'Where's she from?'

'Ainsworth, Nebraska.'

'I'm gonna say it's not her.'

'Oh my god!'

'What? What?'

'There is actually a guy named Lipcock, look.' The boy showed her the screen. Blinding white light, blue text. 'He's a dentist in Brisbane.'

Edna sighed and gripped the wheel. A car was approaching them. She flicked her high beams off, slowed, saw the driver roll down his window as he neared. Adam Bourne hung his thick elbow out the window as the two vehicles came to a stop, their windows aligned. Edna felt her stomach shrink with guilt.

'Aren't you supposed to be driving my Range Rover?' the Indigenous Elder asked. Edna could see Bourne's wife Maggie in the passenger seat, figures in the back seat.

'Ah, we hit a little snag.'

'I know, I know.' Bourne patted the air between their cars. 'I'm sorry. About Stevie.'

Edna felt suddenly choked up. The exhaustion crept into her throat, danced on her eyelids. It had been easy enough to put on a brave face for the kid. But slamming the door on the grief again, saving it for a more convenient time, was a mighty task. 'I can't talk about it.'

'Why aren't you heading east?'

'I kind of am. Big turning circle on this thing.'

'Have you been to the farm? Can you tell us what happened?'

'Yeah, what the bloody hell happened?' someone asked from inside Bourne's car. The back window rolled down. Edna saw a youth in a hoodie, and the small child she'd seen in the street outside the Cooper Creek bank. The kid still had the big remote-controlled monster truck, was rolling its wheels up over the edge of the window as he listened to the adults talk.

'I don't know what you're talking about,' Edna said.

Bourne looked at his wife. Looked back at Edna, blank faced. 'Why not?'

'I'm just a bit behind, Adam, that's all.' Edna shifted up in her seat. 'Tell me what's going on.'

'Well, nobody can get a straight answer on what exactly has gone down,' Bourne said. 'All we know is, searchers are being told to head to the area surrounding the Greatman property. It's west of Thargomindah. A cattle farm. White fellas. Lenny and Daisy. They're saying Harvey Buck was there this afternoon and killed someone.'

'*What?*' Talon dropped Stevenson's phone into the footwell.

'That can't be right,' Edna said.

'This news is fresh out of the pot. Came in ten minutes ago.' Bourne shrugged. 'I got the call from one of my guys who works for the Thargomindah coppers. He says they got a call this afternoon from Daisy Greatman. At first the coppers thought it was some kind of accident. Daisy was hysterical on the phone. Says her father-in-law had been killed and she wanted the cops out there, quick smart. Takes them forty minutes to get there. Meanwhile she's not answering the phone. Then when they arrive, they find mum and kids are barricaded in the house and dad's there roaming the wilds trying to hunt down a . . . a couple they said were responsible for killing the old man.'

Edna looked at Talon. 'A *couple*?'

'It wasn't a farming accident, is what he's saying.' Maggie leant across her husband. 'They murdered him.'

'None of this makes sense to me,' Edna said. 'Who's the couple?'

'Harvey Buck and Clare Holland.'

'*What?*' Now it was Edna's turn to drop something: her jaw. 'What are you saying? They're out there? Buck and Clare? They're . . . *together*?'

'You know as much as I do, now.' Bourne put both hands out the window, lifted them to the sky.

'When did all this happen? You said this afternoon?'

'About two o'clock.'

'Why are we only hearing about this now?'

'I dunno. Christ, Ed, this is not my circus.' Bourne frowned at her. 'Took the boys a while to get out there. Then they had to make sure the property was safe, I guess. Then, they only figured out it was Buck and Clare when somebody thought to show the Greatman fella some photos of the two. They gave fake names.'

'The Greatmans didn't get the alerts on their phones? We sent a "Keep A Look Out For" text on both of them. Buck, at least, went out, I know that. Everybody from here to Sydney should have received it.'

'I said I told you all I know, Edna.' Bourne put his hands back on his steering wheel. 'We're just being ordered to haul our arses over Thargomindah way. Now.'

CHAPTER 35

'I think I know what the plan is,' Harvey said.

Clare lay next to him. The ringing silence gave Harvey extra senses. He could tell from the sound of her breathing and the heat of her body that she was lying exactly as he was, face upwards, staring unseeing at the ceiling of the truck.

'The big-bang finish?' Clare said.

'He was vague,' Harvey said. 'But he mentioned kids. Twice. I feel like he . . . he kind of leant on the words. Like he wanted me to figure it out.'

'Jesus, don't tell me he's going to use us to bomb a school.'

'There wouldn't be a school around here with enough kids in it. Outback schools, it's a dozen kids or less,' Harvey said. He sat up, thoughts zinging together. 'But I'm asking myself the same question that I asked you. About your husband. Why did it have to be now?'

'What do you mean?'

'Darryl said he and the other guys had been watching me for a year. Planning all this. So why did they hit the go-button yesterday?'

'Because of the bomb scares,' Clare said. 'At the airports.'

'That was them.'

'Jesus Christ.'

'They know me. They know I'm not a guy who sits around an airport for four hours waiting for another flight when I could be on the move. I would have been in such a rush to get to Sydney, to get to Shayna, I would have driven, at least to Durham or Birdsville or some other airport.'

'What are you getting at?' Clare sat up beside him. He could feel her breath on his face.

'There was another reason it had to be now,' Harvey said. 'And I think I know what that reason is.'

'What?'

'Operation Burke and Wills.'

'What the hell is that?' Clare was frowning at him. 'You mean Burke and Wills the explorers?'

'Yes. Sort of. It's also a military operation,' Harvey said. 'Or, it's meant to look like one, at least.'

Clare was silent.

'When you join the army,' Harvey said, 'they send you to Blamey Barracks. It's in Kapooka. That's if you're joining as a soldier, anyway. Officers go somewhere else. If you sign up as a grunt, you do your twelve weeks at Kapooka, and if you don't wash out, you graduate. Then you go and do your specialist training somewhere else.'

'Okay . . .?'

'In order to graduate, you've got to do a two-week training exercise in the desert. Operation Burke and Wills. It's like a fake military exercise they put on, where they throw a bunch of challenges at you and see if you have what it takes as a soldier. Really it's just an excuse for training officers to take you out into the desert and fuck with you a little. Yell at you. Tire you out. Play war games. During the operation, there's a pack march that takes in some of the track used by Burke and Wills when they went out into the middle of Australia looking for an inland sea. It's two hundred k's from the Torowoto Swamp in New South Wales to the Bulloo River in Queensland.'

'How many recruits are we talking about?'

'My intake had about a hundred and fifty.'

'So you're telling me we might be headed into the middle of a pack of young army recruits on training camp?' Clare's voice trembled. 'Wearing bomb vests?'

'They'll be out in the middle of the desert, protected by nothing but their instructors,' Harvey said. 'Ten or twelve old guys who haven't been active in two decades. It'll be the largest contingent of army personnel outside of a base in the country.'

'And the recruits will all be young?' Clare said.

'Most of them will be. There'll be the odd mature-age recruit, or officer changeover. But in general, yes. It'll be kids in their late teens and early twenties.' Harvey held his head. 'Kids playing pretend soldier.'

They sat together in the dark, Harvey remembering those days. The excitement and dread he'd felt being bussed into the desert from Kapooka to the drop-off zone in at the edge of the Torowoto Swamp, smack bang in the middle of nowhere. It had been 3 a.m. He'd been sitting up since 1 a.m., waiting for the fire alarm in the army dorm room to go off, for the instructors to come in shouting. He'd never packed his gear so carefully in his life. His spit-polished boots had been gleaming. Harvey had been twenty-one years old, still zinging with energy at having found what he thought was his purpose, caught in the fantasy that this was what real life in the service was going to be like. And yes, he'd come away from the Burke and Wills exercise thrilled at having passed the test. Sweat-soaked, exhausted, dusty and triumphant, he and his intake had descended on the base camp on the edge of the Bulloo River to drink the night away. He thought he'd achieved something, then. Pushed hard, showed integrity and courage.

But nothing he'd experienced at Kapooka had prepared him for the monotony, bureaucracy and outright horror of being a real, deployed army soldier. The leadership games and mud-crawling with the other recruits had been happy days, where they competed for house points and slagged their instructors, buzz-cut and snuggled in their swags in their hoochie tents listening for the footfall of other recruits playing enemy soldiers. The fantasy hadn't broken for Harvey until maybe a year later, when an officer in the Randwick Barracks where he'd been completing specialist training shot his superior dead in the computer lab following weeks of reported bullying, then shot himself. The fantasy was dissolved further still after the Boxing Day Tsunami response, when, after six weeks of dragging women and children's bodies out of the swampy water, Harvey had sat with twenty-five other guys for their 'group psychological assessment', a forty-five-minute circle-jerk which comprised the only counselling he was ever offered following the mission.

Then there was Afghanistan.

The kids out there on the Burke and Wills track wouldn't have had any experience with the heartache and devastation the service offered, wouldn't understand how easily the job could take their lives, or make them want to do that to themselves or others. They couldn't dream what it was like to raid an Afghan family's home and flash their torches and the aim of their high-powered rifles over infants in cribs. Screaming grandmothers and whimpering family dogs.

They would be starry-eyed, those baby soldiers. Dreaming of graduation, of March Out Day, where they could perform drill manoeuvres in front of their parents.

And there was Harvey Michael Buck, jaded war hero on a twisted killing spree, coming to murder them all.

'We can't do this,' Clare said. 'We've come this far. And we've tried, we've really tried, to save ourselves. But, Harvey, we . . . we can't let him bring us anywhere near those people.'

Harvey nodded.

'If I'd known those kids at the farmhouse were going to run out at us,' Clare sniffed. 'I mean, as soon as I saw it *was* a farmhouse, I should have turned and run back . . .'

'We can't undo what's happened,' Harvey said. 'But we can stop what's coming, maybe.'

Clare blew out a long breath. 'How . . . how do we do it?' she asked. Her voice was tiny.

Harvey shook his head. 'We just rip the zipper down. Yours or mine. It won't matter.' He paused to imagine it. The zipper catching as it united two wires inside the vest, the zap of white light as the connection was made.

And then nothing. Everything that he was. Everything he would ever have been. It would all be gone. Even if his death now prevented the murder of hundreds of young soldiers on Operation Burke and Wills, Darryl, Tizza and Parker's mission would still have been accomplished. He would still be known forever now as a madman, a traitor and a killer.

When Clare's voice came, it was low and dark. 'We're not doing it until we know we'll take Darryl with us.'

Harvey felt a shiver of uneasiness up his spine. 'Right,' he said.

A click, a creak, and a *thunk*. Harvey and Clare froze in the darkness, listening. They heard Darryl's boots crunch onto the dry earth outside. The driver's-side door of the truck slammed. Then footsteps came as their last captor made his way out into the night. Harvey stretched his hand out, found Clare's forearm, followed it to her hand. He gripped her fingers.

'I don't know how to tell you how sorry I am that we're here.'

He waited for a response. Was surprised to feel her slip into his arms. He wrapped his arms around her and held her to him, this woman he hardly knew, her cheek against his cheek and the memory of her gasps in the dark still fresh in his mind. Harvey wondered, as she held onto him, about who she was outside of this time they'd had together, the worst twenty-four hours of either of their lives. All he knew about her was her vengeful fury, her deep, deep tolerance for pain, her raw defiant unwillingness to die at the hands of a man. Harvey wondered what she thought about him. With what she knew of his history, before and after this. He guessed she knew him as a person with the capacity, the natural skill, to hurt. She knew exactly what atrocities he'd wreaked upon Parker, Lipton, Darryl and Tizza in the containers. She knew he'd killed in war. She'd seen him beat and torment their captors, murder Parker, pull a bomb vest onto a struggling old man so that he could be blown to pieces. She'd seen him slaughter Nathan Tizza like an animal. Why didn't she think of him as a monster? Why did she stroke the hair at the nape of his neck now? Why did she kiss his mouth?

Harvey was still trying to unravel who she was, even after knowing her as intimately as he had the past few hours. He was starting to wonder if there was something in her that felt comfortable around monsters.

Long minutes passed. They put their foreheads together, and Harvey heard Darryl's footsteps approach the side of the truck, to the driver's door to the cabin. Then he stopped, turned, and began heading down the side of the truck again.

Harvey felt Clare take the zipper tab at the neck of the vest, high between his shoulder blades.

'Should you do it or . . .' she managed, fiddling with the tab. 'Or . . . I mean. Should I?'

Harvey took hold of the zipper at the back of her neck. Wondered how a person did this. Ended their own life. Her zipper clicked down one tooth just with the weight of his fingers on it, and it was enough to snap him out of the exhausted, upside-down thinking that had brought him to this moment. 'No.' Harvey dropped his hand. Pulled away so that Clare dropped hers. 'We don't give up. Not yet.'

The levers on the truck door squeaked and slid sideways, slowly.

'It's two on one,' Harvey said. 'Okay, so he has a gun and the detonator to our vests. But we have—'

'Survival instinct.'

'Right,' Harvey said. 'Until we're right up on those recruits, we've got to keep trying. Every chance we get, we try to get on either side of Darryl. Catch him in a pincer movement. Even if all we have left is to give each other a signal and throw ourselves at him.'

'Okay.' Clare gripped his arms. 'Okay. I'm with you. We can do this.'

'We have to do this.'

The door of the truck creaked gently open.

Harvey felt Clare tighten her grip on his arms.

'Hey?' a voice called.

The captives looked towards the open truck door. A silhouette stood there, shorter and rounder than Darryl.

'Anybody in there?' the man asked.

CHAPTER 36

There were cars on the Wire. Edna saw them up ahead, criss-crossing the barren landscape, desert-dwelling cars with high clearance and huge steel bull bars that would make pulp of kangaroos or wild pigs that traversed the path of the giant machines. Edna had seen a local resident and police response like this only once in her time in Clifton Hills. A kombi van full of Christian missionaries had gone missing somewhere in the vastness between the upper edge of Lake Blanche and Gidgealpa, where they'd been headed. At the time, Edna had heard they were on their way. Residents of Gidgealpa, Clifton Hills and Cooper Creek had been complaining to her of phone calls from the missionaries, in which they were attempting to set up public meetings with residents of the Indigenous communities. Then she'd heard the van had been spotted somewhere north of the lake, only one occupant present with it, the bonnet of the vehicle open. Before long, she found herself standing with a crowd of locals, SES, police and specialist personnel at a slowly growing camp near the lake. The team leader had let the crew know that the area they were interested in was approximately 78,000 square kilometres, or about the size of the

Czech Republic. It included dry river beds, cave systems, clusters of woodland and crevasses that were half a kilometre deep in parts.

They'd never found the missionaries. They had been swallowed by the never-never, kombi and all.

Edna turned off the Wire, heading for the Greatman property, then turned north, finding its westernmost wire fence line and parking in the dark under a lean, clawed gumtree.

She stepped out into the night wind. The helicopter that had been coasting along the horizon had turned back now and was working its way down its grid pattern, a red eye blinking rhythmically. She stood with Talon and watched the distant farmhouse. There was no sound. To the right of the property, some distance down a gentle slope, Edna could see the white lights of another crime scene being rigged up, the flashing blue and red of police vehicles.

'How are we going to do this?' Talon asked her. 'Won't the cops just turn us away as soon as we show our faces?'

'We're just going to have to make sure we *don't* show our faces,' Edna said. 'I don't know how that'll work, but we need the real story about what happened here. We can't rely on third-hand gossip. There might be something Buck did or said while he was here that will tell us where he'd head next. Or what he plans to do with Clare.'

'Or if that even *was* Clare.' Talon followed Edna's lead as she bent and slipped carefully between the wires of the fence, taking care to slide beneath the top wire, which was marked as electric. They walked across the plain. 'Maybe Buck had a woman with him. It made it easier to tempt Clare into the car with him, when he picked her up. Sometimes couples do that, you know. Serial killers. They work together as husband and wife.'

'Oh, god.' Edna stopped.

'What?'

'I stepped in cow shit,' she sighed. 'It's in my socks.'

CHAPTER 37

Harvey sprang to his feet. He thought it was the dehydration and the sudden movement that made lights blast into his vision. But he opened his eyes, and found the whole truck filled with light. Tizza's blood was on his forearms, almost black now, as he shielded himself.

'Jesus, fuck!' the man at the doors said. 'It *is* you!'

Harvey heard the metallic double-snap of a pistol being actioned.

'Don't fucking move.'

'Help!' Clare threw her hands up, got to her feet beside Harvey. 'You've got to help us.'

'I'm here, lady. I'm here,' the guy said. 'You're safe now. Step away from him.'

'No, no, no, no, he's with me! He's okay! He's with me!' Clare waved her hands frantically at the silhouetted figure at the end of the truck.

'What?'

'Turn the light off!' Clare hissed. 'Turn the light off, *now*!'

The truck went dark. Blindingly, chokingly black. Harvey crouched and felt his way forward. 'We're hostages. Both of us. We've been captive for about twenty-four hours.'

'By Harvey Buck?' the voice in the dark said. 'Aren't you him?'

'I am him.'

'But—'

'We don't have time to talk about it,' Clare said. Harvey felt her brush by him, scrambling out of the truck even faster than he could. 'How did you get here? Where's your car? Take us there.'

The guy waited for them both to get down, then started jogging. Clare and Harvey followed. As his eyes adjusted, Harvey could see the guy was squat, beer-bellied, boxy-headed. A distinctly Queensland accent twanged in Harvey's ears.

'I don't get what's going on here. Who's held you captive?'

'We can explain later,' Harvey said. 'Right now we need to move.'

'I've got a semi parked up on the ridgeline.' The guy pointed. 'I've been hearin' about youse since about six o'clock this mornin'. It's all over the radio. All day. Where's the guy who's got youse captured?'

'He's out here somewhere,' Harvey said. 'Give me the gun.'

'Nah, mate, I can't—'

'Give me the fucking gun.' Harvey put a hand out. The man slowed his jog, thought about it, handed the gun over. 'I know you're trying to do the right thing here. And we're really grateful. But I'm trying to get us all out of this alive.'

'It's just . . . It's just . . .' The man was huffing with the effort of running for the cluster of hills before them. 'You are Clare Holland, right?'

'Yes.'

'The cops is on the radio sayin' *you've* been taken hostage by *him*.'

Harvey nodded. 'Sounds about right.'

They stopped at the foot of the hills, by a boulder the size of a small car. It seemed the natural place to pause, get their bearings. They crouched, a huffing, gasping trio. 'We'll explain everything when we're out of here,' Harvey said. 'Right now we need to figure out where Darryl is.'

'Harvey, we should just go,' Clare pleaded. 'Forget Darryl. He said his truck's just up there.'

'Yeah, and a lot of good it'll do us when we climb in and Darryl realises we're gone and he blows us to pieces five minutes down the road.' Harvey examined the gun in the pale moonlight. A little 9 millimetre pistol. Small, but not nothing. He felt the weight of the cartridge inside. Fully loaded. 'The box truck he's been keeping us in will catch up to a semi-trailer in no time. We need to end this now.'

'No, please, *please*.' Clare sobbed hard, just once, swallowing the sound quickly. 'Harvey, we have to take a chance. Darryl and the others – they might have been bullshitting us. Surely he can't – I mean – he *can't* set our vests off from anywhere. He just can't. That was a lie. I'm telling you. We need to go. We need to go! Please!'

'What vests?' their saviour asked.

Harvey didn't answer. He watched the box truck in the distance, the one they'd just fled. The left-hand door was hanging open. Clouds shifted over the moon, dialling the night up and down, a pale blue lens shrouding the vast landscape. Nothing moved. Harvey cast his eye along the pockets of shadow in the hills to his left, seeing hundreds of potential hiding spots. The impossibility of finding Darryl in the night landscape pressed down on him. He squeezed the gun, tapping the trigger guard as he thought. Seconds were clicking away.

If Darryl didn't know already that they'd fled the truck, he would at any second.

'What's your name?' Harvey asked the man crouching beside him.

'Wayne Preston.'

'Wayne, I'm gonna try to cover you while you get back to your semi-trailer,' Harvey said. 'You're going to get in and start driving.'

'Harvey, please don't do this.' Clare's fingernails dug into his forearm. 'We can go with him. We can make it!'

'Get to a town. Tell everyone you can that Clare and I are both hostages,' Harvey said. 'And we're heading towards the Burke and Wills track with bomb vests on.'

'*What?*'

'Go!' Harvey shoved the heavy man towards the slope. He listened to small rocks tumbling as the trucker clambered upwards.

'I'm going with him.'

'I wish you wouldn't.'

'Fuck you.' Clare's voice was heavy with terror. 'I can't help you here.'

'That's bullshit and we both know it,' Harvey said. 'You've shown nothing but killer capability in the past twenty-four hours, Clare. You're smart, resourceful and determined, and you'll be damned if you're going to be sitting in that truck with that guy rolling away from here and twiddling your thumbs while you wonder if your vest is about to blow because I've failed my mission here.'

Clare's breath was thin and rasping in the silence of the night. 'Fuck. *You.*'

'If you want to survive Garreth you'll have to survive Darryl first,' Harvey said. She didn't answer. 'Come on. Keep your eyes on the hills that way. I'll cover the east.'

They followed Wayne Preston. The trucker was huffing his way up the slope twenty metres ahead, watching the landscape on either side of him for movement. Harvey could see where he'd originally come down; disturbed red earth making a distinct footfall pattern in a wide slab of soft sand. It would have been an easy route down. Now, Wayne, the long-haul trucker and potential hero to a damsel in distress, had to find a more solid way back up, picking handholds between the spiky desert plants.

Harvey expected the light on his vest to come on any second. Or Clare's. Or both of them. How many minutes had passed now? Surely Darryl had returned to the truck. At least seen it from a distance. He'd use the three-step detonation system to blow their cover, to tell him where they were hiding. First lights, then the alarm. Harvey and Clare would be sitting ducks. Darryl would come and try to recapture them. If they were lucky. If they weren't, he'd blow them both, taking a Good Samaritan with them.

Harvey climbed, covering Wayne from all sides. No sound came. No red light. Harvey wondered if Clare had been right; if the whole idea that Darryl could detonate their vests even out of line-of-sight range was bullshit. Hope stirred in his chest. Something slithered along a rock ledge away from his fingers, just as Harvey gripped the chalky stone. He stopped every few seconds, scanning the dark, seeing nothing.

At the top of the ridge, Wayne ran for the semi's cab door and stepped up using a little ladder embedded in the side of the big hauler. The slamming of the truck cabin door echoed out into the night. Harvey's fragmented mind tried to leave the stress of the situation he was in, to consider the possibilities of what Wayne had been hauling that would make him use the Wire to avoid police attention as he drove. He and Clare arrived at the side of the truck. Harvey was snapped back to reality when the trucker popped the door of the cabin open again and hopped down beside Clare. Some kind of big slurpy cup fell down with him, knocked out of the footwell.

'I got nothin',' Wayne said.

Harvey turned. 'What do you mean?'

'There's no power. No radio. Must be the battery. But I didn't—'

The hairs on the back of Harvey's neck all rose at once. He looked at the end of the semi, the front. He backed up, his gun raised, scanning the hills below. 'Wayne, *run*!'

Two pops, not from any of the places Harvey had focused on, but from above them, inside the cabin. Harvey saw Darryl's outline against the muzzle flare, sitting behind the driver's seat, an arm hanging out the smaller, tinted window, pointed directly at the trucker on the ground. Wayne fell and curled into a ball, gripping at his stomach. Harvey raised his own pistol and fired three shots in quick succession at Darryl's window, but he knew after round one that something was wrong. The recoil was soft. The shots, which had been directly on target, had no effect. Harvey lowered the pistol and pointed it at one of the truck's tyres while Wayne lay groaning and panting in the dirt. He fired twice. The gun bucked and banged and flashed, but the tyre remained undamaged.

In the golden light, Darryl moved from the sleeper's cabin into the front cabin and slid into the driver's seat. Harvey took the opportunity to slip his hand into his pocket, pull out Tizza's dog chains, and drop them carefully into the dirt at his feet. He stood on them. Darryl jumped down from the truck cabin onto the dirt, right beside the innocent man he'd just shot. Harvey watched his captor put his hand into his pocket, and then the edges of his vision grew pink as the light on his chest came on. Darryl smiled sadly at Harvey as he pointed at the pistol at his chest.

'Drop it right there.' Darryl gestured to the ground between them. Harvey tossed his useless gun. It clattered on the earth. 'Blanks. Unlucky, Harv.'

Darryl tossed him a bullet. Harvey tried to examine it in his palm, but a cloud shifted over the moon, leaving him in darkness. He chucked the bullet away, didn't need to see it to know what it was.

'I found the cartridge box in the truck,' Darryl said.

Harvey was so crushed, he felt like crying. Like sitting in the dirt and holding his head and rocking and crying. So he did what he always did when a feeling like that came over him. He locked eyes with his enemy, set his jaw, and smiled gently. Like it was all a game. Like a good man wasn't dying in the dirt nearby, the kind of man who, even though he seemed to have chosen the criminal life, couldn't even bring himself to defend that life with real bullets. The kind of man who had probably just fallen on bad times, a regular trucker, probably with a wife, a couple of kids, who had bent to the pressure of drug runners to use his vehicle to move their goods. The kind of man who had been traversing the High Wire and had heard about a woman in peril, had spotted Darryl's truck from the ridgeline, and decided to go investigate with nothing but a gun loaded with blanks to defend himself with. Harvey kept his eyes on Darryl as Clare bent over the dying trucker, holding his head and crying and trying to offer him comfort as his consciousness slipped away.

CHAPTER 38

Cows. Dozens of them, by what Edna could smell, approaching an awning that was the length of a football field and edged with water troughs. They stepped carefully in the dark, Edna leading, walking along the back of the awning towards the distant house. Huge beasts shuffled and snored and huffed as she and Talon went by. The earthy, slightly acidic smell of their faeces was in her nose and mouth, the occasional fly butting against her cheek and brow in the dark. There was gravel between the awning and the house. They turned off, walked in darkness towards the back of the little property.

The wide verandah was lit by a single lantern besieged by moths and lacewings. Edna could see tools on steel shelves, empty feed buckets, a row of kids' bikes leaning against a pillar. She was so tense she almost yipped when Talon grabbed her elbow.

'We can't stand here all night.'

'Just let me get my bearings.' Edna put her hands out. She was waiting for a plan to form. None had. 'We can't just walk into the lounge room and present ourselves.'

The screen door of the verandah before them opened. A stocky man in an Akubra pushed his way out, let it slam behind him, went to the bowed steps to the dusty gravel and sat down. Edna and Talon were frozen, a couple of feet back from the edge of the lantern light, watching as the man drew a packet of cigarettes from the pocket of his jeans and lit one. Edna felt Talon put a huge hand on her shoulder. She didn't move. The boy gave it a second or two, and then he shoved her.

Edna stumbled into the light and whipped around, her face burning with fury.

'Who's there?'

The man on the verandah was standing now. Edna noticed a rifle leaning against the pillar beside where he sat. His fingers were trailing towards it.

'It's okay.' Edna stepped further into the light. She put her hands up. Kept her voice low. 'I'm Edna Norris. I'm a police officer.'

The man frowned, took in Talon slowly as he approached, letting his eyes linger on the makeshift bandage wrapped around the boy's biceps, the undersized T-shirt. 'The rest of the coppers are down the hill. You two lost?'

'We came in through the side fence.' Talon pointed.

'Why?'

'Because we're sort of . . . separate . . . to that party.' Edna gestured to the front of the house. The hill. The crime scene. Her former police brethren. 'Mr Greatman, I'm going to have to ask you to trust me. My partner and I are not with the police who have been attending to you today, but we are really invested in finding out what happened here and tracking down who's responsible.'

'Journalists,' Lenny Greatman said. 'You must be. The cops said you'd come sniffing around, saying all kinds of things. I didn't expect you to pretend to be cops. Isn't that a crime?'

'I'm not lying to you, Mr Greatman. I'm a police officer.'

'He isn't.' Lenny pointed at Talon. 'You look fresh out of high school, mate.'

'I'm . . . her bodyguard,' Talon blurted.

Lenny Greatman cocked his head at Edna, the cigarette burning to a long cylinder of ash in his fingers. 'You gotta be shitting me.'

'Sort of.' The kid shrugged.

'Talon has been assisting me today,' Edna struggled, looked at the kid. How to explain it all. 'He's . . .'

'Like a trainee?' Lenny raised an eyebrow.

'Yeah.' Talon smiled, turned to Edna. The boy seemed to rise an inch in height. 'Work experience.'

Lenny pointed with his cigarette hand to the wound on Talon's arm. 'You got that on work experience?'

'It's a bullet wound.' Talon rose another inch. 'I got it trying to find Clare Holland.'

'None of this rings true to me.' Lenny pinched the bridge of his wide, round nose. 'But that's in keeping with my whole day so far, I s'pose.'

'Will you tell us about Clare?' Edna asked. 'You saw her?'

'Yeah, she was here.' Lenny sunk slowly down to the steps, weary bones put to action for too long. The cattle farmer seemed to have resigned himself to the fact that whoever Edna and Talon really were, they weren't a threat to him. Adrenaline was replaced by his need to rest. His belly hung between his thighs as he flicked the ash away and took a long drag. 'She was callin' herself "Sally". But she was the one in the picture the cops have been showing me. No doubt about it. And she was here with that Buck character. He was the same as the picture, too, but he had glasses on. Black ones.'

'Like reading glasses?'

'Yeah, thick frames. Clark Kent style.'

'Did they just walk up to the house, or . . .?' Edna asked.

'Yep. Just strolled right in.' Lenny shook his head bitterly. 'Said their car had broken down. A Mazda 6. I let 'em sit at my table. Offered 'em my food. That Buck fella sat right next to my Frannie. Looked nervous as hell, both of 'em. I didn't see it at the time but I realised afterwards, that's what it was. Nerves.'

'What *did* you think at the time? Did you sense something was going on?'

'I thought maybe they'd had a fight or something, over the car,' Lenny said. 'There were a couple of looks exchanged between them. Weird looks. They were tense.'

'Why do you think they came here?' Talon asked.

'I got no bloody idea.' Lenny threw his cigarette away. 'Seemed hell-bent on leaving as soon as they arrived. She tried to go. The woman. Clare. Got all the way out to the verandah, saying she felt sick. He went after her. Brought her back in. They both wore jackets the whole time, even in this heat. I guess he had a gun under there, pointed at her, maybe.'

'So they asked for your help with the car?'

'I offered it. But my father stepped in. They took him off down the hill.' Lenny studied his chubby, sun-browned hands. 'Still can't believe it. Doesn't . . . Just doesn't feel real.'

Edna and Talon waited. Crickets had started up around the house, in the struggling grass at the bottom of a nearby water tank. Echoing in the guttering.

'My son, too.'

'Your son went with them?'

'Yeah. Only he tripped and hurt himself, so they had to send him back.'

'Jesus,' Talon whispered.

'The cops . . .' Lenny fell silent. Shrugged, bewildered. 'The cops are saying they blew him up.'

'Your father? What do you mean they blew him up?'

'They took my father and my son off down the hill. My kid comes back wailing, so I'm seeing to that, when I heard a great roaring bang. Shook the ground, it did. I went down there myself, once I'd got the wife and the kids settled. Fark, man. *Fark.*' He pushed back his hat, wiped his brow. 'I didn't know what I was looking at. At the bottom of the hill there were . . . There were just . . . pieces. Blood and bone and . . . *pieces*. I thought it was an animal. I'm thinking, *Okay. So they fixed the car, took it for a spin, and they hit an animal.* But that wasn't right. Wasn't possible. There was fire and ash. And there was fabric. And a boot.'

Lenny Greatman stared at the horizon, the words tumbling out of him.

'So then I'm thinking, *Where's my dad? Because this . . . this ain't my dad.* I ran back to the house and everybody there was panicking, of course, when I told them what I'd seen. Daisy bailed the kids up. I did a bit of a drive around. I was thinking maybe they'd snatched my dad up.'

'The police are saying the remains definitely belonged to your father, though?' Edna said carefully. 'The body down at the crime scene . . . It wasn't Buck or Clare?'

'They showed me a finger. Burnt. With a weddin' ring on it.' Lenny nodded, his eyes fixed. 'And the boot was his. For sure. Been wearin' those same boots for about twenty years.'

Silence fell over the group.

'And there was another guy,' Lenny said.

'Where? What do you mean?'

'I mean there was another guy. A body.' Lenny looked at Edna. 'My brain was so messed up when I went down the hill the first time, I didn't even notice him. But then the second time, I seen him lying there. Wasn't Buck. It was some small guy that I've never seen before. He'd been shot, I think. Badly. There was blood everywhere.'

'Did you hear the gunshot? Could that have been the roaring bang you heard?'

'No, the bang was much bigger. Like a thunderclap. It rattled the windows.'

'So did you hear a gunshot as well?'

'I don't remember.'

Edna and Talon looked at each other, neither able to speak. Edna's mind was trying to form connections. Play out scenarios. But none of them seemed plausible.

'The cops won't let me go back down there,' Lenny said, nodding towards the slope, the distant hill. 'Say it's a crime scene. They've got to work on it. They told us to leave altogether but . . .' he gestured to the horizon, 'where do we go? The nearest hotel is probably in Alice. And somebody's got to see to the cattle.'

Edna and Talon turned as the screen door to the verandah opened again. A small girl in nothing but a pair of underpants emerged from the dark house, her loose, toffee-coloured hair tumbling off her shoulders. She froze at the sight of Edna and Talon standing at the edge of the night.

'Daddy?'

'What are you doing up? You should be in bed, Fran.' Lenny beckoned her over despite his words, held her against his side, cupping her round naked belly in his big hand. 'Is your mum asleep?'

'She's in the big bed. I want to sleep in there with you guys.'

'Yeah, yeah. Okay. Go on. Climb in. I'll be just a minute.'

'Who are they?'

Edna put a hand up, smiled at the girl. 'We're no one. Don't worry about us. We're just leaving.'

Lenny Greatman hugged his daughter, his big arm around her back. Edna took a breath to thank the traumatised father, but he spoke first, his hand travelling down the little girl's arm to her wrist. 'What is this still doing here?'

The girl snatched her wrist away. Lenny dragged it back, his tone darkening. 'You were told to take that off, Fran.'

'I can't *get* it off.' The girl covered her wrist. 'And I like it, Dad. I want to keep it.'

'The police probably need it.' Lenny rose to his feet. 'I'm not gonna tell you again.'

'What's going on?' Talon stepped forward.

'That prick, Harvey Buck.' Lenny's lip curled in a snarl. 'Frannie was sitting there at the lunch table doing her beads. He took some beads and made a bracelet and tied it on her.'

'Can I see it?' Talon asked.

'You can take it with you.' Lenny slid a pen knife from the back pocket of his jeans, pinched out the blade. 'Because it's coming off, Fran. You can't keep that.'

'But I want to!'

'I said no!'

'Can I see it, please?'

The child dissolved into tears, her mouth downturned, eyes scrunched shut. Talon went to the child, held her wrist for a half a second before the child snatched it away again. Edna tugged at the back of the boy's loaned T-shirt. 'Just leave them to it, Talon,' she said. 'We've got to go.'

Talon turned. Edna pulled him on. As they walked into the night, the boy was speechless, watching the earth pass beneath them. Edna listened to the sounds of Lenny Greatman arguing with his daughter, the child squalling and protesting, Lenny's voice rising to barks. The screen door slapped open and shut again. A woman's voice on the wind.

Edna and Talon walked across the empty plains. On the horizon to the west, a storm was flickering. Sheet lightning.

Talon stopped walking. 'Three small, three big, three small,' he said.

Edna stopped. They were by the cow sheds again. 'Huh?'

'The bracelet. I saw it. It was three small beads, three big beads, then three small beads again.'

'Okay? So what?'

'So that was the same order the pens went in.'

Edna stared at the boy. Against the farmhouse, Talon was an enormous silhouette, his close-cropped hair dusted gold. 'What do you mean? What "order", Talon?'

'The pens at the bank,' he said. 'The ones Buck arranged. They went 0.2, 0.2, 0.2, then 0.4, 0.4, 0.4, then 0.2, 0.2, 0.2. If you think of 0.2 being *half* of 0.4, then you've got three halves, then three wholes, then three halves. Or three smalls, then three bigs, then three smalls.'

Edna waited for more. None came.

'Buck deliberately arranged those pens at the bank, and he deliberately tied that bracelet to that kid.' Talon pointed back towards the farmhouse. 'To send us a message. A coded message. We have to figure out what it is.'

Edna swallowed a sigh and walked on, trying to keep her exhaustion and scepticism out of her tone. 'We've got bigger problems, Talon.'

'Maybe the numbers themselves didn't have anything to do with it,' the boy was murmuring, watching the ground, his step fast. 'It was about ratios. Sizes. Half-half-half. Full-full-full. Half-half-half. The beads were all different colours. And the pens were all black. So I'm thinking the colour didn't matter. But maybe it did. Fuck. I should have taken a photo of the bracelet while it was still on the kid's wrist. The dad's probably cut it off by now.'

'Try to focus on what we do have,' Edna said. 'On what's solid, Talon. Lenny said Buck "blew up" his father. Left the guy in pieces. How could he have done that? How is that even possible? And who was the man who was with them? The short guy. Lenny said he'd been shot.'

The boy didn't answer.

'And why come to the farmhouse at all?' Edna slipped through the electric fence, leaving the boy on the other side, staring at the earth. 'Why didn't she blurt out that she was a hostage? Lenny and his father, Daisy as well, perhaps – they could have taken Buck down, working together. Was Clare so terrified that she played along with the ruse of being Buck's travelling partner?'

The boy didn't answer. Edna beckoned him.

'Come through.' She pressed down the second wire from

the bottom of the fence with her boot, pulled up the third wire. 'Mind the shock cable.'

The electric fence warning sign flapped as the boy slipped through. They turned towards the car. It was the moonlight glinting off the slanted rooftop that told Edna something was wrong. She stood at the bonnet of the vehicle, watching that sliver of light, trying to compute what she was seeing. But twenty-four hours of constant adrenaline spikes, the violent death of her partner, and a deeply ingrained dread for her future and that of the boy got the better of her in that moment. Even the hissing of the two punctured tyres, both on the passenger side of the vehicle, did nothing to shift her into action.

When Garreth Holland stepped out of the shadows by the scraggly gumtree, she watched him come with her hands hanging by her sides and her mouth dry as dust, thinking of times death had arrived unannounced in her life like this. The brown snake that slithered out of her bedroom wardrobe one evening. The lightning that struck the earth two feet in front of her vehicle on a drive into town. The ordinary morning she'd walked past Alicia in the front garden of her terrace house in Adelaide, where the girl crouched in her big straw hat, waiting to take Edna's place on the morgue table. All those times, as the shadow of death passed over her, Edna had been left feeling cold. Yet now a hellfire was prickling outward from her heart, and she felt her teeth locked together as she spoke before Garreth Holland even could.

'No,' she snarled.

Holland lifted the rifle from his side, pointed it at her from his hip. The slide bolt gave a well-oiled *ca-shlunk* as he shoved it forward and yanked it back, loading the bullet that would kill her into the chamber. 'Excuse me?'

'I said "No".' Edna set her feet. 'This is not happening. Not today.'

Edna heard Talon release a huff of breath beside her. The boy tried to step in front of her, but Edna shoved him aside again.

'Do you have any idea of the sort of things I've seen out here?' Edna asked Holland, her eyes narrowed and her voice dark and low. 'I've seen bushfires eat houses with people inside them, like waves swallowing rocks. I've seen semi-trailers squash family sedans as flat as paper. Do you know how many cold-blooded, venomous, predatory things have come after me out here? Only half of them were human, Garreth. Everything with a heartbeat from here to the border is out to kill you. You think I've been living in the middle of that for this long without a scratch, just so you can stride in and take me down? You've got to be out of your bloody mind. You're not going to shoot me down by a fucking cow fence like I'm an injured roo, Commissioner Holland. Not today. Not ever.'

'I'm not?' Holland's stiff face broke for a lopsided grin.

'No,' Edna said. 'Because it would be meaningless. Whether you kill us tonight or not, an inquiry into Stevie's death will note that her vehicle didn't break down. That it was deliberately shot and immobilised from a distance, in the same manner that Clare's vehicle was, by someone with an extraordinary level of experience with firearms. It will prove that someone attended the scene after she herself was killed. Someone with your shoe size. Some techy bastard working for the South Australia Police will be able to trace the purchase of a high-powered tracking device to you, Garreth. I'd bet my life on it.'

'None of that proves I shot Sergeant Stevenson,' Holland said. 'And nothing's going to prove I shot you two, a few moments from now. It's just like you said, Senior Sergeant Norris. There are plenty of bad people out here. Madmen who fire at cars from the hillsides. Guys who roll up and shoot cops and kids for no reason at all.'

The hissing of the slashed tyres had eased, but was still there. Edna thought of vipers, of carbon monoxide snuffing out sleepers in their beds. Holland lifted the rifle and pointed it at Talon. Edna saw a flash of Alicia smiling from under her hat, the last sunshine she'd ever feel dancing on her clear, clean skin as she lifted her face to say goodbye.

Edna heard Talon's last intake of breath, a thin gasp. Then she heard the click of Holland's trigger as it met the back of the trigger guard.

The gun shunted.

Nothing happened.

Holland looked down, turned the weapon in his hands. He tried to shift the slide bolt. It jammed in place.

'Oi!' someone yelled.

Edna jolted at the sound. So did Holland. The trio turned, and out of the darkness just beyond the cow sheds a figure emerged. Lenny Greatman walking quickly, his head down, the Akubra shielding his eyes. In one hand he carried a rifle by the stock. His other fist was clenched. Edna felt a wave of dizziness pass through her as she met Garreth Holland's eyes, the tall man lowering his rifle beside his thigh. She saw malice in her would-be murderer's eyes that sent sparkles of electric pain rippling up from the base of her spine.

Lenny lifted his head as he reached them. He barely took Garreth Holland in, stuck a fist through the fence instead and jutted his chin at Talon. 'Take this, would you?' Lenny said. 'I'm not supposed to go anywhere near the bottom of the hill.'

Talon reached out. Edna heard the little plastic beads tumble from Lenny Greatman's hands into his palm.

'Th-thanks,' the boy said.

'I don't want anything from that guy left over in my house,' Lenny said stiffly, his jaw tight. 'My daughter doesn't understand any of it yet. She doesn't know he was a killer.'

'Okay,' Talon said. 'Okay.'

'And there's somethin' else.' Lenny's eyes travelled up and down Holland, from his head to the rifle, settling nowhere. Because a man carrying a rifle in the outback was as ordinary as a man wearing a hat. And Edna supposed that Lenny assumed all the locals would be walking armed, with all the trouble going on. 'Tommerton's Ag Supplies.'

'Yeah?' Edna said, hardly listening.

'They're a business. Based in town. I was expecting a delivery from them about an hour after Buck and Clare were here. By the time they came, I was out there looking around, trying to find my dad or . . . or Buck or whatever.'

Talon nodded.

'I met them out on the road, long before the house. Turned them back. But I was just thinking, as I walked across here . . .' Lenny shrugged. 'Ray Tommerton was talking about getting a dash cam for the truck. Last year, maybe. Because he hit a roo, and the insurance people didn't believe him, because of how much damage there was. I don't know if he ever got the camera installed or not. But if he did . . .'

'Maybe he passed them.' Talon picked up the thread, nodding, looking at Holland. The boy chewed his lip. 'It's a good idea.'

'That was all.' Lenny lifted a hand in parting.

'Don't go!' Talon said. Edna saw Holland lick his teeth, his jaw muscles flexing. Lenny Greatman turned back, took a step towards the fence.

'We, um . . . We were just talking rifles.' Talon smiled. He gestured to Edna, to Holland. 'Everyone seems to have one out here. I'm dead jealous. Do you mind me asking what type you've got there?'

Lenny Greatman lifted his gun, turned it in the moonlight. 'This?'

'Yeah.'

'It's just a Winchester, nothing special.' Lenny made a move to hand the rifle over, glanced at Edna. 'Is the work experience kid allowed to handle guns?'

'Edna,' Holland said; jerked his thumb stiffly towards the horizon. 'I'm gonna head out.'

'You stay right there, Garreth,' Edna said. 'I'm not done with you yet.'

The police commissioner twitched, the cords in his neck pulling tight against the skin for an instant, as Lenny Greatman handed the rifle between the wires of the fence, under the electric line and over the ordinary wires. Talon took the rifle with a smile, gave it a brief look-over and handed it to Edna.

Edna slid the bolt-action back, shunted it forward, locked it into place and raised it.

Then she shot Garreth Holland in the kneecap.

CHAPTER 39

They were descending. Harvey felt himself tugged gently to one side, closer into Clare's body as he lay with his arms around her. The truck stopped, and for the first time, he heard the peeling of its reverse alarm. They were jostled and disturbed into sitting, the two exhausted captives steadying themselves as the truck inched forward and then back, settling finally on an odd angle, the left-hand wheels higher that the right. Harvey lay back down again, ignoring the throbbing in his cracked ribs as the truck engine turned off.

In the distance, the *whump* of helicopter blades. Harvey heard them rise, then fall away. The sound had brought him comfort, once. It felt like a million years ago. He imagined himself in his bunk in Tarin Kot, trying to catch a nap between watches.

'Why haven't they found us yet?' Clare asked.

'Hmm?'

'The choppers,' she said. 'The searchers. The desert must be flooded with them by now. They'd have started when they found my car burning. Ramped it up when you robbed the bank in Cooper Creek. With the old man dead at the cattle farm, and now Wayne . . .'

'It's not as simple as that,' Harvey said. 'You're talking about an area that's tens of thousands of kilometres wide. From a chopper moving at search-grid height you can see about two hundred k's all around at any one time. That's a fraction of the total land mass. From ground level you can see even less. It would have taken a few hours to get searches coordinated properly. They'd be in full swing now, yeah. But it's night. Which about triples how hard it'll be to spot us.'

Clare was silent.

'Plus, they'll be searching all the wrong areas,' Harvey said. 'When you went missing from your car, they'd have started looking in that area. But by then, you were long gone. Then, when I popped up in Cooper Creek, they'd have focused on that area. Same again.'

Harvey imagined himself walking across the desert between Durik and Tarin Kot. A speck in the vastness, far from where he was expected to be. He had to believe that Leasing's men had searched for him in the mountains around the ambush site. That there had been chopper fly-overs, a couple of teams dropped to examine the site. That's what he'd been told. But in truth, Harvey wouldn't have blamed Leasing for thinking such an effort wasn't worth the risk. Lipton, Parker, Darryl and Tizza had told Command that there were no survivors of the massacre, and the foothills where the ambush had occurred were a rabbit warren of Taliban tunnels. And a search, however grand a gesture, wouldn't have helped Harvey anyway. The whole reason he'd gone out into the desert was because it was an insane move. A suicide mission. Both the Taliban, and Australian forces, would have expected him to hunker down in a cave somewhere. It was the only reason he'd made it home, because they had no idea where to look for him.

'Aren't we following the High Wire?' Clare huffed. 'I mean, they should have a *sense* of where we are.'

'You're searching for a particular paperclip – having the sense that it's inside a particular office building won't help matters much.'

'Harvey.'

'I don't think we're directly on the Wire,' Harvey said. 'We might be within a stone's throw of it. But the ride's been pretty rough for a while now. I'd say we've been bush bashing for the past hour at least. The back-and-forth just now was probably Darryl trying to park us under an overhang, in case a lucky chopper spots our heat signature, or an unlucky trucker eyeballs us again.'

Harvey got up, walked to the top of the truck bed and lay back down. He scooted until his boots were against the wall, his legs at a right angle. Then he pounded the sheet metal, stomping one foot at a time, the noise rippling up and around the truck cabin. He stomped for ten seconds. The silence rang afterwards.

'What the hell are you doing?'

'Darryl will be in the cabin trying to sleep,' Harvey said. The effort of stomping had exhausted him. His stomach ached with hunger. 'Fuck him.'

Clare scooted across the truck floor until she was beside Harvey. She gripped his forearm to position herself. Harvey felt the stickiness of Wayne the trucker's blood on her fingers as it met the hair on his arm. Hair that was itchy and matted with Nathan Tizza's blood. The two captives lay and stomped on the sheet metal together. Harvey wondered what they looked like, two filthy, reeking, blood-smeared people pounding on a truck wall in the dark.

They heard the driver's door open and slam. Darryl's flat palm on the side of the truck, rippling the metal as he bashed it. 'What the hell do you want?'

'Coffee!' Harvey yelled back. 'White, no sugar!'

'I want a shot of scotch in mine!' Clare yelled from beside him. Harvey smiled in the dark. It felt like lifting a bathtub full of bricks.

Darryl got back into the truck, slammed the door.

They began to pound.

CHAPTER 40

'Holy shit!' Talon said.

Edna started the engine in Garreth Holland's Mercedes. The vehicle lit up, purred pleasantly to life. Talon gripped the handle of the door, turned to watch the farm fence line disappear as they peeled away from the place a hundred metres from where they'd left a stunned Lenny Greatman and a screaming Garreth Holland.

Talon had one hand over his mouth, muffling the words. 'Holy shit. Holy shit. *Holy shiiiit!*'

'I know.' Edna reached over and patted the boy's knee. 'It's okay. We're fine. We made it out.'

'Fine? We're not fine. You just *shot* a guy!' Talon's eyes were huge in the glow of the console. 'Oh my god. You just blew his knee away. I saw bone.'

'Calm down.'

'*I-saw-bone-I-saw-bone-I-saw-bone.*'

'He'll be fine. They can work wonders with knees. You're up and walking the day after surgery.'

'You *shot* him!'

'I also stole his car.'

'They'll be after us now. The police.'

'Maybe,' Edna said. 'But it was worth it.'

'*Holy shiiiit!*'

'Look, they won't come for us right away,' Edna said. 'Because there'll be journos in the mix by now. If they haven't arrived already they'll be on the road or arriving at Durham. The first thing they'll be doing is hooking into the communication system on site. Hitting the radio and the phones. If Zhang puts it out on the radio now that one of her cops has just shot another of her cops, everybody will hear it. She won't do that.'

'Why not?'

'Because she'll want to know what happened. If the story needs finessing. It's the police way. Contain and neutralise.'

They pulled onto the sandy road leading away from the Greatman farm.

'She won't let you just get away, though.'

'No. We'll have to be careful,' Edna said. 'Because the message will be out there on the down-low. Passed by word of mouth only. That they want me. That I'm to be held in place if I'm encountered, with Command alerted immediately to my location.'

'You're never going to, like, recover from this,' Talon said. 'They can't let you be a cop again after something like that, right? You can't shoot a police commissioner.'

'I've heard of people coming back from worse,' Edna snorted, flicking the high beams on.

'No way.'

'Here's what's going to happen,' Edna said. 'Lenny Greatman is going to run down the hill and tell the crime scene teams what I did. Garreth Holland is going to be hauled off for medical treatment. He'll have to go into surgery. In the course of that surgery, it's going to be revealed that he has a second, untreated gunshot wound that's at least a day old.'

Talon sat thinking.

'His clothes will also be confiscated before he goes onto the table,' Edna said. 'Including his shoes. And because he's just been involved in a serious crime, those clothes will be bagged and tagged as evidence.'

'Really?'

'Hell yeah,' Edna said. 'What I just did was grievous bodily harm at least. Maybe attempted murder, if you get the right prosecutor. There are arteries and stuff in your legs.'

Talon nodded.

'Zhang and her people, if they're worth their salt, will be starting to get curious by then,' Edna said. 'They'll take a look at Holland's shoes, and how those shoes compare to the print at Stevie's crime scene. They'll be interested in that rifle, too. And whether it matches the calibre of weapon used to kill Stevie. I would be surprised if someone wasn't sent to the Holland residence to see what can be found there. Signs of a struggle preceding Clare's disappearance, for example.'

They drove on. Edna's words seemed thin in the never-ending darkness. 'It'll all come out in the wash. When they realise what Holland's done. It'll be clear that, standing there in the dark with his rifle, he wasn't coming to have a peaceful little chat with you and me. And that's all we'll need; for Lenny Greatman to say he saw Holland standing there with his rifle. It'll be self-defence. The charges will be dropped and I'll be back on the desk at the Clifton Hills cop shop by next Thursday.'

'But that's only if they realise what he's done,' Talon said. 'For that, we need them to not believe him, when he comes up with some story to explain away all that stuff. What if he says he went to Stevie's crime scene because he came upon it after us? What if he explains away the struggle at his house? He could say he was cleaning his personal weapon and shot himself accidentally.'

'There you go with that wonderful imagination,' Edna said. 'Poking holes in circumstances. You're a born lawyer, Talon.'

'What we really need is for Clare to say he was after her, that he came out here to kill her.'

'No problem.' Edna shrugged. 'We just have to find her and bring her home alive.'

'Should we do what Lenny said?' the boy asked. 'Try to get hold of the Tommerton dash cam footage? If he even had a dash cam.'

'If this Tommerton guy isn't out on the search, he'll be home in bed,' Edna said. 'Call the number anyway. It's worth trying.'

Talon tapped the number on his screen and dialled. No answer. He ended the call and began typing away on the phone. They drove in the dark, heading south-east towards the Wire. Edna passed a Jeep with tinted windows, gripped the wheel tightly, waiting for it to turn in her rear-view mirror and come after her. It didn't. Her mind wandered. She tried to imagine Harvey Buck and Clare Holland sitting at a lunch table with Lenny Greatman's family, the little girl by his side, the story about the broken-down Mazda 6. Why had they come to the farmhouse? Had Buck always intended to murder Greatman's father, and if so, why? Edna tried to fit the information Lenny

Greatman had given her into the theory she felt like she had been holding for years now, about Buck as Clare Holland's would-be rapist and murderer, who went on, for some reason, to rob a bank. Nothing about the happenings at the Greatman farm lined up with that theory. And then there was the body of the second man. Or the third, if Edna counted the body they'd found at Buck's car. Had 'Small Man', as she'd come to think of him, held Clare Holland captive while Buck robbed the Cooper Creek bank? And what had transpired between the two abductors that meant that Small Man had to die outside the Greatman farm? Edna saw Buck and Small Man arguing. One determined to do . . . whatever they'd done to Lenny Greatman's father. The other opposed. Buck shooting Small Man dead.

And then what? Edna frowned in the dark.

The cops are saying they blew him up.

I heard a great roaring bang.

Edna strummed the wheel. She'd seen some things in the desert, as she'd told Holland, and one of them, an almost weekly sight, was a kangaroo reduced to mincemeat by a road train. The enormous vehicles, their incredible speed, and the tragic tenderness of flesh and bone meant that sometimes, yes, animals hit by those vehicles out here ended up as 'just pieces'. But that didn't explain the flames Greatman had described. Or an explosion so loud it could be heard well up at the farmhouse as a 'great roaring bang'. One that shook the windows and the floors. Had the police at the bottom of the hill been correct in their assessment of how Lenny's father died? Had he been exploded with some kind of . . . *bomb*?

'Okay,' Talon said. 'Listen to this.'

'I'm listening.'

'I put in the dates. The ones from the tattoo on the balaclava guy. The "Lippo" memorial. I was wondering if, like, Buck killed Lippo back in the day, whoever he was. And maybe that's why the balaclava guy came after him.'

'Okay.' Edna raised her eyebrows. 'Not bad.'

'It's not the same *day*,' Talon said. 'But within the same *week*, in Afghanistan, Harvey Michael Buck did his war hero thing.'

'What war hero thing?'

'I tried to tell you about it before.' Talon squinted at the screen, scrolling. 'But it sort of fell by the wayside.'

'So tell me now.'

'When Buck was in the army, he got caught up in a big ambush. There was a convoy going through this mountain range in like Afghanistan or whatever. Taliban guys started shooting at them. It ended up being the largest loss of Australian soldiers in the whole war. Fourteen people dead in total.'

'Shit.' Edna looked over.

'Buck and five guys escaped the actual fight in the mountains. Four guys fought their way out and drove home to the base. Buck and another guy, Geon Bak-Li, they trekked through the desert for three days to get home.'

'Wow.'

'But get this.' Talon batted her arm with the back of his hand. 'The four survivors, the guy who drove home? All Australians. We got Nathan Tizza, Henry Darryl, Martin Parker and Greg Lipton.'

'Lippo.' Edna's mouth fell open. 'So . . . he survived the massacre. The same one Buck was in. Then he dies later that week.'

'Five days later.'

'How did he die, then?'

'It doesn't say,' Talon said. 'His death is just listed in a round-up of deaths in Afghanistan of Australian soldiers. There's the big massacre, with the fourteen killed. Then three days later, Bak-Li dies. So I guess he was wounded in the battle or maybe walking through the desert killed him.'

'Hmm.'

'Then two days after *that*, Lipton dies.' Talon shook his head. 'Jesus. Why the hell didn't we take off the guy's balaclava? We could have compared his face to some of the people we're talking about here. I mean; Tizza, Darryl and Parker . . . was he one of them? Or some other army guy?'

Edna's mind was sizzling, hissing, shutter-snapping with energy. The edge of the road seemed to glow in the headlights. She pulled over, tried to breathe through it.

'You okay?' Talon asked.

'I'm okay,' she nodded. 'It's just. I'm trying to figure it out. I feel like we're so close. I also haven't eaten in a whole day. Neither have you. Did you even notice?'

'I had other things on my mind.' Talon flicked the overhead light on, opened the glove box, rummaged about. Seemed to find nothing. Edna sat thinking as the boy fished around the car.

'It's all army-related,' Edna said. 'Shayna. Buck's girlfriend or whatever. In Sydney. She was army. We've got to assume this guy with the Lippo tattoo was army. A guy doesn't get a memorial tattoo for another guy unless they're brothers or lovers or best fucking friends. Everything about that scene is screaming military to me now. The road spikes. The two shots. That was a serious ambush we were looking at back there. We thought it was an ambush of Buck by someone he didn't know.

But maybe he did know him. Maybe they were in Afghanistan together. Whoever the guy in the balaclava was, he was the link between Buck and Lippo.'

Talon drew a crackling packet out of a compartment in the centre console between himself and Edna. 'Almonds?' he sighed. 'Urgh.'

'Maybe Buck wasn't alone when he drove out here,' Edna said. 'Him and Small Man. From the Greatman farm. They were travelling together and they picked up Clare . . . And the guy in the balaclava, who had it in for them, tried to ambush them. To stop them, maybe, from going on their crime spree. It didn't work. He got nailed. Buck and Small Man kept going. Small Man kept Clare hostage while Buck went into Cooper Creek to try to get them some cash. They bailed out of there. Rolled up at the Greatman farm. One of them, Buck, I suppose, had the idea to kill someone. To blow him up.'

'They'd know about explosives.' Talon poured a handful of almonds into Edna's palm, his jaws working as he uneasily munched some of his own. 'If we're saying that Small Man is army as well.'

'There was an argument. Buck killed Small Man. Either before or after they blew up Greatman.'

'Maybe they didn't argue, though. Maybe, like, it wasn't a gunshot. Lenny Greatman said he wasn't sure if he heard a gunshot or not. Or if the guy had been shot or something else had happened to him. He said he *thought* he'd been shot.'

Edna cleared her throat, almost said something about shrapnel but didn't. 'Doesn't matter how he died. He died, and now Buck's still out there with Clare, heading towards the next thing.'

'So what *is* the next thing?'

'I have no idea.' Edna rubbed her eyes. There were pieces of almond stuck between her teeth. She needed water. 'I don't even understand the last thing.'

'There has to be more food around here.' Talon twisted in the seat, stopped at what he saw in the rear of the vehicle. He reached into the back seat and brought out a box. 'What's this?'

Edna looked. 'Oh. That's a two-way. Holland would have had it on, monitoring where everyone was during the search.' She reached over and fished around in the semi-dark for a cord, plugged the radio into the dashboard of the Mercedes. Holland's radio was identical to the backup model she had in her cruiser. Edna flicked the radio on and turned the volume all the way up. 'Put it down there at your feet.'

There was silence in the car. In time, Edna pulled back onto the road. They rumbled in darkness, each waiting for the inevitable blip of the radio. In time, a crackle of static came. But after ten minutes, no voices had come through.

'There's probably an official search channel and they might have changed it when I shot Holland,' Edna said. 'They probably know I have his car. Probably know he had a radio. They'll be wanting to keep me in the dark. Reach down, would you, and look for the dial on the front of the unit. Flick it around a few times. See what you can find.'

Talon did as he was told. Almost immediately, foreign voices rattled inside the quiet car.

'. . . *believed to be travelling in a late-model Mercedes, registration DX-511. If search personnel could advise Senior Sergeant Norris to make contact with the command team, and alert the command team to Senior Sergeant Norris's whereabouts, that would be much appreciated.'*

'*Team Five, copy that.*'

'*We copy you. Team Two here.*'

'See?' Edna said. 'The Make Contact call. It's how you know someone's in deep shit.' She smiled. 'I've had a few of those in my life, I can tell you.'

Talon nodded.

The radio crackled. Five minutes passed. It crackled again. They listened.

'*Hello? Is anybody . . . there?*'

Talon looked at Edna. 'Who's that?'

'No idea. One of the search team people, I suppose.'

'*Is anybody there? Please? Please. I need help.*'

Edna felt her skin come alive, as surely as she had been blasted by a winter breeze. Talon was watching her, listening. 'Should we answer?'

'*Help needed, here. Please answer. I need help.*'

'*Go ahead, caller. This is Detective Inspector Luqi Zhang with the South Australia Police. Do you need emergency assistance?*'

'*I've been shot. I'm with my truck. My name is Wayne. Preston.*'

'*Where are you? Who shot you?*'

'*I'm at . . . I'm . . . I'm out in the sticks.*'

'*Where? Give us your exact location.*'

'*I'm about five minutes north . . . of the rock forest.*'

'*Sorry, can you give us that location again?*'

'I know where that is,' Edna said. She swung the wheel.

CHAPTER 41

The truck cabin door opened and they heard Darryl's footsteps in the dirt moving swiftly away from the vehicle. Harvey and Clare still had their boots up on the wall. The footsteps receded until there was silence.

'This is where we hear a bang,' Clare said in the dark beside him. 'A single gunshot. Pop. And it's all over.'

Harvey thought of the way soldiers under his care had spoken in Afghanistan, about gunshots and lives taken like they were numbers in chalk on a board. Then he reminded himself that people will say anything when their lives are hanging over the abyss.

'He'll try to sleep out there. On the earth. It won't work.' Harvey let his legs slide down the wall until they rested flat on the floor, his knees bent. 'There'll be crawling things. Or the impression of them. And the things that crawl on you out here aren't playing games. He'll be back in ten minutes or so, and we'll be on our way.'

The truck ticked gently, still losing heat from the day, even as a distinct chill was making goosebumps rise on Harvey's forearms and thighs. He guessed, this time of year, the temperature in the desert in the early hours would be in the single digits. As though sensing his thoughts, Clare shifted closer to him.

'Do you think he'll do it tonight?' she asked. 'Roll us up on the camp while they're sleeping?'

'No,' Harvey said.

'Why not?'

'Because something as spectacular as this is designed for the daytime. Think of every major terrorist attack you've ever seen footage of. September 11. The Boston Marathon. The London Bombings. Bright, sparkling daylight. This kind of stuff just doesn't have the same effect when all the news crews have to show people is red and blue lights flashing in the dark and shapes moving about.'

'So we have time. Maybe one more shot at getting him,' Clare's voice quickened. Hopeful energy. 'He might let us out again between now and morning and we can make a move for the detonator.'

'It must be in his pocket,' Harvey said. 'If I had to guess, I'd say it's a key fob. Makes that *ca-click* sound key fobs do. Easy enough to hold in your hand and alter to respond to something in the vests. And they have three buttons, right? Lock, unlock and boot.'

'If it's a key fob,' Clare said, 'then it's sending a signal the way a key fob does, right? Like a little radio wave that the car picks up.'

'Mmm hmm.'

'So . . . maybe they *were* lying when they said they can get us from anywhere. The key fob for your car, it has to be pretty close by for it to work.'

'We can't be sure,' Harvey said. 'Just because the trigger is housed in a key fob, doesn't mean it's operating through those little radio waves. It could be that Tiz had taken apart two basic mobile phones. Cut them down to their bare parts. In the key fob, he has the "dial" function fitted, with just one number programmed in. In the vests, he has the "call receiver" function, which will basically just be an electrical circuit that completes when the device attempts to make a ringing sound. He presses the button on the fob. That makes the call from the fob to the vest. The vest tries to ring. Boom.'

'If these vests are programmed with two mobile phones,' Clare said, 'what's to stop someone else randomly dialling that number and setting us off? A robocaller. Or a spam text. We could explode any second because someone sends out one of those scam texts to three million numbers.'

'Exploding at any given second, whether Darryl and Tizza want us to or not, has always been a possibility,' Harvey said. 'From the moment we put these vests on.'

They heard footsteps. Darryl trudging back to the truck.

'What do you think he's going to do to us?' Clare asked. 'When we arrive? Will he walk us into the middle of them?'

'If I had to guess,' Harvey said, 'I'd say he's going to park somewhere that the recruits will arrive at in just a few minutes. Sideways, across the road. He should be able to figure out where they'll be. The Duntroon officers, they run this exercise every year, always the same dates, always the same route. The hike takes two weeks total. Total distance minus days remaining in the exercise, and Darryl should be able to put us within the ballpark of where the recruits and their instructors will be. He'll order me up into the driver's seat of the truck. Cable-tie my wrists to the steering wheel. He'll probably gag me somehow, so I can't warn the others. The recruits and their instructors will come up to the vehicle and find me in the driver's seat, distressed, tied. You in the back, making a ruckus. He might even set the truck on fire. Bring a sense of urgency into the whole situation. A whole bunch of people will converge around the truck. Some trying to break the cabin windows and free me. Others trying to get you out of the back. Or fight the fire. Or just figure out what the hell has happened here. Some of the recruits will start filming the whole thing on their phones in the bright sparkling daylight. You're not supposed to bring phones on the exercise, but you know some of them will have. They're kids.'

Clare was silent.

'Darryl will wait until enough people are within proximity of the vehicle, then he'll blow our vests. Kill us, and them, and maim anyone unlucky enough to be nearby.'

Harvey heard the lifelessness in his voice. The dangerous levels of resignation. Because it was there again, the temptation to give up. The same temptation that had shadowed him, footstep by footstep, through the desert with Bak-Li on his shoulders. Because giving up then, dumping his fellow soldier and carrying on by himself, would have been understandable. He could have justified it in a million different ways. And allowing what was going to happen to him now to happen was also so very, very tempting. The fight had gone out of him. It had fled, like a vapour escaping his nostrils, his mouth.

But he decided, there in the dark, that he would go on, anyway. Even without strength, or fight, or a solid sense of how he could change his outcome. Because going always onward, even if it was directly towards pain, was better than the pain of lying down and wondering in his final moments what one more step could have brought him.

Thoughts zinged together. He played the next few hours out in his mind.

'We need a plan,' Clare said.

'I've got one cooking.' Harvey squinted in the dark. The truck engine started up and roared. He turned towards her. 'This is our last shot at this, Clare. Let me run you through something, and you tell me what you think.'

CHAPTER 42

Flat earth. A slab of desert sand blown smooth and featureless by wind channelled between two narrow gaps in a faraway mountain range. The Mercedes was already eerily quiet compared to what Edna was accustomed to – her roaring cruiser, the rattling four-wheeler she used to get around her property, the borrowed SUVs she'd driven that day. Now, as the luxury car sailed onto the sand, it quietened further. Talon, who had been dozing in the seat beside her, sat up sharply.

The rock forest came out of nowhere. She slowed. Before them, a sudden, sprawling sea of wide, flat stones. The stones were stacked into knee-high mountains, little temples of rock no more than two or three metres apart. The small towers cast long, winding shadows that moved like the arms of a strange gigantic clock, or moon dial, as they made their way through. Edna's breath was stolen by it, as it always was, the enormity of the forest, which receded into the dark, unbroken in all directions. Its unspoken meaning toyed with her. Because the way she had heard it, locals could not account for who had stacked the thousands upon thousands of rocks in their uniform piles out here in the nothingness, or how the arrangement had occurred. Only days before a drover from Bulloo Downs first stumbled upon the forest, the land had been traversed by geologists looking for good mining ground. No one from their party, when questioned, had mentioned it.

Talon leant forward in his seat, watching the towers pass as Edna carefully picked her way through, probably thinking what she was thinking. That this looked like the work of hundreds of people. Yet it was so remote, it had probably only ever been seen by a handful of long-term desert dwellers like her and the other permanent residents.

Edna watched the Mercedes' clock. At the five-minute mark, she slowed to a stop, rolled down their windows, switched the headlights and the engine off. They sat in the blankness of outer space, drifting, listening to the silence. Edna tried to discern the horizon as her vision adjusted. The lowest star, almost as soon as her eyes settled upon it, began to blink.

'There.' Talon pointed, seeing the blinking almost at the same time she did. Edna started the engine up. She hit the accelerator hard. The semi-trailer loomed, growing, its fish-belly-white side materialising, streaked with red desert dust. The flicking of the headlights stopped. The man inside the semi must have heard their vehicle. As she parked, Edna's headlights rolled over the blood. It was on the open door of the semi's high cabin. On the side of the bed. On the wheel well of the huge tyre. The bonnet of the semi was tilted forward, exposing the enormous engine, the headlights reflecting off the filthy interior of the bowed bonnet. Edna followed the blood, deciding someone badly injured had opened the bonnet and then climbed up into the cabin. Talon jogged around the side of the vehicle. Edna heard him open the passenger door as she climbed the ladder to the driver's side, which was hanging ajar and awash with red.

A wall of cigarette stink, body odour, and the metallic smell of blood. Wayne Preston was slumped in the driver's seat, slid forward so that his hips were under the wheel and his chin was against his chest. His eyes were closed, and his face was the grey of freezer-burnt meat. Edna looked into Talon's wide eyes and prepared to tell the boy that they were seconds too late. That he was seeing his third dead body of the day. But the pot-bellied man opened his eyes and gave a gurgle and Edna took his blood-soaked hand as he reached for her.

'You're okay now,' Edna lied.

'Is he . . .' Talon had crawled up into the truck's cabin. He struggled for words. 'Is he gonna make it?'

Edna widened her eyes at the kid. Talon backed off. She reached through the tiny slot window behind the driver's seat, fished around, and yanked out the first piece of fabric she laid her hand on. A T-shirt. The trucker's whole torso was so wet with blood, there was no telling where the gunshot wound actually was without undressing him. But Edna figured he had only minutes left. She wiped the blood running from the man's mouth as he tried to clear his throat, his head lifting as he attempted to swallow.

'Buck . . . is not,' the guy wheezed.

Edna watched his eyes, nodding. 'It's okay, mate. Try not to talk.'

'He's . . . *not* . . .' Wayne shook his head.

Edna nodded again, squeezed his hand.

The trucker took one long, wet, rattling breath. 'Burke,' he said. 'Wills.'

Talon's eyes were huge, searching Edna's for answers. She didn't have any.

'The track?' Edna asked. 'Are you talking about the Burke and Wills track?'

'Where is that?' Talon asked.

'It's a track that runs south to north, couple of hours from here,' Edna said. 'Tourists follow it in their four-wheel drives.'

'Is that where you're from?' Talon asked the trucker. 'Is that where you were headed?' The wounded man shook his head. 'What then?'

The radio crackled somewhere in the enormous console. Not Zhang, but someone else.

'*Wayne? Are you there? We've got a unit about ten minutes away. Hang on.*'

Talon was looking everywhere but at the dying man. At the horizon. At the ceiling. At the semi's cabin lit in the pale green glow of the dashboard. There was a stuffed toy crocodile affixed to the headrest of the passenger seat. Stickers, postcards, paperwork and spent cigarettes littered the dash. The partition between the front seats and the sleeping area was stuck with hundreds of items – sun-coiled, handwritten lists, photocopied maps, menus from takeaway places as far away as Darwin. Edna followed the boy's eyes as she realised they were locked on a battered piece of paper in the upper right-hand corner of the cabin, a list printed in big Comic Sans font.

Official Aussie Trucker CB Codes

CODE 4: Organ Donors Ahead! (Motorcyclists)

CODE 5: Negative on Jumpy Juice (This place has terrible coffee!)

CODE 6: Affirmative on Nap Trap (Upcoming hotel has vacancies)
CODE 69: Car full of Seat Warmers (Attractive women)
MAYDAY MAYDAY: Code 69 women have flat tyre, need help!

Always remember: Rhythmic short horn blasts and a rocking truck means STAY AWAY!!!!

The boy gasped sharply. Edna looked up. Talon swallowed, his eyes flicking all over the cabin, hand reaching for the phone in his pocket. The kid thought better of it, of pursuing whatever it was he was thinking. He took Wayne Preston's other hand, and looked at Edna, and she nodded. They sat with the trucker as the last faint breaths rattled out of him.

No sooner had Edna's feet hit the ground than Talon skidded to a stop in the dirt beside her, having run from the other side of the vehicle. He was frantically thumbing something into his phone, his jaw working, pulse ticking in his neck. In the distance, Edna could see blue and red lights flickering, a tiny pair of specks coming through the rock forest.

Talon pocketed the phone and seized Edna by the arms and she yowled in shock and pain. 'Holy shit, Ed! I was right!'

'Jesus!' Edna snapped. 'What about?'

'SOS!' the boy said. When she didn't respond fast enough, he shook her, almost lifted her off her feet. 'Half-half-half, full-full-full, half-half-half. It's Morse code. They use it in the army. It means SOS!'

Edna stood there, watching the kid's eyes, knowing that the seconds were ticking by between then and when she would need to leave. Because she would be arrested when the approaching unit arrived. She knew that much. But something was happening, and the enormous reversal of thinking was rooting her on the spot, even after the kid let her go. She couldn't move, or plan, or think until she came to terms with what he was saying. Until she fit it into her already overcrowded brain. 'You're saying *Buck* has been signalling for help?'

'I think . . . so?' Talon's voice was disbelieving now, the words half-strength, being tested on the air. 'It fits. The sequence of the pens and the beads on the bracelet. They're the same. And if you apply that to Morse code, it spells out those letters. SOS. It's not a coincidence.'

'But why would Buck need help? What does he need saving from? He's the abductor!'

'But *is he*?' Talon asked.

The faint sound of a siren. Edna's mind quickened. Because all her questions were tumbling around in her brain and being answered, one by one, as the seconds passed. If Buck wasn't the abductor, then who was? The guy in the balaclava? Small Man? Maybe someone else?

'Are you telling me . . .?' Edna stammered. 'Buck . . . He's . . . It's *Clare* who's got *him* hostage?'

'No. Can't be.' Talon shook his head. 'Lenny Greatman said Clare tried to get away from him. Onto the verandah. Buck chased after her and brought her back.'

'So . . . they're *both* hostages?'

'Maybe.' Talon gave a hard sigh, his mind appearing to spin. 'Maybe, like, there was a group of them. At the ambush.

The guy in the balaclava and Small Man and someone else. In the ambush, Buck killed the guy in the balaclava. Then, at the Greatman farm, he killed Small Man. But then maybe there's another. *A third guy.*'

'But . . . I mean . . . where are they now? Who is that third guy?' Edna couldn't believe what she was saying, couldn't keep up with own racing thoughts. 'If . . . If Balaclava Dude and Small Man were holding Harvey and Clare hostage, and those guys are both dead . . . do we even know for sure that there *is* someone else?'

'There must be someone else. Because they haven't handed themselves in, Buck and Clare. They haven't got to safety. And if Buck's a good guy, and Clare's a good guy, then who killed Wayne Preston?' He gestured to the truck. 'They must still be in danger, Buck and Clare.'

'But if someone still has them, who is it? Who's the third guy?'

'I don't know!' Talon lifted his hands. 'Why are you asking me? I don't have all the answers!'

'You have *some*,' Edna said. 'That's for sure. This code thing. I've . . . I've been discounting it from the start, Talon.'

'Well,' the kid's mouth twitched, 'that wasn't very imaginative.'

'If we can figure out who the third guy is—'

'Maybe we can figure out where they're going.'

'But we don't even know who the first two were.' Edna rubbed her temples. 'How the hell are we gonna—'

'Dash cam.' Talon shook a finger at her. Looked up at the truck. 'We didn't go after Tommerton's dash cam, because we didn't know if it even existed and it was too late in the day. But maybe—'

'Go.' Edna pushed him towards the semi. The boy scrambled up the ladder. Edna's boot crunched on something in the dirt, made metal grind on metal. She reached down, picked up a chain with two thin steel objects attached to it. A circle and a hexagon. Dog tags. Before she could really examine them, the boy dropped back down beside her, his eyes on the approaching cruiser.

'But . . . I guess we should leave this for them,' Talon said, holding up a small grey camera with a suction cup. He glanced at the approaching police cruiser. 'It's evidence.'

'No, we'll examine it ourselves,' Edna said. 'On the road. Whatever we learn, we'll call and tell them. Get in the car.'

'But—'

'We don't have a chance in hell of them believing us, Talon. About Buck, about the Morse code, about the third guy,' Edna said. 'The best we can do is keep pushing on as our own team trying to solve this. Explaining ourselves is only going to slow us down. We'll share any insight we have. Of course we will. But we can't stop in our tracks or they'll stick us in a holding cell somewhere and that'll be the end of us.' She pushed the kid along. 'Go.'

They climbed into the Mercedes. Edna started it up and hit the accelerator, kicking up a cloud of dust as she turned in to the empty desert. Talon hung on, looking strangely distant, even as they raced away from the danger of arrest, leaving their fifth or sixth crime scene of the day, Edna couldn't be sure. She supposed the horror of what they were doing, of what they had seen, would come over the boy in waves as adrenaline ebbed and flowed. He seemed to shake himself out of his reverie, turning the little plastic dash camera in his hands, searching for an on switch.

'Even if we find out who the third guy is,' Talon said, 'we have no idea where they're going.'

'Yeah we do,' Edna said. 'The Burke and Wills track.'

CHAPTER 43

They drove for forty minutes, maybe an hour. Harvey and Clare talked. As he listened to her in the dark, Harvey picked at the gash in his skull, the one above his ear, where the drone had flown into the side of his head. When he felt blood flowing, warm and thin, he found a spot on the wall beside him and painted what he hoped in the blinding darkness were three dots, followed by three dashes, followed by three dots. When their talk was complete, they lay down again and started kicking at the fabricated steel barrier at the top of the truck bed. The truck came to a stop. Harvey watched the vertical slice of night appear at the rear of the truck, then widen. The door creaked open and Darryl stepped back. Harvey couldn't see if the gun was in his hand, but he bet that it was. He bet the other hand was in the man's pocket, wrapped around the detonator to their vests.

'She's sick,' Harvey said. He nodded to Clare, sitting with her back against the wall beside him. 'She's gonna throw up. Give her some air.'

'Fuck you,' Darryl said. He slammed the truck doors shut and latched them. The truck started and rumbled on. After half an hour or so, they lay down and started kicking again. They kicked and kicked, taking turns, ten minutes passing before the truck stopped and Darryl's boots crunched onto the earth by the driver's-side door.

'*What?*' Darryl yelled through the metal side of the truck.

'She's sick!' Harvey yelled back.

'We've been on the road for twenty-four hours,' Darryl barked. Harvey listened carefully to the voice, muffled through sheets of steel, still unmistakably thinner and higher than it had been a day ago. 'You think I'm falling for this shit, Buck? There hasn't been a single peep about motion sickness in all that time. Shut the *fuck up*.'

Darryl climbed back into the truck. Harvey readied his legs against the steel wall. The vehicle roared to life. The constant pounding was making his ears ache, making his hips throb with effort. Clare was breathing hard, grunting as she bashed her shoes against the steel, stomping and stomping, the thunderous noise rippling up over the roof of the truck.

They drove for another ten minutes. Harvey heard the faint, tinny squealing of a radio as Darryl tried to drown out the noise. Harvey tried to pick the song. 'Thunderstruck' by AC/DC. He liked the song. Had heard it hundreds of times, pumping out across radios in army garages and around bases and in tactical vehicles. A gear-up-and-roll-out song, which was probably exactly what Darryl was using it for. To prepare himself mentally for that coming time, the no-turning-back time, when drums and thunder and guns would arrive on the innocent army recruits making their way up the Burke and Wills track. As the songs followed, one after the other, Harvey counted them off, remembered times and places he'd heard them. 'Bodies' by Drowning Pool. 'Killing in the Name' by Rage Against the Machine. 'Break Stuff' by Limp Bizkit. 'Chop Suey!' by System of a Down. He and Darryl's minds were one, touring dark and chaotic musical lands, where it rained bodies and snowed hatred on death-deserving angels. He breathed, and stomped the wall, and tried not to be taken backwards. Tried to focus on the plan. When the truck stopped again, Clare came up onto her knees, stuck her fingers down her throat and vomited onto the floor.

Darryl must have heard the sound, because he stopped, got out and trudged around to the back of the truck, threw open one of the doors and shone a torch inside. 'This is bullshit,' he said.

'Is it?' Harvey asked. Clare dry-heaved and wiped her mouth on her hand.

'It is,' Darryl said. 'You think you're going to take one last shot at me, by having me let her out and turning my back on you to see that she's all right. Guess what, it ain't happening.'

'If you weren't concerned that she's all right, you wouldn't have stopped the truck again,' Harvey said. He waited for Darryl to come up with a counterargument. He didn't. 'Truth is, you are concerned, and you should be.'

'Why?'

'Because she could die back here,' Harvey said.

'So what?' Darryl was a silhouette behind the bright white torchlight. 'I'm literally driving the two of you to your deaths right now. I've told you that.'

'Maybe so,' Harvey said. 'But if she dies in the next five minutes, instead of when we arrive, that's one less asset you'll have for the next phase of the plan. Can you really afford that?'

Again, Darryl didn't answer.

'You lost Parker,' Harvey said. 'Then you lost Tizza. Those were two major failings in your plan. Now it's just you, and you have to ask yourself what major failings lie ahead. Because maybe we'll arrive at the Burke and Wills track and you'll park the truck and finish us both off and everything will go exactly as you want it to. It'll be hellfire and carnage. Your dream realised. But maybe it won't happen like that. I'm here, right now, telling you it won't. And I'm right. I was right about Parker. I was right about Tizza.'

'Fuck you,' Darryl snapped.

'Everything is falling apart, Darryl. Your plan is falling apart. Disaster is coming. And if you let heat stroke and trauma and dehydration and possible underlying medical conditions she hasn't told you about kill Clare five minutes from now, you're going to have half the amount of assets available to you to deal with that coming disaster.'

'She doesn't have any underlying medical conditions,' Darryl scoffed.

'Do you know that for sure?' Harvey asked.

'I just need some air,' Clare begged. 'And some water. Please. If you don't trust him, just don't let him out of the truck! It's that simple!'

She vomited again. Harvey watched Darryl, who was barely a solid shape behind the torchlight. Silence fanned out across the truck.

Darryl slammed the doors, shunted the levers closed. Harvey held his breath. Counted the seconds. Harvey didn't believe in mind-meld or telepathy or any of that woo-woo stuff, though he'd had reason to in the past. He'd seen whole groups of men, moulded together by time, stress and circumstance, make the same decision at the same time. Soldiers finishing each other's sentences, anticipating each other's moves, sensing each other's emotions or desires when there was no outward indication of what lay inside each mind. He guessed there were rational explanations for it all. Pheromones or micro-gestures or animal instinct or whatever. But as he and Clare sat in the dark, and the smell of her stomach acid burnt in his nostrils, Harvey tried to connect to Darryl's mind. Tried to take him back to the wretched, sobbing, miserable creature he had been in the containers, the one who hated himself for not protecting his daughter. Harvey knew Darryl had already resigned himself to the decision to kill Clare. But not letting her out of the truck for a breath of fresh air when she was tired and sick and traumatised was an unnecessary cruelty. A cruelty that was below him, who he was as a man. He closed his eyes and silently willed Darryl to think of it as such.

The sound of the boots. The driver's-side door opening and closing again after a few seconds. The boots again. The levers. The truck doors opened. Darryl pointed his gun at Clare. 'You,' he said. 'Only you.'

Clare scooted on her butt down the length of the truck bed, avoiding the patch of vomit. She was shivering visibly as she reached the edge. Harvey squinted into the light of Darryl's torch and saw what he hoped to see. One hand clutching the torch and a dark object balled in the last two fingers of his hand, almost certainly the vest's detonator. The gun, clutched in Darryl's other hand, now pointed at Harvey. Darryl was trying to do the work of at least two men as he kept the light on Clare and the gun on Harvey. He looked jittery, exhausted, on edge.

Harvey shifted forward on his butt, just a metre, moving swiftly and silently when Darryl's head was turned. Clare slid down from the edge of the truck bed and hit the gravel. Darryl pointed to something on the dirt, too far out into the dark for Harvey to see.

'There,' Darryl said. 'Pick it up. Drink it.'

'I just need a second,' Clare said. She pressed the back of her hand to her mouth, leaning hard against the edge of the truck bed. She wobbled, gagged again. 'I think . . . I think I'm gonna be sick again.'

'So drink the fucking water,' Darryl snapped. 'That's what it's for.'

Harvey shifted forward another metre.

'You keep hurling your guts up without taking in more fluids and you'll—' Darryl started. But his words trailed off as Clare took a step towards the water bottle, faltered, and collapsed into a heap.

Darryl stared at her dark shape on the ground for a good two and a half seconds. Harvey counted them as he shifted forward. Then the older soldier flicked the aim of both his torch and gun back at Harvey. 'Don't fucking move, Buck!'

'I'm not moving.'

'You've shifted forward. Shift back. Now. All the way back.'

Harvey didn't move. 'Is she unconscious?' he asked.

'She's fine.'

'Looks like she fainted,' Harvey said, trying to keep the predatory iciness out of his voice. He shifted up onto the balls of his feet, still low, in a squat. 'Should have stopped an hour ago and got her that water.'

'She's faking it,' Darryl said. He swept the aim of the gun and the torch back to Clare, then to Harvey, an almost 180-degree arc he was desperately trying to cover. 'I know what this is. Okay? I know what this is. This is a play. It's not gonna work. Get the *fuck up*, bitch!'

Clare didn't move. Darryl stepped towards her, shoved her shoulder with his foot, made her whole body rock limply against the earth. Harvey took those precious microseconds while his focus was on her body to rise and take a step forward, bringing him within reach of the edge of the truck bed.

'I said get back!' Darryl shifted the gun back to Harvey.

'I'm not making a play.' Harvey put his hands out. 'I'm concerned for my friend. Is she breathing?'

'Who gives a fuck if she's breathing?' Darryl snapped. 'Get back in the truck. We're leaving her here.'

'You don't wanna do that,' Harvey said.

'Don't tell me what I should and shouldn't do.'

'Why not?' Harvey took another step forward, right to the edge of the truck bed. 'You clearly need help. Everything's falling apart, Darryl.'

'No it isn't.'

'You've got two options,' Harvey said. 'Get her back in the truck, or get her vest off.'

Darryl stood panting, his face twisted as he tried to think.

'Because if you leave her here with her vest on,' Harvey said, 'guaranteed, she'll be found. And they'll know your plan then, Darryl. They'll know I must have a vest on, too. All it'll take is a phone call. Or one of those police alert text messages saying "Do not approach – may be carrying explosives". You don't want that, do you? Because your whole plan is to activate my vest while I'm surrounded by innocent people.'

Harvey crouched, then sat on the edge of the truck. He slid down, stood on the earth. He knew what was coming.

Tried not to think about it. Because he was already in so much pain, and the thought of volunteering himself for more seemed ludicrous. He tried to side-step Darryl, to back him up against where Clare lay. But Darryl twisted out of his attempted corral, stepped back and kept his aim centred on Harvey.

'Pick her up and put her in the truck,' Darryl commanded.

'No,' Harvey said.

'Do it now.'

'No.'

'I'll blow your fucking vest, Harvey Buck, I swear to god!' Darryl roared. 'Pick her up, and put her in the truck!'

'You're not gonna blow my vest this close to the end.' Harvey took a step towards Darryl, causing him to take a step back. 'Not when you're so close to realising your dream. You don't have any leverage here, Darryl. You're backed into a corner.'

'Oh, I am?' Darryl asked. He smiled suddenly: a hard, icy smile.

Then he pointed the gun at Harvey and pulled the trigger.

CHAPTER 44

'Pull over,' Talon said.

Edna slowed, stopped under a gum tree. This one actually had leaves. They were heading out of the miserable, desolate sand and scrub that constituted the crown lands, where unfortunate cows that wandered from their herds further south found only baking rocks and certain death. In the distance, she could see the shape of what could only be a copse of trees, a lonely island in the nothingness. More would come. They were heading south-east towards the tiny town of Thargomindah, the land getting better as they went, only the dying whispers of a half-conscious trucker to drive them onward. Edna felt weighed down by hopelessness. Thought about Burke and Wills and their horrific, doomed-from-the-start mission out here to find a sea that didn't exist. The silent minutes while Talon tried to figure out how to work the dash cam left her time to pick holes in his whole theory about the codes Buck had apparently left for them. Could they really rest such a heavy working theory, about Buck's innocence and the presence of a third man, on a handful of beads tied to a child and some of pens placed on a counter? Her head swam. Talon shoved the camera in her face, and she found herself blinded in the dark by its hard white light.

'Check it out,' the boy said.

Nothingness. A blank, pale grey slab of earth, dusted with rocks. Edna could discern the smooth, curved nose of the semi-trailer's bonnet just edging into the bottom of the screen. The camera must have been positioned to record what lay immediately in front of the vehicle, up to about a hundred metres. Designed to capture rear-enders, she guessed, or accidents with pedestrians or wildlife. A man came into the frame; tall, muscular, shaven-headed, white. He put a hand on a hold in the centre of the bonnet, leant back, and hauled the enormous engine cover forward, exposing the semi's innards and blocking himself from the camera's view. Edna watched as the man popped back into view, obviously standing on a foothold in the semi's side, fishing around in the engine block.

'He disconnects the battery, I reckon,' Talon said, stopping the video and skipping backwards. He paused the feed on the man's face as he gripped the bonnet. 'He spends a few seconds in there, then he shuts the bonnet and disappears for a while. Next thing we see is Wayne Preston maybe an hour later. He's injured badly. Trying to open the bonnet and undo whatever this guy did. It takes him a while.' Talon rubbed his eyes. 'It was hard to watch, to be honest.'

'Is this the third guy, then?' Edna leant in to look at the man who was not Wayne on the screen.

'Must be.'

'So who is he?' Edna said. 'Did you check him against—'

'Against those guys who survived the massacre?' Talon nodded. 'Lippo and the others.' He turned his phone towards Edna, showed her a picture of the same man in full colour. It was an old picture. He was younger, fuller-faced, scowling with a rifle leaning against his shoulder.

'Henry Darryl,' Edna read. A sparkle of energy hit her. She slapped her forehead, fished around in her pocket. 'Jesus, in all the chaos, I forgot all about this. I picked this up at Wayne's truck. We were in a hurry. I just stuffed it in my pocket.'

She held out her hand, showing Talon the dog tags. The boy reached up and turned on the overhead light. Squinting and examining the words printed there in the unflattering gloom, with exhaustion hanging heavy on him, Talon looked ten years older. Still young, but further along his journey into becoming whatever it was that he would be. Edna felt a pang of mixed, hurtful emotions. Pride. Regret. Talon tapped at his phone, showed her another picture. A narrow, weasel-faced man standing in a group, his oversized helmet clamped to his head like a mushroom.

'Small Man,' Edna said. 'Nathan Tizza.'

'The guy in the balaclava must have been this one. Parker.'

'Okay. So we know who they are,' Edna said. 'Now we have to figure out what they're doing.'

'Yeah.' Talon nodded. 'What's their problem with Buck? I mean, what happened? Was it something during the ambush? Did Buck set the whole thing up? Did he try to feed them to the Taliban?'

'Whatever their reasons for taking Buck hostage,' Edna said, 'our focus needs to be on their plan. What does the Burke and Wills track mean to these guys? Why were they taking Buck there?'

They pulled back onto the road.

Edna dialled Zhang, then found herself wincing as the line connected.

'Tell me this is you calling to negotiate a surrender,' Zhang said.

'You make it sound like I'm the one out there robbing banks and blowing people up.'

'You're sure blowing up something. Your career is basically vapourised right now, Norris. You grievously wounded the commissioner of the Northern Territory Police.'

'I was provoked.'

'That's not what the witness says.'

'It'll be what the evidence says.'

'I'm being told by officers at Wayne Preston's semi-trailer that you just left an active crime scene. Again.'

'Not only that,' Edna said. 'But I've taken evidence with me. Again.'

'You *what*?'

'Listen,' Edna gripped the wheel, steeled herself, 'my capacity to act in this case has been jeopardised from the start. I was stripped of my weapons and my authority in a targeted bureaucratic attack, so in order to keep pursuing what I believe is the right course of action to stop people being killed, I went off road. And I'm still off road.'

'Off road, baby!' Talon cheered.

'Jesus, Edna,' Zhang sighed.

'But I won't hamper your investigation,' Edna said. 'I'm going to send you some stills from Wayne Preston's dash cam. And a picture of some dog tags I found at the site. We've already identified the man in the images. His name is Henry Darryl. He was in the army with Buck. So was Nathan Tizza, the owner of the tags. And we believe that the man at the crime scene at Buck's car was Martin Parker. Our investigation has also led us to believe that Clare Holland and Harvey Buck have both been held captive by this crew.'

Zhang was silent. Edna explained their theory, the distress messages left by Buck at the bank in Cooper Creek and the Greatman farm. She told Zhang about Wayne Preston's final words, his mention of the Burke and Wills track. There was only silence on the line.

'Are you still there?' Edna asked.

'I'm here,' Zhang said. 'I'm just . . . Honestly, I'm lost for words, Edna. Cop to cop? I mean, I get it. I've been emailed about you by your old chief back in Adelaide. I know what happened to you, and I think something like that would fuck anybody up. But that doesn't mean you get to ride around with a teenage sidekick shooting people and jeopardising evidence and cooking up weird theories about hidden symbols and codes.'

Edna laughed. An angry noise. 'Cop to cop,' she told Zhang, 'your law-enforcement instincts should tell you to hedge your bets here. Because as crazy as all this sounds, there's always the possibility that I'm right. So if you're good at your job, Zhang, you'll bag Commissioner Holland's shoes when he gets dragged into hospital. You'll look at his rifle to see if it was recently fired, and if the ballistics match Sergeant Stevenson's crime scene. You'll have officers search his house for signs of a struggle with his wife, and you'll go into his online accounts looking for the purchase of a tracking device. A good cop *always* hedges their bets.'

'Uh-huh,' Zhang sighed. 'I've got a shoot-to-kill order out on Buck, Edna. And an arrest-on-sight order on you. Please don't make things difficult when you're apprehended.'

Edna hung up. Talon was watching her from the dark of the passenger seat.

'We're on our own?' he asked.

'Always were.' Edna straightened in her seat. 'The track. Let's talk about the Burke and Wills track. There are towns along it, but they're tiny. Thargomindah, for example. There's a pub and a medical centre. Okay, so the population is only like three hundred people. But those properties are spread out. We don't want to be looking for Buck and Clare and Darryl over that great an area when we can narrow them down to a single destination.'

Talon struggled, his brow low. 'Maybe there's a specific person they're going to meet up with. Another army guy. Someone else from the massacre . . . Or . . . Are there any events there? Like, what's the date? Could there be more people in the town than there usually is?'

'There's a race every year, and a music festival, and neither of them are now.'

'So what else happens there?'

'People trade cattle and drink beer and sweat into their Levi's.' Edna rubbed her aching eyes. 'We need to find the connection. Between Buck and Darryl and the track.'

'I'll do a deep dive on Darryl.' Talon tapped at his phone. 'Maybe he has a property there or . . . a business.' The car rumbled through the desert. 'Jesus. These army people. They hate the internet. He doesn't even have a LinkedIn.'

'Is there anything army-related that connects to the Burke and Wills track?' Edna squinted at the horizon. Ahead, a red dot blinked, tracking the horizon. A helicopter or drone, she couldn't tell. 'What about army bases nearby? Or . . . the Birdsville Airport. Does it house army choppers or anything?'

'I'm going to put in "Australian Army" and "Burke and Wills track" into a search,' Talon said. There was silence. Edna thought about turning on the radio, clueing back into the search efforts. She wondered if it would keep her awake.

'Hang on,' Talon said. 'I think I've got something.'

CHAPTER 45

Harvey took the shot exactly where he expected to. Front of the thigh, slightly to the right of the bone, maybe ten centimetres above the knee. It was the smartest place for Darryl to shoot him. A gunshot to the leg, in the thick, large quadricep muscles and away from the arteries, wasn't going to cause Harvey to bleed out or go into catatonic shock or anything that would impede Darryl's next movements. But it was going to stun and incapacitate him, and that's exactly what happened.

What Harvey hadn't expected was the pain. He'd heard what getting shot was like from guys who had taken bullets in the army. The blinding thump into his flesh, that took his leg right out from underneath him, caused him to spin and flop to the ground. The shuddering wave of energy that rippled throughout his entire frame as the bullet hit, his whole body like a gong, ripples echoing out from the impact point. Then came the swelling, searing pain that crept up from the wound into his very throat, shutting it off, stifling his ability to scream. He was not prepared for that. Because those guys in the army hadn't been expecting the bullets that had marked them, and they'd been on the run, full of fight-or-flight chemical goodness, half-numbed to what had happened by the need to survive. They'd talked tough about getting shot. But this wasn't fun. Not fun at all. Harvey curled up and gripped his leg and ground his teeth until Darryl came over the top of him and wrenched his arm behind his back.

Harvey howled in protest to cover the sound of Clare getting up, lifting the rock he'd told her to try to spot as she got out of the truck in the dark. He'd told her to try to collapse by a rock that was big, but not too big, something she could heft with one hand but would get the job done in one strike. Rockmelon-sized, they'd agreed. Their hopes had been heavy. Full of dread. Because for all his luck, Harvey knew, they could have stopped on bare sand. Now Harvey turned his head, spotted Darryl's gun hand lying by his shoulder, steadying the man as he ground a knee into Harvey's spine.

When he heard the inevitable thump of the rock into the back of Darryl's skull, Harvey reached up, grabbed the gun, twisted it out of Darryl's loosening grip as the older man slumped on top of him. Harvey rolled out from under Darryl, flipped him over, pressed the gun to his temple. Darryl was still awake. The heavy-lidded, grey eyes slid towards Harvey, trying to register what had happened, sliding away to try to focus on Clare kneeling there with the bloodied lump of sandstone in her hand.

Harvey didn't say anything. Not a goodbye, or a fuck you. He just pressed the gun against Darryl's temple as hard as he could, sandwiching his skull between the pistol and the unforgiving desert plain, and he pulled the trigger. He put him down like an animal. Because that's what Henry Darryl deserved.

Harvey and Clare knelt there together then, wind whistling by them, dragging with it the urgency and terror of the past few moments, the fear that had left them both sweating and gasping and huffing now, struggling for calm. The pain in Harvey's leg, as it lay stretched before him, had subsided to a dreadful ache, the kind that threatened to erupt and take him if he dared move a single inch. But moving was necessary, for both of them. Clare dropped the rock she'd just helped murder a man with, and raked her fingers up into her hair, and bent her head and made a despairing sound. Harvey shifted over to her, breathing through the lightning in his leg, gripped her wrist and squeezed it. It was all he could manage. Some neglected corner of his mind was telling him he should be feeling relief. But none had come.

The first light was touching the horizon, bathing everything in a thin blue glow. Harvey shifted over again and reached into Darryl's pocket, ignored the feel of his still-warm body, and fished out an object. It was a pair of black plastic car key fobs, connected by a single key ring. Each fob had three buttons on it, the former 'unlock', 'lock' and 'unlock boot' functions. The fobs were exactly as Harvey had expected them to be. From the top of the key, to the bottom, the three vertical buttons housed small dome-shaped pieces of plastic glued in place. Harvey supposed the little dome-shaped bumps provided a kind of brail for Darryl, so that he could keep the fob in his pocket out of Harvey and Clare's view, but still feel which stage of the detonation process he was about to initiate. The top button, with one dome, Harvey supposed was stage one. The light. The second, stage two, the alarm. Harvey looked at the former 'unlock boot' button, which housed three small domes in a row. The third stage. *Ka-boom*. He ran a finger lightly over the bumps, feeling a chill creep into his stomach, as he noted one key fob's shape was decidedly different to the other's. One was from a Toyota. The other from a Hyundai. He reached into Darryl's other pocket, looking for a phone or another key fob, the fob belonging to the vest that had killed the old man, Warren Greatman. He found nothing. Harvey realised Clare was watching over his shoulder as he examined the fobs again. He handed them to her when she put out her hand.

'My god,' Clare whispered. 'I can't believe I'm holding them.'

Harvey dragged himself to his feet, pushing off his good knee, chewing his bottom lip as the pain pulsed through him again. 'We're nearly there,' he said. 'But we're not there yet. We need to get to the front of the truck, see if we can find Darryl's phone. You're going to tell the cops the situation. That I'm not a threat to you. That we need explosives specialists to deactivate our vests. Hopefully they'll believe you. About me, I mean. Hopefully they won't just shoot me on sight as soon as they arrive.'

Harvey limped to the back of the truck, leant against the bed, tried to put his full weight on his wounded leg. The pain whumped into him, bad, but not as bad as getting up from the ground. Progress.

'Which one of these fobs is my vest and which one is yours, do you think?' Clare asked. She was standing now, holding the connected fobs in one hand. 'Am I the Toyota or are you the Toyota?'

'No idea,' Harvey said. He had limped a little into the landscape. Discerned the edge of an embankment in the near distance. They were parked beside a wide, bare slab of earth flattened by the passage of vehicles. Was this the Burke and

Wills track? He couldn't remember what it looked like. He had a flash of trudging on muddy sand, recruits ahead of him and behind. Grey skies. Instructors shouting at them. Then the vision was gone. The aftershock of being shot was shuddering through him, turning his thoughts to fragments. 'It doesn't matter, does it?'

Clare didn't answer. Harvey looked back. She kept her eyes on him as she bent slowly and retrieved the gun from where Harvey had set it, beside Darryl's limp, dead hand. She rose slowly to her feet, and Harvey turned to her, the pain in his leg forgotten as he recognised the guilt flickering in her eyes.

'Clare?'

'Listen,' she said. He took an agonising step forward. Clare took two large ones back. 'Listen to me, Harvey. J-j-just listen for a second. Okay?'

'Clare,' Harvey eased the word out, heard it tremble on the wind. 'What are you doing?'

'You said it yourself.' Clare adjusted her grip on the gun. Nervously. Shakily. Dangerously. 'We're nearly there. But we're not there yet. I'm sorry, Harvey. But I . . . I need some leverage, too.'

'What are you *talking* about?'

'When we make that call, telling them where we are,' Clare said. 'We . . . It could be that the first person to arrive on scene here is Garreth. Okay? Because he'll be out there. I know he will. He'll be searching for me, and wanting to end this cleanly, and I know he'll have his ear to the ground with all the-the-the cops and the rescuers wanting to know where I am. Harvey, he's . . . he's going to kill me. Okay? He's going to kill me before

I can tell them that we've . . . he's . . . that he's been trying to kill *me* all this time! He'll cook up any story he has to in order to explain what happened. He'll say you came at him, and he fired, and he accidentally got me.'

'Clare.'

'And you'll be dead, Harvey. He'll kill you, too.'

'Clare.' Harvey took another step forward. Clare took three backwards. 'Don't do this.'

'I'm scared, Harvey. I'm scared of this man. You don't know him. It's going to take more than a gun to get away from him, okay? I tried that. I have proven that already. I want to make sure I'm safe and away before—'

'*Clare!*' Harvey's voice was heavy with fury. 'Put the gun down! Put the key fobs down! There are other options here!'

'I just need to hold onto these until—'

'Put them down!' Harvey roared. His whole body was shaking. Clare stepped back into the desert, leaving him at the edge of the road. 'We can drive to Thargomindah. Make sure we're not alone when we make the call. If there are other people around, it won't matter what Garreth says. There will be witnesses. Or we can explain, over the phone, that we won't reveal our location until we can guarantee—'

'There's no time, Harvey. *Please!*' Clare's gun arm was shaking. She pointed the barrel at his vest. Her finger was sliding on the trigger, wet with Darryl's blood. 'They could stop us on the road. Garreth could be with them. I want you to get in the back of the truck and I'll drive us somewhere safe.'

'I'm not doing that,' Harvey said. 'Clare, it's me. It's *me*. It's Harvey. I'm a person. Work with me, here. I can keep you safe. I've done it for this long!'

'I have to do this, Harvey. I'm sorry. But if it comes down to it, I will use you to kill Garreth.'

Harvey stared at her.

'I want him dead,' Clare said. 'And this is my chance.'

'Are you saying you're trying to get away from him, or that you're trying to kill him, Clare?'

'Both.'

'Jesus Christ.' Harvey looked at the horizon. It was all coming back to him. The swift right angles in her personality. The woman who rescued dolls and made thousands of dollars. Who regrew roses and secreted herself gifts. Who lived in terror of her husband as she watched him down pills that could kill him. Harvey realised in horror how badly he had misjudged this woman. How stupid it had been to keep watching his perception of her slip through his fingers each time he thought he had a grip on who she was.

'Harvey, you're . . . You're a nice guy, but I have to do what I have to do. Get in the truck.'

'No.' Harvey shook his head. 'No, Clare.'

'Stop where you are. Stop coming towards me. I know what you're like, Harvey. You're not getting within twenty feet of me.'

Harvey stepped forward.

'I need you to get in the truck, Harvey!' Clare screamed. '*Now!*'

'I'm not doing that,' he said again. He limped forward.

Clare took her eyes off him for a second, looked at the fobs in her hand, pressed her thumb down on a button on one of the fobs. Harvey heard the *ca-click* of the button being depressed, then coming back up. Then the vision of the woman in front of him, her gun hand and her fob hand outstretched towards him, was consumed in a ball of white light and heat and sound, and there was only a roaring in his ears and a nothingness that swallowed him whole.

CHAPTER 46

He swam in the nothingness for a long time, shifting through layers of pain and exhaustion. Maybe an hour passed, or two. He had no idea. Energy came, bringing with it light, sensation, sounds. The wind tussled his hair. He twitched, felt dirt under his face. Then he was dragged down again, under that same earth, into a thick and swirling, muddy painfulness where there was no sound and even breathing felt like a heavy, exhausting effort. As he rose for the hundredth time out of that darkness, non-urgent wonderings slid around him. About Clare pressing the button at the top of the fob. The highest in the vertical row of three. The button with the single raised bump glued to its surface. Because, of course, stage one of the detonation process would be marked with a single bump. One stage. One bump. Harvey had assumed the same. But then, Harvey remembered Tizza standing by as they watched Darryl detonate Warren Greatman's vest in the desert outside his cattle farm. How the evil, weasel-faced man had counted down, not up.

Three.

Ca-click.

Two.

Ca-click.

One.

The one bump button had actually corresponded to stage three.

Detonation.

Harvey's mind turned and twirled, circled the possibilities entwined in Clare's accidental detonation of her vest. She'd been trying to enact the relatively harmless first stage, in which one of the vest's lights would come on. His or hers, it didn't matter. Not knowing which fob belonged to which vest, she'd invertedly chosen the one corresponding to her own. The thought fluttered through Harvey's mind that the chances had been fifty-fifty of Clare choosing his vest and accidentally blowing him up. But that hadn't happened. He was alive. Wasn't he? Harvey turned his face, felt sand grind against his cheekbone. He sucked in a breath, found there was ash in his lungs. Pain. Fire. He coughed, rolled onto his side, glimpsed brightness, felt warm blood dripping in his eyes.

Voices began to swim into his consciousness.

'. . . say they're about ten minutes away.'

'Okay.'

'What do we do in the meantime? Should we look for him?'

'Dunno, mate. He's obviously off his nut. I don't like the idea of tangoing with him, to be honest. I've got a wife and kids at home. And if half the nation's coppers haven't managed to take him down yet, I'm not placing much faith on you and me.'

'True.'

'So long as we got those army recruits turning back, and the cops on the way, I say we just hold tight until the experts get here and tell us what to do.'

'You're probably right.'

Harvey opened his eyes. White, pre-dawn sky. The distant edge of a rocky, sandy embankment, turning and ticking back as dizziness worked its way through him. He shifted carefully onto his back, turned his head, spied desert. The voices must have been from up on the road. He rolled onto his other side, shifted up into an awkward half-crouch, his bad leg outstretched. Blood from the bullet wound had adhered his jeans to his leg from the thigh down. He felt no pain from the wound now. There were fresh injuries, perhaps from the explosion. Skin off, or burnt, on his arms and hands. Lumps and grazes in his face and head. Harvey flattened on the embankment, slithered carefully up, until he could see the road.

The truck. And two move vehicles now, a van and a ute, the latter carrying four sheep, who were lounging and sleeping in the bed, flies buzzing around them. Harvey fancied he could smell them from where he lay, they were so close. The men who were talking were standing at the van's bonnet, looking down at an object on the road, each holding a rifle by the stock. He followed their gaze to Clare's shoe, which lay between them on its side. Harvey realised with a quiet horror that the shoe was full. He looked across the road, beyond the wheels of the van. He could just make the shape of Darryl's body lying in a heap beyond the truck. He did a quick calculation, realised he must have been blown clear across the road by the impact of the explosion from Clare's vest.

'You ever seen anything like this before, mate?' one farmer asked the other.

'Oh, god. I actually have.'

'You have?'

'Yeah. I used to be an arborist.'

'A what?'

'Tree lopper.'

'Right.'

'Saw a guy get pulled into a chipper once.'

'Jeez.'

'Yeah.'

Harvey slid back from the embankment, began crawling, with his teeth clamped against the pain, away from the men along the length of the rocky dip from the road. His burnt hands picked up dirt and grit, and blood ran from his chin down his throat and into the vest. He pressed on for what felt like an eternity, the voices of the men fading. Then he pushed himself up, and in a low crouch, made his way towards a small hill, listening all the time for gunshots, or the voices of the men behind him shouting. None came. When he got to the hill, he stopped for a rest, counting out twenty full, slow breaths, before he went on.

CHAPTER 47

A chopper roared overhead. Edna and Talon leant forward together to watch it pass so close Edna felt the beating of its blades in her chest. The Burke and Wills track was wide and clear, a path traversed by tourist vehicles, on-foot endurance adventurers and, apparently, a contingent of young army recruits twice a year completing their initial phase training. Edna had seen no sign of them, and had no idea whether Zhang had alerted the army instructors running the operation of her theory. That Harvey Buck, Clare Holland and Henry Darryl were heading their way. She hoped Zhang had. She hoped the army personnel had evacuated the area.

Edna was heading down a two-hundred-kilometre section of track with only a vague sense of where those innocent people might be, based on the dates in which the operation ran every year. She and Talon had guessed that, over the two-week stretch, the young recruits would traverse equal portions of the track each day, winding up at the Bulloo River on the final day. That meant her area of interest was about thirty-five kilometres long.

Talon sat rigid in his seat beside her, watching as a mob of kangaroos left the path ahead, heading for their morning feeding grounds. The distant vehicles began as pinprick inconsistencies in the otherwise sparse horizon, which grew into tiny boxes, then morphed into a ute, a van and a truck. The vehicles were abandoned, alone.

Edna shunted the Mercedes to a stop and they got out. She took in the scene; the body lying at the back of the truck, the skull caved in, and more remains that lay not far from the dead man; a single arm, a boot, a clump of blonde hair and skull. There was a gun and a pair of key fobs. Talon's face was grey, his mouth downturned. The boy leapt up into the bed of the box truck in a single bound, barely touching the truck wall to steady himself. Edna clambered in after him. They looked around the empty vehicle, spied a container, blankets, empty water bottles, food wrappers. Someone had been housed here. The place reeked of body odour and vomit. Talon pointed to the markings in blood on the wall.

Three dots. Three dashes. Three dots.

'So where are they?' Edna said. She was suddenly breathless, her temples pulsing. 'Is the dead guy Buck, or Darryl?'

'Buzzcut. It's gotta be Darryl.'

'So where's Buck? And who owns those cars?'

Edna went to the edge of the truck bed and hopped down. She saw blood on the road, followed the smear to an embankment, where there was more. A red-brown pool drying in the soil.

'Come on,' she beckoned the boy.

CHAPTER 48

Harvey stopped. There was a helicopter working its way along the distant Burke and Wills track, and its steady thumping rhythm had masked the footfall of the men behind him. Now, as it receded, he heard the unmistakeable crunch of dry, thin bracken. The country they were in was littered with struggling gums. Harvey turned slowly, heaving his bad leg with him, and saw the two farmers frozen and watching him from some twenty metres away.

'All right, mate,' the first said. He was a short, portly guy wearing a green chequered flanno. The other, a young man with a ponytail, was visibly trembling. Both had rifles in their hands, pointed at Harvey's chest. 'Just chill out.'

Harvey said nothing.

'We saw you,' the bloke in the green flanno said. He flicked the nose of the rifle sideways. 'From the road. You're injured, bad. It's time to give up and just come quietly.'

'Okay,' Harvey said. He put his hands up. 'Okay.'

He said nothing about the bomb vest. Nothing about his innocence. Nothing except those two words. And that was because he wanted the men with the guns to do exactly what they did next. They took a step towards him. Harvey went down carefully on his good knee.

'Lie down on your stomach,' green flanno said.

'Okay.'

'Don't give us any shit.'

'I won't.'

Harvey admired the men. Their reluctant bravery. He pictured them deciding that they wouldn't be heroes, then spotting him limping into the distance. Figuring they had to try. To save more lives. To do the right thing. He waited until the one with a bit more gall came forward, as Harvey knew he would, and took his wrist. Harvey popped back up on the knee he'd gone down on, and in the same motion, batted the rifle sideways out of the farmer's hand. He gripped the barrel, yanked hard, and palmed the guy hard in the collarbone, a blow that would knock the breath out of him and would numb the arm that held the gun. The rifle came out of the guy's grip, and Harvey spun it clockwise in his hands, and pointed it right back at the sun-browned face of the shell-shocked farmer. The move took less than a second. Harvey cocked the slide-bolt and saw, out of the corner of his eye, the younger farmer with the ponytail give a full-body jolt at the sound.

'Drop it,' Harvey said.

He didn't look at the kid. But he clocked the boy placing the rifle carefully on the ground out of the corner of his eye. Harvey backed the older farmer up a couple of steps, shifted sideways, reached down and took the second rifle by the stock. 'Lie down on your stomach, interlock your fingers behind your head, and count to a hundred,' Harvey said. 'Both of you.'

The farmers looked at each other, still trying to figure out how the two of them had been so quickly and successfully disarmed by a single wounded man, to catch up to the instructions they'd been given. They went down, slowly and carefully, onto the sand. Harvey backed away.

He limped through the wasteland of dead trees and crunchy scrub, jettisoning the second rifle after only a minute, the instrument weighing a tonne and sliding in his blood-wet fingers. There was no plan, just as it had been coming out of the foothills below Durjit, nothing but survival on his mind and a need to get away from the terror behind him.

The helicopter's thumping rose, fell away, seemed to rise again. Harvey wasn't game to look back. The trees were thinning out before him, and between them, he could see the spectre of his nightmares; the howling expanse that had never really left him. Wide, sunlit, featureless desert. There were sirens on the wind. Voices. He heard a woman shouting, and paused at the edge of the nothingness, sucking in great gasping breaths as the helicopter noise thumped louder and louder.

'Talon! Talon, wait!' the woman cried. '*Wait!*'

Harvey turned. There was a huge young man running full pelt towards him through the trees, a big kid with a barrel chest and arms like the pistons in some enormous machine pumping back and forth. Harvey raised the rifle. He took aim at the kid's chest.

But the young guy was too fast. He was on him before Harvey could even begin to make the decision to fire. The kid seemed to ignore the rifle completely, rushed up and swaddled Harvey in an embrace that was so violent and all-encompassing that it squeezed the air out of him. The two of them smashed into a tree. Harvey was pinned there, the kid hugging him, the rifle flung from his fingers as the helicopter that had been pursuing them swung to a stop just beyond the reach of the dead trees and the shooter riding in the open cabin window looked down at Harvey with a machine gun raised and ready to fire.

Through the wind, over the big kid's shoulder, Harvey saw a small woman in a tan police uniform. No hat. Punky, short-cut silver hair. She was waving madly at the chopper, the sniper seated within it.

'Don't shoot! Don't shoot! Don't shoot!'

Harvey held on to the huge, panting youth who had him and felt weak in the knees. He couldn't be sure, but he got the sense that these two people were with him. That they had the situation under control. And to relinquish that control now gave him a taste of the relief he'd thought he'd feel when Darryl died. The kid who held him smelt as terrible as he did. Harvey gripped the kid's T-shirt and felt tears in his eyes.

'Who the hell are you two?' he yelled over the noise of the chopper.

'I'm Talon, and this is Edna,' the big kid yelled back. 'We're . . . We're the off-road team!'

CHAPTER 49

The remote-controlled monster truck turned in a tight circle, shunted to a stop, kicking up red dirt before it buzzed and spun its tyres. It was being driven by an adult, someone from the Adelaide team. The officers were clustered around a police cruiser that marked the middle of the roadside gathering. Edna and Talon, standing a few metres away, watched the officer drive the monster truck away from the gathering of people, down a shallow slope, along the same path the toy truck had cut ten or twelve times already. It went through the dead gum forest, past a boulder and a fallen log, approaching a big, gnarled gum tree.

Harvey Buck sat leaning against the tree trunk. He woke from the little doze he'd been having, his legs flopped out and his hands on his thighs. Edna, Talon and a hundred or so other people watched as Buck unhooked the little bundle that had been haphazardly sticky-taped to the top of the remote-controlled truck. In the bundle were a razor blade, some wires, some scissors, and a few other bits and pieces cobbled together from the vehicles that had arrived since Buck was discovered five hours earlier. Buck had been sitting against the tree the whole time. No one had got closer than fifty metres to him, save for Talon, who'd used his body as a human shield to protect Buck from being shot by a police sniper, and Edna, who'd helped the boy walk the wounded man back to within view of the roadside. Since then, the army veteran had been dozing, talking, drinking water and eating snacks that were delivered to him via the toy truck. His T-shirt was off, and the bomb vest was exposed. His gunshot leg was wrapped tightly in a compression bandage that had arrived from somewhere.

As Edna surveyed the scene, she spotted Zhang talking to officers from her own outpost, partway along the assembly of locals, journalists, police and search responders. Zhang was commanding this scene and the one a little further down the road, where the truck and the remains of Clare Holland and Henry Darryl had been covered with tents. Zhang was telling someone to try to push the journalists, who were steadily creeping closer to Buck at the outer edges of the gathering, back into line. She was also listening in as the young Indigenous officer beside her communicated back and forth on the phone with an officer in Perth, who had infiltrated Nathan Tizza's home address. The officers were working through Tizza's design plans of the bomb vest, which were in plain sight in the dead man's office.

Listening in, nearby but not too close, Edna felt at once part of the effort to save Buck, and completely detached from it. Now and then she caught an icy glare from Zhang. Or a sneer from one of Zhang's subordinates. A slight sense of smugness fluttered about Edna, because she knew, with so many journalists on scene, that she wouldn't be arrested. But pain was on the horizon. Inquiries. Interrogations. Miles and miles of reports and hours and hours of meetings. She told herself not to let the dread take her away from this moment. There were more pressing matters at hand. She ignored the looks from where she sat perched on the bonnet of someone's little grey Subaru. Talon stood beside her, leaning against the vehicle.

'Mr Buck,' Zhang said through a megaphone, 'we think we're ready to make some moves on this thing.'

In the distance, Buck raised a thumb.

'Just to be clear—' Zhang drew a deep breath. Edna saw her glance sideways at the crowd. 'We've agreed, with your current medical condition and the urgent need for you to receive treatment, that the best course of action here is to have you deactivate the vest yourself. You're not being pressured to do this. It was, in fact, your suggestion.'

Buck nodded, raised his thumb again.

'You feel confident in doing so, Mr Buck?' Zhang pressed. 'You don't want to wait for a specialist from Sydney?'

'Let's do it,' Buck called.

Talon snorted. 'What a badass.'

Edna looked the kid over. Wanted to remind him that he'd put himself between a bomb best and a machine gun only hours earlier to save the life of a man he'd never met, brushing aside a loaded rifle to do so. But she didn't. She didn't want to embarrass him in front of the crowd by lavishing praise upon him.

'We want you to take the razor blade you've been provided with,' Zhang said into the megaphone, 'and carefully slit the front of the vest, from shoulder to shoulder, along the neckline. You shouldn't encounter any wires at all during this procedure. From there, we'll get you to lift the Kevlar up and cut the front of the vest down the sides of the breastplate, creating a flap.'

Buck did as he was instructed. Cameras clicked. The procedure was painstakingly slow. Buck's hands were burnt and trembling, the razor stopping and starting as it cut through the thick Kevlar. As the front of the vest came down, and the innards were exposed, a low moan of horror and intrigue came up from the crowd. Edna saw rectangular blocks which she guessed were plastic explosive housed in their own individual Kevlar pouches, stacked like cartoon abdominal muscles down Buck's belly. Uniform grey wires were there in their dozens, sprawling out from the blocks like vines, reaching up and over the shoulders of the vest and around the ribs towards the back.

'What we're hoping to do,' Zhang said, 'is bypass the electrical circuit that goes up over your left shoulder. We'll disconnect that shoulder completely, and you should be able to cut through the wires and the fabric. From there, you might be able to slide out of the vest through the widened neck hole.'

'Fingers crossed,' Buck yelled in response. A small murmur of uncertain laughter went up from the crowd. Talon smiled. Edna bumped his shoulder with her own.

They watched Buck as he followed the instructions. Shaving down wires with the razor blade. Connecting new wires into the stack. A pair of journalists stood beside Edna, clicking away madly on cameras with lenses as long as her arm.

'If he makes it out of that thing, this'll be in the history books,' one said.

'Even if he blows himself up, it'll *still* be in the history books,' the other responded, squinting into his camera's lens. 'First to file with this gets a Walkley Award.'

'You can bet your arse.'

Edna turned as a vehicle came down the track, trying to nose its way into the crowd of creeping gawkers at the edges of the gathering. An ambulance. Buck had finished with the razor blade and the bypass wires and was taking up the scissors. People shuffled, some taking a few discreet steps backwards, others outright moving behind the cover of vehicles. Zhang wiped sweat from her neck into the collar of her shirt.

'Hold on to your hats, everybody,' the journalist beside Edna said.

EPILOGUE

Edna Norris was not at work the following Thursday. Or the Thursday after that. It was, in fact, twenty-six consecutive Thursdays before she found herself slamming the door of her cruiser on Alan Jacob Horn, who shuffled awkwardly along the bench seat, trying to find a comfortable spot for his handcuffed wrists against the tough leather. It was 5 a.m., because Edna had been waiting three weeks for the approval to effect the man's arrest, checking her email every morning as she woke for the green light. She'd raced straight to the address. It was with a quiet sense of glee that she now went around the cruiser and opened her own door, sliding into the driver's seat with a self-satisfied sigh. Horn didn't miss the sound's intention. He was glaring at her in the rear-view mirror, eyes cold and bleak like the day outside.

She started the engine and drove. The endless expanse of red earth welcomed her, drawing her into its arms, and when Horn refused her polite attempts at conversation, she was happy enough to drive silently. It was going to be a quiet day. She'd formally question Horn on the charges of using a carrier service to solicit a minor, using a carrier service to send sexually explicit images to a minor, using a carrier service to receive sexually explicit images of a minor, and incorrectly stowing a loaded weapon in a residential property. When Horn was locked up and fed, she would return to his property alone and effect the search warrant she had obtained for his home, computer and phone.

Edna imagined that after the whole thing with Harvey Michael Buck, Horn had lapsed into a false sense of security about getting arrested. As she drove, she envisioned what he might have seen of her life in the media over the previous six months. The journos had taken a while to catch up to every detail of the extraordinary cross-country hostage crisis and killing spree in the desert, but they were quick to cover her involvement and the consequences. She had been immediately stood down from her position as lead police officer in Clifton Hills Station and surrounds, and replaced with two officers from Adelaide. While on the face of it, Edna refused any and all requests for interviews about what had happened, details of her actions somehow surfaced regardless.

It was reported that she had, in the company of a volunteer member of the public, taken the extraordinary measure of grievously wounding the commissioner of the Northern Territory Police in order to intercept him on what had later been discovered to be a hell-bent mission to kill his wife and to ultimately escape justice from murdering Officer Rebecca Stevenson from Cooper Creek. It was also reported that despite concerted efforts to inform police of the catastrophic predicament of onc Harvey Michael Buck, Edna and her volunteer member of the public had run into the line of fire and gravely endangered themselves to save Buck's life. It was reported that, after several inquiries, six months' unpaid leave and a significant reduction in rank, Officer Edna Norris was re-employed as the duty officer at Clifton Hills Police Station. A suitable replacement as lead officer in this region had not yet been found.

Edna wondered if, having read all those articles, seen *A Current Affair*'s special and the *60 Minutes* special and perhaps perused the many podcasts that had covered the events, Alan Jacob Horn had grown nervous. Because while he was rarely mentioned by name, Talon David Crest had now and then popped up in the coverage of the outback hostage crisis. The media wasn't forgetting about him. Edna, certainly, wouldn't forget about him. And that meant the police, in fact, might not forget about him. And what had happened. Why, indeed, he'd been in the region in the first place. Edna had banged on Horn's door at 5 a.m. on the dot, and although she hadn't seen his waking expression, she hoped it was one of terror. Stories about the outback hostage crisis had begun to die down. There was room, now, for a double-page spread in a top national newspaper about a sad little man in the middle of the desert pretending to be a teenage girl and manipulating kids online.

Edna thought about Talon as she reached over, opened the glove box, took out a Twix and unwrapped it, steering the cruiser with her knees. The seat beside her was empty. She felt the silent car rumble around her and remembered those first days after Alicia when her terrace house in Adelaide had felt impossibly bigger and emptier, now that she was gone.

Edna pulled up at the Clifton Hills Police Station, opened the door and hauled Horn out. She marched him up the sun-warped wooden steps and inside. The place still smelt of the officers who had replaced Edna while she was in the doghouse.

One had a penchant for microwaved curry and the other had worn too much cologne. She went around the counter and opened the window beside her computer, leaving Horn to stand awkwardly in his handcuffs in the little waiting area on the other side of the counter.

She left Horn there while she filled in his booking sheet, made herself a coffee and drank half of it. Then she took his arm and led him down the hall towards the holding cells. Voices floated up the corridor towards them.

'How about this?' Talon said. 'You say you were outside the shed and you heard something inside that sounded like a scream. You broke in because you felt like someone might have been in danger.'

'Huh. Okay. That could work.'

Edna brought Horn around the corner. Talon, who was leaning on the bars of the holding cell from the outside, stepped back when he saw the older man so that Edna could unlock the door. The young, bearded guy Edna had arrested the night before stood up and moved to the corner of the cell, just on the other side of the bars to Talon, and the two younger men watched Horn take his seat on the steel bench. Talon looked Horn over through the bars with a muted expression of distaste. He didn't say anything. Edna was proud. She'd been drilling into the kid, since he moved in with her, that the best course of action when dealing with someone of Horn's stature was to remain silent. *You can't educate pond scum*, she'd told him. Edna knew that Talon was going to learn a thing or two about the beauty and power of silence as he progressed through his study of the law, but as far as she knew, he was still rounding out his higher school certificate by correspondence, which he'd dropped out of a couple of years earlier to be at home with his mother.

Talon resumed his place with his wrists hanging over the crossbar of the holding cell, and his incarcerated friend took up his place on the bench beside Horn. 'I'm pretty sure you'd be clear on the break-and-enter charge if you said you were gaining forcible entry to the premises under the belief someone was in peril,' Talon said. 'But I'd have to look it up.'

'Well, so, how do I explain why I've got their ride-on mower in my backyard, then?' the young guy asked. 'The one that went missing from the shed? You got a story you can cook up for that one, mate?'

Talon glanced at Edna, gave a sigh. 'We need to get creative here,' he said and stroked his starter-moustache. 'Give me a minute.'

'Nah, I'm fucked, mate,' the man said. 'It was theft, plain as day.'

Talon smiled as an idea came to him. He raised a finger. 'Unleeessss . . .'

Harvey pulled to a stop outside the little house at the foot of the mountain, his tyres popping gravel and sending something slithering into the long grass at the side of the old carport. Behind the weathered house, the mountain created an early sunset for the overgrown patch of land on a long, dirt road in Doctors Gap. The real estate agent must have heard his car, because she opened the screen door just as he switched off the engine and waited quietly, if a little awkwardly, as he limped up the drive. Harvey had just said goodbye to the walking stick he'd been using since the goings-on out in the desert months earlier, and he was still reaching for its reassuring presence for long distances. The agent, Fiona, took his arm as he made the top step. She was like that. A warm and touchy person, with big eyes. Country real estate agent, he supposed, far from the inner-city sharks with their cockroach cruncher shoes and immaculate fade haircuts.

'Look at you.' Fiona beamed. 'You made it.'

She took him on a tour of the house, but he didn't see anything he didn't expect to see. A deceased estate, the elderly former occupant's furniture had left telltale marks in the carpet and on the walls. Harvey could see the ghostly outline of an old dresser with a mirror in the musty bedroom, the phantom of a picture on the living room wall. There was still ash in the pot-belly stove and the floors creaked loudly in every room. He smiled and nodded along as Fiona talked about the property's potential, the sunrise over the trees, the local legends of wombats as big as German Shepherds. Harvey saw there was a sprawling back deck looking up at the mountain and a dog door installed in the laundry. That was really all he cared about. He knew installing a dog door in solid oak was a pain in the arse.

'Do you think I could be cheeky and shoot you over the contract this afternoon?' Fiona nudged him with her elbow. 'You could take a squiz over the weekend and we could have this all wrapped up by mid next week.'

'Sure,' he said and shook her hand. He saw happiness sparkling in her eyes. Wondered if she could see its embers glowing cautiously in his. 'I'll call you Monday.'

•

Harvey started the car and pulled onto the dirt road, going the opposite direction to the real estate agent. Before he could go far, his phone dinged. He stopped and reached for it on the passenger seat. It was another notification from Sydney Dogs and Cats Home. *We have someone we'd like you to meet!* Harvey felt curiosity prickling in his chest. He started driving again, the lush forest hugging the road tightly on either side of him, receding to blackness mere metres beyond the first row of trees. He decided he would get dinner at the local pub, look at the notification about the rescue dog, wait for the inevitable email from Fiona. She'd send it as soon as she got home. Country real estate agents. You didn't have to chase them.

The night grew and he flicked on his headlights. Ahead of him, around a corner, they picked up the reflective metal of a numberplate, and he slowed, seeing the shape of a car between the ghost gums.

Harvey gripped the wheel, pressed on and arrived at the scene quickly. A convertible with the bonnet up, a man and a woman standing staring at the engine bay. As Harvey approached, the guy stepped out, a hopeful hand raised. Harvey stomped on the accelerator, drove around the scene and continued on.

A minute or two down the road, he stopped and let his hands flop down from the steering wheel into his lap. He glanced at the secret holster in the door by his knee, the one that held his gun. Then he looked up at the rear-view mirror, the dirt road leading back to the stranded couple, the thick, inky blue darkness of approaching night.

He had two choices. Drive on. Or turn back. He sat there, weighing things, his dust cloud making swirling patterns in the beams of his headlights.

Harvey let out a sigh.

ACKNOWLEDGEMENTS

When I first met Lee Child, I was a baby writer in New York attending my first big American literary festival. He was in the banquet hall, making slow progress traversing the crowd of authors and guests, a giraffe wading through a sea of happy gazelle. I steeled myself, approached him and told him how much I loved him and his work. He thanked me and posed for a selfie, and I darted away, exhilarated. I was so exhilarated, in fact, that I blurted out to a man who was standing at the side of the room, 'I just went up and talked to Lee Child!'

He snorted in response. 'What? Lee? You don't know Lee? He's here every year. *Hey, Lee!*' he called. To my mortification, Lee looked over. The man made a gesture with two fingers at his mouth, like he was puffing on a cigarette, and cocked his head towards the doors. Lee nodded enthusiastically. 'We're just about go out for a cigarette. You want to come? Do you smoke?' the guy asked.

I reminded myself to breathe. 'Of course I do!' I lied.

Long story short, I ended up on the smokers balcony with Lee Child and a host of other hugely powerful authors, frantically scrabbling to keep up with the conversation and doing my best to pretend I was smoking the cigarette I'd bummed off someone. Our friendship grew from there. He has been extremely kind, generous and supportive of me throughout my career, asking for nothing in return, and I have heard that he is that way with many people. Like his globally beloved Jack Reacher, Lee seems to be someone who will lend a hand to anyone, no matter how powerless they are or how hopeless their case.

High Wire is a bit of an Australian-flavoured love letter to Lee and Reacher. As is the case in Lee's novels, here the lone male hero, so cherished in Western storytelling, is surrounded by women who are equally brave and fierce.

Thank you, Lee, for being so cool. I hope you love the book.

I couldn't do what I do without having learned the craft from the very best at the University of the Sunshine Coast, the University of Queensland and the University of Notre Dame, Sydney. Clare Zizza was there for me when I needed a friendly ear for this novel, and she also inadvertently lent me a character name. So, thank you Clare, and sorry about the spoilers . . . and your fate. Lauren Gadson helps me with my medical details, and for this book, Matt Schroder of the Royal Australian Navy helped me with a search and rescue query. I'm represented in Australia by the glamorous Gaby Naher, and in the US by the incomparable Steve Fisher and the majestic Lisa Gallagher. My books get into the hands of you, the readers, through the tireless efforts of Beverley Cousins, Holly Toohey, Jessica Malpass, Kathryn Knight, Rod Morrison, Veronica Eze, Linda Quinton, Kristin Sevick, Robert Allen, Thomas Wortche and a host of others publishing professionals.

And, as always, emotional, logistical, domestic, culinary and caffeinated support services during the writing of this novel were provided to me by my darling husband, Tim. My endlessly clever daughter, Violet, was head of department on humour, kisses, snuggles, afternoon naps, procrastination, girls' club, idea generation, artistic development and cola-flavoured lollipop procurement. My dog, Noggy, barked a lot to keep away the imaginary murderers who must be constantly besieging the house, so that was something.

ABOUT THE AUTHOR

Candice Fox is the author of twelve crime novels and the winner of three prestigious Ned Kelly Awards. In fact, she is the only author to have been shortlisted for that award for every single novel. She has also co-written seven *New York Times* bestsellers with James Patterson, the world's bestselling thriller writer.

Candice's novels *Crimson Lake* and *Redemption Point* have been adapted into the major ABC TV series *Troppo*.

A meticulous researcher, Candice has interviewed a serial killer on death row, been to prison three times (for work purposes) and while on honeymoon in the US took a road trip to famous crime scenes looking for clues. She has also dined with a former President of the United States, filmed a cameo role in her latest screen adaptation and, as a volunteer for WIRES, has rescued countless wild animals.

She lives in Sydney.

Read on for a sneak peak of DEVIL'S KITCHEN by Candice Fox

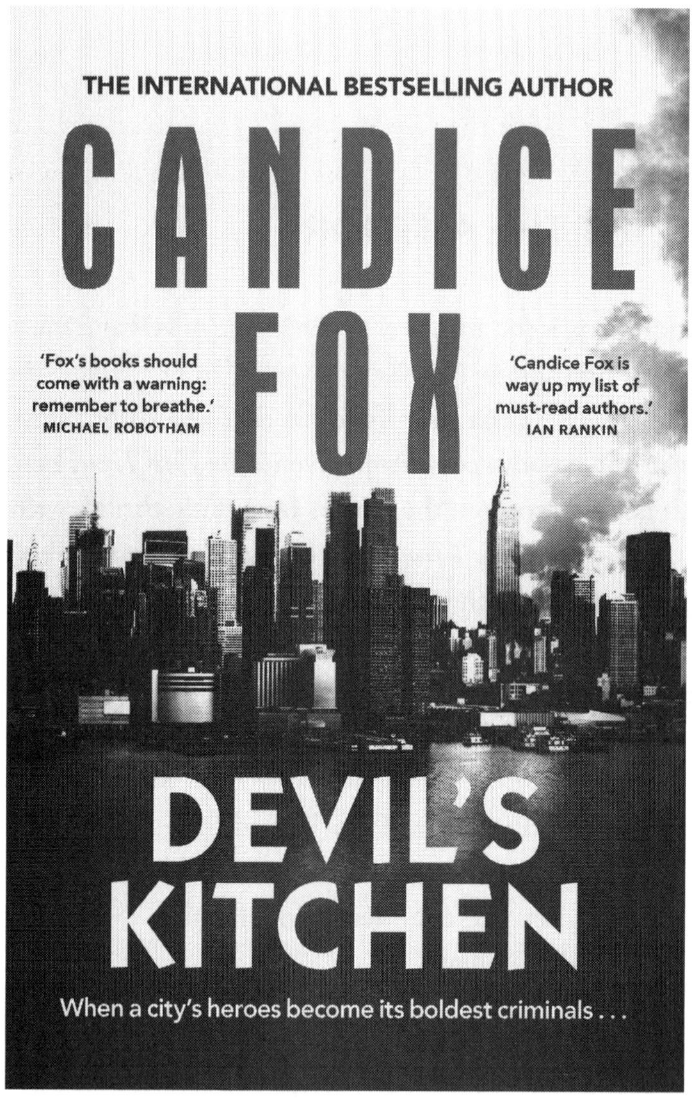

Available now

When a city's heroes become its boldest criminals . . .

For years the firefighters of New York's Engine 99 have rushed fearlessly into hot zones, saving countless lives and stopping devastating blazes in their tracks.

They've also stolen millions from banks, jewellery stores and art galleries. With their inside knowledge and specialist equipment, they've become the most successful heist crew on the East Coast.

Their newest member, Andrea 'Andy' Nearland, is not what she seems either. She's an undercover operative, hunting the men of Engine 99 for a host of crimes – including the murder of an off-duty cop and the disappearance of a mother and child.

As the clock counts down to the gang's most daring heist yet, loyalties begin to fray and mistrust boils over. Andy's career is all smoke and mirrors, but infiltrating this crew of 'heroes' might prove to be her most dangerous job of all . . .

'Candice Fox books should come with a warning label: remember to breathe.' MICHAEL ROBOTHAM

'Breathless and enthralling, with a premise like no other, *Devil's Kitchen* is one of the best crime novels I've read in years. Candice Fox just goes from strength to strength.' ANNA DOWNES

'Imagine Michael Mann's cinematic masterpiece *Heat* but with Fox's indelible storytelling swagger. *Devil's Kitchen* is a relentless, action-packed thrill ride . . . Candice Fox is a titan of the genre.' SIMON McDONALD

ANDY

'We know you're a cop,' Matt said.

Andrea had been waiting for those words. All the way out to the forest, as they pulled off the highway and onto the thin dirt road. The unsteady headlights between Matt's and Engo's shoulders cast the trees in a strangely festive gold. The killing fields. In a way, Andy had been waiting for the words a lot longer than that. Every morning and every night for almost three months. The potential of them clinging to the lining of her stomach like an acid.

We know.

Now she was kneeling on the bare boards of a run-down portable building in the woods, the sound of boats on the Hudson nearby competing with the moan of skin-peeling wind. The corrugated-iron roof rattled above all their heads. The property – a massive, abandoned slab of woods that probably belonged to some absent billionaire who'd had ideas of building a house here once – was dead silent beyond the little shack. Andy knew she was in a black spot on the river's otherwise glittering edges, so close to safety, yet so far away. Ben was breathing hard beside Andy, sweating into his firefighting bunker uniform. The reflective yellow stripes on his arms were trying to suck up any and all available light. There wasn't much. Matt, Engo and Jake were faceless silhouettes crowding her and Ben in. Strange what a person will long for at the end. A sliver of light. To breathe the sour air unfettered, as Ben did. They'd taped her mouth.

Matt put his gun to Ben's forehead, nudged it hard so that his head snapped back.

'You brought a *fucking cop* into the crew.'

'She's not a cop! I swear to god, man!'

'I *raised* you,' Matt growled. 'I found you in a hole and I dug you out and this is how you want to play me?'

'Matt, Matt, listen to me—'

'Benji, Benji, Benji.' Engo stepped forward, put his three-fingered hand on Ben's shoulder. 'We *know*. Okay? It's over. You got a choice now, brother. You admit what you've done, and maybe we can talk about what happens next.'

'*She's not a cop!*'

I'm not a fucking cop! Andy growled through the tape. Because it's what she would say. Andrea 'Andy' Nearland, her mask. She wouldn't go down quiet. She would fight to the end.

Engo came over to her and tried to start in with the same faux pleasantries and soothings and bargains. She flopped hard on her hip, swung her legs around and kicked out at his shins. He went down on his ass and she let off a string of obscenities behind the tape. Andy had always hated Engo. Andy the mask. And the real *Her*, too. Jake got between them. Little Jakey, who had until now been hovering in the corner of the dilapidated portable and gnawing on the end of an unlit cigarette, muttering worrisome nothings to himself.

'Get her back on her knees.'

Jake approached and helped her up. His hand was clammy on her neck.

Don't fucking touch me!

'Benji,' Big Matt said. 'There's an out here. I'm *giving you* an out. You gotta take it.'

'I don't—'

'Tell us that you turned on us. That's all you have to do, man.'

'She's not a cop!'

'Just tell us!'

'Matt, please!'

'Tell us, or I'm gonna have to do this thing. I don't want to do it. But I will.'

Andy looked at Ben. Met his frantic gaze. She saw it in his eyes, the scene playing out. Andy taking the bullet in the brain. Her body rag-dolling on the floor. Ben next. All the vigour going out of him, as if his plug had been yanked from the socket. Matt, Engo and Jake strapping firefighting helmets onto their dead bodies and lighting the place up around them. Driving back to the station car parked at Peanut Leap. They'd make the anonymous call to 911. Then respond to the dispatch officer when the job came over the radio.

Hey, Dispatch, we're up here anyway. Engine 99 crew. We took the station car for a cruise and we have basic equipment on us. We'll head out there while the local guys get their asses into gear.

It would look like an accident. The crew had taken the station car out for a spin, parked to watch the lights on the river and sink beers, and picked up a run-of-the-mill spot-fire call. They'd rolled up to the property, spotted the portable that had probably served as a construction site office once starting to smoke out. Ben and Andy had taken the spare gear from the back of the car and rushed in ahead of Matt and the rest of the crew, no idea that the blazing building was full of gas bottles and jerry cans that some local cuckoo had been hoarding.

Kaboom.

A tragedy.

Oh, there'd be an inquiry, of course. Wrists would be slapped – about the rec run with the station car, the beers, the half-cocked entry. There would be whispers, too. Especially after what happened to Titus.

But then everybody would cry and forget about it.

Matt and his crew did that: they made people forget.

Andy watched Ben weigh his loyalties. His crew, against the cop he'd brought in to destroy them.

'I don't want to do this, Ben,' Matt said. The huge man's voice was strained. He shifted his grip on the gun. 'Just tell us the truth.'

The wind howled around the shack and the boats clanged on the river and Little Jakey started to cry.

THREE MONTHS EARLIER

BEN

Fire is loud. It calls to people. Probably had been doing that since the dawn of time, Ben guessed. When it was old enough, when it had evolved through its hissing and creeping and licking phase and was a good-sized beast learning to roar – that's when they came. Stood. Watched. Felt the heat on their cheeks and felt alive and part of something, or some hippie shit like that.

By the time Ben's boots landed on the wet sidewalk of West Thirty-Seventh Street there were huddles of people in darkened doorways across the street and gawkers hanging out of apartment windows above them. The pinprick white lights of phone cameras. He hardly noticed, was hauling and dumping gear onto the concrete, his mind tangled up with the next eighteen steps. Engo, with a cigar clamped between his teeth and drenched in sweat, started stretching the line.

'This is a mistake,' Ben told Matt as the chief jumped down from the engine. The flashing lights were making Matt's angry red neck stubble a sickly purple.

'It'll be fine.'

'A fucking fabric store?' Ben ripped open the hatch on the side of the engine and started grabbing tools fast and efficiently. A looter in a floodlands Target. 'It's a tinderbox.'

'The building is right on our path. It's the best way in.'

Clouds of singed nylon were pouring out of the building above them. 'It'll go up. And Engo and Jakey won't be able to—'

'Stop bitching, Benji.'

Ben stopped bitching, because you didn't bitch too long at Matt. By now, two windows on the third floor of the fabric store had blown out and the crowd in the street had doubled. The windows were glowing up there, not just the ones that were blown. Ben had been doing this ten years, maybe longer. The window glow told him the fire was big enough that it was probably into the foundations.

He tanked up, slapped on his helmet, shouldered a gear bag and went in. Engo was in front, of course, his chin up, the hose hanging over his arm like a great limp dick. A guy walking into a fancy museum. Engo made a show of marching into fires like that, like it was all routine. Like nothing was a big deal. *What happened? Granny left the iron on?* Ben had seen the guy step over bodies as if they were kinks in a rug. His tank was unhooked because smoke worried him the way water worried fish.

Ben dropped his hose, split from Jake and Engo and went down the stairs while they went up towards the fire. Things passed before him, curiosities his mind would pick over later as he tried to sleep. Walls of buttons in a thousand shapes and colours. Giant golden scissors. Cutting tools and rulers. There were stacks of leather lying folded on shelves, colours he hadn't imagined possible. He was glad they'd decided to set the spark device that ignited the fire on the third floor. It was all fur and feathers on the basement level – this part of the store was going to vaporise when it caught.

Ben dropped his bag and helmet. The bag was so heavy with tools it shook the floor, made a jar of pins jump off the nearby cutting counter. He took a knife from his belt, slit a square in the carpet, raked it back and exposed the boards. Lifting up six floorboards with the Halligan tool took fifteen seconds. He dropped his gear bag down onto the bare earth below the building and slipped in after it, landing right on top of the concrete manhole. He didn't have a pit lid lifter but the Halligan did the job, slid nicely into the iron handle of the 40-pound manhole cover. He adjusted his mask, worked his jaw to make sure it was sealed tight before he popped open the cover and stepped down into the blackness.

Something about being surrounded by toxic gas makes a guy breathe harder. He'd thought about that for the first time as he hauled bodies for overworked paramedics in COVID times, then while putting out car fires while the NYPD doused the streets in pepper spray during the George Floyd days. Now, in the dark, working his way along the disused, hand-bricked tunnel beneath West Thirty-Seventh Street, he thought of the hydrogen sulfide swirling in the air around him, built up from decades of moss and sewage and whatever the hell else percolating in the old, sealed subway access. It made him suck on the oxygen like a hungry baby at the tit.

He didn't use the flashlight down here. Engo had tried to argue that H_2S wasn't that flammable, and an LED didn't spark like that anyway, but Ben wasn't going to turn that corner of New York into Pompeii because he didn't like the dark. He had about eleven minutes to get where he was going, do the job and get back again. The blindness would make the timing tight. The radio crackling in his ear canal with the voices of the crew behind him made him twitchy.

'*Engo, you on site?*'

'*Yeah, boss. We got a nice little campfire here.*'

'*Ben?*'

'Checking for a secondary ignition site,' Ben lied. His voice felt trapped behind the mask.

'*We better black out the whole block,*' Matt said. '*We don't know who shares a distributor.*'

Ben fast-walked, imagining Matt on the street, ordering the backup crews, who were probably already arriving from Engine 97 and Ladder 98, to shut down the power to the whole Garment District. The guys from 97 and 98 would probably think that was over the top, that blacking out the single block would do. But Matt needed to make sure that not only the fabric store was powered off, but also the jewellery store on West Thirty-Fifth, where Ben was heading.

Left, right, left, he reminded himself. Just like the marching call. He turned the last corner, walked for three minutes, his gloved fingers trailing the wall, all sorts of landscapes passing under his boots, most of them wet and squelching. He found the steppers he was looking for – rusty iron rungs concreted into the wall – dropped his gear bag and went up. His arms were shaking as he lifted the second manhole cover. Nerves.

It had been a year or more since they'd done a high-end job like this, something that required blueprints to be memorised and onsite scouting in the lead-up. A dry spell ended. Ben didn't like these kinds of jobs: scores they *needed.* Don't rob when you're broke. That was a mantra he'd always believed in. Desperation makes guys stupid, dissolves trust. Because at the end of the day, did Ben really know for sure that Matt had got the best fence for this take? Someone who could move what they stole tonight without making ripples? Or had Matt settled, because the crew chief had three ex-wives with their hands out and a bun in the oven with baby mama number four? And did Ben really know for sure that Jake had double-checked on all the construction sites in the Garment District for late-night workers who might be in the tunnels? Did Jake know the local police response times? Or was the kid into the horses again? Was he hocking old PlayStation games to fend off loan sharks?

Ben realised, as he hauled his gear up through the manhole and into the two-foot-tall crawl space beneath an apartment building on Thirty-Fifth, that he didn't trust his own crew on a job anymore.

And that was bad.

But there were worse kinds of mistrust.

There was the one that had made him write the letter to the detective.

Ben lifted the manhole cover back into place, raked his oxygen mask off and lay panting on the compacted dirt floor. The crawl space was as black as the tunnel, but years of working in roof cavities and basements and tunnels and collapsed buildings had given Ben the ability to manoeuvre in the dark like a night creature. He found the flashlight on his belt, clicked it on and got his bearings. Wide, raw-cut floor beams stretched into the nothingness just inches above where he lay. They'd probably been built when they still called this place the Devil's Arcade and it was an army of prostitutes and bootleggers, and not fancy types shopping for diamonds, stamping over them. Ben started crawling west, found a gap in the brick foundations that separated one building from another, and kept on. A hundred yards from the manhole, three buildings over, the subsurface power distribution board belonging to the jewellery store was just where he expected it to be, bolted to a brick strut.

He pulled wire cutters, a charge tester and the bug device from a vest strapped under his turnout coat, started working the board to insert the bug. Sweat ran into his eyes. His mind kept trying to wander away from what his fingers were doing and drift two blocks over to the fabric store, to 23-year-old Jake, shoulder to shoulder with an eight-fingered, pot-bellied psychopath who wanted to die in a blaze of glory. The two of them battling a decidedly glorious blaze. The men trying to let the magnificent thing eat through enough cotton and satin and jersey and whatever else to give Ben the time he needed to do what he had to do, but not so long it would become a monster and turn and eat them, too.

Ben finished installing the bug in the jewellery store's security system and was shifting around to crawl back to his gear bag and tank and the manhole three buildings away when he heard a woman's voice.

'Hello?'

Ben froze. Instinct made him flatten on the dirt like a threatened lizard. His toes were curled in his boots. His eyes bulged and his lungs expelled all the air that was in them. He heard the floorboards somewhere to the right of where he lay creak with footsteps.

The radio in his ear crackled.

'*Engo and Jakey, you got it in hand?*'

'*Yep. Yep. We got it.*'

'*It don't look like it from here.*'

'*I said we got it.*'

'*Ben, give me an ETA. They need you up there.*'

Ben didn't breathe. Whoever was in the jewellery store above him walked across the boards right over his head. He heard a muffled snap, and then, even through the layers of carpet on the boards above him, he saw the glow of a light.

'Fuuuuuuck,' he mouthed.

'Hello?'

'*Ben, give me a sitrep*,' Matt insisted.

He didn't speak. Slowly, achingly, he lifted his hand from the dirt and reached for the radio on his shoulder. He clicked the talk button twice, the code for trouble.

There was a long pause. Ben counted his breaths. The counting made him think of time. Seconds ticking off. With a recognition so filled with dread it sent a bolt of pain through his spine, he remembered the PASS alarm on his belt and reached down and shook the safety device so it wouldn't sound a pealing alarm at his immobility. Sweat was dripping off his eyelashes.

'*Two for hold, three for abort*,' Matt finally said. Ben could hear the tightness in his chief's voice. He clicked the radio twice.

Another three minutes. Ben counted them. The woman in the jewellery store moved some stuff around, opened and closed a cabinet.

'*Ladder 98 crew are comin' up to join you, Engo*,' Matt said. Ben could hear the quiet fury in his voice now.

'*Tell those pricks we got it!*'

'*I'm telling you to haul ass!*' Matt said. '*They're comin'!*'

Ben swore under his breath. It probably sounded to anyone monitoring the radios that Matt had been talking to Engo, encouraging him to get the fire under control before another crew came in and claimed the knockdown of the fire. But Ben heard the real message. Matt was telling him to haul ass out from under the jewellery store and back to the fire before the guys from 98 geared up and entered the site, climbed to the second floor and asked where the hell Engine 99's third guy was.

Or – worse – they came looking for him. In the basement, maybe, where he'd opened up the hole in the floor to access the tunnel.

The light clicked off above him. Ben guessed whoever was in the store had decided the sound she heard wasn't a person. He counted off ten breaths, then slithered for his life back to the manhole, tanked up and popped the cover and dropped his gear into the shaft.

He was sprinting so hard down the home stretch his fingers almost missed the steppers on the wall under the fabric store. He grabbed on and yanked himself to a stop, almost slipped in the toxic sludge. Ben climbed to the top of the ladder, shouldered open the manhole, got out and threw it back into place, then heaved himself up through the hole he'd cut in the floor. His body was screaming at him to just lie there, take a minute. Three-quarters of his oxygen tank was gone just from his panicked breathing. The air in the mask tasted rubbery and thick. Soon it would start shuddering on his face, a sign he was about to max out. He rolled over instead, got up and dragged a heap of furs to the edge of the hole. He lit them with a cigarette lighter and bolted up the stairs.

He arrived in the foyer as the Ladder 98 guys were marching up the stairs to the second floor. Ben came up behind them.

He couldn't think what else to do. A guy he didn't recognise whirled around on him.

'Da fuck?'

'We got a secondary ignition site in the basement,' Ben said. The Ladder 98 guys looked at each other for a moment, probably trying to decipher how the hell a secondary fire could start on the basement level of the building when the main fire was on the third floor. And what the hell Ben was doing down there looking for a secondary site before his crew had taken hold of the primary site? But they shook it off. They probably guessed Engo was behind the split in manpower, and they'd all seen stranger things happen with ignition sites. Fires creeping through walls and popping up in two apartments on opposite sides of the same building. Fires reigniting two weeks after they were put out. Fire had no rules. It was the only magic left in the world.

'Go to your crew,' the 98s guy said. 'We'll take the basement.'

Ben watched them go. He could see flames licking up the walls of the basement stairwell. Just as he'd predicted, the basement was already just a room full of ash and memories.

It was 4 am and they were in the squad room before anybody could talk about it. Matt's crew had a room of their own, mainly because nobody from the other crews could stand the idea of Matt coming in and sitting down to watch the TV and them having to sit there with him like there was a full-sized lion lounging on the end of the couch. Ben and the guys, they all stank. Ash and sweat and monoammonium phosphate. Engo was in his armchair nursing his paunch, a wet basketball under his T-shirt. Matt was throwing shit around in the kitchenette. Jake stood by the door, wincing like he was expecting to be the next thing picked up and hurled against the wall.

'Who *the fuck* was she?' Matt bellowed.

'How do I know?' Ben shrugged. 'Hard to make her out through the floorboards.'

'It was *your* job to watch the ins and outs.' Matt turned and stabbed a sausage-sized finger at Engo. 'You said nobody would be there.'

'So somebody pulled an all-nighter,' Engo said. 'What do you want from me? I watched the store for two months. Nobody ever stayed past nine.'

'*Did* you watch the store?' Ben piled on. 'Or did you sit in your car eating burgers and jerking off?'

'This guy.' Engo shook his head sadly at Ben.

''Member that time you landed that nineteen-year-old on Snapchat? You let those security guards creep up on us at the Atrium.'

Engo sat grinning at him.

'What if we'd put you on watch duty at the fabric store instead of the jewellery store? Huh?' Ben asked. 'What if someone pulled an all-nighter there, and you didn't notice them? We could have had a civilian on the second floor when the fire started. Or in the basement, when I was cutting through the goddamn floor.'

'You're really mad, huh?'

Ben held his head.

'Would it help you feel better if you took a swing at me, babycakes?' Engo tapped his stubbled chin. 'Because you're welcome to try.'

'Jesus Christ.'

'Yeah. That's what I thought.'

'We can't go on with this job.' Ben's hair was still plastered to his skull with sweat. He thought about giving up and going home to bed. He made one last appeal to Matt. 'The 98s saw that I was split off from my crew. They'll know something was up. They're going to wonder why I went looking for a second site when the primary site was getting so out of control.'

'It was never out of control,' Engo said.

'If I hadn't got back when I did, you and Jakey would be sandwich meat between the third and fourth floors of that place right now.'

'You're delusional.'

'It was into the foundations!'

'No it wasn't.'

'Maybe we should think about it,' Jake piped up, already glowing red in the neck and cheeks like a parakeet. 'Because there was, uh . . . You know. There was the radio call, too. "Hold or abort." That'll be on the record. That's not good.'

'We're not pulling the pin on this job,' Matt finally said. 'We're too deep.'

'We've been deeper before and walked away,' Ben reasoned.

No one spoke.

'The woman. What if she figures the noises under the carpet were rats?' Ben asked. 'Maybe she sends a pest guy down there.'

Matt was white-knuckling the kitchen sink, staring out the window at the training yard. 'Some dumbass rat guy's not going to know anybody else was down there messing with the electrics. He'll be looking for rats, not bugs.'

'"Rats, not bugs."' Engo laughed. 'That's funny.'

'What if she *doesn't* figure it's rats?' Ben said. 'We hit the jewellery store in three weeks, and she remembers the noises she heard under the floor. Reads about the fabric store fire in the papers. Sees it was the same night she heard the noises.'

'So, we wait a month,' Matt said.

'We can't go ahead,' Ben insisted. 'A job this size has got to be perfec—'

'*I said we're doing it!*' Matt grabbed a mug off the counter, gripped its rim and handle and sides like it was a baseball. Or a grenade. 'You got a hearing problem I don't know about, Benji?'

He didn't answer. No one did.

In the end, Ben just shrugged, because he was tired and he didn't need a coffee mug to the temple right then.

And what did he care, anyway? They were all going to jail, whether it was a month from now or sooner.

'One of the best thrillers of the year.'
THE AUSTRALIAN

'Brilliant premise and masterful storytelling.'
GOOD READING

THE INTERNATIONAL BESTSELLING AUTHOR

CANDICE FOX

FIRE WITH FIRE

Their daughter's case went cold. Now they're raising hell.

FIRE WITH FIRE

Candice Fox

A married couple launch a deadly plan to find their missing child.
A half-dead man washes up on a Los Angeles beach.
A rookie cop is fired on her first day.

Ryan and Elsie Delaney don't accept the official line that their young daughter drowned on Santa Monica beach. Her body has never been found and their pleas for a proper investigation are rejected.

So now the desperate pair are raining hellfire on the police.

Taking three hostages at the Hertzberg-Davis Forensic Science Center, they give law enforcement an ultimatum: if Tilly isn't located in the next twenty-four hours, they will destroy evidence in several major cases.

Detective Charlie Hoskins only just survived five years embedded with the ruthless gang known as the Death Machines. All his work is in that lab. If the police won't look for Tilly, he will. Even if that means accepting help from Lynette Lamb, the rookie officer sacked for blowing his cover – and having him thrown to the sharks.

Finding Tilly is now a matter of life and death – for the Delaneys, for their hostages, for Charlie and Lamb, and for the little girl who one day simply vanished . . .

'Clever investigative drama at its finest, with a brilliant premise and masterful storytelling.' *GOOD READING*

'That rarest of things – a thriller that completely exceeds the promise of a remarkable premise. This is breakneck stuff, and you'll need to remind yourself to take a breath.' LISA JEWELL

'One of Australia's finest new-gen crime writers.'
SYDNEY MORNING HERALD

'Masterful.'
SYDNEY MORNING HERALD

'Pulse-spiking.'
APPLE

'Constantly surprising.'
HERALD SUN

THE INTERNATIONAL BESTSELLING AUTHOR

CANDICE FOX

WINNER
THE NED KELLY AWARDS

THE CHASE

600 prisoners escaping justice. And one hunting it.

THE CHASE

Candice Fox

Winner of the Ned Kelly Award 2022 for Best Crime Novel

When more than six hundred of the world's most violent human beings pour out from Pronghorn Correctional Facility into the Nevada Desert, the biggest manhunt in US history begins.

But for John Kradle, this is his one chance to prove his innocence, five years after the murder of his wife and child.

He just needs to stay one step ahead of the teams of law enforcement officers he knows will be chasing down the escapees.

Death row supervisor turned fugitive-hunter Celine Osbourne is single-minded in her mission to catch Kradle. She has very personal reasons for hating him – and she knows exactly where he's heading . . .

'Candice Fox's new book further cements her position as one of the world's most original thriller writers . . . I was blown away by the clever twists and quirky characters, all overlaid with Fox's characteristic dark humour.' *READER'S DIGEST*

'*The Chase* is her most assured solo crime novel to date and it is masterful.' *SYDNEY MORNING HERALD*

'Action-packed, constantly surprising, suspenseful . . . this reviewer found it hard to put down.' *HERALD SUN*

'One of Australia's finest new gen crime writers.'
SYDNEY MORNING HERALD

'A master of the genre.'
THE SATURDAY PAPER

THE INTERNATIONAL BESTSELLING AUTHOR

CANDICE FOX

GATHERING DARK

A killer. A thief. A crime lord. A cop.

GATHERING DARK

Candice Fox

Blair Harbour, once a wealthy, respected surgeon in Los Angeles, is now an ex-con down on her luck. She's determined to keep her nose clean to win back custody of her son.

But when her former cellmate, Sneak Lawlor, begs for help to find her missing daughter, Blair is compelled to put her new-found freedom on the line. Joined by LA's most feared underworld figure, Ada Maverick, the crew of criminals bring outlaw tactics to the search for Dayly.

Detective Jessica Sanchez has always had a difficult relationship with the LAPD. And her inheritance of a $7 million mansion as a reward for catching a killer has just made her police enemy number one.

It's been ten years since Jessica arrested Blair for the cold-blooded murder of her neighbour. So when Jessica opens the door to the disgraced doctor and her friends early one morning she expects abuse, maybe even violence.

What comes instead is a plea for help.

'Candice Fox's brilliant crime novel set in LA will surely garner her a whole new set of readers . . . It's that good.'
SYDNEY MORNING HERALD

'One of the best crime thrillers of the year.'
LEE CHILD

'A masterful novel.'
HARLAN COBEN

THE INTERNATIONAL BESTSELLING AUTHOR

CANDICE FOX

NOW A MAJOR ABC DRAMA

TROPPO

CRIMSON LAKE

Where people come to disappear . . .

CRIMSON LAKE

Candice Fox

Now a major ABC TV drama series, *Troppo*, starring Thomas Jane and Nicole Chamoun

Six minutes.

That's all it takes to ruin Detective Ted Conkaffey's life. Accused but not convicted of abducting a teenage girl, he escapes north, to the steamy, croc-infested wetlands of Crimson Lake.

Amanda Pharrell knows what it's like to be public enemy number one. Maybe it's her murderous past that makes her so good as a private investigator, tracking lost souls in the wilderness. Her latest target, missing author Jake Scully, has a life more shrouded in secrets than her own – so she enlists help from the one person in town more hated than she is: Ted Conkaffey.

But the residents of Crimson Lake are watching the pair's every move. And for Ted, a man already at breaking point, this town is offering no place to hide . . .

'One of the best crime thrillers of the year.'
LEE CHILD

'In her willingness to go to the dark side and turn it upside down, Fox is a daring antipodean original.'
SYDNEY MORNING HERALD

'This is terrific crime writing.'
HERALD SUN

'A brilliant and original thriller.'
SUNDAY TIMES

THE INTERNATIONAL BESTSELLING AUTHOR

CANDICE FOX

NOW A MAJOR ABC DRAMA

TROPPO

REDEMPTION POINT

Clearing his name may cost him his life.

REDEMPTION POINT

Candice Fox

When former police detective Ted Conkaffey was wrongly accused of abducting thirteen-year-old Claire Bingley, he hoped the Queensland rainforest town of Crimson Lake would be a good place to disappear. But nowhere is safe from Claire's devastated father.

Dale Bingley has a brutal revenge plan all worked out – and if Ted doesn't help find the real abductor, he'll be its first casualty.

Meanwhile, in a dark roadside hovel called the Barking Frog Inn, the bodies of two young bartenders lie on the beer-sodden floor. It's Detective Inspector Pip Sweeney's first homicide investigation – complicated by the arrival of private detective Amanda Pharrell to 'assist' on the case. Amanda's conviction for murder a decade ago has left her with some odd behavioural traits, top-to-toe tatts – and a keen eye for killers.

For Ted and Amanda, the hunt for the truth will draw them into a violent dance with evil. Redemption is certainly on the cards – but it may well cost them their lives . . .

'If you like great thrillers, you'll love Candice Fox.'
LEE CHILD

'Perfectly paced, super-addictive crime fiction.'
HERALD SUN

'A rollercoaster ride full of twists and turns.'
COURIER MAIL

THE INTERNATIONAL BESTSELLING AUTHOR

CANDICE FOX

GONE BY MIDNIGHT

They left four children upstairs. They came back to three.

GONE BY MIDNIGHT

Candice Fox

Crimson Lake is where bad people come to disappear – and where eight-year-old boys vanish into thin air . . .

On the fifth floor of the White Caps Hotel, four young friends are left alone while their parents dine downstairs. But when Sara Farrow checks on the children at midnight, her son is missing. The boys swear they stayed in their room, and CCTV confirms Richie has not left the building. Despite a thorough search, no trace of the child is found.

Distrustful of the police, Sara turns to Crimson Lake's unlikeliest private investigators: disgraced cop Ted Conkaffey and convicted killer Amanda Pharrell. This case is just the sort of twisted puzzle that gets Amanda's blood pumping.

For Ted, the case couldn't have come at a worse time. Two years ago, a false accusation robbed him of his career, his reputation and most importantly his family. But now Lillian, the daughter he barely knows, is coming to stay in his ramshackle cottage by the lake.

Ted must dredge up the area's worst characters to find a missing boy. And the kind of danger he uncovers could well put his own child in deadly peril . . .

'Terrific crime writing.' *HERALD SUN*

'The queen of the creepily compulsive thriller.' *WHO* magazine

'One of our best crime writers.' *CANBERRA WEEKLY*

'Bright new star of crime fiction.'
JAMES PATTERSON

'Definitely a writer to watch.'
HARLAN COBEN

THE INTERNATIONAL BESTSELLING AUTHOR

CANDICE FOX

WINNER
THE NED KELLY AWARDS

HADES

There's a fine line between good and evil . . .

HADES

Candice Fox

Winner of the Ned Kelly Award 2014
for Best Debut Crime Novel

Homicide detective Frank Bennett feels like the luckiest man on the force when he meets his new partner, the dark and beautiful Eden Archer.

But there's something strange about Eden and her brother, Eric. Something he can't quite put his finger on.

At first, as they race to catch a very different kind of serial killer, his partner's sharp instincts come in handy. But soon Frank's wondering if she's as dangerous as the man they hunt.

'Definitely a writer to watch.'
HARLAN COBEN

'One of the stand-out crime thrillers of the past few years.'
THE CHRONICLE

'Fox has hit gold . . . a name to be reckoned with.'
PRIMO LIFE

'Breathtaking.' SYDNEY MORNING HERALD

'Nail-biting riverting.' PUBLISHERS WEEKLY

'Sizzling page-turner.' DAILY TELEGRAPH

THE INTERNATIONAL BESTSELLING AUTHOR

CANDICE FOX

WINNER THE NED KELLY AWARDS

EDEN

Justice is good. Revenge is better.

EDEN

Candice Fox

Winner of the Ned Kelly Award 2015 for Best Crime Novel

Most police duos run on trust, loyalty and the desire to see killers in court. But Detective Frank Bennett's partner, the enigmatic Eden Archer, has nothing to offer him but darkness and danger.

Eden doesn't mind catching killers – but it's not in the courthouse where her justice is served.

Now she is about to head undercover and it's up to Frank to watch over her.

But as the darkness around Eden gathers, Frank begins to ask himself: is Eden saving lives, or taking them?

'*Hades* announced an important new voice in crime fiction . . . *Eden* is equally breathtaking.'
SYDNEY MORNING HERALD

'Fox again grabs her reader by the throat from the get-go and does not relinquish her grip . . . Gripping, confronting and powerful.'
WESTERN ADVOCATE

'A sizzling page-turner.'
DAILY TELEGRAPH

'If you love great thrillers you'll love Candice Fox!'
LEE CHILD

'Inventive, thrilling and totally addictive.'
JAMES PATTERSON

THE INTERNATIONAL BESTSELLING AUTHOR

CANDICE FOX

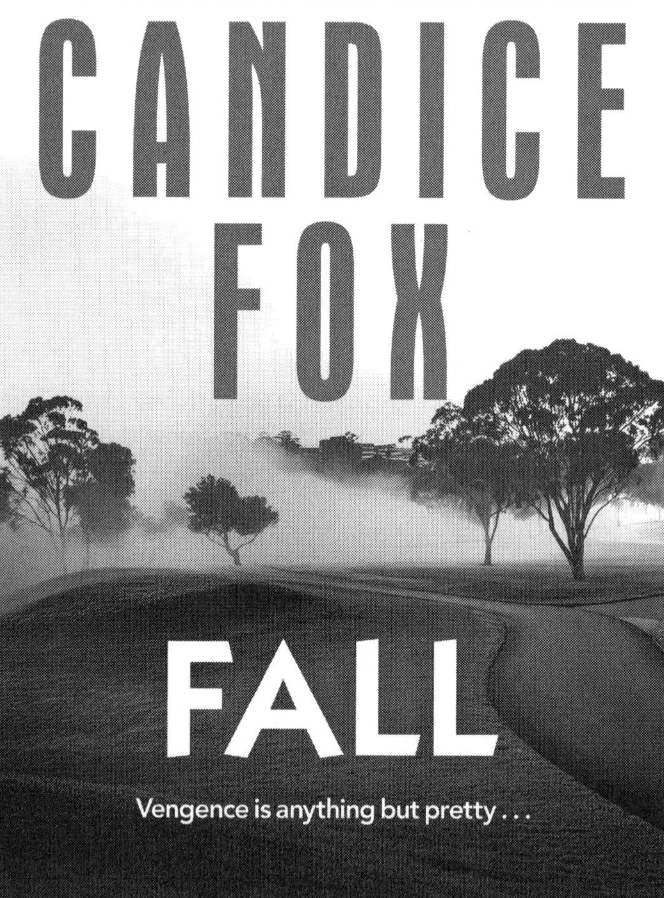

FALL

Vengence is anything but pretty . . .

FALL

Candice Fox

If Detective Frank Bennett tries hard enough, he can sometimes forget that Eden Archer, his partner in the Homicide Department, is also a moonlighting serial killer . . .

Thankfully their latest case is proving a good distraction. For, on the city's rain-soaked running tracks, a predator is lurking.

Meanwhile, Frank's new girlfriend Imogen is determined to solve the disappearance of the two young Tanner children more than twenty years earlier. But the trail is leading to Eden's door.

And asking too many questions about Eden Archer can get you buried as deep as her past . . .

'Fox has taken crime fiction by the scruff of
the neck in recent years.'
WEEKEND AUSTRALIAN

'Tough and thrilling, this will keep you reading
well into the night.'
SUNDAY CANBERRA TIMES